RACE WITH THE BLACK DEATH

BLACK DEATH TALES

BOOK 2

WILLIAM J. CONNELL

A Wild Ink Publishing Original

Wild Ink Publishing

https://wild-ink-publishing.com

Editing by Leila Sanders & Kristen Rethy

ALSO BY WILLIAM J. CONNELL

THE BLACK DEATH TALES

Mask of Death

A Race with the Black Death

HELLO!

You've returned! How nice to see you. I presume you liked the last tale?

The story was foul and horrid. It was not one with the happiest of endings, though from my perspective, it was appropriate.

Yet here you are. Why?

Ahh, the little girl, Maddalena. What happened to her? To her family? Are you sure you wish to hear this tale? As a poor young girl, the daughter of a concubine, and with the Black Death swirling, her life expectancy would not be long. Especially as the target of ravenous and deadly flesh eaters.

I understand.

You must know.

Well, I will only say—there may be more to the story than you think. Let me set the scene.

Our story begins in the mid-14th century, during the height of early summer. The Black Death, or the Great Mortality as it is sometimes called, continues to ravage what you know as Europe.

In our story, many different personages will appear, but our focus will be on two somewhat unfortunate children. One is Bartolome, a loving, if somewhat simple, young boy who passes through life without many cares. The other child is the one inquired about, Bartolome's slightly older sister Maddalena. She is slow to speak but observant.

As our story opens, the children are traveling with their mother and their uncle under papal guard, from Rome to Avignon, but very shortly these two will begin a journey with another group—a set of troubadours who you will also get to know. The members of this troupe are racing from the plague, and—for now, let's just say there are others who want the children. And do you know all those silly legends about strange and evil creatures that prowl the night, looking for the hapless and the isolated?

Many such legends are based on fact.

Would you like to hear more? Then by all means, turn the page.

[1]
GOOD NIGHT

A valley in Piedmont, Northwestern Italy

Baby Dear, good night, good night,
doggie lies in slumbers bright
hush a bye, my treasure trove,
don't you wake though! If you do,
pups will bark, and puss will mew,
go to sleep, and never fear,
mother will come when morning's near.[i]

I LOVE LISTENING to my momma's voice. So sweet, so gentle, and soft.

Mother cradles me in her arms as we lie in our wagon, near the fire.

"I'm too old to be rocked," I protest, but mother knows I lie. I can see her smile, even though I cannot see her face. Next to me, I can barely see Bartolome as he stirs in his slumber.

---

i Old English Lullaby. Adapted from http://rhymeslyrics.blogspot.com/2008/01/baby-dear-good-night-good-night.html

"Your brother is tired, Maddalena," Mother says. "It's been a long journey for him." She squeezes me. "And it has been a long journey for you, too, hasn't it?" She speaks next to my ear. I giggle. When she holds me close, I can smell the posies she wears in her dress. I love their smell—sweet and radiant, like Mother.

"Mother," I ask, "how much further is it to Avignon?"

There's a pause before she answers.

"I don't know, Maddalena," she says, and I hear a slight weakening in her voice. "This isn't the way we came down. But don't worry, your uncle knows. He'll protect us."

"Yes, and the soldiers," I add.

I stare into the fire burning near our wagons. I don't like the soldiers. Usually, they just dismiss Bartolome and me. We are under their feet, like rocks on the road, something to be avoided or kicked. I don't mind so much. I stay out of their way. But there are times, some of them, they look at me. And I don't like how they do that. They don't look at Bartolome that way.

My uncle is an important man and has provided for us since our father died, though he seldom speaks to us. He has news for Pope Clement, news of the plague. And of the others.

Mother pulls me close again, tightening the woolen blankets around my body, and kisses my head, then notices something in the firelight.

"Did you scratch your arm?"

"Yes. I was reaching for a firethorn. I'm surprised you can see it."

"It is faint. But I am your mother. You're usually so careful."

"It was high in the bush, and I was getting it for an elderly Romani woman who asked me for help. The scratch was worse, but the woman licked it. See, now it is healed."

Mother is quiet.

"Good night, Princess. It is time for you to sleep," she whispers.

I feel the warmth from her body.

"Tonight is a harvest moon," Mother says, and it fills the sky.

I am not frightened of the soldiers, or of the plague, or of the vampires that follow us.

"And stay close to me."

I fall asleep while Mother hums another lullaby.

Horror!

We are rushing through a thicket. My arm is in pain. Mother is panting as she drags Bartolome and I. Behind us, I hear screaming. I smell smoke in the air. I say nothing. I want to turn, but I am afraid. If we pause a moment, we are dead. I know.

Bartolome cries as a branch snaps beneath him.

"Quiet, children!" Mother says. I hear her fear. "Run for your lives. Dear God, let it be here."

The moonlight allows us to see a short way. The screams behind us are overtaken by howling and other noises I cannot make out.

I trip on my dress, and my mother follows me to the ground.

She grunts out, then cuts it short, looking around. I steal a glance back. Our wagons are burning. I can see *things* moving through the flames.

We are on our feet again, Bartolome and I at the side of our mother. There are other sounds. Something is breaking through behind us.

"It must be here," Mother says. "Oh, Mother Mary, please let it be here."

I hear water running.

Bartolome cries again and disappears. He has fallen. Mother calls his name, and still clinging to me, we tumble downward as the ground drops from beneath us. My hand slips from Mother's. My face hits the earth, and I slide until the ground flattens. There's a splash and the sound of running water—my right side is cold and wet.

"Maddalena!" Mother calls. "Where are you?"

"Here, Momma," I say. I feel Mother's hand grab my arm and pull me. One of my boots gets lost in the mud along the bank of a river. I see tree branches carried along by its current.

"Bartolome," Mother calls.

"Mother," Bartolome answers, somewhere ahead. "Help me!"

The brush has cut him.

Mother struggles through the reeds in shallow water and heads in the direction of his voice. "I'm coming. Keep talking, but keep your voice low, child." Mother looks back.

I see something thrashing in the water.

"Over there," I say.

Mother drags me through the water.

Bartolome has fallen into the river and is tangled in brush.

"Mother, help me!" Bartolome yells again. Mother and I reach the edge of the bank. Several broken trees have been caught at this bend by the river. We wade through them, slipping in the water. It is hard to move because the muck grabs our soles. I lost my other boot. The water soaks my stockings, and it is cold, very cold. Mother tells me I must not look back. When we reach Bartolome, he is sobbing loudly.

"Easy, child, mother is here." She steadies my shoulders. I shiver.

Mother speaks to me calmly.

"Are you stuck, Maddalena? No? Good. Get steady. Now hold your brother's hands."

The limb Bartolome is pinned under is actually a small tree. Mother reaches over and pulls on Bartolome's legs, but he whimpers. Momma begins singing again through the cold night air.

Baby Dear, good night, good night.

She struggles to pull Bartolome's feet. One seems to come loose.

Doggie lies in—ugh—slumbers—bright.

The tree begins to move. I am bent over, pulling Bartolome to me. Mother turns and tells Bartolome to pull with all his might. Bartolome is crying, but I yell at him to pull. The tree shifts again. The brush cut my lips. The water is so cold. Mother disappears under the river.

Now it is my turn to cry out.

"Mother!"

Bartolome wrenches forward, his foot released. His head strikes mine, and he yelps in pain, but I silently grab his elbows. Mother rises, water dripping off her. She reaches over to hug us, but can only touch our hands.

Her leg is caught.

Bartolome's face is pressed against me. He stops crying. His eyes widen, and he leans from me to Mother, but I do not let him go.

"Hold on!" I say.

"Mother—they're coming!" he says.

Mother glances back one time.

I dare not.

Mother tells us to close our eyes. I do so. I hear her singing.

Hush a bye, my treasure trove.

Something wet is slopped on my wrists. Mother has removed the sash from her waist and is tying our hands to the tree.

Don't you wake, though! If you do.

"No!" I scream. And now I look back.

Along the shore, hulking figures—not men but things that look like men—and women—are walking toward us.

I know what they are.

Fleshers! The dead who eat human flesh.

The sash bites into the skin.

"Don't leave us!" I scream. Bartolome stares backward,shaking.

"I love you, children," Mother says, and pushes on the log. The current begins to pull it outward, but halts.

We hear the things march in our direction. Mother struggles and pushes the branch again.

"GOODBYE, MY LOVES," she says.

There's a loud snap, and the branch floats away from the shore, with Bartolome and I holding each other's arms, bound together. We are both crying as we are carried into the river.

BACK ON THE RIVERBANK, SHORTLY AFTERWARD, AT THE SCENE OF THE ATTACK

"Janosz," Elizabeth began, "tell me the children didn't get away."

Janosz Ujvary was aware that Elizabeth was angry. Were he capable of greater passion, he might have been more aroused by the sight of his mistress storming along the banks, her scarlet hair being blown back by the night wind, just above her riding cape. Before the plague, he had been a man of discipline, a man of war, but also a man robust appetite, and one who loved life. A woman of Elizabeth's stature and, yes, her beauty, which she still retained, might have spurred arousal, yet never fear. But that was before. Since he had suffered and died, such feelings were no longer part of his constitution. Indeed, he had no memories of such feelings. He felt only a sense of obedience, for he must do as he was commanded. And also a sense of fear. That sense had not been destroyed.

"I cannot," he replied. "Mother and children reached the river. Mother pushed the children in."

He was bowed on one knee, and his mind, though feeble, instinctively braced for something. A flood of commands? Or maybe his destruction. It did not occur to him to move. He would accept whatever was delivered.

He felt a gentle slap across his cheek. That was all.

"Then let's go look at the river," Elizabeth said, turning toward the water. Obediently, Janosz rose and walked behind her.

They walked to the riverbank. For this instant, Elizabeth reflected on Janosz.

His vocalizations have progressed remarkably. He can improve. So many of the others slowly rot away. He'll tear the head off an enemy with those massive hands. Useful, and dangerous. I might need to destroy him at some point.

Her focus returned to the matter at hand. The current was strong, and her kind never did well in running water. A simple stream could throw them off. She did not know why, but water was deadly to them. The children's mother knew that as well. She'd been wise to get the children thrown into the river.

"If they drowned," Elizabeth mused, "and their bodies are underwater, they'll be bloated. They'll become food for the pike and other water parasites, and then what? All our work will be for nothing, and we will die. Again."

She laughed. "Wouldn't that be a shame, Janosz?"

He averted her eyes.

He knows a sense of failure.

"Take me to the mother."

Janosz led his mistress over to the reeds, past a pair of youths serving as some sort of guard. to a body draped on a granite slab. The head was turned away, but the long brunette hair and woolen skirt suggested a female. A linen shirt was saturated in blood. Elizabeth reached forth and stroked the hair, then pulled the head up. The body sagged underneath at an angle that could only be reached with a broken neck. The woman's eyes were closed. Her face was drained of color.

"You were wise to get your children into the water. I wish you had survived."

Elizabeth noticed the darkest concentration of blood was under the left shoulder. She ripped open the blouse, revealing that a large chunk of flesh had been torn from under the left scapula. Bite marks were visible on the bone. Elizabeth contemplated this.

"Were my orders unclear, Janosz?" she finally asked.

"No," he replied. "I had gone—up river—when—"

She raised a hand.

"You can't control *all* our soldiers, can you, Janosz?" A wound like this causes bleeding. And if she bleeds enough, then this is nothing to me but a worthless husk. We can't have that, can we?"

"There was much blood at the attack," Janosz said. "We—they —no control."

Elizabeth struck Janosz sharply with the back of her hand. Janosz remained stoic.

Elizabeth assumed a calm demeanor.

"Get the wagon. I want this body in the barrel as soon as possible. But while we wait for it, where is the one who did this?"

"Back." Janosz led her back over the slope.

The woods were populated with great firs, cypresses, and pine trees, and were overgrown with vines and brush. They walked through effortlessly, Janosz's vision being better than any other than Elizabeth's. She smelled the laurel bushes and the pines, which were pleasant, but then she detected that odious sweet scent and wiped her nose.

"Wild posies. I despise their smell."

They passed others who had been men and women of various ages and sorts in their prior lives, including nobles and serfs, knights and monks, prostitutes, even a duchess. In their former lives, many of them would never deign to associate in the same room with the others. But the great mortality had created a great equalization among classes. For those select few who died and—*returned*—their state WAS the same. Most of these creatures were gnawing on some sort of human remains left from the attack on the caravan, oblivious to what was anywhere other than in front of them, but in varying degrees, all recoiled at Elizabeth's entrance.

Janosz led Elizabeth to a torch-lit spot where a man, or what had been a man, thrashed on the ground, bound by ropes between two trees. He wore the cloak of a papal guard. He foamed at the mouth and snapped his jaws.

"Cut him loose."

Janosz gestured, and two creatures shambled over and held the prisoner down clumsily on his back. Janosz walked over, pulled out a cutting knife, and slit the ropes. The newly freed prisoner broke away from the two undead who had held him, rolled onto all fours, and with a primal gurgle, bounded towards Elizabeth. She raised her hand and, while few could see it, furrowed her brow. The iris of her eyes turned from blue to burnt orange.

The man stopped, completely silent, save for a heaving breath, and sat before her. Elizabeth inserted her hand into his mouth and rubbed a finger against the inside of his cheek. He sat docile and motionless. Elizabeth removed her finger and touched it to her lips. She was aware that a small group of the undead had clustered around the perimeter of the torchlight, observing, yet keeping a distance.

"I understand. You're a mindless fart. You couldn't help yourself. And it was my job to control you."

She pointed her fingers in emphasis. "But I needed her alive. And her being dead makes me angry."

Of course, none of the creatures comprehended anything she said, save for Janosz on a very rudimentary level. No matter. Others were looking on, from the shadows, *and that did matter.* Fear was an instinct, one that survived death.

Elizabeth flicked her wrist and turned away. The man reared up and then bashed his head into the ground. The skull cracked open. The body twitched.

The fool would lie there and eventually cease to exist even as a flesher.

But he would be there for a long time.

Elizabeth paused by Janosz and said, "I want the mother prepared as we discussed."

Janosz bowed. "Yessss," he managed.

Elizabeth's lips curled up ever so slightly.

"Try not to worry too much, my friend. If we preserve the

mother's body and find the children alive, there should be enough left. If the sisters have spoken true."

She looked back towards the river. The partial loss of the mother's blood was cause for concern, real concern. Though she had prepared for it, she had wanted all three alive.

She spoke aloud to herself, as she would when in deep thought.

"You're the fool. You know how hard they are to control when there's blood. You overestimated your own abilities after Sacra di San Michele. Learn from it."

No one approached Elizabeth save for one. The only one who was so allowed. A frail girl who had been on the cusp of womanhood when she was struck down by the plague. She wore a hooded purple cape, which covered her face, and shuffled awkwardly using a piece of olivewood as a type of crutch. Her head was bent down.

"You're getting better with that, Nicola." Elizabeth gently kicked the olivewood.

Nicola held out her right fist.

"What have you got there?"

Nicola dropped something into Elizabeth's palm. "This is just a used bandage."

Nicola remained silent but stayed in her spot.

Elizabeth studied the bandage more closely. She held it to her nose and then licked it. "The bandage I placed on Maddalena." Elizabeth's face brightened, and she embraced Nicola. Then she turned to Janosz

"I don't think the boy and girl drowned. Nicola senses they are alive. I do too. They're still alive. And so am I."

Her fingers ran through her auburn hair, and then she looked at her hand. Red strands clung to her palm. A not-so-subtle reminder, she thought. Unlike the vampires, the other undead, her body was slowly but steadily wearing and withering.

Yet that one trace of the child's blood portended great possibilities. It invigorated her.

"Janosz, we're going to find them," she declared.

MADDALENA

All is blackness. I had a most horrible dream. I must wake up.

My body is cold. I am so tired. I—cannot move my hands.

I force my eyes open. It is morning. I can see some leafless trees. There is water flowing around me, but I am numb; I feel nothing. Bartolome's hand is tied to mine. His body is on the other side of the bough. He is not moving.

It was not a dream. I am dead.

Behind me, something splashes in the water. Someone is coming toward us.

I am dead.

I do not want to, but I open my eyes. I see a large Nubian man reaching for me.

I close my eyes. Please let it end.

I thought I heard a human voice, but I...

I'm warm now. I am lying on my back. As I breathe, there's a weight on my breast. My body aches everywhere.

Am I dead?

"So, you are alive." I hear a woman's voice, firm and strong.

I look up. She is crouching by a fire. An Oriental with black hair to her shoulders. I've only seen women Orientals as slaves or companions to ladies. This one seems to be alone. She stands and walks to me, holding a copper cup. Her features are weathered, but there is something striking about her. She is somewhat pretty, with green eyes I have seldom seen.

"I don't like to waste time," she says. "My friend Mansa thought you might be useful to us, so we fished you out of the river." She speaks in Occitan, a language I know well, though with a slightly strange accent.

She crouches beside me and hands me the cup. "Tea," she says. "You better drink. There are herbs in there that will help you."

I push up on my elbows and take a drink. It is a little bitter, but it is preferable to the river water I've swallowed.

"Where is my brother?" I ask.

"He's fine," she replies. "He woke earlier. Mansa took him, and they are looking for some supplies. You'll meet them later."

I remember the events of last night.

"These woods aren't safe," I say. "They're filled with—"

"I know, I know," the woman says, walking to a mule. "Wild boars, hungry bears, rabid skunks." She reaches the mule and begins to put something in a side bag, and then adds, "Or were you thinking about the vampires? Or the fleshers?"

I sit silently.

"Oh yes, child, we know of them." She pulls a dagger out of the bag and begins drawing it against a polishing stone. "But it's daylight, and those things are night creatures. Don't fear for your brother, he's in good hands. You didn't drown, so you must be lucky. Now tell me, child, how is it the two of you found yourself strapped together on a log and floating down a raging river?"

I want to cry, but it is not my nature. I stare ahead.

"No matter. You've been on the water for an entire day. Your brother gave us some idea. Your name is—Maddalena?"

I nod.

"I am Jai Ling," the woman continues. She sharpens her knife. The metal scraping against the stone has a rhythm. I do not know how long I sit there.

"That tea will let you rest," she said. "You need to recover from the water. Tomorrow we must be off, and if you don't want to be left behind, you must be able to ride this mule."

This cannot be happening.

"I have to find my mother and uncle."

The woman holds up a dagger. The metal glistens. She returns to her bag and pulls out some other sticks with metal tips. Arrowheads. She begins to polish them with a cloth.

"We both know that's not possible. Your brother gave us the story. Your mother put you both in the river to escape a flesher attack. She was wise. But among those left behind—fleshers leave nothing when they attack."

I take another sip of the tea. I will not weep.

Maybe it would be better for me to have drowned.

I understand that may have been unsettling.

Would you prefer to stop now? Something else, perhaps a tale of a wonderful princess held in a tower or a castle by an evil stepmother, stepsister, step-something, who is rescued by a tall, enigmatic, and bland prince, would be more to your liking? I highly recommend a writer named Perrault.

No, you want more of this tale? I must warn you, this journey may not be pleasant.

Very well. We shall continue.

[2]

A CITY OF DANGER

A DUNGEON IN A WALLED CITY

IT IS AMUSING how some sounds are universal. The hollow clang of the metal gate being shut in a prison is one of those sounds, especially in a dark and damp chamber. Dioneo heard the guards coming. Sitting with his back against the stone wall, he raised his head just enough to see two pairs of pointed boots before him. Black, made from thick chamois leather, the kind favored by the king's guard in this kingdom.

"Those are beautiful patterns," Dioneo commented. "Are they made in this town? Do you think you could find me a pair while you're busy raping some poor miller's daughter?"

Dioneo looked up. One guard seemed younger than him, with a scraggly beard. The other older, with a fuller, grayer beard and the hint of a hunchback.

"You insult us?" said the older guard, poking at Dioneo with a metal baton. "Who's a prisoner down here?"

"You do have a point there, friend," Dioneo said. "But insults are not my intention, great lords. I'm only admiring the skills of the women's bootmakers of your village." Dioneo flashed them his brilliant smile. "They look lovely. Could I get some for the arena?"

The younger guard drew his foot back to deliver a kick, but a deep voice from the shadows commanded, "Do not strike him."

Both guards were startled by the speaker. Definitely a man's voice. The smile never left Dioneo's face, but he was mildly troubled. How long had the speaker been there?

"Ah, a new friend," quipped Dioneo. "I didn't see you come in."

"Help the defendant up," the voice said, and the two guards grabbed Dioneo's shoulders.

"Gently now, gently," Dioneo instructed.

Again, the voice spoke. "The defendant is correct. He must be treated fairly before his trial."

The two guards unbound Dioneo's feet and, grabbing his shoulders again, stood him up. Dioneo's hands remained bound behind his back.

"Thanks, friends. And thanks to you too, my dear—"

As he looked toward the unseen voice, Dioneo heard, "Do not turn around—*my friend*."

Dioneo surveyed the situation. The older guard was slightly hunched over, and the younger one a bit straighter, but Dioneo was taller than either, even standing in his hose. He could probably bowl the younger one over and drag the older one down. With hands bound at his back, he'd have to strike with his feet. He couldn't be sure where the owner of the voice was located.

Still, it might be worth a try.

The guards had loosened their hold on his arms.

Dioneo somersaultedand broke the grip of the younger guard. The older one tumbled, fell on all fours, and then grabbed for a dagger in his belt. Dioneo kicked the elder guard's jaw. The guard's head jerked back, blood flowing from his nose. The younger guard moved on Dioneo while the older one shook his head at the ground. Dioneo feinted like he was going to jump, but he kicked forward. The younger guard ran his gut into Dioneo's bare feet, buckling over. His face fell inches in front of Dioneo.

"Hello." Dioneo smiled and pushed out, propelling the guard

backwards into the far wall. The older guard had recovered enough to pull out a longer sword and was crawling towards Dioneo. Then from the shadows of the hold came, "Enough!"

All three combatants froze.

Dioneo scowled. The voice was beside him.

"I don't mean to be rude, but how did you get back there?" he asked.

"Please do not move, my young friend," said the voice.

Dioneo cracked his back and said, "I'm not so young anymore, but thanks for saying so."

Dioneo felt a blade touch his neck.

"Please. Do not move," repeated the voice.

"How can I refuse?" Dioneo replied. He felt a nudge or tug at the ropes binding him. His shoulders felt loose and—his arms were free.

This was startling. Some ropes were still wrapped around his wrists. As he held up his hands, the remaining ropes slid off. He rubbed his shoulders and laughed.

"A very nice cut, sir," he said.

The figure walked into the torchlight and stood before Dioneo, while the younger guard, rubbing his nose, helped the other guard to his feet.

Dioneo thought the stranger wide-shouldered, and he wore a tunic and headscarf favored in the east. The man's complexion was dark, as were his eyes, and Dioneo recalled seeing men like this during his own days in the Holy Land. He stood as tall as Dioneo, although given the stranger was wearing footwear, Dioneo probably had a slight advantage in height. The stranger's Italian vernacular was of the kind spoken in Mantua. Although perfect in enunciation, his speech was measured, again suggesting an eastern origin. The tunic's cut revealed large, rounded muscles in the upper arms, and while not so strongly defined as Dioneo, the stranger possessed a greater bulk.

But it was what the stranger carried in his right hand that most caught Dioneo's attention—a wide scimitar. And its upturned edge appeared quite sharp.

"You don't come from here," Dioneo said. "But the tenor of your voice—I've been in lands where people speak that way. Perhaps you hail from—Acre?"

The figure gave a slight bow to Dioneo, while the guards showed disgust in their bloodied faces, the younger one propping up the older.

"My voice betrays me," the stranger said, looking up from his bow. "The defendant is most perceptive. I actually hail from a village several days' travel from Acre, but your guess is closer than I would expect. Very impressive. Such perception may assist you in the arena."

Dioneo glanced at his wrists. The skin was red from the ropes but otherwise untouched.

"You're rather impressive yourself, with that big knife of yours. But thanks for cutting the ropes and eh—leaving me my hands," said Dioneo, again flashing his grin. "Of course, I couldn't very well open a door to the tigers without them. Who are you anyway?"

The figure gently brought his weapon down and clasped a free hand over his sword wrist, then smiled back. Not so wide a smile as Dioneo's, just a mild upturn of the lips.

"I am known as the Discourager of Hesitancy," the figure replied. "I serve my majesty. As a stranger, you may not realize what an honor it is to participate in the functions of our royal court, although the height of this honor is known throughout this land. Many would give their entire lives' provisions for the privilege of appearing before our King and to benefit from his infinite largess."

Dioneo laughed and snapped back, "Yes, I'm sure they would. Walk in the arena and open the right door, and you'll find a lovely maiden chosen just for you. Pick the wrong one, and you wind up in a tiger's belly. You simply have to make sure you get that door right."

The Discourager smiled.

"You appreciate our justice. But there are those rare occasions when a guest invited to engage in one of our functions, at some point, may question whether to *participate* as he, or on occasion she, should. It is my function to remind such guests of how great an honor it is to be a part of such functions and to discourage such *hesitation*."

Dioneo listened carefully. That scimitar was twice as wide as a normal one, and should have been unwieldy. The Discourager of Hesitancy knew how to use his tools.

"What about Ricciardo?" Dioneo asked. "Does he get the honor of having his own Discourager of Hesitancy?"

The Discourager of Hesitancy's smile changed into something less pleasant.

"No. Your friend goes willingly into the court. His fear of disobedience *and his love of the princess* will be sufficient motivation."

Dioneo chuckled.

"The love of the princess," he said. "Yeah. And not to mention, your guards, and of course, your archers. Oh, I'm sorry, the king's archers. But you're right. The little bastard is a fool for love. Maybe that makes him better off than you or me. The sad part is he's probably going to die out there for what he thinks is love."

"Perhaps, if that is fate's wish. The justice of the arena is swift and resolute."

The Discourager took a step closer to Dioneo and looked in Dioneo's eyes, asking, "But you—what will you die for?"

"The only thing worth dying for today," came Dioneo's reply. "Money."

The Discourager looked Dioneo up and down and held his sword to Dioneo's ear. "His Majesty is always wise, but I think especially so in having me see to you." He gestured toward the metal bars, then brushed the blade against Dioneo's face.

"Soon it will be time for the fates to judge you."

Dioneo didn't flinch as the saber kissed his skin.

"You seem very skilled with your blade," Dioneo said. "Maybe later we'll get a chance to see how you are without it."

The Discourager of Hesitancy's eyes narrowed but then relaxed. He gestured for the other two guards to leave the room.

"Perhaps you will find a way out of the arena yet." The Discourager backed his way out of the cell and closed the door.

"But I do not foresee it."

MADDALENA

I hear the voice of this woman, Jai Ling, call my name. It is prime, and the sun's light is beginning to rise. Have I slept another day? I remember I awoke briefly to see Bartolome and this woman's companion, a large Nubian she called "Mansa." I spoke little to Bartolome but fell asleep. I was awoken again at matins by this woman, who said we must go. We travelled for a while, with me riding the mule laden with several bags, she leading them along a footpath in these woods. We reached the end of the forest, and there was an immense clearing. Jai Ling made me dismount.

Now we are walking quickly, across open land toward a great barrier surrounding a city. It looks like the walls of Paris, but higher. Jai Ling is leading the mule, with me walking behind her, carrying a sack slung over my shoulder. It is heavy. I do not know what is in it.

The city entrance is a tall double-doored wooden gate. The sun has been up for a little while, but there are no travelers at this entrance.

There are some tax collectors at the gate, all men, and some who wear military outfits like the soldiers who were with my uncle's caravan. A box sits on a table to receive the entry tithes. Jai Ling stops and lifts me onto the mule, then tightens the burka around me so only a small portion of my face shows. She speaks to me.

"Maddalena, say nothing. Let me speak."

She leads the mule by its snout into the entrance. I can smell the drink on the guards' breath. The soldiers swarm around Jai Ling and make her open her tunic and pull up her shirtdress and drop her sheath to display her body. I look away, but before I do, I glimpse a red scar across Jai Ling's belly. One of the men points to the scar and asks about it, but another says that's a sword wound. The men laugh and make her stand there longer than necessary before letting her drop her shirtdress. She places two coins on the table and grabs the mule's ropes.

Then I hear one of the men ask about me. I feel my throat tighten, and my heart beat. Jai Ling slaps another coin onto the tax box and says that I am very young and that this should be a good enough inspection. The men take the coin and let us through.

Now that we are in the city, I see people hurrying in the same direction we are going. The streets are filled with the usual animals —cats, ducks, geese, chickens, a few pigs, some dogs, and rats. We turn onto a large street. It is paved with cobblestones, but in the center runs a trough of filth. I have seen these in large cities. It stinks from the waste in these troughs. But ahead, I can see a great structure, rising over the village as a round bowl. Many voices come from there.

"That's where we are heading," Jai Ling says. "Stay near me, Maddalena. Do not lose me."

I stay on the mule. I have nothing to do. It is as if I am dead. I follow because I am told.

Uwe squeezed the apron and felt the cloth slide against the flu he had coated the railings with. No one had seen the hunchback enter the arena and brush selected areas with his special combination of flu and sulfur that would ignite with the right spark. He grinned to himself. Fire was a wonderful thing. It consumed and cleaned. His only concern was that an errant spark from a sword against the stone or some other unforeseen happenstance could ignite this before it was time. This area was limited to the royal archers, who would be forbidden to smoke or do anything but stand ready to do the king's bidding. There shouldn't be any flames. Until necessary.

From above, he heard a human wail. One of the hired mourners was already up on the parapet, practicing his wailings with the illusion of sympathy. In a short while, other mourners would be scattered along the outer rim of the arena. Uwe didn't like the sound of the mourners, or even the idea of a professional crier. Why, with the sun just beginning to rise, Uwe could easily climb up the battlement and snap the bastard's neck, and who would be the wiser?

"What are you doing here, freak?"

Uwe looked back to see two of the king's guards approaching. Maybe he could break their necks. He recognized one as the captain of archers. More guards were approaching from behind the captain.

The dwarf grunted and gestured towards the apron.

"I've seen this one, it's the king's latest fool," said the subordinate guard, a tall, gruff-looking man with a scar across his nose. "They have *him* laying out the box linens? Damn, he's an ugly bastard."

The archer chief looked at Uwe and spat. "He's right, you are an ugly bastard. It hurts my balls to see your face. Get out of here."

The dwarf raised his hands apologetically and ran to a nearby stairwell.

MADDALENA

We are surrounded, a mixture of men and women and children, mostly dressed in drab colors. Many different languages are being spoken. From what I understand, the arena is full, but many are still trying to get in. The people speak of some sort of trial. Voices argue about a lady or a tiger.

Jai Ling leads the mule into an alley that has no people on the ground. On the buildings, shutters are closed on all but the top floors above us. She pulls me off the animal, looks inside the pack on my back, then smiles at me.

"Don't get near any fire, Maddalena," she says, and winks at me.

She hoists the other two bags from the mule and throws them over her shoulder. Jai Ling seems stronger than you would think. Her hand clasps mine. I don't wish to move, and I stumble, falling forward. She pulls me, but I lie on the floor.

She bends and grabs my elbows. I see anger in her eyes.

"I don't have time for this! I should have left you back at the river."

I stare emptily away.

Jai Ling slaps me.

"You're drifting. Stop it. I cannot wait for you; I must hurry. If you don't come now, I will leave you. This is a bad world, child, and especially so for a pretty young woman who is alone. You don't want to be left here."

Her eyes slightly soften.

"My parents were killed when I was young. It is a truly cruel world we were born into. But if one is in it, it is better not to be alone in it. I don't want to leave you, but I must hurry. I do have friends, and you can be with us. Come with me, Maddalena."

I look back at her.

"What about our mule? I ask.

"He's done his job."

Jai Ling slaps the creature on the rear. It utters a bray and wanders into the street.

I allow Jai Ling to lead me outside back into the crowd.

Throngs of people crush against the walls of the arena. Many want to get in. Around several portals, guards block the entrance. There is some mention that the coliseum is full. People crowd and yell and offer deniers and shillings to gain access. Almost all are adults, though I see a few children my age. We shall never enter it.

Jai Ling is dragging me along. I keep my focus on her. She is agile, and as I follow her, we shift, slide, and slither through the great masses. The crowd looks impenetrable, but we ooze through the slightest openings, and when we push against someone, we disappear before we can be detected.

Suddenly, our hands slip. I feel the crowd jostling me, and I am moved in a different direction. I fall backwards to the ground, and I thought my pack would shield my fall, but my hood slides back.

"What's this!" A loud and piercing voice.

A set of large hands encircle my waist and hoist me upwards. I see a vile man with an ugly face, one eye, and brown teeth.

"What a beauty you are!" he laughs while his fingers squeeze my hips. His breath reeks. "Look at this!"

I scream, "Jai Ling!" I didn't mean to, but I am too startled.

"Yer mine now!" he yells and displays me like a doll. "Look what I found!

Suddenly, his eye grows enflamed, and he screams in pain as he drops me. I land on my feet and stumble, but he falls to his knees and buries his head into the cobblestone, groping at the back of his leg. I can see blood spilling. Then a familiar grasp encircles my waist.

"I told you not to let go," Jai Ling scolds. I see her slipping the handle of a bloodied dagger underneath her tunic. I look at the man. No one seems too concerned.

"He'll live," Jai Ling says.

Then we are gone.

Jai Ling holds my wrist tighter. We reach the exterior of the arena and follow its curved stone. People here seem resigned to not entering. Various beggars are huddled against the wall. A blind old crone clutches a stick, waving a cup in the air. Two young children call out for Dineens, ropes tied around them and held by a one-armed woman crouching against the wall. A man with two stumps for legs reaches out to me and asks for food. These kinds seem to grow from the ground. I have seen such people before. If Mother were here, I would ask her to give them money. Mother is more generous than Uncle with such things.

The crowd has formed a circle around a small, dwarfish girl, dressed in a jade tunic that fits her well. She is beautiful, about my height, perhaps slightly older. The features of her face are perfectly sculpted, yet tiny, very much like a doll's. Up close, I see her face is painted with sprinkles that shine off her cheekbones. Her hair is rolled up high, much like the wealthy ladies at the Court of Avignon. She dances around a hat to the notes and beat of music played by a man sitting at one end of the circle. He plays a flute pipe with one hand and beats a tambourine with the other. Like the dancer, he too appears to be a dwarf, yet he is a terribly grotesque figure, as ugly as the dancer is beautiful. I see him rocking back and forth as he plays, providing a beat for the young dancer to move to. He is a hunchback with small lower limbs, but he has a disproportionately larger upper body with hands and arms that seem far too big for the instruments. As for his features, his nose and mouth seem set at odd places on his face. Yet he draws little notice. The people are fixated on the girl as she spins on one leg, her head pulled back and gazing to the heavens, making each circle faster as her companion plays a quicker pace. Hands in the crowd clap with the melody.

The music abruptly halts mid-note. The girl twirls in silence and then pauses mid-turn, her face cocked to the side, and—just for a moment—she smiles right at me. It is the first warm look I have received in this city. With a shrill note from the flute pipe, the music returns, and she resumes her dancing.

We depart.

The pack has grown heavy, and I grow tired of carrying it. I want to throw it down and run. I don't like this city. I don't like my companion. I wonder what has happened to Bartolome.

We enter a narrow alley that is walled on both sides. No one is here—these are the rears of the buildings. Here, there is an open trench for the sewer, a watery muck that is a muddy mix of sewage, shit, and pea. The stench is horrible.

We follow it. I now see a half-arch in the arena wall, out of which the trench flows.

"The Cloaca Maximus," I say under my breath, thinking of the great canal in Rome.

"You're well educated, Maddalena," Jai Ling says.

"It stinks here," I say. "Worse than the streets."

Jai Ling laughs. "It does, my child, doesn't it? That helps keep out the undesirables. But we're not undesirables, are we?"

She looks backward. A few people scurry past the top of the alley, but no one pays us any interest. Above, the windows are shuttered, no doubt because of the disgusting odor. Jai Ling pulls two cloths from the bag on my back and ties one cloth around my face, just over my nose. It has been scented with something I can't tell—like a lemon, but very strong. It weakens the stink from the pit. Jai Ling wraps another around her face, makes me pinch my nose, and then she jumps into the trench, pushing me with her.

Immediately upon entrance into the chamber, the air becomes drastically cooler. My pattens become stuck in the muck. Just inside the entrance, there is a stone ledge running along the side of the sewer wall, something not apparent from the outside.

Jai Ling lifts me onto it and then pulls herself up. We're only an arm's length over the trench, but at least we are not in the filth. We scurry a short way and soon outrun the farthest reach of the daylight. The stone is slippery under our feet, but it is better than wading in the city's manure. The dark has engulfed us. I call out to wait. Jai Ling lights a torch, and she pulls my wrist.

We make our way through a series of vaults and passages through which sewage flows. Thank God for the lemon-scented cloths! Still, I am beginning to feel sick. I sense we are moving upward. We reach a small, damp chamber that is away from the river of filth. Jai Ling tells me to lower my bag, then lights a candle that has been put in the room. She puts the torch in a sconce, drops everything else she was carrying, and begins to undress. As she does so, she takes my bag. It is filled with clothing. She hands me a pair of low boots and hose and, laughing, tells me that these are a present, and to put them on because my feet stink. I sit down and peel off my clothes, which smell of waste. Jai Ling tosses me a linen cloth to wipe my face and hands, which I do, and then I put on the new hose and boots.

At the same time, Jai Ling strips off her clothes and dresses in a stockinette shirt and leggings with stirrups on the bottom, all black, and a pair of boots. I have never seen such a dress on a woman. In the shadows of torchlight, I see she ties her hair back with a piece of cloth and smiles at me. Then she wraps a cloak around her and tugs me along.

"This way, Maddalena."

We pass through the dark. The torch has been left behind. It is as if night had fallen.

Ahead, I hear noise. The sound of people. We emerge from a seam in the wall. It is a large hall—no, a corridor, with people running about. Large archways lead to the outside. I see great stairways jammed with people. Everyone is looking towards the arena, and no one notices us.

We move quickly. Jai Ling stops and tilts her head to the right. Two young men are walking by, one with his arm around the other, both very handsome, both laughing. One takes no interest in us, but the one with his arm around his companion looks back. His face is beautiful, his features sharp and olive-skinned, but in his eyes there is a look of fear and hatred. It is only for an instant, and then he turns. Both men continue laughing.

I look at Jai Ling. She clutches the handle of her dagger.

Strangely, at that moment, I understand.

"That boy," I say to her, "he's a vampire, isn't he?"

"You *are* a very perceptive girl, Maddalena." She releases her grip on the blade. "But we've no time to deal with his like. Let's go."

We continue to move through the people, but unlike in the sewers below, Jai Ling stays behind me.

The small girl dwarf who was dancing earlier, known as Trippetta, stood by her horse, a young, swift gelding. Her arms were wrapped around Uwe, the other dwarf, he of the great upper body strength. He gently but firmly pushed Trippetta away. She resisted a moment, then released her embrace. She wiped a tear with her dainty hand and gave him a kiss on his cheek.

"Good luck," she said, mounted her horse, and gently kicked. Although Trippetta was a tiny figure, she handled the reins skillfully, and the horse responded to her direction and galloped down the empty street. Uwe watched her turn a corner. Then he climbed up a drain pipe to the roof of a building and began for the arena, navigating among the rooftops.

For her part, Trippetta rode out through the front gates of the city unnoticed.

A small woman riding her horse gently along the outside of the kingdom's walls might on some days have elicited some notice, but not today, when a trial was to be held in the arena. Trippetta rode close to the exterior of the highest walls in the kingdom, which attached in the rear to the arena, forming a border to the outside world. The sun was coming up behind her. Someone would have to look directly down to see her, and even if they did, what would they care?

But looks can be deceiving. For though young in appearance, and often childlike in demeanor, Trippetta was over twenty years of age. She paused her gelding at one part of the outside wall of the arena. The granite stones were well cut and laid. Granite is a hard stone, very hard; mortar, which is used between the stones, is made from lime, soil, and water, not so much. Trippetta leaned forward and saw the holes that Uwe and she had dug into the mortar two nights ago. They had packed these holes with Uwe's own concoctions, a flexible putty material. She moved her horse further along. More X's. Then, a circle, at the base of the wall. Farther along, another, and then another. Then two more circles higher up, and a final two, the highest of all, dug into the granite.

The sun was now right over the tip of the arena. There might be a guard posted on the ramparts above, but if there were any, they were looking inward. The sun shielded her. For a long distance, at least a six-minute ride at full gallop, there was nothing but white sands and some brush. A veritable kill zone that had been created by the barbaric king's barbaric ancestors long ago. Out on this plain was a small group of people on a wagon, with horses nearby. They seemed to be working on a broken wheel.

Trippetta cupped her hands over her eyes and saw a tall African man stand up and wave to her.

"Hope you're right, Mansa," she said.

She pulled from the shift she had on over her dancing outfit several sticks with sulfur tips coated by a dried mix Uwe made from powdered sand.

"Fire sticks," she said, and dismounted. She struck a fire stick against the granite wall, and a flame sparked from the clay tip. Then she inserted the stick into the farthest hole on the right at the bottom of the wall. The mixture of sulfur and other chemicals began to sparkle.

Trippetta methodically went to each hole and lit each one. Then she mounted her horse and lit the two middle holes, waiting each time to be sure they were sparkling. For the highest two, she had to balance herself atop the horse's back and rise on her toes—for Trippetta, a relatively easy task.

With the last hole burning, she sat on the horse and watched the sparkles coming from the walls, burning *into* the rock.

Trippetta giggled and clapped, quite proud. Then she rode out onto the white sands towards the wagon, which, if anyone noticed, now had all its wheels fixed.

Going upward through the great arena, steadily pushing Maddalena before her, Jai Ling was conscious of her surroundings but focused her eyes in front of her. People were running back and forth, crowding the archways to see a glimpse of the trial. Jai Ling did not notice a woman wearing a black wool cloak, covered by a hood, observing from a recess in the exterior wall of the arena. The woman was breathing deeply—the morning sun was warm, and her covering made her warmer. Without it, she could move better, but she did not want to be observed. She marveled at the gracefulness of the Oriental woman working her way through the crowd.

"Jai Ling. *What a pretty name.*"

Damn.

Elizabeth had only meant to touch the woman's mind gently, not comment or speak.

But the thought had come out.

It was a mistake on Elizabeth's part. Quite lazy, really, but she had not mastered the nuances of mind-reading. Jai Ling flinched and cast a sharp look to her left, pausing for an instant, but then kept moving.

Elizabeth realized she herself was vulnerable here. The Oriental was strong, a vampire killer, someone to be reckoned with. Oh, she could bite several others and turn the entire place into a carnage house, but getting the girl out of here alive would be impossible.

But she was close to the girl. And the boy was near too.

[3]
LADIES AND TIGERS

MADDALENA

My God. I've never seen such a spectacle. It is as a great bowl, or circle, with arches spaced apart. The circle is filled; the entire city must be here. There are people everywhere. Most of the circle is open, but at the far side, directly across from us, is a large covering where, underneath, sit some people with colorful clothing. It looks like there are many soldiers surrounding them.

I am standing in a hall at the top of this great arena. It is a giant bowl and rivals the Coliseum of Rome. There are archways all along the top, supported by columns shaped in the form of gods. In the one below us, a goddess holds a large vat with fire burning in her hand. The flames flicker at the edge.

Jai Ling goes to a stone gargoyle statue and reaches behind it. She pulls out a large package wrapped in black blankets. She unfolds the blankets. There is a crossbow, a longbow, a quiver, and a small vial of liquid. The arrows are strange—there are small pouches tightly wrapped around the shafts of each one, and a wick is attached to each pouch. Jai Ling takes the longbow up and pulls its cord, testing it. She then takes the vial, opens it, and wets the bow strings with the liquid. After this, she holds the bow to her ear and pulls the string again, and the rhythm of the bow sounds different.

"Much better."

"You just found that?" I ask.

"No," she answers. "It's a present left for us from a little friend. Best he could find in here. Hope it is accurate."

Jai Ling has laid my bag down. She opens it and pulls out a bunch of short sticks and lays them beside the arrows. Some are wooden, some are metal. They are tubes and have a wick standing out, just like on the longer arrows.

"Arrows?" ask.

Jai Ling smiles, wets a finger, and runs it up and down one of the arrows.

"Bolts, actually. Arrows are fired by bows, and bolts are for crossbows. These are our presents for the king, Maddalena. It's something special that comes from my home. He's going to get a real bang out of it." She looks at me. "It is going to get dangerous soon, Maddalena. You can leave and take your chances, if you want, or stay with me. It's up to you."

"Where would I go?" I ask.

"I don't know. But it is your choice to stay. Make sure you don't get the arrows or the bolts too close to the sunlight. We don't want them to get hot."

I hear trumpets. I rise back to the portal. Two men stand at the end of the arena to our right. The sun beats on them. They are distant, I can't make out their face, but one seems anxious, looking in many directions at the crowd, while the other stands stolid.

I feel Jai Ling beside me. She is holding the longbow and has an arrow drawn.

Dioneo stood at one end of the arena, a few feet to the left and slightly behind Ricciardo. The crowd's cheers rang in Dioneo's ears. In his mind, the crowd could be broken into three groups (he'd had plenty of time on his hands to think about such things while in the dungeon). One, probably the smallest group, was appalled at the "trial." In almost every crowd, there was always some humanity, and no doubt some peasants and, to a lesser degree, nobles, were here solely out of fear of possible retribution that could come from not being present. Ricciardo was a native here. Surely some sympathized with the young man's plight, having committed the most egregious crimes imaginable in this kingdom, that of falling in love with the king's daughter. Or perhaps, as Dioneo said, at least thinking he had fallen in love.

Then there was also a second group, those who probably loathed the young lover. Ricciardo was a good-looking boy who'd had the audacity of actually romancing the most desired beauty in the kingdom. Whether jealous of his appearance, his boldness, or his (apparent) success in wooing the princess, Lucrezia, these people were hoping to see Ricciardo receive his just "reward" at the jaws and claws of the tigers.

And still others fell into Dioneo's third group. They were the ones who were content to go along with the festivities. These people had been indoctrinated into the ways of the king and his penchant for "creative" justice. They neither hated nor loved Ricciardo, but looked forward to the spectacle of the arena. And what would happen, indeed? It would be interesting.

Dioneo squinted. Though still early, the sun was above the arena's top level. The doors at the far end of the arena were placed at the eastern end of the oval. The rays blinded a defendant in the arena, prohibiting someone from seeing a tell-tale wiggle or jarring of one of the doors caused by a tiger throwing itself against it, although Dioneo thought it unlikely His Majesty would allow such an oversight to enter into his game. The doors were purposefully heavily carpeted to encase any sound within their chambers, and the tigers were held back by chains that released by the opening of a door.

The crowd noise stopped. The king was making a speech to the crowd, thanking them for their attendance and extolling the virtues of their justice system. Something about fate having brought the defendants here, and how fate would decide how they would leave.

Dioneo looked over at Ricciardo. They'd had time to talk in the dungeon. Ricciardo was a pleasant enough, if naïve, boy. In the dungeon, he'd been remarkably calm, with faith that his beloved Lucrezia would be his salvation. But standing at one end of the arena, looking around at the bloodthirsty audience, bedecked in white linen pants which set off his olive skin, Ricciardo seemed more like a skinny, frail, and frightened child. Yet he was bolstered by what he thought was real love.

When the boy looked over to Dioneo, his face was fearful. The king's voice and the crowd seemed to grow very distant at that moment.

"Wonderful weather, wouldn't you say?" Dioneo chimed.

"I'm sorry you're here, Dioneo," Ricciardo said. "I don't know why you are sentenced to be with me. I should be here alone. But..." He paused and looked to the ground. "I—I guess—right now I—" He looked up, and there were tears in his eyes. "I'm glad I'm not alone."

Dioneo's heart was quite mercenary. As he'd said, he was there for money, or at least profit, and nothing more. He'd learned years ago that was the only thing worth caring for in this world. But he felt a slight twinge of pity. In a few moments, Ricciardo would either be dead (along with Dioneo) or heartbroken. He lost either way. For Dioneo, it was much more of a win-or-lose proposition. Dioneo flashed his teeth and walked to his compatriot's side.

"Have faith, Ricciardo," Dioneo said, placing his arm around the younger boy's shoulder. "Look at these beautiful garments they've given us. Linen feels so nice on the body, it breathes, don't you agree?" Dioneo felt the boy shudder under his hand, so he made a broad wave to the crowd.

"I think you and me, we're going to get out of this," Dioneo said. "And we're going to show the king a thing or two about justice."

Ricciardo looked back at the ground and said, "I have faith. And I know we will be safe. Lucrezia will not fail us."

As a circus performer, Dioneo knew the importance of putting on a good face. And his face never changed its positive expression towards Ricciardo, which, under the circumstances, he thought, should have qualified for an award at the Venice Festival—whenever or if ever it were held again.

"It is arranged," Ricciardo whispered. "I know this is short, but it is our first chance to speak since we went to the dungeon. Lucrezia will sit with hands clasped. But she will raise one finger. To the west means the door on the right. To the east, the door on the left. And I shall open the door she points to. I was told to say nothing to you. But as both our lives shall be judged, I feel I must. You must let me choose the door. Yet now I must ask you—Do you trust Lucrezia and me?"

"My boy," said Dioneo, squeezing Ricciardo's shoulder tighter, "I trust that I know exactly what both of you will do."

Ricciardo gave a very nervous trace of a smile.

Dioneo then released his grip and gave Ricciardo the slightest push forward. Ricciardo looked up at the crowd and made a weak wave, to which the crowd roared even greater approval. He began striding across the arena floor.

"Nobody ever runs *to* the fire," Dioneo thought, and he set off behind Ricciardo.

From atop the highest portions of the arena, Lora watched Dioneo and Ricciardo walk across the arena to the two doors opposite them. Masquerading here as a professional mourner (or celebrant, depending on the results), she had the highest vantage point of the proceedings. Although spaced far apart on the parapets, it might be possible for one of the other mourners to see her if that person were searching for her. But all eyes were focused on the two men crossing the sands of the coliseum towards their fate.

If all was well, Jai Ling and that girl were in the alcove directly across. If not, Dioneo would wind up dead. Probably Lora, too. Yet Lora was not one to fear death. Not after losing so much to the sickness known as the great mortality. Still, there was the issue of the task at hand.

Everyone was looking at the arena, not high in the sky above. To be especially careful, Lora had positioned herself atop the eastern-most pillar, so anyone giving her a casual glance would be blinded by the sun. No one noticed as she pulled off the coverings of the cages beside her. Leo and Francine sat in their respective compartments. Her prize peregrine falcons were beautiful creatures, much as Lora had once been. Francine, with a red nape on the back of her head, and Leo, with an all-green feathered head and red quills on his tail. Sometimes he was mistaken for a red-tailed hawk. After checking their talons, she took each one out and placed it gently on her arm, which was covered with a leather wrap. The falcons tightened their talons into the leather covering on her forearm. Lora looked again and saw that Dioneo and Ricciardo were striding for the doors. It was time. She slipped a glass vial into their claws, and each bird dutifully clenched its package. Then she removed Leo's hood first, then Francine's, and shook her arm. Both falcons took flight in opposite directions, encircling the vast amphitheater and clasping their containers.

Ricciardo hesitated. He'd seen Lucrezia's signal. He knew with all his heart that this was the door she had directed him to. Pausing in front of it, he took note of its vast size. Both doors stood side by side, each with a metal ring hanging from it to pull. No sound came from behind either one.

Ricciardo straightened his back and reached for the handle on the right-side door.

The next thing he heard was Dioneo's voice in his ear.

"Son, never trust a woman with your life."

Ricciardo was pushed into the wall space between the doors.

The king had watched as Dioneo stayed several feet behind Ricciardo. Yet at the moment while Ricciardo opened the door, Dioneo sprang in and pushed him forward.

"Kill Dioneo," the king commanded.

While Dioneo pushed Ricciardo forward, he reached out with both his arms and, grabbing the great metal rings, yanked both doors open simultaneously and pulled them around, forming a momentary shield around Ricciardo and himself from the archers. Immediately, he felt the vibration of arrows striking against the door from the king's box. The archers were good, but the doors were made of iron and really were deeply carpeted on the inside, which now faced outward. Good thing too—the arrows were front weighted and metal-tipped, designed to penetrate armor.

But arrows were not the only danger. The air was filled with roars as tigers leapt out from both open portals, their massive bodies passing within inches of the men in the arena who were hidden behind the doors. The animals burst onto the coliseum floor from both doors and seemed momentarily stunned that they had not been greeted by a shocked victim waiting to receive the warm embrace of the carnivorous judges. Dioneo glanced back and counted their number at six.

It would not take the animals long to detect the scent of nearby flesh.

As the tigers prowled, no one noticed the two falcons swooping in from the east, obscured in the blind of the morning sun. Leo arrived first and released his package. It dropped to the ground and burst into a great gaseous substance. Pink, of all colors. Francine followed suit and dropped one that erupted into a greater cloud of black smoke. The smoke had a strong odor, and the tigers were engulfed in it. They were disoriented and ran away to the edges of the arena.

While the falcons dove, other archers waited for a clear shot. The smoke made a direct sighting impossible.

"Kill them!" bellowed the king above the roaring crowd.

At that instant, a flaming arrow streaked across the arena. Almost no one saw it. The Discourager of Hesitancy caught sight at the last moment and placed a strong arm on the king's shoulder.

"Stay down," he ordered.

The arrow struck with an explosion right in front of the gallery where a group of the king's own archers stood. The force of the concussion sent several guards reeling backwards. There were other rows of archers above them, but a great flame burst open on the draped coverings over the railings, and it spread quickly, feeding on the drapes and blocking what had been a clear view down into the arena.

A second arrow struck higher up in the stands. Several soldiers were dismembered by the explosion, and others collapsed into one another, unable to detect where the attack was coming from. The fire below raced up the rails lining the stairways. A third arrow struck near the top of the arena and exploded, toppling several more guards from their parapets to the streets below.

The king had been forced by the Discourager to the right of the flames and into a safe alcove. The king stood from the side, to the right of the main force of the fire, and dug his nails into the wooden archway.

"Find that shooter!" he growled to the Discourager. "And don't let those men escape the arena."

The Discourager heard his majesty's words, but his attention was across the arena, peering through the flames around him. This shooter had to be in a concealed place in the upper echelons of the stadium. His eyes searched. Then they rested on a small crevice near the top, strangely uncrowded, with no guards nearby. He walked a few steps down.

Diagonally across the arena, Jai Ling's eyes zeroed in on the king. "You deserve to die today, too, fat boy," she said, releasing an arrow directly at the king's belly.

The Discourager peered furtively over the area. Even if one knew where to look, it was hard to see as people were now screaming and rushing from the arena, along with smoke. Still, the arrows were coming almost dead on. The archer had to be at a particular angle, directly across them, and from above. A flick of movement from the crevice he was looking at—something coming towards them.

The king was screaming at the captain of the archers, who stood between him and the Discourager. There was no time for the Discourager to speak, only to react. The Discourager leaned over, grabbed the Captain of Archers with one hand, and thrust him in front of the king.

Even for the Discourager, this was a bold move, and the king was about to chastise him when he saw the archer captain's face jerk forward, frozen in mid-speech. Then his head fell to the side, and the king saw an arrowhead bursting out from his chest. The Discourager threw the body into the ring, where it exploded as it fell. One of the tigers pounced on an arm that had been blown off and trotted away with it.

"We must get you to safety, your majesty," said the Discourager.

"Where is my daughter?" he bellowed in defiance. He was the

king, and this entire attack was an affront to his rule. Then he noticed blood on his robes and hands.

"She ran to the protection of the stairs," answered the Discourager. "But you must be removed from this position of vulnerability."

While the Discourager moved the king further into an escape path in the interior of the stadium, he glanced back towards the upper alcoves.

"Sergeant at Arms," he called, pointing upward, "your assassin is at the top level across from us. Find him!"

And what of the two men in the arena, you might ask? Dioneo had waited while the tigers were distracted and the archers attacked. Ricciardo, as one may expect, was somewhat discombobulated.

"Time to go, Ricciardo," said Dioneo. He could see the boy was paralyzed with confusion. "Sorry to have to do this, but it's for your own good."

Dioneo smacked the boy on the side of the head to stun him, then threw Ricciardo over his shoulders. He started to close the right door, but an arrow flew by his head, so he pulled it back to shield himself. Some people from above were jeering at him, but most were trying to flee the arena. Then he slipped around the left door carrying Ricciardo and ran into the chamber, slamming the door behind him.

Uwe watched the flames run along the paths he had set for them. The area where the king's archers sat was now like a great torch, burning away. Flames had also traveled to the top of the arena, where other guards had been stationed. The fire was not spreading rapidly into the other areas of the stadium, as he'd been careful where he set the combustible fuel under the lush velvet drapes. Of course, a person's outer garments could catch fire, and then they might go up quickly. But for now, most of the peasantry should be able to exit. Still, the crowd only saw the flames. People were screaming and pushing everywhere, but crouched low with an arm wrapped against a metal railing in the stairwell, Uwe was as immobile as a rock, and others bumped into and tripped over him.

Someone on fire fell into the arena. He wore the leather armor of an archer. One of the tigers ran off with his limb.

Uwe was proud of his work.

Jai Ling cursed when she saw the bodyguard thrust forward another to protect the king. Her aim was on target, and the king would've been dead otherwise. She thought of firing again, but noticed Dioneo had left the arena.

The stands opposite her were in flames. The king's bodyguard had pointed in her general direction. Regular guards would be coming. She'd done her job.

"Time to leave, Maddalena."

"Going somewhere, my dear?"

The olive-skinned boy they'd passed earlier in the gallery stood in the shadows at the far end of the chamber, clutching Maddalena across her chest and covering her mouth. He had another hand stroking her neck. Maddalena was frozen.

"About now, you must be in a hurry," he said through fanged teeth. "And this lovely girl—oh, I can smell it, taste it, royal blood." He licked Maddalena's neck, but kept a wary eye on Jai Ling. "And she's not your daughter or sister. No, you're not related at all, are you?"

Jai Ling looked at the arrows sitting in the bag at her feet.

"No no no," said the boy, and though appearing to be of slight build, he raised Maddalena with a single arm so that she shielded his upper body.

"You've fulfilled what you came here to do. My guess is you now plan on blending into the crowd. Who'd suspect a woman of being so good with a bow? And an Oriental at that! You just need to leave here, and this girl is nothing to you. She'll only slow you down. You can stay and deal with me, but think of the time. Some nasty people are coming for you."

In the background, Jai Ling could hear much yelling and screaming, but she made out someone saying, "Up there." Her eyes met Maddalena's, whose face was otherwise covered by the vampire's hand.

"Sorry, child," Jai Ling said and, picking up her cloak, slipped out the back of the alcove.

MADDALENA

She left me.

I'm being carried back into the darkness.

I'm-going-to-die.

"You're a heavy little bastard," Dioneo thought as he raced into the chamber with Ricciardo draped over his shoulder. An interior portcullis was shut, with a small opening at the top, just the way he'd been told it would be. Dioneo dropped the young lover and leaped onto the metal grating. With the ease that he possessed as an acrobat, he climbed up and over the gate, grabbed hold of the metal release, and slid down the other side, drawing the gate up as he did so. He ran back and grabbed Ricciardo, who was starting to stir.

"Ricciardo, can you run?"

"My head," he said, rubbing it. "Am I—did I die?"

"Not yet," Dioneo said, throwing Ricciardo over his shoulder. Further up, the— They hadn't closed the other door in the arena.

Dioneo ran deeper into the depths of the fortress. The corridor was a sandy bottom lined with limestone. Torches burned along the way—after all, once in a while, a maiden really was led along this path to wait at the end in case her door would be opened. Or the animal wranglers would lead the tigers along here, fiercely chained, to be deposited behind the metal grate and to await their victim.

Ricciardo was growing more alert.

"Dioneo? What are you doing? Where's the maiden? Where's the maiden?"

"The maidens are waiting for you in Valhalla, or whatever place you choose to believe in," said Dioneo, "but they aren't here."

Ricciardo began to squirm.

"Lucrezia pointed me to the right door."

"She pointed you to the door she wanted to all right," said Dioneo, still running. "But there wasn't any maiden behind either.. Your lover sold you out, my friend."

Ricciardo protested, "No, she couldn't have known," and hit Dioneo in the back.

Dioneo dropped his passenger down with a thump.

"We're in the bottom of the arena, Ricciardo. We opened both doors, and a bunch of big, hungry cats jumped out. And tigers have a great sense of smell, so we left the doors open, and we might see one of them pattering right down this tunnel. Plus, I have a feeling that he's not going to be very happy with you or me, so I expect there will be some angry guards rushing down here ."

Ricciardo was shaking his head and pounding his fist to the ground. "No no no—Lucrezia wouldn't betray me."

Dioneo grunted and, grabbing the front of Ricciardo's shirt, dragged him along.

The passageway opened into a circular chamber, well-lit by torches on the walls, and lofty. Its interior walls were smooth and formed a dome, with several other portals on the opposite side. A pair of parapets ran around the dome above the floor, forming several layers, and a stone stairway led upward. Dioneo stopped.

"The first step's a long drop, my friend," Dioneo said, gesturing to the ground. The floor of the room was not solid, but a huge stone grate over a pit. The area underneath was dark. Something was moving below.

"What is that?" Ricciardo asked.

"That's where they keep the tigers. But we're going over there to the left hallway."

The stone lattice bars were roughly a foot wide, more than enough to get a foothold on, but the spaces were spread so that a person who slipped could easily fall through. The air was tdamp here, chillingly so, and the grates were covered in moss.

"I can't cross it," Ricciardo said, recoiling from the pit.

"Son, that's not an option." With that, Dioneo threw Ricciardo over his shoulder again and commenced crossing. Ricciardo looked heard s growling below. He could make out one of the tigers sitting on its haunches, watching them.

Fate has shone on Venturo today, the vampire thought as he moved down the narrow stone stairs, cradling the girl in his right arm.

The fates be damned. They had told him today was one to exert caution, to avoid risky judgments. He thought that perhaps picking up the boy from Mantua, Benvolio, may have been what the stars warned of. But when he passed the girl in the hall earlier, his olfactory senses exploded. He immediately knew. And when he'd seen her, alone but for her companion, he had to have her. Undoubtedly, the other one was a vampire hunter, and a female one at that. When their eyes had met, he sensed she was skilled. Also, she was an Oriental, rare but always dangerous. Yet as sure as Venturo recognized the sweet, intoxicating scent of royal blood, he also sensed that the hunter was here for another purpose. To her, the young girl was only a means to an end. The huntress wouldn't fight a pitched battle to protect the child.

Realizing all this, he quickly dispatched Benvolio in a nearby alcove and stashed the body away for later. *'Twas a shame*, Venturo thought, as the youth was beautiful, and could have been a source of much pleasure, but the chance for a prize as valuable as this girl was too good to pass up. He'd followed the two and bided his time for the proper moment.

And when it came, he found he had been right. About the girl and the huntress. As he watched the huntress draw arrows, it was clear her target was the king, or at least his guards. When confronted with either delay and a fight, or quick flight, she had relinquished her charge to him rather than risk being trapped. The huntress didn't know how special this girl was. Now he could savor this child.

He squeezed the child against his chest; the aroma of her blood filled his senses, dazzling him in ecstasy. Perhaps he could save *her* for later.

He slowed his gait and walked through the black halls. "You're very precious," he whispered to her. "You don't know how precious you are. I'm not going to kill you. I'm going to keep you." With that, he licked her neck. Delectable. She didn't even struggle but lay limp in his arms.

Shock. Such a common response.

The pleasure he felt was intoxicating. So young a child! And of such ancestry. Why, the pleasure swelling in his loins and in his lungs was so great as to be almost painful. Dazzling images filled his thoughts, of erotic and unspeakable pleasure and pain. The line between the two was truly a fine one, he'd found. His fangs sprouted instinctively from his jaws, and he couldn't restrain his hunger any longer.

Then another image jutted into view—that of the huntress's face in the dark, upside down in front of him.

A strange hallucination, he thought.

Then he realized the pleasure he felt was indeed pain, that of a silver dagger penetrating his heart from the back. The blade thrust up, shredding the most vital internal organ. Venturo felt his life force spraying out from him, just as in the many stories he'd heard told. He dropped the girl with the realization that his lust had so engulfed him that he'd wandered right beneath where the huntress had been waiting for him.

Venturo heard the huntress whisper, "This is how we Orientals say good-bye to your kind." As he died, his last thoughts were he was too beautiful to end like this, and the fates had been right, and he would have been fine if he'd only been content to stay with that boy from Mantua.

Jai Ling grabbed hold of the wooden beam she'd been suspended from and dropped beside the vampire's corpse. Maddalena lay crumpled on the floor. Jai Ling reached for her, but the child pushed back.

"You left me to die," Maddalena said.

"I came back," retorted Jai Ling, extracting her knife from the vampire's back and wiping the blood with a cloth. She was still in her form-fitting black stockingnet, with no hood or cloak, and quite bloodied.

"You helped me get in and carried my things._I saved you from him and the river. We're even. You want to cry, stay here and find someone who'll listen to you sob. I'm leaving. "

The degree of difficulty experienced in balancing oneself on the edges of a stone grate that covers a pit of hungry tigers depends on the individual. For a skilled acrobat as Dioneo, it would ordinarily be so rudimentary a task as to not even qualify as an exertion. But factoring in that he had been imprisoned for the previous night, and adding the body of Ricciardo, plus the added possibility of pursuit from several sources, had increased the exertion needed to execute the crossing. At least, that was what Dioneo was thinking as he crossed over the stone lattice and entered the corridor on the far left.

It was dark in this passage. Dioneo said, "We're going to make it Ricciardo," as he walked in. He smelled the odor of sulfur, as made by a fire, yet there was no light. Why weren't the torches on? The tiger wranglers would have been through here and would have left the hallway lit. Unless someone had just extinguished the torches.

Dioneo stopped in his tracks. Coming from a lit chamber (and the glaring morning sun a few moments earlier), his eyes had taken a second to readjust to the dark, but he could make out a sword being turned towards him. Dioneo threw his buttocks backward and arched his back, watching the arc of a swinging sword just miss slicing his belly open. Dioneo dropped Ricciardo to the ground and rolled to his feet, pushing Ricciardo to the side.

"Gentlemen," he said, and waltzed backwards into the chamber and onto the stone grill. He stood on one of the parallel bars and spread his hands out.

Ignoring Ricciardo, two soldiers came out, a younger one with a sword, the other an older, slightly hunchbacked one carrying a pike. Dioneo recognized his friends from the dungeon.

"Such a pleasure to see you again."

"You're going to die this time, you bastard!" said the younger one. Both guards hesitated to venture onto the slippery stone grate, glancing nervously below.

"It *is* a pleasure to see you again, stranger," came a voice from above. A large-shouldered man looking down

from a level above, a leg propped up on the railing and leaning forward.

"The Discourager of Hesitancy himself," said Dioneo, taking another step backward. "Tell me, how is His Majesty feeling right now?

"I must confess, he has had better moments," said the Discourager, who was resting his hands on his knees and still had not drawn his scimitar. "And how are you, stranger? You are the first man I've ever seen leave the arena in quite that manner."

"I'm just full of surprises," said Dioneo, now edging near the center of the chamber. "Are you going to come down and join us?"

"That remains to be seen, Dioneo," said the Discourager. "But I don't think that will be necessary."

Dioneo's instincts told him to turn. The younger soldier had come out gingerly, glancing down before nervously inching another foot forward. The grates were wide enough to stand on, but there was also enough space to fall through. He held his pike outward, brandishing its sharp head towards Dioneo. The older hunchback stood at the edge of the grate and yelled, "Slice 'em up!"

The younger soldier thrust the pike in front of him. Dioneo sidestepped its head and grabbed the shaft. He pulled it out of the younger soldier's hands, who slipped and fell backwards through one of the holes in the grate. Immediately, there was a cacophony of growls from below. The soldier's hands grasped at the edge, and Dioneo saw his eyes widen in fear as he struggled to pull himself up. Suddenly, the soldier's hand slipped off a moist stone, and he disappeared through the floor. There was a yell interrupted by the sound of his body hitting the floor, then the roar of animals whose appetite had been stoked over the last week.

"Hell's balls," snarled the older guard, who had crept along the edge of the room. Then he added, "Let's just hold 'em here; he can't run."

Dioneo swung around to face the Discourager, who now had his scimitar up and was descending the staircase to the room.

"Idiots," the Discourager spat out. But he quickly regained his composure. "I guess I shall have the pleasure of dealing with the stranger myself."

Dioneo tensed and clutched the pike. The Discourager's skill with his sword was formidable, and Dioneo was on uncertain footing. The other guard wasn't coming out, but he had to be accounted for. Then he heard a growling coming from one of the other tunnels—the one connected to the main arena. He looked towards the corridor where Ricciardo had been—and where Ricciardo now stood.

"Get back!" yelled Dioneo, and the boy slunk out of sight. The older soldier still had his sword out but kept one arm against the wall, precariously balanced on the edge, and made no move forward. The Discourager was halfway down the steps. While holding the pike, Dioneo smiled at the Discourager, then at the guard by the wall, and jumped through a hole in the grates.

Many people with knowledge of wild animals gained primarily through writings and illustrations often underestimate the actual size of such creatures and are surprised upon seeing these animals in the flesh, close enough to smell the animal (of course, in most cases, the animal can also smell you long before then). The same effect can be felt when seeing an animal one has observed in the past from a distance, in an up-close setting. The average adult male Bengal Tiger grows to a size of nine feet in length. Maggo, the older soldier, experienced this startling revelation in one instant, specifically being the instant when one such Bengal leaped through the space Dioneo had occupied a moment earlier, front paws outstretched. Mercifully for Maggo, this was all his mind had time to process as his upper torso caught the full brunt of the animal's lunge.

Dioneo saw an orange blur passing overhead. He clung tightly to the pike, which straddled the grate, and heard the tiger rip into Maggo with a roar. Another tiger entered the chamber and paused at the edge, sniffing the air. It briefly looked through the grate and swatted at Dioneo's hands. Dioneo switched his grip to avoid having his hand ripped off. Then the creature turned its head in the direction of the Discourager of Hesitancy, who was retreating back up the stairs. The tiger growled and ran at the stairway in the Discourager's direction.

Hanging here under the floor, Dioneo had momentarily forgotten what was in the dark beneath him. He swung his legs up and felt something swipe the air beneath him, accompanied by a roar of disgust.

"Sorry, kitties. " Dioneo slipped his shins through and locked his feet around the grate. then pulled himself out. The large cat was lying on the cement, front paws draped over Maggo's body, feeding. Dioneo held the pike and gingerly moved back to the far-left corridor. Inside, Dioneo found Ricciardo lying on the ground just outside the torchlight of the chamber.

"I've never seen anything like—" Ricciardo began, but Dioneo threw his hands over the boy's mouth and pulled him further.

"Our animal friends may still be hungry," said Dioneo.

Uwe hopped through a hall on the south side of the arena, one level below where the king's box burned. He used his arms to push himself along. Several guards had run by him, but with smoke billowing throughout, he was hard to see. Flames burned from the ceiling. Uwe smiled. Fire on the ceilings was especially disorienting.

He reached his spot, located on the second level, south side of the coliseum, where he had hidden a coil of rope under a barrel earlier. The rope was there, one end anchored tightly around a stone ornament. Grabbing the free end, he went to the open arch and tossed the rope over the edge.

"You bastard!"

Uwe turned to see the subordinate guard, the one who had insulted him earlier, looking at him with hatred. The guard was fairly tall, armored with a chest plate and helmet, and held a spiked Morningstar mace on a long chain.

Uwe gnashed his teeth and waved himaway.

"You did this!" the guard yelled. He ran at Uwe and swung the mace at Uwe's head. Uwe ducked and avoided the ball, which gave off sparks as it struck the stone wall behind him.

"I'll kill you!" The guard pulled the mace back and struck again

Uwe ducked but howled. One of the spikes had caught his shoulder.

The guard was throwing his arm back to swing again. Uwe, already on the ground, hit the guard's right leg with one hand. This threw the man's leg out from under him, and he fell backward. Uwe sprang onto him and pounded his fist into the guard's face. There was a cracking sound as facial bones broke.

The guard's body lay still.

Uwe hopped on the rampart and tugged at the rope. It held. He scrambled over the wall and slid down into the city, leaving bloody handprints behind. When he reached the ground, Lora_was waiting for him with two horses. Each took a mount, and they galloped for the outskirts of the city.

Dioneo peered carefully into the next area, thrusting a torch into it. The corridor opened into this larger space. The light from Dioneo's torch could not reach the ceiling. What the flames did reveal were walls composed of immense blocks of stone throughout the chamber, some clearly formed, most broken, and a few stacked atop each other.

"What is this place?" he asked.

"It's old," said Dioneo. "Maybe it was used like a quarry to cut stones for the keep. Maybe it was used to torture your countrymen who weren't happy about paying His Majesty's taxes." Dioneo saw the youth gazing upwards into the unseen blackness. He slapped the boy on his shoulder.

"My boy," Dioneo said, "don't look up there, look there." He guided the boy's face towards the wall in front of them and said, "That is the edge of the arena. On the other side of that wall is our freedom. Assuming our friends hit the right spot."

"Ricciardo!" came a call to their side, from behind a wall. Not that of a swordsman or a soldier, nor even the Discourager of Hesitancy.

"Lucrezia!" cried Ricciardo, who turned around towards the voice.

Dioneo shook his head and wiped a hand across his face. "God's balls, women," he muttered.

"I'm here," they heard Lucrezia say, stepping out from behind one of the upturned stone blocks. Ricciardo ran towards her.

The lovers embraced, while Dioneo stood back.

"Lucrezia," Ricciardo said, and kissed her again. "My love. For just a moment, I thought I was going to die."

"Ricciardo," said the king's daughter, "I knew you wouldn't. I knew the fates wouldn't keep us apart."

"You're in danger coming here," said Ricciardo, still hugging her. "If your father finds us together, it will be bad for us both."

"I couldn't let you perish, not in the arena, not in this place," she said, rubbing her face against his shoulder.

He had to give it to the kid, Dioneo thought; he had guts, romancing the king's daughter. And it was understandable—Lucrezia had the long and lithe look of a beauty produced by a life of privilege, one protected from the ravages of the world beyond these walls. But Lucrezia was not so innocent a youth as Ricciardo. Her father was the king, of course, and while she had beauty to spare, through her veins flowed her father's blood and the blood of her ancestors. Dioneo allowed them a moment together, debating what to do. He must be getting weak because he weighed, if only for a second, leaving Ricciardo's dreams intact and bringing both along.

Lucrezia stole a quick glance at Dioneo. In that one look, Dioneo saw the hardened face of a woman who may not have loved Ricciardo, but who did love her possessions. Above all, she was jealous of her possessions.

"No, princess, you couldn't let him perish here," Dioneo said. "But in the arena, that was another story, wasn't it?"

Lucrezia's eyes narrowed. She pulled Ricciardo closer.

"I thank you, stranger, for bringing the love of my life back to me," she said in a halting voice. "But it is time you both part ways." Lucrezia maneuvered behind Ricciardo, plaçing him between her and Dioneo.

Time was short. But there was a little time for this.

"I told you before, Ricciardo, she sold you out. There wasn't any maiden behind either door for you. Just tigers."

Ricciardo rose to his tallest height. Dioneo could see confusion in his eyes, but Dioneo continued.

"Lucrezia couldn't bear to see you with another woman."

"Dioneo is a common thief," Lucrezia said, her voice deepening. "A liar. Don't listen to him."

"Or maybe I should say, she couldn't bear to have the kingdom see you married to another woman, right in front of her. That's what really would have hurt, wouldn't it? To see Ricciardo married to someone else, someone from your own court, even, and to have everyone in the kingdom join in the celebration—except you, of course."

"Shut up," Lucrezia snarled through her teeth.

Ricciardo seemed to wilt before Dioneo, but was fighting. He murmured, “Why do you torture us, Dioneo?”

“It really wasn’t a hard choice, was it?” Dioneo said, smiling at Lucrezia. “That image of everyone in the crowd cheering while Ricciardo and Angelique were married. Better to endure a few moments of sadness watching Ricciardo be mauled to death than to live with him in another woman’s arms. So you suggested putting animals behind both doors.”

He leaned toward Lucrezia and added, “Isn’t that right, your highness?”

Ricciardo swung at Dioneo. He thought Ricciardo was too weak to give much of a punch. But the kid’s blow did sting. Another sign he was getting old. Dioneo rubbed his chin and shook his head, then smiled. Ricciardo was frozen.

“You’ve had a hard morning so far, my boy. I’ll let you have that one. But as for the rest, ask the princess.”

Lucrezia’s eyes burned afire, and she venomously spat at Dioneo.

“Why didn’t you die in the arena like you were supposed to?”

“And why wasn’t Angelique behind the door she was chosen for?”

“Angelique?” Ricciardo injected. He looked back at Lucrezia. “Was it to be Angelique behind the door for me?”

“She was a whore!” snarled Lucrezia, but then her demeanor changed. “Ricciardo, run with me before my father’s guards come. I have friends in the court, we can hide, and then we can go away together.”

It could have been the torchlight, of course, that often played tricks on the eyes. But Dioneo had seen something new in Lucrezia’s face. And with that, a lingering question was emphatically answered.

“Where is Angelique?” asked Ricciardo.

Lucrezia met his eyes and was crying. “That’s who you’re worried about? AngeliqueWhy?”

"She's dead," interjected Dioneo. "She was dressing in the royal bridal chamber last night when someone came in and stuck a knitting pin through her neck."

With Ricciardo trembling, Lucrezia pointed an accusing finger at Dioneo. "Murdered," she said. "Probably by his friends. The ones who tried to kill my father."

Dioneo stroked his chin and started to laugh. "Not quite, Your Highness."

Lucrezia pulled Ricciardo's face towards her. "Ricciardo, I did not know of this. I thought Angelique was at the door to the right. Just as I signaled you."

Ricciardo stared into Lucrezia's eyes and asked, "What do you say is true, Dioneo?"

"Angelique is dead, kid."

Ricciardo asked, "By your friends?"

Lucrezia pressed her head against Ricciardo's chest, but glared with hate at Dioneo.

"No. We were hired to get you and you alone out of the arena, Ricciardo," Dioneo replied. "But my friends, well, the milk of human kindness runs through their veins a little more than mine. They did try to reach Angelique. You know when I head-butted the guard? The idea was to attract attention to that part of the palace. Which it did. My friends tried to get to Angelique then. They went to her bedroom chamber. But someone else reached her first and strangled her."

Dioneo walked away from the couple.

"Don't believe him, Ricciardo," Lucrezia hissed. "He's a liar. He cares nothing for us."

Dioneo walked past them deeper into the chamber, navigating around the large stone blocks and holding his torch to the walls, but staying away from them. "Yeah, well, that may be. But my friends better hurry," he said.

Ricciardo observed, "You seem to be looking for something."

"In a breezy manner, Dioneo asked, "Your romance is forbidden, so you always meet in secret, don't you?

"Back alcoves, hidden passages, secret bedchambers, or outside the castle at night—always in the dark, so to speak."

Dioneo glanced at the wall. There was a spark in the blackness, which hissed and burned. Ricciardo let go of Lucrezia's embrace and turned to see a small flame peak through the stone. Lucrezia remained focused on Dioneo, who turned, flashing his broadest smile.

"You don't like the daylight too much, do you, your highness?"

MADDALENA

We are plunging down the outside of a castle wall, a rope attached to each of us. Jai Ling violently pulls me aside. An arrow brushes by my arm.

"How could you miss?" screams a voice from above.

Jai Ling pushes off the wall with her feet. We swing out and away from the opening above and—

BOOM!

There's a giant sound, and we are rocked against the walls, then we fall. Jai Ling is holding me, and we strike the ground. She covers me for a moment.

I can hear things falling around us. Then—horses approaching. I look up.

Two of the guards lie on the ground next to us. They do not move.

Behind me, the dwarf from the arena—the dwarf man with the huge arms—he has ridden on a horse and brings us another one, a large black stallion. Another woman with a veil over her face rides beside the dwarf.

"Come on!" Jai Ling yells and pushes me onto the horse. Then she climbs in front of me and tells me to hold. I grab her waist and hold for my life, as our three horses gallop along the base of the castle walls. I am pressed against Jai Ling's back. My hold is not strong, but if I let go, I shall fall and be crushed by the other horse.

The hills are on the horizon. Why not head there?

The dwarf's horse pulls beside us. Then another sound of an explosion, like before, only louder, and the stone walls of the arena rattle. The earth shakes beneath us. The dwarf's horse stumbles, and he slips to the side. I think he might fall, but he holds on to the animal's neck. Jai Ling kicks her horse, and it responds, pressing past the dwarves.

We round the corner and see a yawning hole at the base of the castle wall. A wagon pulled by horses has raced up to it. There's a strange object on the back of it.

Dioneo climbed over the fallen rubble blindly. The dust and other debris in the air were thick, like being in a dense fog. He followed a coughing sound and found Ricciardo under some fallen mortar. Shaken and a bit scratched, but all right.

"You'll live," said Dioneo, pulling him up under his armpits and heading for the light. "Good thing you dropped when I told you to."

"Where's Lucrezia?" he asked.

"Hiding, I'd say," Dioneo chuckled, viewing the open plane outside the wall. "That carried a little more punch than I expected."

Ricciardo shook his head. "Now what do—" but his voice trailed off as a wagon, drawn by four horses, pulled in front of the cavity. It turned around and backed up to the entrance, leaving a cage before them.

"That's our ride," said Dioneo.

"In the cage?" Ricciardo asked, gesturing forward.

"No, that was just—"

Dioneo was interrupted by a call from the side.

"Ricciardo!"

He turned and saw Lucrezia standing in the shadows, just outside the sun's strokes that had crept in. Her white dress was bloodied, and the skin on her right arm was burned. She held out her left hand to Ricciardo, pushing against the edge of sunlight, and spoke between fanged teeth.

"You belong to me."

Dioneo pushed Ricciardo away and added. "You'd better treat that sunburn."

From the recesses of the chamber came the now familiar growls of a pursuing tiger.

"Oh shit me!" said Dioneo. Half-carrying Ricciardo, Dioneo raced the two into the cage's wall. Ricciardo started to cry out, but as the two men struck the cage, its front side slid up, and they were atop it, leaving the rear open. The tiger ran forward and barreled headfirstinside. Before the animal could turn, the door slammed back down, trapping the big cat inside.

MADDALENA

Confusion. There is dust everywhere, and sand is in my face. I can't see ahead of me, but I know we're racing away from the kingdom. My fingers hurt from holding on to Jai Ling. My head is pressed against her back; I dare not move it. I only see to the side. The dwarf and his horse are with us, the veiled woman, and there are others. There's a wagon driven by the Nubian who found me with Jai Ling, and there's a cage on it with a tiger inside. One—no two men are clinging to the top of the cage. There are some others riding with us on the other side.

One of the men on top of the cage—I think he might have been in the arena. He looks over at me and—he smiles and waves. His teeth seem to sparkle, even now. I think I nod—barely. I can't recall.

Elizabeth watched the parties escaping from the shade of a garden of fig trees. The heat bothered her more than she expected this morning. Her own body felt weary, and today's sun was burning. It was not that she couldn't move in the sun, but she might not have overpowered Jai Ling, not here, not yet. And even if she had, with the fire, she never would have gotten out with the girl alive. No, Elizabeth had trusted her instincts to seek, but not take, not today, despite what had been told to her.

She knew the three sisters possessed great knowledge, but they spoke half-truths and were never to be fully trusted.

The king had ordered all members of his court to the throne room. The typical combination of courtiers and concubines, artisans and scribes, eunuchs and lawyers—all did their best to evade His Majesty's visage as it swept the great hall. o appear may have been to risk death, but to not appear was to actively seek it as boldly as Ricciardo had pursued Lucrezia. Throngs of people lined three sides of the room, while the king sat on his throne at the fourth end, elevated above all on a raised dais.

His Majesty appeared deep in thought, his face showing calculation, stroking his beard as he was wont to do on such occasions. The Discourager of Hesitancy stood by His Majesty's side, head bowed, the scimitar, bloodied, clutched in both his hands downward. Scattered across the room were the recently decapitated bodies of the keeper of the tigers, as well as the king's personal seer, who had predicted a wonderful day for his majesty and his lawgiver. Each had lost their respective heads while explaining the day's events. The tiger keepers had mercifully rolled under a table, and the seer's had landed into a wide bowl of fruit where it still lay, much to the disgust of those eating at thattable. No one was quite sure where the lawmakers had wound up. Not that any voice rose in complaint.

The crowd stood in silence while the king stared down. This period was broken when the king asked, "Has Lucrezia been found yet?"

His voice was not menacing, but indifferent, at best a little worn. The question was not directed to anyone in particular. And in response, no one spoke.

"I asked about Lucrezia's whereabouts." This time, the inquiry had more force. "Doesn't anyone know where she is?"

One of the eunuchs spoke. "She was found near the tiger chambers, your excellency. She is resting in her bed chambers at this moment."

The king nodded the slightest of nods, one that would be imperceptible to all but the most ardent observer. At that moment, all inhabitants of the chamber would qualify as such. The king was known for his infinite justice and mercy, but as everyone knows, mercy can be a mercurial thing.

The king scowled and slowly said, "My lawgiver said that there were tigers behind both doors. But that cannot be. That cannot be."

The king rose to his feet and held out his hands, walking among the people as if imploring his subjects for advice. "If that were true, it says the arena is unjust, it is unfair, and how can that be? What decisions can be more fair, more determinate, than the court of fate? What did we see? Can we be sure of what we see? Yet there is our law, isn't there? The law of this kingdom requires we record the truth of each trial in the arena, does it not?"

"If I may," came a voice from behind the throng, and from their midst there stepped out what looked like a well-traveled adventurer, of medium height but light-skinned, a stranger to all in the room, but he carried the air of confidence. He was dressed in long robes more commonly found in residents of the eastern kingdoms, but spoke with the accent of those from the northern provinces. "Perhaps I may be of assistance."

Such boldness was quite dangerous, as all in the room were aware, but sometimes boldness at the right time leads to greatness. Indeed, advancement in the kingdom was through the king, as treacherous a road as that was, and often advancement was at the expense of another's head (as indeed, the office of the chief solicitor had very recently become vacant). The adventurer sensed an opportunity. The king's attention focused on him.

"Who speaks to the king thus?"

"A stranger to your lands, Your Majesty. But I have had the opportunity to witness the magnificence of your justice system. And I've also studied your laws. The law requires that the truth be recorded, does it not?"

The king gave a sly smile and nodded. Regardless of whether this adventurer might soon find himself dispatched to the next life, the king needed to hear something interesting. "You are correct. Go on."

"But the law does not say the results must be recorded, only the truth," continued the stranger, confidently walking before the king but being careful to avoid his gaze. And to not trip over the two corpses.

"So let us record the truth, and not the result. Is it not enough for the world to know that a young man of inappropriate station dared to love the king's daughter? That such a man was placed in the arena and put to the test? The system was fair, but those who implemented it were derelict in their duties. Why speak of the failures of some of your servants? Instead, why not pose the question for all posterity? Why can't the record state the day's events and then leave it to the reader to decide which emerged, the lady or the tiger?"

The king was clearly pleased at this solution to his problem and beckoned a scribe to approach. "Write it as this man has said."

The king stepped over the tiger keeper's corpse and approached close to the adventurer. "No, better still. Let this man write the story," he proclaimed. "You, sir, you record the day's events. If I am pleased, you will be well rewarded. And if not, we do not tolerate failure well."

The king, his anger sated for the moment, commanded that the royal record of the day be given to the stranger for editing as suggested. The king then ordered the room cleared. The stranger was escorted away with a pair of concubines on each arm. Eunuch servants dragged the dead bodies away, while relieved members of the court silently withdrew until only the king and the Discourager of Hesitancy remained.

"I shall take my leave of you, my lord," said the Discourager, who bowed and began to turn, but was stopped by the king.

"Wait," said the king. "The adventurer's story may present a solution to the problem with our law. But it still does not resolve the question of justice *in the arena.*"

The king placed his hand on the Discourager's shoulder and drew him closer with an evil smile.

"We must rectify that. I have a special mission for you."

[4]
THE PRISONER

Somewhere in a commune called Cuneo, located near the beginnings of six mountain passes.
Around the same time as the prior story.

We will watch how a vampire tries to enter a monastery. You may not yet see how these people relate to our last story, but for now, trust in me, your humble narrator, when I say that they will.

ABBOT DOM FELICE felt his joints ache as he shuffled through the subterranean wine cellar of the Saint Michael-du-Anjou monastery. The dampness may have been good for preserving wine, but not human tissue. Even the torches struggled to stay lit.

At least he did not have to stay long down here.

He travelled further into the catacombs where the monastery's honored dead were entombed. Upon turning a corner, he saw a papal guard standing erect across from a bricked-up alcove. There was a small open space in the wall at eye level.

Gesturing to two bricks on the ground, the abbot asked, "Why are these not in place?"

The guard stooped to pick up the bricks and replied, "Abbot, they were on the ground when I arrived. I thought you had ordered them removed."

The abbot raised his hand, indicating for the guard to stop. The sentry placed a nearby stool directly in front of the brick wall, assisted the abbot in sitting down, then stepped back.

As the abbot took a deep breath, cool air entered his lungs, and he coughed.

A deep voice spoke from behind the bricks. "You don't sound so good today, my friend. Maybe you need to spend more time with Lisabetta, no? The country girl, she never says no, is true?"

The abbot banged his chest and waved the guard off.

"Cesare. Why torture yourself and me? Tell me where your laboratory is. And why did you come here? We can work with you. I can speak to the Holy Father for you. Help us, and I am sure he will allow you a more humane existence."

The abbot heard laughing from behind the wall.

"Of course, my friend. I tell you all you want to know. I help you with completing *my* experiments. And we all forget about your special toys, your special experiments for vampires, yes? Remember, when I first came here? You demonstrated them all to me."

There was more laughing.

"Cesare! Millions are dying!"

"Yes, millions," the voice shot back. "But no, my people, not so much. Your kind? Many. Not everyone eats so well as you do here. My friend. I think my being here bothers you more than me."

The abbot stood and motioned for the guard to take his stool when Cesare interrupted.

"My good abbot. I think I will be out of here soon. You not kill me, so I give you one chance. If I were you, I would get away from here. Because when I get out and find you, I may not be in such a generous mood. So you go now. While you can."

Cesare began his guttural laughing again.

Abbot Dom Felice shook his head and, turning to the guard, said, "Put the bricks back in." The guard complied and resumed his station.

As the abbot made his way back above ground, he made a mental note to double the guards at Cesare's cell.

Cesare Borgia—as he was known to the guards now—sat on the ground inside the pitch blackness of his cell. Cesare stroked the fluffy cheeks of the green conure who had flown in earlier.

"Thank you for the message, my friend."

Pietro Gualtieri approached the bridge carefully. The thunderclaps were now almost directly overhead, and the horses were already spooked enough by their transport. He firmly pulled the reins, keeping the animals from breaking their formation, and tightened the strings on his coif. Cold from the wind-swept rain cut through his cape, which he had drawn close around him, and he muttered a curse at the dampness. The moment the words left his lips, he shuddered, not knowing how his passenger would react, but she remained a silent, motionless figure next to him, as she'd been most of the trip. Bowed over, head covered with a hood from her heavy woolen cloak, one would have thought she was dead, and he couldn't help a little grin at the irony of that thought.

"Is something funny, Pietro?" came a question from under the hood.

His passenger's voice ran through Pietro Gualtieri's body more sharply than the dampness. Even amidst the rain and the clip-clop of the horses' hooves and the wagon wheels grinding through the mud, her voice was clear and strong. He couldn't resist trembling, and one of the horses paused and neighed, as if startled. Gualtieri sensed the horse preparing to buck up and pulled sharply on the reins to keep the animal in line. Thankfully, the horse responded and continued to move. Delays would not be tolerated.

"N-n-no," he said, unable to keep from stammering.

"Remain calm," she replied in the same firm voice. "I need you right now. Just keep going, and we'll all be fine."

The wagon approached the small bridge spanning the moat surrounding the Saint Michael-du-Anjou monastery. Its walls towered over their approach, and the road led to a single wooden gate the height of four men. Gualtieri's horses had brought supplies down this road so many times that the animals could probably make the trip without him. This idea also frightened him. He wondered if his passenger had thought of that. He guessed she had. Gualtieri was a simple man. He wasn't here because she didn't know how to get here. He was needed. That was some comfort. Maybe he would live to see his wife and children again.

The sound of the horses' hooves changed as they struck the wooden planks of the bridge. This span was about five cart lengths long, wide enough only for a single wagon to pass. Gualtieri looked over at the water. It was high and fast for this time of year, with the rain contributing to that. He could sense a change in his passenger as they crossed over it, a tensing, and he wondered if the stories were true. Her focus was on the water. And her face was covered. Perhaps for just a moment with her guard down, she could be shoved into the river and plunge to her death. Perhaps. Would he dare try it? No. Gualtieri was a simple man.

They went across the bridge.

"You made a smart choice, Pietro," she said to him. "You've made many smart choices up to this point. Now keep making them."

"Halt," came a command from up ahead. Two men approached from the gate to the monastery. They wore helmets and metal mesh tunics bearing the insignia of the papal guards. One carried a long pole axe, while the other held a short sword. The one with the pole axe stood a few feet from the cart, while the one with the short sword walked on the other side, towards his passenger. Gualtieri recognized this guard, although he didn't know the name. The guard gave him a cursory look, then unsheathed his sword and pointed it at the passenger. She kept her head bowed underneath her cloak.

"Who's your friend?" he spat out.

"A new servant," Gualtieri answered. "From the village."

"New, eh?" asked the guard. "Why won't he show his face? Does he have the plague?"

The guard moved closer, his sword cautiously thrust before him, and tapped his weapon on the passenger's lap.

"Hey, you," he snarled. "What's the matter? Are you covered in boils? Do you want to bring damnation on all of us? Show yourself."

Gualtieri felt his heart pounding through his chest. He expected the worst. And then, to his surprise, his passenger straightened up and pulled her hood back.

The guard gasped. He'd expected a sore-riddled beggar man, or perhaps a youth of tender years. Instead, before him sat a raven-haired beauty. Long black hair flowed from her head and draped out of the cloak, surrounding a countenance with sharp features. The falling rain fell on and then off flawless alabaster skin. And the eyes—bright blue, sitting above a pair of brilliant crimson lips, whose color was accentuated by the white skin.

"My name is Carmen Teresa," she said, gazing into the guard's eyes herself. "What is yours?"

The guard stood on his spot, having dropped his sword and been mesmerized by equal parts shock, lust, and, although he was not completely aware of it, some unsettling fear.

"His name is Joseph," called the other guard. "And mine is Phillipe, in case you wondered."

Phillipe lowered his axe head at the cart.

"The rain is cold," Carmen Teresa said, turning slowly towards Phillipe. "May I replace my hood?"

"Go ahead," said Phillipe, as he walked closer, also meeting her eyes. Carmen Teresa replaced her hood, but this time left her face uncovered so she could see Phillipe.

Phillipe ordered, "Joseph, check the cart."

The one called Joseph hesitated, then cursed at his own ineptitude. Picking up his sword, he sloshed through the mud and climbed onto the back of the cart, where he saw five large barrels, along with some material covered by burlap. Gualtieri's hands perspired, and he began to turn around when he heard Carmen Teresa quietly but firmly say, "It's all right, Pietro. Joseph is just sampling the wine."

Joseph went to the barrel closest to the edge of the cart and pried off the cover with his sword, then scooped out some of the liquid with his hand.

After slurping it, he yelled, "You call this piss wine, Gualtieri!" A clap of thunder rolled overhead. "You take advantage of us, peddler. This is not good wine. But out in this pisshole even bad wine is good."

"It is the best our poor land can offer now," Gualtieri said, still leery of what Carmen Teresa might do. If that was her name.

Joseph pulled aside the burlap covers. Underneath were several urns and a few sacks nearly bursting with their contents.

"At least you've brought lots of flour," Joseph called and hopped off the cart. "More so than usual. You manage to bring us enough to eat. And these barrels, they're larger than the ones you brought before. It must have been a good month. If only your wine weren't so poor."

Gualtieri bowed his head. "Like you, I am a humble servant of His Excellency."

Phillipe had not removed his eyes from Carmen Teresa, nor had she from him. She gave him the slightest hint of a smile and said, "Each of the barrels are hogshead. Do you need to check the rest of the wine?"

Phillipe felt the fire from the burn in his loins. There'd been no women from the village in several weeks. The sense of the plague could be felt in the woods. He could have taken her right there—who would stop him? Not the peddler. Joseph could have had her, too, after he did. And the "abbott" wouldn't say anything. No, not on this detail. Still, something in the girl's eyes—she met a man's gaze. And she wore no wimple. And she spoke too well for a village tart. Yet—why rush?

She would be inside the monastery. Night was falling.

"No," he said.

Hearing this, Joseph slid off the cart, stubbing his toe and cursing as he did.

"Go on," Phillipe said with a wave of his arm. Turning to the stone walls, he yelled, "Open the gate." He looked back and added to Carmen Teresa, "Maybe I'll see you later."

Carmen Teresa clearly flashed a broad white smile and said, "I hope so."

As the cart moved forward, the gate's doors parted just wide enough to allow them through. They passed through the entranceway and found themselves within the keep-like inner sanctum of the monastery. Inside, the walls of Saint Michael formed a hexagon, and they seemed even higher than they did from the outside. On the far side was a cluster of larger buildings, the tallest being a four-story brick tower, which most interested Carmen Teresa. In the middle of the yard, there was a well along with a life-size marble statue of the namesake of the monastery. Saint Michael's visage met them as they drove in. Otherwise, the courtyard appeared deserted. The rain began pouring even harder. Carmen Teresa stared at the figure.

"You see. No one wants to be out in this storm," Gualtieri muttered.

Carmen Teresa peered around. "Isn't this the time for Vespers?"

Gualtieri had forgotten the time. “You are right,” he said and began to make the sign of the cross. A force of habit, of course. But he knew he’d made another mistake, one which would not be overlooked.

“I asked you not to do that,” said Carmen Teresa. A toned hand suddenly shot out from under her cloak and clamped onto Gualtieri’s wrist, and he felt excruciating pressure that forced him to buckle over, dropping the reins. Carmen Teresa released her grip and grabbed the reins in mid-air before they fell.

“Please don’t do that again, Pietro,” she said, yanking the reins.

While Gualtieri whimpered and rubbed his wrist, Carmen Teresa guided the horses to the left, past where the grainery should be, if the maps she’d studied were correct, and towards an overhang. The horses obeyed her without resistance. Carmen Teresa then jumped off the wagon and tied the horses to a post.

“Come, Pietro, we’ve much work to do. The wine cellar is over here, yes?”

Gualtieri nodded his head.

“Then hurry.”

Carmen Teresa gave a furtive look around the courtyard. It truly was deserted. The monks would be in Vespers for a while longer, and the guards on duty were trying to avoid the rain. Still, she had revealed herself, and that might stir “interest” in these isolated men. Word was sure to spread that a woman had penetrated into this most unholy of holy men’s enclaves. And the monastic life was quite a lonely one—especially when your main function was to keep watch over a prisoner.

Pietro Gualtieri was perspiring as would one of the small runt pigs he would catch and hold in his arms, just before he would slaughter it for supper. Here he was, carrying the fourth of the urns from the cart. His companion had ordered him to bring them to the farthest depth of the wine cellar. He could hold two in his arms at once, but Carmen Teresa had forbidden him to carry more than one at a time.

One benefit from being a monk was the ready donations of food and wine, whether voluntarily provided or otherwise coerced, and the cavernous cellar was filled with barrels of varying shapes. Pietro had already rolled two of the largest wine barrels into the cellar. It was a long distance from the entrance, but the floor sloped down, allowing the transport of such large vessels to the dank portions of the cellar. The wine sloshed in its container. Pietro had managed to complete this task and ignored the sound of what else was rattling inside them.

Though out of the rain, the dampness here was in some ways worse than outside. It was completely dark, save for a few torches Carmen Teresa had lit along the way for his benefit. The first time down, she, carrying grain sacks over her shoulder, moved with ease, and he couldn't keep up with her. She had gone on, but instructed him to follow. Gualtieri could have dropped the urns and gone to the monks for help. For long stretches, it seemed that she had disappeared. But then, when he thought he was totally alone, Carmen Teresa would appear from the shadows and pass him, bringing different wine and flour sacks from the wagon to the cellar. He'd made a total of four trips when placed the last urn next to the others and sat down.

The urns were in a round room with only two entrances, probably somewhere underneath the monastery's main sanctuary. There was a wine rack on one side and some barrels strewn about in a haphazard fashion. The ceiling seemed to rise a little here. He wondered if they were under the church refectory or kitchen.

Where was Carmen Teresa?

There was a retching sound from behind the wine rack. He walked around it.

Carmen Teresa was on both knees with her back to him, supporting herself with one hand on a wall and one grasping her stomach. She had dropped her cloak and was wearing a thin sheath and her boots, which went to her knees. Gualtieri's momentarily felt a wave of shock and arousal, but his extreme fear overpowered these feelings. Before Carmen Teresa was a pool of red blood and a frothy yellowish slime.

"They were right—you have the plague," he stammered, taking a step back.

"You idiot!" she said, spitting blood through clenched teeth. "Look at my body! Do you see sores? Do you?"

Gualtieri had seen the plague before, and it was true, while she was bent over, her skin was immaculate. Legs, arms, buttocks, and back, all white without any sign of the tell-tale boils or black blotches. Indeed, her skin was remarkably free of any blemish. But the blood and pus flowed out of her mouth.

"Then—"

She spat out words through coughs. "When I took my hood off in the daylight. The sun's rays still shine, even in the rain. Passing by relics. Water. They take their toll, Pietro."

Wincing, she spat up more blood, and Gualtieri, while he did not realize why, was drawn to the contrast between her brilliant crimson lips and white skin.

"Does seeing me like this make you feel better, Pietro?" She forced a smile at him and met his eyes, and he felt fear. The eyes weren't sick. They were hungry. "Maybe it would be better if I did pass."

She retched again, then looked back up.

"But I didn't, Pietro. Not yet. Go get the last jar," she ordered. Gualtieri dutifully turned and returned to the wagon.

Outside, it was still raining, and the night had fallen. Vespers were continuing, or perhaps dinner in the great hall was being served. It wasn't unusual not to encounter anyone. He had come so often his presence was taken for granted here at Saint Michael-du-Anjou. Again, he wondered if he should run to the hall for help. As he held the last urn, contemplating these thoughts, an arm grabbed his shoulder and spun him around.

Standing over him was Philippe, the guard from the front gate. There was alcohol on his breath, and while he no longer had his axe, a short sword hung from his belt. Philippe pressed his face against Pietro.

"Where's your friend, peddler?" Philippe demanded, shaking Pietro and staggering slightly.

"She—she—"

Gualtieri fumbled with his answer.

"You're as dumb as a dwarf," Philippe sneered and shoved Gualtieri aside. Then the guard looked at the wagon and noticed that most of its contents had been removed. Philippe looked over at the dark hallway descending into the wine cellar and grinned.

"She's in there, ah?" he said. "Maybe you can hide her from your fat pig of a wife, but you can't hide her in here. It wasn't wise to bring a woman to this place, Pietro."

Philippe laughed, then whirled and barged into the cellar.

Gualtieri panicked. He'd said nothing. But would Carmen Teresa be angry? He could run and get help. Perhaps he should. There were monks and guards here. Men who could help him. Surely they could overpower her, couldn't they? But how sure was he about her?

These thoughts occurred to Gualtieri all at once. He also suffered from a certain curiosity. He followed the simplest choice, picking up the final jar and carrying it to the wine cellar.

The torches in the central chamber lit it up. Carmen Teresa had lit another one, and the oil was reaching the flaxen, so the torches burned brightly. Gaultieri put the urn down next to the other four.

The chamber was empty.

He peered around the corner. He saw a rift in the wall and looked through. Inside, it held several devices for building and repairing furniture at the monastery. There was a large circle sketched on the floor in the middle. He walked in with his own torch.

Carmen Teresa was bent on all fours, emitting gurgling sounds, like an animal gnawing on a bone. Phillipe's body lay underneath her, arms and legs writhing in convulsions, his head obscured by Carmen Teresa's body. She turned around and met Pietro's eyes. Blood dripped from her mouth. She seemed stronger than before.

And when she opened her mouth, he saw two small but unmistakable fangs protruding from her upper teeth.

Gualtieri stumbled backward, dropped his torch, and turned to run, only to go into a brick wall. He fell against it, then slid down, tears falling from his face.

Time passed. He did not notice as the light approached him. Carmen Teresa stood before him wearing the peasant dress he had first seen her in. She grabbed his belt and pulled him up with one hand.

"You think I'm evil?" she asked. "Come here." She dragged Pietro into the side room, one he'd been told on prior visits not to enter. Her grip was amazingly strong, and he was almost being lifted by her.

Inside was a veritable torture chamber. Two different types of iron maidens, one filled with spikes, the other with holes in it for spears to be thrust into. Tables with heavy ropes and metal restraints, with various sharp cutting instruments scattered about. A rack. No, several. Many sharp implements are strewn about. Metal cages in which hung skeletons. In the corner, a tall, upright frame, with a rope dangling from the top bar down to a large, sharp metal blade.

The fangs were bared, and blood dripped as Carmen Teresa spoke.

"You know what this room is used for, Pietro? Your monks, the priests of your god, they find my kind. You see these stakes?"

She brought him over to three iron spears rising from the floor.

"These are impairment stakes. They coat them with silver and then slide a vampire's body down it. "

She brought him to a wall.

"And they hang us on these hooks, and they burn us on these pyres. This frame device? This rope pulls the blade up. They force the head into this spot, and they decapitate us on these blades. That's what they do here. The men in this fortress are my enemy, and I am theirs. I want to survive as much as they do."

Pietro looked down.

Now sounding much calmer, Carmen Teresa said, "Go tell Joseph that Philippe and I are having a party."

Joseph hurried towards the wine cellar. It was common for one of the town girls to be brought here for the guard's pleasure. But...

Joseph entered the cellar. At the far end of the room stood a tall, cloaked figure with her back to him. Was this the girl he'd seen earlier? She seemed taller now, even though she'd been seated on the cart. He walked toward her. She turned around abruptly, threw back her hood, and as she faced him, he knew in that instant how great a peril he'd just encountered. Carmen Teresa stood several hand lengths over him. While he himself was not a tall man, he was stout and considered a formidable fighter. But the sight of blood out of the side of her mouth frightened him, and as she talked, her fangs were bared.

Joseph had fought many a battle with the Templars in Egypt against the heathens, where he'd lost two fingers from his left hand. But he'd only heard stories about these creatures. He recalled a boast, uttered many years ago in a distant land, fueled by wine, that he hoped to meet one someday. His boast apparently had been heard.

"You know what I am," she said, striding towards him. Joseph reached for the hilt of his sword and began to draw it out. Before it was halfway unsheathed, Carmen Teresa had grabbed his wrist and wrestled the sword from his hand. She held the blade towards the torchlight and studied it, turning her back to Joseph, who stood silent and dumbfounded.

"Iron," she finally said. "An awkward weapon, really. Heavy and hard to use."

Joseph said, "It served me well in the holy lands." Be brave, he thought. It was all he could think.

Carmen Teresa looked over at him and walked to the other side of the room.

"But against me, you're much better served by this."

She pulled out a dagger from a sheath underneath her breast and tossed it at his feet. Joseph crouched down and picked it up. It felt extremely solid, short, and gleamed in the firelight.

"Pure silver," he said, more thinking aloud than anything else, cradling it in both hands.

"Yes," said Carmen Teresa, walking towards the far side of the room. "You know how to use it?"

Joseph stood silent and shaking.

"Of course you do, Joseph. You're a member of the Pontificate Guard. You know how to fight. And you also know you're going to die, unless you plunge that into my heart."

Carmen Teresa faced him from the far side of the room and pointed beneath her left breast. "Right here, Joseph. Thrust it right here. In and up. It's your only chance to get out of this room."

Joseph stumbled back until he pressed against the cellar wall.

"No, please—"

A bell began to ring in the distance.

"The bell for night prayers," said Carmen Teresa coldly. "It rings six times, doesn't it, Joseph?" No sooner had she finished her sentence than the second strike rang.

"You've got to the end of the last ring, Joseph."

Joseph fumbled with the weapon, then found its grip. A third ring.

"Let me serve you," he begged. "Please—"

"Thrust it right here, Joseph," Carmen Teresa said, pointing to the same spot. "It is your only way out."

The bell rang a fourth time. Joseph was a man of war and had seen battle, but he'd never felt this kind of fear.

A fifth ring.

Joseph tightened his grip on the dagger's hilt and braced himself.

The bell was struck a sixth time. As its ring ended, the vampire threw her arms back and flung herself at him.

Gualtieri slumped on the floor, sobbing quietly with his hands wrapped around his knees. How had it come to this? Only a few days ago, he'd been a simple merchant, quietly bringing food on a bi-weekly basis to the monastery from Cuneo. The monastery paid for wine and flour, allowing some measure of subsistence for his family that was better than the fate of the others in the village. Few villagers dared to leave the town limits for fear of the black death. It had crept into the neighboring village of Dansk over a month ago, but there was a great wood and river between his town and Dansk that, till now, had kept the devil's curse away. His wife, Maria, and his three children had been fortunate in being able to conceal Gualtieri's actions, going to black market merchants and the back entrances of barns at night, scouring the countryside for food and wine to please the monks and more especially, the Pontificate Guard. The family had managed to conceal their minimal wealth, remaining inside during the day and not letting others know that they had food and drink, at least to subsist on. But now he was allied with a creature of the night, a creature of pure evil, and he would be damned.

He sensed her presence beside him.

"Your part is almost finished, Pietro." Carmen Teresa's voice sounded even deeper now. Stronger, fuller, revitalized.

"Don't go too far."

The sight that met Pietro Gualtieri's eyes caused him to buckle at the knees. The bodies of Phillippe, Joseph, and another man dangled by their ankles over separate clumps of a yellowish mush and blood. They had been stripped to the waist, and their throats and wrists had been carefully slashed so that blood was still pouring from these openings onto the mixture below. In the center of the room, a fire had been constructed and was burning underneath a small cauldron. The heat seemed to sear Pietro's skin. Carmen Teresa pulled Pietro along to the cauldron.

"Please, please, I mean you no harm," he begged.

"I know, Pietro," Carmen Teresa said. "Your kind and mine are eternal enemies. Those men would just as easily torture me if our situation were reversed. But I've no quarrel with you, Pietro. I need you for one final matter."

Then she pulled Pietro's arm over the cauldron, revealed her fangs, quickly bit into his forearm, and squeezed blood from the punctures into the boiling liquid. Gualtieri started to shriek but was powerless to stop the actions.

"I know you probably can't believe this, but you're fine," Carmen Teresa said, her fangs retracting. "I just punctured the skin. You may be sore for a few days, but that's all." She smiled slyly at him. "You won't become like me, or father any like me, at least not from that. I'm not passing my blood to you."

She laughed and twisted his forearm further. A few more droplets fell into the liquid. She released his arm, and he stumbled back. A great gust of steam burst from the pot. For the first time, Gualtieri looked up. The steam disappeared through some vent into the upper dark heights of the room. If they were below the refectory, it was possible that this vented into the main hearth. The monks would have eaten earlier and would have retired to their cells for night prayers, or would already be asleep. It would not be unheard of for cooks to be working at this hour, preparing a late meal for the Pontificate Guards. Thus, the smoke itself could go unnoticed, or at least not attract attention.

Carmen Teresa grabbed an iron ladle and spooned some of the smoking liquid into a clay urn.

"You may fall asleep for a little while. When you awaken, you'll find a small sack of coins by your body. A token of my appreciation. Leave this monastery at once, back the way we came in. Don't wander and you'll be safe."

Once the pot was filled, she carried it over to the mixtures on the ground and knelt. Carmen Teresa began to utter a combination of droning and higher-pitched cries, most of which Pietro couldn't understand. Some sort of incantation.

Vediovus? Februus? Rimu? Were these names she was calling to? Pietro could not know. But he watched, fascinated, for as Carmen Teresa spoke, she spilled the liquid onto the blood mush mixture. The liquid splattered and flamed up each time it touched the substance. Pietro slumped into unconsciousness, but before he did so, three thoughts filled his mind. The first was that the flames on the floor did not consume the mixture. On the contrary, the substance began to swell, absorbing the flames as if a sponge in water. The second was that the mixtures were laid out in three outlines, each roughly the size of a man. And lastly, he saw, on the other side of the cauldron, four *more* such mixtures.

Besides Carmen Teresa, there were five others—Bernardo, a wiry Tuscan; Federigo, the oldest of them by far, with a pointed bald head which humans found especially fearful (he was also the only one Carmen Teresa knew well); Raphael, the youngest of the group, who looked like a young man; Miguel, the strongest, a large Corsican; Marie, the lone female; and Thomas, a vampire of average height but very quick from Florence. Two others could not be revived. They stretched their limbs and backs. Ideally, one should wait several days after such resurrection before being active, but there was no time. This group had all volunteered. Most were experienced soldiers from the coven, except for Raphael, the youngest of the brood. His eagerness made up for any lack. Federigo, the oldest, had been a confidant of Carmen Teresa's for years, and she had welcomed his counsel, though she was concerned for his age.

"Lady and gentlemen," Carmen Teresa said, "you know what we're here to do."

Abbott Dom Felice stirred from slumber. The strawberry-blonde nymph, Lisabetta, from Cuneo, lay next to his heaving belly. He shared many a night with Lisabetta, and he grimaced looking at her skinny form, although somewhat round in the bosom, gently outlined in the single candle burning on his table. She had first been brought to the monastery by the young and virile Friar Puccio, and Abbott Dom Felice had observed them enter the young monk's cell. Later, Dom Felice made his own personal acquaintance with Lisabetta and found her to be eager to please those in the ministry of the lord. Eager may have been too hard a word. She never said no. She was incapable of conversation, a simpleton who some said was cursed. Dom Felice felt guilty lying with her. But she certainly was discreet.

Both the friar and the abbott had regularly shared the pleasures of her company until the abbott had grown tired of the friar and had him meet the monastery's special guest.

Something didn't seem right. Something was missing. The hour of midnight prayers was approaching. To the untrained ear, the monks of Saint Michael-du-Anjou practiced silence as part of their piety with great precision and would arrive at midnight prayer as silent as a ghostly apparition. After presiding over this monastery for many years, Dom Felice could detect sounds and stirrings of his flock preparing to gather. The faint patter of feet in the corridor below Father Ferondo; the dull thud of Brother Bernarbo's cane, trudging his body across the courtyard to enter the vestry. And the papal soldiers—not one was singing in a drunken stupor? Dom Felice climbed out of his bed and walked to a window.

A light knock was at the door to Dom Felice's cell. Lisabetta stirred in her sleep and perhaps subconsciously pulled the sheets up to cover her breasts. The Abbott gave her a reassuring gesture to avoid fear, and he walked across the room to his door. What matter needed his attention now?

He placed his hand on the lock. As he did so, for some reason, he recalled what Cesare Borgia had said. Apprehension passed over him. Rather than pull, he inquired, "Yes?"

"Most holy one, I need your help." The voice on the other side was of a woman and sounded humble and needy. Abbott Dom Felice opened the door.

A dark hooded figure knelt right outside, so close that he was startled by her presence. The cloak moved, and the same womanly voice said, "Forgive me, Father."

Was this one of the handmaids? He vaguely sensed other persons just outside the torchlight.

"Forgive you Why, my child, what have you done?"

The figure rose and pulled back her hood. Abbott Dom Felice stared into dazzling blue eyes surrounded by a ceramic-white face. Speaking through blood-soaked lips, the figure answered, "What haven't I done?"

Pietro Gualtieri woke in the horrible chamber he'd passed out in, but a blanket had been placed under his head. He rose to his feet.

The flames under the cauldron were dying, only a few embers still smoldering. He stumbled around the room, alternately looking up and down in a half-frenzied state. The bodies of the slain soldiers had been removed, and the mounds that Carmen Teresa had poured the flaming liquid on were gone. All that remained were charcoal outlines on the floor and an assortment of liquid stains. Gualtieri was alone in the depths of Saint Michael's monastery.

"Run," he thought. "Run now."

And so he did. He began to run. Out of the horrid chamber with its torture devices and cauldrons and stench of death.

Abbott Dom Felice choked on a mix of his own blood and gravel. Having been thrown to the floor by one of the vampires, he lay there, deep in the catacombs of the monastery where the dead were entombed. Surrounding him were several vampires, dressed in a motley assortment of rags and tattered clothes, along with their leader, the cloaked one. She carried a torch, for Dom Felice's sake, since, as he knew, the vampires could see well in the dark. The female kneeled beside him.

"Here?" she asked, neither menacingly nor threatening.

The abbott whimpered and began to pray. "Oh my God, I am heartfully sorry for my sins—"

"Abbott, please answer my question," said the female as she reached under his left rib and dug into his ribcage. Dom Felice experienced intense pressure on his lungs. He started coughing, spitting blood onto the vampire's cloak. She took no notice but released her hand ever so slightly. "Where is he?"

The abbott weakly raised a finger towards a wall lined with several crypts. Carmen Teresa tipped her head, and two of her attendants began to scour the row of bricked-up tombs. “Look for one with a small opening,” she said.

Finally, Raphael said, “Over here, Mistress.”

Carmen Teresa handed her torch to Miguel and walked over to Raphael. They were in front of an archway that had been completely bricked over.

“I said to search for an opening,” she said.

“Look here,” Raphael said, and touched the stone. Carmen Teresa peered at it carefully. Near eye level was a cluster of bricks which had distinct cracks surrounding it. Carmen Teresa pressed against it and felt the wall give.

She smiled. “Very good, Raphael. Remove them.”

Grasping the stone, Raphael pulled out two bricks and felt a draft of cool air, along with a stench.

“Cesare?” Carmen asked. “Cesare?”

There was no answer for several moments. Then, a lone voice.

“Who wants to know?”

“Your rescuers,” Carmen Teresa said. “We’ve come for you.”

There was another pause. Then a burst of laughter.

Using a pair of mauls and another pick taken from the torture chamber, the vampires smashed the bricks and quickly opened up the wall into a small alcove. Cesare Borgia sat in a corner, stroking a green conure. His right arm was chained to the wall. A small table had been built up. A shit pot lay in the far corner.

Cesare was dressed in linen, originally a manila color but now quite blackened with dirt and soot. His V-shaped face had a worn leather look, and like his matted hair, it was covered in dirt and grime. But his V his brown eyes danced when he watched Carmen Teresa enter.

“You,” he said. His voice was low and a bit husky. “I knew you would find me. Even when I stood before you at the Vampire Council. But it is good to see you again."

Carmen Teresa looked at the table that had been knocked over when the wall came down. "How did you eat?" she asked.

Cesare smiled back at her. "My friends, they slid food through another hole in the bottom of the wall." He waved his right arm, and the chain jangled. "You see, they left me just enough to reach over." He demonstrated, grabbing an imaginary piece of meat and stuffing it in his mouth. "Plus, I get to pass out the shit pail. They think of everything."

Carmen Teresa smiled and pulled out a flask from beneath her cloak. "You used to like wine, Cesare. Have some." She handed him the bottle, and he drank.

"Ahh, you haven't forgotten," he said. "You're a good friend." Then he began to laugh. "But you're not here out of friendship, are you, M—"

Carmen Teresa threw her hands against his mouth.

"Cesare. You know why I'm here," she said.

Carmen Teresa produced a key she had taken from the abbott's cell and inserted it into the irons. Although it was not the exact match, the key was close enough for her to unlock the chain. Cesare stepped aside and then fell forward, his legs buckling beneath him. He reached out and was caught by Raphael and Carmen Teresa, and he laughed again.

"My legs need a moment," he said. "Sit me down." They lowered him onto the pile of bricks and released him.

Carmen Teresa stared at him. "I've got something else that might make you feel better." She motioned the vampires, and they brought forward Dom Felice. She could see Cesare's brown eyes widen when the abbott was tossed in front of him.

"My good friend Abbott Dom Felice," Cesare said. "You can't imagine how good it is to see you without looking through a hole in the wall."

The abbott moaned fearfully.

"Please. Please, what d-do you want?" he stammered.

Carmen Teresa knelt in front of him.

"Me? Nothing—from you," she said. "I only want Cesare."

The abbott groaned.

"We have much to talk about, the abbott and me," Cesare said.

Carmen Tereas stood up.

"Don't take too long. We have to go places."

"Are you finished?" Carmen Teresa asked, tightening the sash at her waist. Raphael stood nearby, while the others waited far above in the dead still that had become the courtyard of Saint Michael's, just outside the entrance to the dormitory.

"Almost," Cesare said. "I need one more moment. Only one more moment, Mir—"

"Hurry," she said, cutting him off and strapping a sword to her waist. "We've less than two hours left to the night, and these others aren't strong enough to survive in the day. And you'll call me Carmen Teresa."

"Why not just stay—" Cesare began.

"We didn't come here to stay," she retorted. "We're to reach Castle Otranto by tomorrow. It's down the second mountain pass. The plague has visited it in force, so none will bother us there. Here, there may be some occasional wench or youth or pilgrim seeking repose of their beloved soul."

"You fear them?" asked Cesare. "I know you. You fear no... thing. And after taking this monastery?"

"I do fear things, Cesare," Carmen Teresa shot back. "Not the villagers. They're too afraid to leave their hovels. But there are other things, things *we* created, Cesare. You especially. Your sickness created a strain of stronger fleshers. They like the taste of our flesh. You, above all others, know that. And if *they* learn we are here, they may come. Make no mistake, you've been rescued for a purpose, Cesare. The others might want to stop us. Besides," she said, "you might not survive in the daylight either."

Carmen Teresa pulled out the silver dagger she'd given earlier to the guard, Joseph, and began to sharpen it with a pumice stone.

"And Cesare," she added, "I wouldn't want anything to happen to you—just yet."

Cesare took an exaggerated bow.

"Thank you for allowing me to give a proper goodbye to my dear friend, the abbott."

"Be quick about it," Carmen Teresa snapped curtly.

Cesare gave a sly grin and walked back down the corridor. Here, hidden in the depths of the monastery, he paused briefly outside the crypt where he'd been for—just how long? But his pause was short, and he moved along to a smaller crypt. It was short, barely reaching Cesare's mid-section, and its entrance had been recently covered with brick and mortar, save for a small opening at its top. From inside came a muffled crying.

"Dom Felice," he said slowly, savoring each word, "why do you cry so? Have you not been spared, when so many others here lie dead?"

"CESARE!" gasped the abbott. Cesare peered into the small opening at the top. Nine months living in darkness had done much for his night vision. The abbot of Saint Michael's was wedged into this chamber, chained by his feet to the floor. Dom Felice's chest squeezed into his protruding belly, leaving him capable of only a weak gasp.

"You and Pope made a huge mistake. You got rid of that person. The one doing the experiments and saying there are small living things in the air and the body, which caused this disease? He was called a heretic and kicked out of this place. Your pope declared him excommunicated for heresy."

Cesare leaned closer to the opening.

"But he was right. Not completely, but close. He developed something I could not. Something that could eat the living things.

Is amazing, I tried, but could not. He has not finished but is close. But he did not know it."

Cesare opened his saddlebag and showed several vials of white liquid through the opening.

"You see these? *This* is why I came here. Many of these things are now dead, but maybe a few survive. If not, I hope I can recreate them. I did make a simple mistake and was caught. But I knew my friends would find me eventually.

"Kill me," the abbot managed to gasp from the dark. "For the love of God, Cesare."

Cesare laughed, thinking of the irony of the statement. "No. I warn you to leave. You did not. I commend you to *your* god and his mercy."

"P-p-please."

"Nemo me impune lacessit," Cesare said and slid the final brick into place.

"I said to let him go," Carmen Teresa ordered. She stormed up the corridor with Raphael and Federigo trailing her.

Bernardo and Miguel held Pietro Gualtieri by the shoulders in the secret passage leading from the catacombs below into the main dormitory, where most of the monks of Saint Michael lay still and lifeless in their cells. Thomas was out in the courtyard with the horses. Marie had been killed earlier while attacking two men. A pontificate guard managed to slice her head half off with a sword. That was the kind of death that could not be resurrected from. Carmen Teresa finished that guard personally. If Marie had more time to rest, she might not have made that mistake. But time was not a luxury. Everyone knew the risks.

The bodies of the Pontificate Guards were scattered throughout the grounds, though many had been collected in the building which served as their barracks and lay in their beds. To an outsider, it might seem that the plague had struck here quickly, and most of the men had gone to their end in their beds, as so many before them had.

Pietro Gualtieri had witnessed these horrors.

Bernardo and Miguel were eyeing him with intense hunger. Cesare, a saddlebag slung over his shoulder, lurked to the side.

"Stop that!"

As Carmen Teresa approached, the vampires obediently released Pietro Gualtieri. He fell to his knees, clasping his hands together.

Cesare cocked his head to a side alcove and said, "Let us talk for a moment." He began walking away when Carmen Teresa commanded, "No." She looked at the others, who stood in a semicircle around them. "The rest of you, leave us."

Gualtieri sensed the other creatures receding into the depths of the monastery corridor, leaving him on his knees with Carmen Teresa and the one called Cesare.

"You think is wise to leave this one?" Cesare asked.

"I promised no harm if he did as I asked," she shot back. "Do you want me to break my word, Cesare?"

"Your word? To him?" Cesare said, nodding incredulously towards the kneeling Gualtieri. "It means nothing."

"You challenge me, Cesare?"

Cesare slunk back and brushed dust off his shirt. "Never. It is just—no, I do not challenge you or question you," he said, his voice trailing off. As Carmen Teresa turned and began to walk away, Cesare added, "Mircalla."

Carmen Teresa froze in her tracks. Pietro saw her look directly at him. Her brow furrowed, and she looked back at Cesare, then looked to the ground, as if studying the distance between them. Cesare began to speak. "Oh, I-I'm sorry, Mir—"

Carmen Teresa whirled and violently pinned Cesare against the wall, her fangs drawn and dripping near Cesare's scruff-covered neck. Cesare was limp, his toes not touching the ground, and blurted, "I'm sorry, I didn't know." His words contained real pain; there was an air of quiet confidence about them.

Carmen Teresa whispered into his ear. "Cesare, do that again, and I will kill you."

A thin smile crossed Cesare's lips. "And if you do kill me, Mircalla, then all this rescue will for no-thing. And the ones who sent you—they won't be so happy, will they?"

Carmen Teresa snarled.

"Listen to me, Cesare. I don't care. Say my name again, and I'll tear you limb from limb. In the most literal sense."

She shook his head, then whispered into his ear, "And then I'll bring you *back.*"

Carmen Teresa let Cesare fall and strode by the kneeling Pietro Gualtieri. He received a look of pity from her.

She leaned over and whispered, "You should have just left."

Pietro stammered, "I-I had t-to see..." His voice trailed off. Carmen Teresa shook her head and walked down the hall to the dormitory. Pietro watched her fade awayand sobbed out, "Carmen Teresa, please." He was a simple man, but he felt an overwhelming sense of fear in his gut, and he urinated on the floor.

"She is a strong one, no?"

Pietro felt the vampire stroking the back of his hair.

"Don't leave me," Pietro cried.

"I am sorry," said Cesare. "I did not know your arrangement. You see, she," Cesare pointed in Carmen Teresa's direction. "She is unique. A natural leader in her own coven, wise and strong, as you've seen, and most capable. A formidable woman, no? And a necromancer! But you see, our world—it is a very dangerous one, and there are many who would want to find a female vampire who can raise the dead. They are jealous of her and her power. And many of these are not so kind as her. They are *bad.* With a piece of cloth, a tuft of hair, almost anything, they can try to seek her. But with a *name,* those same ones, they could find her, and do harm, or worse."

Carmen Teresa disappeared out of the torchlight.

"You see," Cesare continued in his halting manner of speech, "the name of a vampire is a very important thing. Some of us go to great lengths to keep ours secret. I go by Cesare Borgia now. I have gone by many names. Never my real one. Carmen Teresa? She really meant to let you leave, which is good for you. But I mentioned her real name in your presence."

Cesare pulled Pietro close. "And now *you* know it. That is not good for you."

"I will not speak it! I swear on my children's lives, I will not!"

"You may honestly believe that," said Cesare, as the other vampires began to emerge from the darkness. "But among our kind, there are those we fear, and they have ways of extracting information. Even from those who refuse to talk. And Ms. Mircalla, no matter what she promised you, she cannot risk that. You understand, no?"

Pietro Gualtieri was a simple man. But in that last instant, in his last thoughts, he was very aware of how much evil was in his presence.

Each vampire and vampiress mounted their horses in the middle of the courtyard.

"Less than two hours to sunrise," Carmen Teresa said. "Don't waste time."

Cesare expressed surprise at the animals.

"You've trained these well," he said, climbing onto a saddle.

Carmen Teresa said, "We have made many advances with animals since you went away, Cesare. These nightmares do well for us. Daylight is still a problem, though. Did you get what you needed?"

Cesare patted his saddlebag.

"Yes."

Federigo pointed to the refectory and said, "Look."

A dirty blond-haired waif stood in the doorway to the dining hall and slowly drifted toward them. Federigo began to move toward her, but Carmen Teresa ordered him back and instead rode up to her, then dismounted. The girl looked right at Carmen Teresa, and Carmen Teresa gazed intently into her eyes. The girl began pointing to the moon in the night sky and began babbling, "Eh eh eh eh."

Carmen Teresa noticed a locket around the girl's neck. The vampiress reached for it, and the girl slapped at Carmen Teresa's wrist. Carmen Teresa smiled at the gesture, then touched the girl's hand and gently but forcefully put it down. Then Carmen Teresa looked at the back of the locket and saw a name.

"Lisabetta," she said, and now recognized the woman she'd seen in Dom Felice's cell. The girl made no response.

Carmen Teresa climbed back on her horse and rode to the others.

"Leave her," she said.

"Is that wise?" Cesare asked.

"She's an idiot," Carmen Teresa said tersely, then rode up to Cesare and gave a sharp backhand to his face, drawing blood. His head snapped back, which the other vampires observed, being careful to avoid eye contact with either.

"Any more questions, Cesare?"

Cesare wiped his mouth with the back of his hand and smiled. "No, Carmen Teresa. You are right, of course."

The girl wandered off into the courtyard. The vampires rode out the main entrance, across the wooden bridge, and bid a permanent goodbye to the abbey of Saint Michael-du-Anjou.

[5]
MOMENTS OF REFLECTION

Well, we have three groups as of last count.

FMaddalena, who has become part of a group of adventurers. The troupe has some interesting characters, don't you think? But can they be trusted?

Elizabeth, the leader of a group of flesh-eating ghouls, known as fleshers, who want to get her hands, Maddalena, and her little brother.

Then there is a group of vampires who have rescued one of their kind for reasons that are not entirely clear.

Let's look in on some of our groups.

First, Maddalena.

MADDALENA

OUR JOURNEY IS such a whirl that it is difficult to remember. It is like a set of plays or images flashing before me.

Our group, a collection of vagabonds racing on horseback and with wagons into the foothills. There is some concern for pursuit by others from the kingdom. The land rises higher, growing rockier. We crossed a wooden bridge. Jai Ling and the ugly dwarf stopped to light something. The bridge is blown apart into many splinters. Dust blows everywhere. We continue our ride through the day. Hard riding. No resting.

Jai Ling's horse is a strong corsair; she calls him Bellerophon. But it is small and begins to struggle with two riders. Jai Ling puts me on the wagon next to Bartolome. It is good he is alive. But I still feel empty. The tiger stirs in the cage behind us. We race on.

Night finally comes, and with it, fog. We slow down, pause, and Jai Ling and another rider, a woman wearing a veil, go ahead. Jai Ling comes back and waves us on. I remember passing through the mist, unable to see much beyond our reach. Then, out of the smoke, I see a set of three open coffins. A body lies in each. Two, a man and woman, are lying dressed in fine clothing, while the third, a girl probably my age, lies in a torn shift. Her face is blackened and bruised, split open at spots where boils burst.

I am too tired to be afraid.

Our group stops at a clearing. The fog is still present, but I can see further. At first, it seems empty, but as we venture in, out of the white, a small group of people emerges, waiting. They have wagons. A boy or young man, older than me but not by much, was left with some of the people. Their leader was a tall, elderly man with a long face and striking white beard and hair. Perhaps the boy's father. He reaches for the boy's arm, then stops. An older woman comes up, embraces the boy, then slaps him. The boy seems ashamed.

From out of the mist, another group arrives, larger than the first. More wagons. More horses. More people. Dioneo, Jai Ling, and the others know these people and greet them as friends. Their leader is a tall and thin dark-skinned man with an angular reddish-colored face, a close-cut black beard, and dressed in silk robes. He walks rigidly, like a king.

The boy's father speaks with this tall man. The father complains about the many soldiers killed at the arena, how they will all be made to pay. The tall man says that they had warned him such things could happen, and that the price would be a high one. The ugly dwarf growls that no peasants were killed, only soldiers.

We are given barrels of wine. And food. Fruits, salted meats, fish, and some vegetables. Dioneo's friends take these and put them on their wagons. I now see this is why they saved the boy in the arena. Why we saved the boy. It is a barter. The boy's life for food, drink, and other materials.

A boy my age acts as a squire and leads a pack of horses by a tether. All palfreys, maybe a few larger. The Nubian, Mansa, walks over and chooses three, which he takes from the boy's hand.

Suddenly, the dwarf—Uwe he is called? He is angry, he growls and grinds his teeth while looking into one of the barrels. Jai Ling looks in as well. She, too, is angry. Something about not enough sulfur.

The woman who rode out with us, the one who wore the veil, speaks to Jai Ling. Now with her veil gone, I see—oh my God.

One side of her body, her right side, is beautiful, her limbs strong but feminine. Exquisite is not a strong enough word. But the other side, her left side, is covered in scars and burst buboes. There is a hole in her cheek, and her left eye is crooked.

The white-haired older man is saying there is no more. He pleads with the tall, rigid man and Dioneo. Dioneo says it is not enough, that maybe they'll keep the boy. There is a sudden silence from all.

Then Dioneo laughs and clasps the other two men on the shoulder and asks, "What is some sulfur between such un allegra brigata di amicis?" Neither man seems happy with Dioneo, but the rigid man who seems to be the group leader says they'll take two more horses to settle the account. The white-haired man looks at a woman who may be his wife, and nods. Mansa walks back and takes two more horses from the squire.

The group we gave the boy to seems unhappy, but they do not protest. Eventually, they leave the clearing, disappearing into the fog.

Jai Ling tells me we will rest here for the night. Bartolome and I are led into a wagon where they tell me to sleep. I want to sleep, but I cannot.

"Where's Momma?"

Bartolome cries on my shoulder. We hug each other tight. Now we huddle together in the wagon, trying to make each other feel better. I cry a little, but I stop the tears. I will not let Bartolome see me shed them. Mother taught me to be strong.

"They won't take us back," I say to him. "They say it is too dangerous and that Mother is dead. We only have each other."

My voice sounds strange, not like my own. I feel Bartolome shudder next to me. "She's not dead!" he says, and cries even more. "I want Momma, I want Poppa."

I cannot answer him.

A scratching on the side of the wagon. In climbs the girl we saw in the city yesterday. Smaller than me, though older, and indeed quite beautiful, like the most perfect of dolls. She no longer has her hair up in a coil, but instead it falls across her face, dirty and sand-swept from our recent run from the arena. I see now that she is a dwarf too, though a very pretty one. The others call her Trippetta. She acts as if she has befriended my brother and I.

"Good news," she says with a smile, and I can't help but feel my heart jump. But I should know better than to be hopeful at this point. "El Erreur has said you can stay, at least until he can decide about you," She sees my glumness and sits next to me.

"Do not worry." She pats my leg. "I will speak for you and your brother. And Jai Ling will speak for you, I think. You helped her at the arena, and she will not forget. El Erreur is our leader, but he never crosses Jai Ling if she really wants something."

"Am I supposed to be thankful?" I ask, cradling my brother. "They will not go back to search for our mother."

"I understand," she says, reaching behind me and patting Bartolome's head. "When I was younger than you now, I was taken from my homeland. Stolen. My land was captured by one of King Frido's generals. My father and brother were killed in the fighting. I don't know what happened to my mother, but we were parted, and I never saw her. It was very hard. But I am alive now, though none of my family is. You have your brother. You wish to wander the woods alone? There is danger at every turn, this you know. And food? What do you eat? And plague? How could you run from it?"

I look at her with sad eyes. The dwarf woman takes a cloth and dips it into a bucket near us, which has clean water, and begins to wipe her face.

"Wash yourself," she says, wetting another cloth and handing it to me. "You feel better."

It is understandable how a dwarf as pretty and graceful a dancer as Trippetta might be taken or stolen as a prize. She is unusual, but in a beautiful way, and would be a welcome addition to many courts. Yet she seems cheerful. Too cheerful.

"If you were stolen from your home," I ask, "why don't you go back?"

Trippetta pauses. For a moment, I see the slightest sign of water in her eyes.

"I did," she answers. "Uwe and I were kept at a court as evil as the one we just ran from. I was a dancer, and Uwe was a fool. We were treated as things to make King Frido happy; that was all. Uwe was often badly beaten. For me, the men in the king's court, they like me, I am not beaten so much, but they do—other things to me.

"One night, Uwe and I had our chance, and we escaped. We

finally did get away, back to our homeland. My village was gone. Empty. My friends, my family, everyone. King Frido's invaders were dead from plague. There was nothing to stay for. The black death had come. Hard. It spares few."

She blinks at me and speaks so simply. There is no terror in her voice when she talks. All she does is tell her story.

"And Uwe?" I ask.

"He came from a land next to mine. It was nearly the same in Uwe's home. There were a few who survived, but they were dying. And in hiding."

"From the plague," I said.

Trippetta shook her head. "No, the plague had already raped this land. But there are other sicknesses that follow a plague. The vampires. They fed on people left behind. They feasted! And not the blood vampires. No, these eat flesh. They are called fleshers. The people hid in the day and waited, hoping the fleshers would not come for them at night. They were already dead. Uwe and I were not. So we fled."

"How did you get away from King Frido's court?" I ask.

She continued. "Once, during carnival time, King Frido struck me in front of the court. Uwe saw this. Truthfully, this was not so bad, really. Compared to other things. I never told Uwe or anyone about other things done to me. But when Frido struck me, I had never seen Uwe so angry. Uwe demanded revenge for me and himself. I thought we might escape the land, as we did, or have our deaths. Either was good with me.

"There was to be a costume ball soon. Uwe convinced King Frido and his six closest advisors to dress as grotesque monkeys. O-rangs, I think he called them. Uwe made their costumes out of fur and flax, and they seem so real." Trippetta laughs mischievously.

"Uwe charmed the King and his ministers into being chained together and hoisted above the party. Then Uwe lit them on fire. They burned. I can still smell their skin being eaten by the fire. But it was just. Then Uwe went up the chain and exited through the roof. We have been together since."

She laughs more. "King Frido was at the top of the chain, and the last thing he saw—before the fire ate him—was Uwe and I leaving.

Trippetta giggles, pats my shoulder, and makes to leave, adding, "So you see, everything works out. Be happy you are here and not dead like King Frido."

"That's a horrible story," I say.

"Not at all," replies the dwarf. "King Frido was evil." She winks as she disappears over the wagon rail, then adds, "Uwe's really good with fire."

Jai Ling and Dioneo Go Off by Themselves

Jai Ling stood outside, leaning against one of the wagons, just beyond the ring of light given from the fire, and slicing an apple with one of her daggers. Her bow and a quiver of arrows were still slung behind her back. A small stream trickled by. Earlier, Trippetta and Uwe had strung up nets in the water in hopes of catching some trout, or perhaps a perch.

"Ahh, my dear Jai Ling, you're waiting for me at the appointed place," came a voice behind her, and a figure grabbed her arms. "I may love you, but you must understand that we can never be together."

"Shut up, Dioneo, I'm thinking," she said, slipping out of his grasp.

"You're an oriental goddess, a temptress," Dioneo laughingly said. "Come and kiss me, my dear."

Oblivious to Dioneo's advances, Jai Ling walked to a nearby tree half-rooted in the water and sat down, laying the bow beside her. "Yesterday was close, Dioneo. Nearly lost my head a couple of times. But you—" She gestured with the knife. "When I saw you in that arena, you looked tiny. I thought you had food for the big cats."

"Well," Dioneo laughed again and sat beside her, slapping his knees as he did, "I cheated death again. We all did." He reached to pat Jai Ling's knee, but she pushed his arm away.

"Hmmm," mused Jai Ling, "we just put him off another day. The danse macabre takes all of us in the end." She cut another slice of apple and offered it to Dioneo, who took it from the dagger tip.

"Ricciardo," she said, "he seemed like a nice enough boy."

"I think he was," Dioneo commented as he bit the apple slice. "Mmmmm, not bad."

"For all we did, it ought to be excellent," Jai Ling said. "The wine looks good, too. But we should have insisted on more sulfur. Uwe says we're running low. You shouldn't have settled for two horses."

Dioneo shrugged his shoulders and said, "I wanted more, but I think they gave us all they had. And who cares what Uwe says, he's just a crazy dwarf who likes to burn things." He leaned toward Jai Ling. "Kiss me, baby."

Jai Ling shifted just enough so that she firmly bumped his extended chin with her shoulder. Dioneo mockingly yelled (although there was some force to Jai Ling's move) and rubbed his face.

"I'm not a complete idiot," he said. "I think I left my mind in the arena. Want to help me go back and get it?"

Jai Ling said, "You handled the matter about the boy well. You weren't really going to have El Erreur hold onto him?"

"God no," laughed Dioneo. "He was a whiny little fop. Couldn't wait to get rid of him."

"What about Ricciardo's friend, Angelique?" asked Jai Ling, crunching on the apple. "Trippetta said they tried to reach her, but she was dead."

Dioneo nodded, taking another apple slice off of Jai Ling's

knife. "Yeah. Probably killed by Lucrezia herself. Or at her bidding. She wanted them both dead."

"I thought I saw someone lurking in the background when we blew open the keep," Jai Ling said. "Lucrezia?"

"Yes," Dioneo replied, nodding, and he looked into the night. "Vampirism has arrived there. Probably won't be long before the plague follows."

"So much for their walls," Jai Ling mused. "As if that could keep vampirism or the plague out. But I ran into a vampire, too."

"I heard," said Dioneo. "And you left the poor kid alone. Scared the girl half to death. Surprised she's still alive."

Now Jai Ling shrugged. "I got her back."

Dioneo smiled his famous grin. "That was foolish. You could've been caught. You wasted time chasing after some orphan you don't even know. I wouldn't have bothered."

Now Jai Ling laughed. "No," she said, "I think you would have."

"I don't go back for anyone," Dioneo said. "Except for the right price," he added slyly.

"There's something else," Jai Ling added. "It was strange. The vampire—it grabbed Maddalena. It *wanted* Maddalena. I heard him say she was so precious. Dioneo, when he took her, I started to leave. I was going to run, but even after I decided to go after the girl, I figured my only chance would be to throw a knife from a distance. I guessed which hall he'd go to, and I climbed into the rafters. But he was distracted, Dioneo. He was so excited, he was so *focused* on her, that he walked right under me. I got on top of him, and he didn't even know I was there."

"Don't tease me so much," Dioneo said, as straight-faced as he could.

"Don't bother," snapped Jai Ling.

"Look. It was a male, right?" said Dioneo. "And a younger one. They love little girls. He was crazy for her. And you're the best hunter I've ever seen, at least among humans. You were after him; he was all wild for a young girl. No contest. It's as simple as that."

"True, I did kill him. With this very knife, no less." Jai Ling admired the blade.

Dioneo looked at his hands.

"By the way," Jai Ling continued. "What about Maddalena's caravan? Think any chance the mother and uncle survived?"

Dioneo gave her a look of shock.

"You're kidding, right? They got caught. That's it. Fleshers feed on anything breathing. Their mother got the kids to the river. Good for her. Fleshers leave nothing alive. Besides, vampires or flesh eaters, they're behind us," he said, gesturing one way with his thumb, "and that's why we're going that way to stay ahead of them," and he pointed in the opposite direction. He took another bite of the apple. "I'm not going back to mess with fleshers to look for a mother who is already consumed."

Jai Ling shook her head. She also thought about that moment when she was going through the arena and thought she heard *someone*—a voice in her head called her name.

A hallucination, she thought. *Still....*

"I'm not sure," Jai Ling replied. "There was something about that girl." Then she rose, picking up her bow and drawing an arrow from the quiver. "But you're right about the others being behind us. I'm going to check the crossbow traps. Make sure everyone stays in; I've set some particularly nasty bolts in them."

"Suit yourself, sweetie, I'll be nearby if you get lonely."

Jai Ling gave him a half smile and slowly walked around the perimeter. Dioneo sliced off another piece of apple, then paused before eating it.

"Jai," Dioneo called, and she paused to look at him. "After you killed the vampire."

"Yes?" Jai Ling asked.

"You did wash this knife, didn't you?"

What of Carmen Teresa, Cesare Borgia, and our other vampire friends?
Let us look in.

While standing in a doorway to Castle Otranto, Cesare Borgia stroked his facial growth. One couldn't call it a beard. No, having spent *how long* walled up in a catacomb at Saint Michael's, with only an occasional piece of bloodied meat thrust on a spear through a slim hole in the bricks, what had grown in the black of the tomb was a tangled mass of stubble and hair. Tonight, he'd slept for a few hours, but restless ones. Now he was wandering this deserted structure before the dawn. Cesare laughed to himself. Men followed their religious symbols so *religiously*. They were idiots. Begrudgingly, he could admire the organization of their Church, a vast hierarchy of old men who preyed upon the masses for their own advancement, all on the basis of a fear of some non-existent god. But the Church feared Cesare and his kind, and most especially Cesare. As they should. Don Felice had spent months trying to make Cesare speak and learn his secrets.

A faint pale orange was just beginning to break across the horizon. It had been so long since he'd seen anything like daybreak that he stared, entranced by the beautiful color, even though he would have to retreat from it.

"Going somewhere, Cesare?"

Cesare was more amused than startled, though he had not known she was there. He laughed and said, "You startled me."

Carmen Teresa swung her legs down from the stoop she'd been lying on and sat up.

"You haven't adjusted yet to being let out," she said. "You'll come around soon enough."

Cesare cocked his head. "You've been sitting all night? You think I might try to run away?" He patted his chest. "In my weak condition?"

Carmen Teresa walked towards him, and in the darkness, Cesare was aroused by her presence.

"You might," she replied, turning her back to him. "Not that you'd get very far. You couldn't survive in the daylight right now. But you might think you could."

Cesare shook his head. "You know, when they first brought me to their quaint monastery, Don Felice and his friends, they had many little things to try on me. He found ways to put things in my body that you'd never imagined."

Cesare pulled up his tunic. The candlelight flickered off his bare chest, highlighting the protruding ribs that the skin barely stretched over. Numerous red sores and blotches covered it like some macabre bacchanalian canvas. Even with the vampire's rapid healing process, his body had scarred.

Cesare uttered a laugh. "Don Felice, he was a creative little man of the church, no? But after a while, he decided I wasn't very cooperative. So he placed me in that walled cell you found me in. But I was a problem. How do you keep a vampire alive as a prisoner? Well, they fed me bloodied cattle meat. And do you know what? The first time I tasted it, I retched."

Carmen Teresa felt a swell of desire in her. Cesare had bathed when they arrived. Still, there was a smell to him. It would not wash away quickly. She detested Cesare as much as she hated his awareness that even now, she desired him. But hate was never known to stop a vampire's physical wants.

Cesare continued. "Then a fun-ny thing happened. Our bodies are wonderful things, Carmen. Given no choice, the body, if it does not die, will adapt, at least enough to continue existing. On rare occasions, I think they give me human flesh, as if the good friars thought I could live on that. Don Felice must have paid the local village well for corpses, or perhaps he tricked the fools into entrusting their dead to him with some promise of an indulgence or other riches in heaven. And he promised me more. Living ones. All the young girls I would want, or boys, if I'd only tell him what he wanted to know. And after a while, I began to think, 'why not, I'm going to die here anyway.'"

Cesare waved his fingers upward.

"But then you came along and rescued me. How nice."

He walked closer to Carmen Teresa.

"So after a long night's ride, you are right, I am in no condition to go anywhere. But why would I leave?" He reached for Carmen Teresa's shoulder. "When there are such treasures here in these walls?"

Carmen Teresa let Cesare run his hand up and down her bare shoulder.

"Why bother yourself, Cesare, when you know how I despise you?" she said coldly, but she did not move from his touch.

Cesare moved behind her and grabbed both her shoulders, pulling her to him and drawing his lips to her shoulder. Kissing the nape of her neck, he whispered, "You know, Carmen, the humans are a strange bunch. When the black death comes near, some say, 'our god is angry, we must repent,' and they spend their days in prayer to their gods, and they deny themselves food and water. Or my favorite, they whip their bodies with cat-o'-nine tails. They are funny, no?"

He boldly reached around and grabbed Carmen Teresa's bosom sharply. There was no gentleness in his touch.

"But others," Cesare said, "they embrace the moment, they eat what they find, they make love with whomever they want, they sin as much as they can, and they say 'Eat, drink, be merry, for tomorrow you shall die.' And in the end, it makes no difference; their god takes them all. I think is better to embrace the moment, no?"

Then he pulled her face to the side, caressing it with his fangs but not breaking the skin.

"Your limbs are strong, Carmen," he whispered.

"I could kill you right now," she said, but her body released its tension, and she let him loosen her cloak.

"Of course I know," Cesare said, quite truthfully. Even in this advantageous position, he was well aware that she could turn on him in a moment and do what Don Felice had been unable to. "But that is what makes it worthwhile, no?"

Raphael was confused. Two nights ago, he had felt energized by the events at the monastery. But now he was starving, his whole body craving something.

He turned the corner and saw Carmen Teresa sitting nude on a bench, her back to him, combing her hair. The one they'd come for, Cesare, lay asleep on some sheets in the corner. Raphael glared at the sleeping vampire. No one had told him what made this vampire so important, and now that he'd seen him, Raphael still had no idea. He clenched his fist.

"What is it, Raphael?" Carmen Teresa asked, still combing her hair. "You should be resting. You've had a long journey, and to be raised from your essence is draining on a person."

Raphael released his fist, then held back.

"We're hungry," he said. "We're very hungry."

Carmen Teresa ran her fingers through her hair. She liked Raphael the best of the bunch. He had been a pretty boy in life and had been turned just as he was entering manhood. She would have to spend time with him.

Then she looked at her hand. Her fingers were thin. The previous nights had ravaged her body. Feeding on soldiers, then breathing out her life force to resurrect the others. A single resurrection was difficult, but six? Too many at once. Her body was still adjusting. And the others? All had been weakened by having to kill and then ride here. Except, perhaps, Cesare. His body had actually gone through the least battering of any of them over the past two nights. She was still stronger than him and should remain so, but she would have to be careful. And she had almost forgotten. When one was resurrected, one was not so hungry at first. But after a day or two, the appetite became ravenous.

"You're right, Raphael," she said. "We all need to eat."

She turned and smiled at him. "Tell the others we'll go out tonight."

[6]
THE POWER OF SILVER

Ahh, let us look here. The place is a forgotten village on the border between the Kingdom of France and the Italian city-states. The Black Death ravages across Europe. Nearly half of Europe's human population has been decimated. The main struggle is to survive. People, however, are not the only victims of the plague. Animals, particularly nocturnal ones who feed on other living creatures, are also susceptible

And sometimes, even vampires.

CARMEN TERESA STARED up at the night sky. It was her fault, really, and she knew it. After spending three days at Castle Otranto, they had ridden for three nights in the general direction of southern France. They found shelter during the day, once in an old mine, once in a cave, once in the woods. They had rested at the castle, sufficiently, she had thought, but since then she had pushed too hard. Two of the night mares died, the rest were weakened. But the Vampire Council did not care. A little bird had given her a message. Now that she had Cesare, they wanted the laboratory found as soon as possible. She had to come up with an idea.

The group was fortunate to come across this small village that had been struck hard by the plague. The manor house was set off quite a walk from the other houses. Having found it mostly deserted, they had entered the manor house and allowed their horses to rest in the stable. area. The few villagers still alive were too weak or too afraid to seek them out, so the vampires were left to themselves.

Raphael had recovered quickest. He had been useful in going out on food forages. He had found one woman in the village, a deep scar running from her jawline down her neck, but it was not the scar of buboes, more like that of a vicious bite. Otherwise, she had seemed to be free from the plague, and he was able to lure her to the manor house. Everyone had wanted to drink her blood, but Carmen Teresa had forbidden it, for the girl's smell was not right. Feeding on those infected with the black death could lead to sickness and death for a weakened vampire. The girl was allowed to go. No one from the village came to the manor house the next day to inquire, either from fear or being too sick. Still, this evening, Carmen Teresa had ordered Raphael and Federigo to rely on animals and plants, as they had since leaving Saint Michael's monastery.

Behind her, Cesare Borgia lay on the floor beside a plush bed, his head propped up on a down-filled pillow, drinking from a wine sack.

She had played this game long enough.

"What are you thinking, Carmen Teresa?" Cesare asked.

Carmen Teresa sat down on the bed, over Cesare. "So where is it?" she inquired matter-of-factly.

Cesare shrugged his shoulders and continued drinking from the wine sack. "Where is what?" he repeated.

Carmen Teresa spoke sternly. "You know me too well, Cesare. I won't keep asking."

Cesare laughed.

"Why don't we all leave and I show you?"

"You're not well enough to travel yet," Carmen Teresa said. "And I am not sure about the others, except Raphael. We tried moving from Castle Otranto, and look what happened. You all need to rest here a few days more."

Cesare quietly stared at the night sky. "You brought me here just for me to tell you where the laboratory is. Then I tell you, and you kill me, no? Or if I don't tell you, you kill me and bring me back. Like one of your mindless minions. Then I tell you everything, no? It is smart thing for you to do."

Cesare sat up and threw the wine sack aside. "But that plan, it has one fault. You bring me back, maybe I not remember some things. Maybe I be no good to you. Then where you be?"

Carmen Teresa shook her head. "You misjudge the situation," she said, pointing to Cesare's forehead. "There is far, far too much information in that brain of yours to destroy it. We need you to find a cure for the menace you've created, Cesare. We've sent other poisoners, assassins, killers to the fleshers, and they just don't come back."

Cesare smirked and said, "I not create them. I added your black death. The fleshers, they arise on their own. From the black death, perhaps, but I not their father."

Carmen Teresa crouched in front of Cesare. "Created, spawned, birthed. Parse words as you want. Tell me where the laboratory is. I will ride out to it and find the entrance. I am sure you have it protected. I will then come back to get you—"

"And then we will all go together," Cesare finished. "And I make the antidote for you." He threw his head back and clapped his hands. "Why not, Carmen Teresa? Why not?"

He leaned forward and wrapped his hand around the back of Carmen Teresa's head. She resisted for a moment, then smiled and said, "Why not?"

The vampires, other than Cesare, gathered around an interior room of the manor house.

"He gave us a location," Carmen Teresa said. "About two nights' ride from here. Raphael and I will go search for it. If and when we find it, or if we find nothing, we will return here. Either way, we will ride out and be back in five nights."

"You trust him?" Federigo, the eldest, asked.

"Cesare?" Carmen Teresa said. "Not at all. But he knows if he lies to me, what I will do to him. I need you to watch him carefully."

"We should all go," said Miguel, the large Corsican, pounding the table.

"You need a few more days to rest, as do the night mares," Carmen Teresa said. "I pushed too hard. We can't lose any more horses; they take too long to train."

"And we need to eat," Miguel continued.

"Do not touch the villagers here," Carmen Teresa said. "There's a smell of the plague in the air."

"Bah," Thomas said. "Vampires are not prey to the black death."

"They are if they're weakened," Carmen Teresa said. "And you are. The plague has hit this village. In a few days, you will be able to eat and drink as you want. But not yet."

"You question Carmen Teresa?" Federigo spoke loudly. "You all agreed when you volunteered to follow her, no matter what. And do you, Thomas, do you think you know more about the resurrection than her?"

Carmen Teresa smiled. “Your personalities are coming back. That’s good. But your bodies are still regenerating. You will stay here and keep Cesare company.”

Miguel said, “You take Raphael, this runt?”

“He is the youngest,” Carmen Teresa said. “He has returned the quickest. It is no shame on any of you; it is merely how these things work.”

“Bah, I am ready.”

Carmen Teresa’s hand slapped Miguel’s. He stumbled back, but caught himself before falling. He rubbed his jaw, a trickle of blood flowing down. Carmen Teresa looked at the others, then licked the blood off her fingers.

“Don’t forget who I am. Any more questions?”

No one spoke. Miguel gave an angry glance at Carmen Teresa.

“Good. Federigo is in charge while Raphael and I are gone. Watch Cesare in shifts. I think he is too weak to go far, but I want him in this manor house while we are gone. And do not feed on the villagers.”

There were murmurings of agreement.

Outside, in one of the adjoining rooms, Cesare Borgia listened to each word. He held a small clay bowl or mortar in one hand and a pestle in the other. This would have to be hidden for now.

He had seen Miguel’s look.

Miguel sat at a table, watching a fire in the central hearth of the manor house. Cesare sat in a corner, pounding a powdered substance into a paste.

“How long since they left?” Cesare asked.

“What do you care?” Miguel asked in return, staring at the fire.

“I’m hungry for real food,” Cesare replied. “I have not fed on real food. Not even at the abbey.”

"That's your problem."

Cesare said, "And yours."

Miguel shrugged. "So what?"

"So the girl Raphael brought here was fine, that is what," Cesare said. "You feel fine, no? You look fine, no? She look fine, no?"

Miguel looked at Cesare. "What are you doing over there?"

"This?" Cesare said, holding his bowl up. "This help us eat."

Miguel walked over. Though the flames from the fireplace barely touched this corner, the contents in Cesare's bowl had a silver-hued shine to them.

"It looks like silver shit," Miguel said. "You want us to eat that?"

Cesare laughed gruffly. "Nooo," he said deliberately. "This shit? It detect the plague in people."

"Ehhhh?"

Cesare nodded. "You rub this on the body. It turn black if person has the black death. Is poetic, no?"

Cesare watched Miguel's eyes widen for a moment, but then harden.

"Carmen Teresa told us to avoid eating from the village," Miguel said.

"And Carmen, she not here now, is she?" Cesare observed. "You and I, we go outside." Cesare got to his feet. "I find you some food that is safe. Bring Thomas. Bring all the others. I show you." He leaned into Miguel and added, "I saw where that girl lives."

Carmen Teresa and Raphael rode gently along the moonlit path, one beside the other. Their destination was Rolliere's, a village several miles west of the Durance River, near the southwestern edge of the Alps. They sought another manor house with stone walls cut from marble. Unusual to find in any village. More particularly, there was a cave to be found near the marble house. Cesare had said to seek out the locals. They would know where it was because they avoided it.

"You seemed a bit troubled, Mistress," Raphael said.

"I don't like leaving Cesare alone with the others," Carmen Teresa commented. "But a little bird came to me from the Vampire Council. Now that we have Cesare, they want the lab found. Quickly."

"Miguel is strong; surely he can overcome Cesare?" Raphael asked.

Carmen Teresa looked skyward.

"Yes, Miguel is strong. So are Bernardo and Thomas. And Federigo is wise. But Cesare is crafty, very much so. He has outwitted popes and the vampire doge. He stayed chained in a walled-up cell for months without revealing the location of his laboratory. Yet he told me."

"He knows you are honorable."

After laughing, Carmen Teresa said, "Ahh, young one, that is why you are with me. Do you like salt, Raphael?"

Puzzled, Raphael said, "It can be satisfying at times."

"Well, when you dine at the table with Cesare," Carmen Teresa continued, "he won't pass the salt without getting something greater in return."

Raphael took a drink from his wine sack.

Carmen Teresa had noticed it before. It was the one Cesare had earlier.

Margarita di Molese was on her knees, praying to the Virgin Mary. In the adjoining room, her husband of fifteen years, Talano di Molese, lay naked on a cot, sweating profusely, awaiting his death.

Talano was a decade older than Margarita, but his death would be premature. Margarita had removed all blankets, but in the late summer heat, there was no relief. Talano had been fine only two days ago when he left their home at sunrise to work in the nearby field, which he still cultivated. He returned unexpectedly by late morning, complaining of general weakness. He went to lie down, and at midday, when she checked, he was extremely hot and complaining of heat. She gave him water and gingerly removed his tunic. Late in the day, he still complained of heat. She peeked under his linen tights and saw. His inner thigh and abdomen were marked with egg-shaped buboes. Terrified, she retreated to the other room.

Through the night, she heard his fever-induced moaning. At various times during the night, he begged her for help. Once, she mustered the courage to return to the room and remove his clothes, careful not to look too closely at the body.

In the morning, she peeked in again. The buboes had swelled more and, in some cases, burst, oozing that mixture of blood and watery fluids. One had a chance of surviving these. But now Margarita saw the purplish splotches on the chest and neck of Talano. "God's Tokens," she whispered, and indeed, these were signs that death was near.

She was praying for forgiveness. Forgiveness for not helping her husband more. As each hour had passed, his condition had descended closer and closer to the end. A bloody cough had appeared late on the second day, followed by violent vomiting. The room stank. She wanted to help him more. But God's Tokens were clear. One was not going to survive. Margarita could not leave her husband, but she could not summon the courage to do more.

She also prayed for forgiveness for her transgressions. Only a few nights ago, she was out walking when she recalled meeting a stranger, a virile young man, thin but muscular in a wiry type of way, with sharp brown eyes. He said he was a pilgrim and passing on his way to Avignon. Had it really happened, or had it been a dream? She could not recall. Indeed, she could not recall anything thereafter. Perhaps she had committed a great sin, and she had erased the memory from her mind, but she had no clear recollection of what had happened to her or to the young man. But there were vague—thoughts? Images? Her in the manor house. Others around her. She was stripped and looked at.

What was her greatest sin? That she liked the memory. She could not help but like it. Years ago, her husband had warned her one night not to go out in the evening. Talano had spoken of a vision he had experienced where she would be attacked that night by a great wolf. She ignored him and indeed, thought the worst of him.

He left the house that night to seek out this wolf, but she, not trusting him, followed, thinking that Talano was cheating on her. In the woods, she became disoriented. Just as Talano had predicted, she was attacked by a great wolf. She was rescued from death by a pair of passing shepherds and returned to her husband. Margarita recovered but bore deep scars from her jaw to her collarbone. People stared and winced when she walked by, and no man would ever look at her, save for Talano, who always loved her. So this recent memory of men looking at her with desire, even if it were only a dream, gave her pleasure. And that was sinful.

Knock knock knock.

It came from the door.

Margarita's heart jumped. Was this a sign?

There was a shove against the wooden door. It was barred with a solid maple plank. The plank held.

For a moment.

Then it split apart as the door swung open. Bernardo and Thomas burst through first. Miguel followed, pulling Cesare by his collar. Margarita cowered on the ground, screaming for help. In the next room, her husband, Talano, vomited blood. He was beyond comprehension of what was happening.

Miguel shook Cesare and said, "You said you could prove who was plague-ridden. Now prove it."

Cesare smiled and said, "Just watch me."

Miles away, Raphael was doubled over in pain and gasping for breath on his night mare.

"What's wrong with you?" Carmen Teresa asked urgently.

The young vampire slid out of his saddle and lay on a forest floor of clover. He continued to gasp and was clutching at his heart.

Carmen Teresa swung off her mount and went over to him. There was a glazed look in Raphael's eyes. He arched his back and shuddered. Carmen Teresa saw the wine sack he had been drinking from and grabbed it. She gave it a quick taste, then spat it out.

"Silver nitrate," she muttered. Quickly, her fangs extended. She bit into the back of her forearm and sucked, drawing a good blood flow. Then she shoved the forearm into Raphael's gasping mouth. For a moment, he resisted, but then she ordered, "Drink!"

The vampire began to suck blood from Carmen Teresa's arm.

The four vampires stood over Talano di Molese. He was on his side, trapped in his own excrement, and half slumped off his bed, a hand resting in a pool of blood and vomit.

"It stinks in here," said Thomas.

"These creatures are so weak," Bernado said. "Look how the pestilence eats them."

"This one has the purple patches," Miguel cried. "He's already dead. Why do you show us him?"

"Waaatch," Cesare said. "He is not dead yet." Cesare poked at

Talano. The old man groaned and shifted slightly. Cesare pulled a sack out of his tunic and sprinkled a white-silver power on Talanao's arm. Then Cesare took out a pestle and rubbed it up and down on Talano's skin, leaving a large white streak mark all along his arm.

"You are crazy," Thomas said.

"Just watch," Cesare said in his deep voice.

As they stared, the powder on Talano's arm turned from silver to black.

"You see?" Cesare said, pointing. "The powder reacts with his body. If it turns black, he has the black plague. Poetic, no?"

"This proves nothing," Bernardo said, storming out of the room.

Thomas silently followed.

Miguel pulled Cesare out of the room, threw him aside, and said, "So what, we all could see he had the plague."

"And what about her?" Cesare asked, gathering himself and gesturing to Margarita. "Does she have the smell of the plague about her?"

The other vampires went over and encircled her. Margarita stayed on the ground. Then Thomas pulled her up and licked her on the neck, the side that was not scarred.

"She seems all right," he said.

Margarita was repeating the Hail Mary over and over and looked to the thatched roof of her cottage.

"Let me show you."

Cesare applied the white-silver powder to Margarita as he had done to her husband. She moaned slightly.

"If she is without plague, it will turn to silver," Cesare said.

The vampires watched. In a minute, there was a very bright silver streak on Margarita's arm.

"You see?" Cesare asked. "Are you convinced now?"

Thomas grinned, but Miguel asked, "Why did Carmen Teresa tell us not to feed on her?"

Cesare stared right at Miguel and said, "Carmen Teresa know many things. But she not know the black plague as well as me. Or how it works. Or how to find it. Is true."

"And you want us to eat silver?" Miguel bellowed down at Cesare. "You want to kill us."

Cesare looked at their hungry faces and calmly said, "You not feed at the arm." Cesare sensed their desire to feed, but their fear of the silver. "The silver on the skin, it no bother you," Cesare assured them. "You no believe me? Then watch."

Cesare took Margarita in his arms and, while she continued praying, he said, "Keep asking your Mary for help." Then he bit down on her neck and drew blood.

Margarita swooned into unconsciousness. Cesare handed her limp body to Bernardo, but Miguel pushed in and drank. Bernardo began to feed from the scarred side of Margarita's neck. Thomas, the smallest of these three, held back, but when Miguel released his bite and withdrew, Thomas moved in. They drank their fill from Margarita. She was unconscious the entire time and died after approximately one-half hour of this exchange.

Telano expired in the adjoining room a few minutes later.

Raphael sat on the ground, rubbing his forehead. Carmen Teresa was feeding straw to the night mares.

"What happened?" Raphael asked.

"Silver poisoning," Carmen Teresa responded, walking to him. She held up the wine sack he had been drinking from.

"You got this from Cesare, correct?"

Raphael nodded, noticing that her arm was bandaged.

"He gave it to me before we left, when we were getting provisions."

"Of course he did." She threw the sack at him. "The water has been laced with a silver nitrate. A very carefully ground powder, it almost disappears in water. It goes right to the heart and grips it."

Raphael shook his head and said, "I can't believe I didn't taste it."

Carmen Teresa was tightening the saddles on the horses.

"You wouldn't. It has a very faint odor, but Cesare knows how to disguise it. I could smell it, but you couldn't. It is hard to detect, and it might not kill a stronger vampire, but you were only resurrected a few days ago. Cesare knew that. He must have found some or made some when we were in the cave."

He noticed her arm was bandaged.

"Thank you," he said apologetically.

"Don't thank me, I need your help. You may be my only companion left. Get ready to ride, we are heading back to the manor house."

"What about the marble house?" Raphael asked, rising to his feet.

"A ruse. Cesar wanted me gone."

They mounted the night mares, though Raphael was a bit unsteady. Carmen Teresa threw a cloak over him. "Get your hood up, we're going to have to ride a little while in daylight," she said.

"What about you?"

Carmen Teresa went to her horse.

"I have a blanket, that's all I need. hate to risk the horses, but I am sure Cesare is making a move. I hope we find someone who is still alive back there."

Miguel was collapsed on his hands and knees just inside the manor house, heaving deeply and coughing up blood. His heart felt as if there were a stake in it. Bernardo and Thomas lay outside in the woods, dead.

When they drained the woman of her blood, they felt filled. The four vampires had left the house, leaving the wife crumpled on the floor. Cesare had begun to walk away from the group, back to the manor house. The other three pursued, thinking they would run him down quickly. Bernardo had dropped in mid-stride, dead. Thomas and Miguel felt pain in their hearts and stomachs, pain that doubled them over. Thomas had got within sight of the manor house when he fell and convulsed for several moments before expiring. Miguel collapsed outside the manor house, but had crawled to get inside before the pressure on his heart was too great, and the blood coughing started.

Cesare walked into the room, several bags slung over his shoulder. Miguel grabbed his ankle. Cesare shook free relatively easily, then crouched down.

"I afraid I have made mistake," Cesare said. "The silver color mean a person has plague. But not full. You see, is strange. Some humans, they carry plague in their blood, but it not show in them. That woman, she give it to her husband, but she, she no show. Those people, they show silver. *White* mean person no have plague. I sorry."

Miguel coughed and said, "Help me."

Cesare said, "There no help for you now, my large friend. Just lie here. It be over soon."

Then Cesare got to his feet and headed towards the door.

"You drank from her," Miguel spat out.

Cesare stopped.

"When I was a guest at Saint Michael-du-Anjou, my good host, Abbott Dom Felice, he feed me many things. Sometimes animals, maybe some dead humans, I not know. He not want me dead, but sometime I taste, I know the plague had been in the food. I ate it anyway. If I died I died. But fun-ny thing happen. I get sick, I was sick, but I no die. And then I get better. The plague no bother me now."

Miguel managed to get up on his elbows.

"I'll kill you."

Then Miguel collapsed fully. As he hit the floor, he vomited blood and viscera.

"I think no," Cesare said, walking out the doorway.. "Oh, don't worry about Federigo, I take care of him. I also take both horses. I no think you need them. Adios."

Carmen Teresa and Raphael made it to the village less than two hours after sunrise. The road was heavily forested, providing lots of shade. Carmen Teresa had learned the trick of covering the head and neck of the night mares with blankets, which allowed them to go in some sunlight.

Bernardo and Thomas lay along a pathway, both contorted, both covered with burst buboes, and both lying in still-wet pools of body fluids. Raphael nearly fell off his horse, but Carmen Teresa steadied him.

"Rancid," was all he could mutter.

On reaching the manor house, they dismounted and found Miguel's body inside, his face half-up. His eyes and mouth were open.

"Just like the others," observed Raphael. "And their jaws."

The lips were curled back to expose well below the gumline.

Raphael took a cloth and reached down, but Carmen Teresa warned, "Don't touch them. They fed on someone with the plague."

She pushed him along, saying, "Take the horses to the stable. I am going to search the house."

Raphael hesitated, but Carmen Teresa said, "Don't worry, Cesare is long gone."

Raphael left and did as he was told. Carmen strode through the house, looking for any signs of where Cesare might have gone.

Raphael called for her in a frightened voice. Was Cesare still here?

She ran outside.

Out in the back, Federigo was tied down to the ground, face up, in a gavel-strewn clearing. Though it was less than two hours after sunrise in this location, he had been exposed to the sunrays nearly all that time. His pale body was burned in several places, but he was alive. Raphael and Carmen Teresa untied Federigo and brought him into the manor house, laying him on the down-feathered bed of the master bedroom. There was some wine left in the pantry that Carmen Teresa sniffed. It seemed all right. She poured some in a cup, held it up to Federigo's lips, and said, "Drink this slowly, old friend."

Federigo breathed heavily and drank.

"He told me he was going to look for someone," Federigo said hoarsely. "Two children."

"Two children?" Raphael repeated.

"The ones," Federigo said. "The ones the woman is looking for." Federigo drank some more.

"The woman?" Raphael again repeated.

"You rest now," Carmen Teresa said, giving Federigo the cup and pushing him back onto the bed. She gestured for Raphael to leave, and they both started to exit. As they did, Federigo said, "I suspect he thought I would not survive."

Carmen Teresa turned and said, "He underestimated you, old friend." Then she walked out, saying under her breath, "As I underestimated him."

Outside the room, Raphael asked, "Who is this woman?"

"The flesher," Carmen Teresa said. "The red-haired one who leads the others. Elizabeth. She wants two children. The coven knows what she wants, but not why. Right now, we need to find the children. When we do, we'll find Cesare."

"How does he know all this?' Raphael asked.

"I think Abbott Dom Felice frequently spoke with him. I think the guards spoke to him. Sort of a torture, letting him know what was happening. Also, if your sight is turned useless, your other senses develop. I am sure Cesare heard many things as a prisoner in the abbey."

"How do we find these children?" Raphael asked.

"I don't know," Carmen Teresa answered. "But we will be alert and keep our ears open. When someone is being hunted like that, word gets around—even in times like these."

[7]
NORTH OF TOULON

MADDALENA

WE RIDE along in our wagons. There must be eight of them, and they all have some covering set up. Most of us travel in these wagons, though a few, including Dioneo and Jai Ling, ride their own mounts while the others lead pack animals. Mansa drives the last wagon, where he has several animals caged, notably the tigers we picked up before. Rain falls, not too heavy, but more than enough to create a rhythm on the canvas. I am in the third one with Bartolome.

I sit near the back of the wagon. Lying across from me is the one they call Lora, sleeping on her side, as always. She is such a strange creature. One half of her face is beautiful—exquisite. As beautiful as any noblewoman of Venice. But the other half is repulsive. Her face is scarred and pockmarked. The same is true of her arms, shoulders, and legs, with one half beautiful, the other pitted and damaged. Even her hair is golden and luscious on one side and gray-streaked and straggly on the other. Her birds are with us, sitting in their covered cages. Further down is Bartolome, along with three other people I have not met, who are also sleeping.

Trippetta hops off her horse and into the wagon. Besides people, there are boxes and barrels crammed with food and drink, weapons and musical instruments, but t Trippetta nimbly dances over them and slides beside me.

"Hello," she says. "Do you want to play a game? It's called Cats and Hounds."

She reaches into a box, pulls out a sack, and spills the contents on the floor. Out comes a wooden board marked with colored squares, several animal figures finely carved out of a black stone, and a smaller pouch, which she shows me to be filled with colorful stones. They appear to be translucent. I have never seen such stones used in play—usually they are found on fancy brooches and other fine jewelry.

"I don't know how to play," I say.

"No matter, I will show you. I like to play while it rains."

Trippetta sets the board between us and places two figures, one of a great dog, possibly a mastiff, and the other a beautiful cat, on one end of the board. She pulls out a ruby-colored stone and, with glee, moves the dog to a square on the board that has a similar color.

"See? Now you try."

I look around the wagon. There are crossbows and longbows, maces and swords, but also food and drink. There are festive items such as flutes and mandolins.

A tear comes from my eye. I wipe it.

"You are sad?" Trippetta asks.

I stare at the game, but I nod.

"Why?" she asks.

I find her annoying, but she means no harm. "My mother plays the mandolin," I say.

She stares at me for a moment and then says, "I am sorry. I forget. You see, so many of us have lost ones. We see it so much."

I stare at the board. "You have your friend Uwe."

"And you have your brother Bartolome," she says. "And Jai Ling. And me. We're your family now."

I feel my throat beginning to choke, and I hold back. I reach for a red wool scarf and throw it around my neck.

"Maddalena," Trippetta continues, "so many people have died in black death. We see it everywhere. And even those who survive —look at Lora." She gestures to the sleeping woman.

"She was one of the beautiful women in Florence. Then the great mortality struck. It only struck half her body, but see. She lost everyone close. Now she is with us."

I can't help but be stunned at the strangeness of Lora. Trippetta touches my wrists—I was tugging the edges of the red scarf hard against my neck and was not even aware. I relax.

Trippetta adds, "Many of your age die. You have friends here. Do not forget."

Her words are mildly comforting, for the moment. I say, "Your group is a strange combination of troubadours and warriors."

Trippetta laughs her high-pitched pitched giddy laugh, like a girl younger than I, though she is much older than me. "We are a strange group," she says, "and life can be very short at best. But I think for today we will survive."

I wipe my eyes with the scarf.

We played the game for some time. Then I find myself drifting off to sleep.

MADDALENA

Jai Ling calls me, and I stir. She is at the back of the wagon on her horse, beckoning me. Lora is gone, as is Trippetta. I crawl over. The others are up and eating. The wagon has stopped, as has the rain. No, not quite—there is a thin mist that still falls from the sky. I sit up, and my neck is warm. I can see slivers of light appearing behind the trees. I slept all night with the red scarf on.

"I want you to ride with me," Jai Ling says. "Climb on the back of my horse."

I do as I am told. Jai Ling's longbow and a loaded crossbow are strapped to opposite sides of her horse. It is cool for the summer, so I still wear the scarf.

"Hold onto the saddle and keep your eyes on the lookout."

I mumble, "For what?

"An empty golden palace with a lifetime supply of food would be nice." She looks back at me and adds, "But if you see anything not so nice, then that too."

We ride slowly beside the wagon. The ground is muddy, and some is kicked up on my legs. It is cool. We are on the outskirts of a small village, which looks like it was pretty at one time. It is situated just outside some heavy woods. There's a watermill at the far side of the village, up on a berm overlooking a river. I can see several small houses with outbuildings situated on tofts and crofts with overgrown wheat and grass. At this point in the year, more of it should have been cut for hay, and the large gristmill should be grinding wheat. But there is no sign of movement.

Wait. A pair of foxes stares at us from the woods, then runs back into them.

Lora rides up to us with her falcons swooping by her. She says Dioneo and Uwe rode ahead; she will scout the right, and Jai Ling agrees to check the left. We all ride to the first wagon. El Erreur, the leader of the group, is standing by it, and Neferri, his wife, is beside him. I see displeasure in his eyes when he realizes I am behind Jai Ling.

"Why is she with you?" he asks.

"Because I don't have Lora's falcons or Dioneo's luck, and I need a set of eyes in the back of my head."

El Erreur is about to protest, but Jai Ling kicks her horse, and we are off to the village. After we are out of El Erreur's hearing, she says, "He's such an old fart."

We ride a short yo the town's houses. They are basic wattle and daub walls with thatch roofs. Looking closer, the village no longer appears so pretty. It is a poor mill village. I ask her what this place is called. Jai Ling says she doesn't know the name. She also asks where the bodies are.

"What are we looking for?" I ask.

"Whatever we can find that we can use. Food, perhaps, but one has to be careful what to eat from a place of the dead. Tools and weapons—those are safe. You'd be surprised what some of these villages have. Of course, we can only carry so much, so it has to be something worth taking."

"What about the owners?" I ask, half-knowing the answer.

"If they're alive, we will barter," she says. "Everyone is looking for something. If they are dead, they won't grieve over what we take."

Our horse carefully makes its way off the main path. The mud is thicker here. A wheelbarrow is turned on its side. Buckets are strewn near a well. Other items lay on the ground, weeds growing over them. This is the harvest season. If there were people here, we would see some of them in the fields working to bring the hay in. In the distance, I see a cow standing in a field, looking at us. We turn a corner and see the body of a man lying face down outside the entrance of a small home. Pieces of clay—a shattered water pot —are around his head. It is as if he were carrying water to his home and collapsed.

"Maybe there will be more bodies inside," Jai Ling says. "I'm going to look. Do not move from here."

She climbs off her horse and enters the house for a while. Then she comes out carrying a bucket holding wooden shafts and some glass goblets.

Getting back on the horse and handing me the bucket, she says. "Don't drop these."

We ride to some houses set further back from the road, and Jai Ling goes into each one. She does not find any people, but she pulls out some more pieces of wood and leaves them outside.

"We can turn these into arrows," she says.

We ride farther and come to what she thinks is the last one, but then we see a larger house, set just inside the woods. Jai Ling studies it with caution.

"Strange place for a manor house. But worth looking into. Feeling adventurous, Maddalena?"

"I suppose."

We ride to the manor house. It is inside the tree line, just far enough in so it cannot be seen from the road. Jai Ling again dismounts and says she will only be a moment, to stay out here and call if anything happens. She takes her weapons with her and heads inside.

I grow tired of waiting.

How long have I been here?

What is that?

Something moved.

I see someone. Wearing a red hooded cloak, it is a girl. She is staring at me from behind the corner of the manor house. She disappears behind the house.

The water mist seems to be turning into heavier rain. Yet it—no, it is not the rain, it is something—a thicker mist. It is flowing around me. I feel lightheaded.

What's that? The sound of a branch breaking. I look out at the mill. There's someone! It is the same red-cloaked girl.

"Jai Ling," I call. There's no answer from the house.

The girl starts to run down the bank to the river, but before she is out of sight, she stops and turns.

She stares into my eyes.

She looks much like me.

I think of when I was running through the woods with my mother and Bartolome, running from the fleshers.

She must be scared.

Then she disappears behind the mill, towards the waterwheel.

"Jai Ling, come here."

Dioneo paused his horse at the edge of the hill, overlooking a sheltered cove downriver from the gristmill. He'd ridden ahead while Lora and Jai Ling checked the actual village. Uwe was around somewhere. Then Dioneo looked closer. The cove was littered with human remains piled atop each other.

Uwe rode up beside him and saw the same thing.

"Fleshers?" Uwe grunted.

"Look," Dioneo said back.

It was a flotsam and jetsam of dead and undead. The water lapped against a rocky shore, moving limbs gently, making it hard to determine if anyone was moving on their own power.

"Plague pit," Uwe grunted.

"No, "Dioneo said. "They realized fleshers can crawl out of a plague pit. They don't know enough to stay buried. But water? They don't deal with water. So somebody said, Let's toss the dead bodies in the river. If any come back, they aren't getting out. Still," he paused, looking behind him, "It doesn't look like this village learned in time. Or if anyone did, they cleared out."

Dioneo slapped Uwe's shoulder and pointed to the right. An elderly woman, her torso trapped between other bodies, was trying to chew on limbs that hung near her. She seemed toothless and was making no progress in the water.

"Any chance for her?" Uwe asked, nodding to the woman.

"Don't see how," Dioneo replied. "She's a flesher. But she won't get out of there. I don't know how long they live, but if they can't eat, they die. Again, that is."

Lora rode up with Leo on her shoulder.

Dioneo asked her, "Anything in the village?"

"A few dead bodies," she said. "An old cemetery with lots of new graves. The usual pattern—start burying the dead, then dispose of them in a pit when you can't keep up, and then people fall in their tracks."

"Anything worth taking?" Uwe asked.

"A few tools in the cemetery—shovels, picks. There's an old wagon we might salvage."

"We'd better get all that stuff and my dear Jai Ling and move on," Dioneo said. "The plague is here. I don't know about you, but it doesn't seem to me that we're outrunning it."

"Jai Ling went on the other side with Maddalena," Lora said. "Anyone see them?"

"No," Dioneo answered. "That kid is dead weight. There could be more fleshers around. We need to find Jai. Come on."

Jai Ling wandered through the manor house in darkness, her short bow in one hand, two arrows in the other. She could see—her eyes adjusted well to the dark. Often, she laughed that there had to be a cat in her family history somewhere. But this was no place to laugh right now; she needed to keep her focus. The house seemed larger on the inside than she expected—wider rooms, more depth. She reached an interior room with no windows, which led to another room farther into the center of the house.

Out of the corner of her eye, a fleeting image of a red cloak on something ran around a corner away from her. Jai Ling must have just walked by it.

"What the hell," she whispered.

Whatever it was had crouched in the shadows and let her pass.

Not much ever hid from Jai Ling. But this had.

"What the hell," she whispered again, turning the corner with two arrows drawn on her bow. She was entering the third interior room. Farther from any windows, it was especially dark.

Jai Ling stood motionless in the room and closed her eyes, aurally scanning the room from one side to the other. The monks at the Shaolin Temple had trained her well.

The floor boards opened up, and she broke through, managing to stop herself from completely going under by grabbing floor beams at the last moment. Her bow had slipped across the floor and was out of reach, and she'd dropped her arrows. She glanced down. Below it was dark, a dug cellar, at least twenty feet deep. But Jai Ling could see bodies swirled and writhing in the darkness underneath, unable to rise, but waiting with hunger for her to fall.

I'm on the other side of the berm. How did I get here? Where is my horse? I hear the creaking of the gristmill turning. I must not get too close.

"Stay," a voice says. It is quiet. I can't be sure if it is in or out of my head. Something makes me turn around. The girl in the red cloak is a few feet away from me.

"It's you," I say. She is very pale, and her eyes are sad.

I take a step toward her, but something stops me.

"Stay," she says aloud. "I am so alone."

"Come with us," I say.

"I cannot. Your companions won't allow it."

As she speaks, I see she is missing a tooth. Though the rain is falling harder, she pulls back her hood and her hair to show that her left ear is gone. Despite such disfigurements, she resembles me in age and looks much like me, but she is dead. She reaches out and touches my scarf.

"It is soft," she says. I can hear her voice in my head.

"I was forced to bring you here for the others," she says. "But I want you to be with us. They are like me, but they are not like me. I have no one to talk to."

As she says this, I become aware of movement. The pair of animals I thought were foxes or dogs—they are wolves. They are sickly thin, as if they have not eaten in a long time, but they have long teeth. They emit a deep growl. In the grass behind me. Crawling up the riverbank. Fleshers. Coming for me.

"You can be like me," the girl says. "But hurry, I cannot stop them unless you are like me. You must—"

A flesher is almost on me. I step back.

"Don't run," she says.

But that is what I do. I turn and stumble—the girl reaches for my scarf, and it falls off, but I get up and start to run up the hill. The mud is loose, and I slip again. I do not look back, but I kick. My mouth fills with mud and grass. No one can see me down here.

Something flies by my head so close that I am cut. I grab my forehead and slide over. There's a flesher right next to me—I didn't know it was so close. It lies on its side, an arrow through its forehead. Another pair of fleshers is crawling my way. One rises to her knees. She looks at me with an open mouth, her jaw hanging from her face, when an arrow splits her skull apart. The other one, a boy crawling at me, jerks as an arrow strikes him, pinning him to the ground. It is not a head shot; it pierces his back, so the body flails in the mud.

Jai Ling slides beside me and pushes me down. I am surprised, but then I see her pull her crossbow up, and she fires it at one of the wolves while it leaps through the air. The wolf drops in front of us, the bolt having struck the wolf's underside by its front leg. It twitches on the ground.

She drops the crossbow and raises her short bow. The other fleshers are crawling from the river, but they are slow. I see the girl who spoke to me, and her face is now a snarl at Jai Ling, and she bends her knees to the ground, arms stretched to the side. Jai Ling takes aim, but I grab her arm and say no. The arrow flies to the left of the girl. She makes an inhuman animal cry and runs into the woods, with the other wolf following her.

Jai Ling looks at me angrily, then gets to her feet. She walks over to the three fleshers she shot and pulls her arrows out of their heads. For the boy impaled on the ground, she shoots the back of his skull with a crossbow bolt, which results in a big splatter of blood. Then she picks off several of the other undead crawling up the bank with her short bow.

She comes back to me and pulls me up. Her boots are pointed and heeled in a way that allows her to get a grip on the mud and get over the hill easily, pulling me along. I see her legs are scratched, as if something pawed or clawed at them.

Dioneo, Uwe, and Lora are riding towards us.

All Jai Ling says to me is, "Let's get out of here."

Several hours later, after taking what they could find of value in the village, including the tools and a new wagon, the caravan continued through the woods. Dioneo rode up beside Jai Ling. It was getting close to dusk, and they would be camping soon.

"You seem melancholy, my dear Jai. Is your new younger sister getting to you?"

Jai Ling gave a quiet laugh. "No. If she wants to get herself killed, that's her pleasure. What bothers me is what she said. There was a flesher back there—a small girl in a red riding cloak. She looked a little like Maddalena. Maddalena said she spoke to her. She spoke to her, Dioneo."

"Vampires do that," Dioneo said.

"But she—she was a flesher. Or a combination. You know where I was raised, we call them jiangshi. Jiangshi doesn't think. They smell human flesh and go eat it. That's it. They have no mind —they're the reborn dead, dammit."

"We're gone from there, don't worry."

"You don't understand. I was lured into a house by something in a red cloak. It messed with my mind. Probably the same girl Maddalena said talked to her. I fell through a floor, and there were fleshers underneath. If I went down and broke a leg, they could have had me."

Dioneo laughed, saying, "I doubt that, you would have thought of something."

"But you still don't understand. Maddalena was lured over to the water mill. She said her mind went blank. That flesher was luring her to where the weaker ones were. A flesher who thinks, Dioneo. That is dangerous."

"If you are so worried, tell our fearless leader," Dioneo quipped.

"El Erreur is a fool," she replied.

"I know, but he knows more than any of us," Dioneo said with resignation. "He's been around forever, and whether we like him or not, he's smart. You are talking to him tonight."

The wagons have been circled for the night. A few of the others are on watch. Mansa's tigers growl, restless at night, but their sounds will keep many potential intruders away. The tigers and the black bear are all set outside the camp, chained to iron stakes. Mansa pounds into the ground. It gets the animals out of their cages. Several fires burn in the enclosure, but the largest is in the center, where El Erreur holds court. Jai Ling speaks to him. Dioneo stands behind her, off to the side, looking uncomfortable. A few others are on logs pulled around the fire, including Lora, Uwe, and others I do not know. I am sitting on a log next to Trippetta. It is odd how El Erreur is dressed in majestic robes appropriate for Egyptian royalty.

"Is he really a king?" I whisper to Trippetta.

"He says yes," Tripptetta answers. "He was great king in old land. He say he was poisoned. He was made into mummy. But he is alive. I not know of Neferri, but she is old too. They know much. Very wise. That why we follow."

"Do you believe him?"

Trippetta answers, "Others do. So I do."

I do not think Jai Ling does.

"I tell you, it was a flesher," Jai Ling said. "It lured me into the manor house, and it tricked Maddalena off my horse."

There was a small group gathered around a fire as they often did at night. The unofficial leaders of the group. The other members of the troupe knew to stay away unless asked to appear. El Erreur and Nefferi. Jai Ling and Dioneo. Mansa and Lora. Uwe. Trippetta was welcome in this circle, but as of late, she had been spending time with Maddalena. Those two were huddled next to each other, just outside the circle.

El Erruer's gaunt, weathered face looked irritated.

"All these creatures have existed since time immemorial," he said in a low monotone. "In my land, when I was king, we had instances of mummified royalty walking our earth. The reanimated dead. Those embalmed, or buried, before their time. These creatures arose from their slumber and walked the desert sands at night, seeking living beings to feast on. Some were known to lure people to them for death or to set fires. But they are limited to where they can inhabit."

Jai Ling muttered, "You sure your memory is correct?"

Dioneo started to laugh and stopped himself.

El Erreur's eyes narrowed, and he smiled, but there was nothing warm in it. "My memory is fine, Jai Ling. Is yours?"

Jai Ling turned and bumped Dioneo's shoulder as she went by.

Dioneo yelled, "Ouch!"

"Poor you," Jai Ling said as she pulled Maddalena in front of El Erreur. "Tell them what happened."

Maddalena related the afternoon's events as best she could recall.

"She was on my horse," Jai Ling said, "and then she was on the other side of the watermill, out of sight of anyone looking from the road."

"Jai, the creature was a vampire," Nefferi interjected.

"She led me into a trap for fleshers. Vampires don't protect fleshers. And when I found Maddalena on the other side of the hill, there were fleshers crawling for her. Vampires don't do that. And why didn't my horse bolt?"

"Some vampires control animals," El Erreur said.

"Dioneo, what did you see?" Nefferi asked. El Erreur gave her a quick disapproving glance, but she ignored him.

Dioneo stepped closer to Jai Ling, and Uwe and Lora shifted to join him.

"We found a pond that had been used as a body pit. They were piled high, a big one. I saw at least one flesher in the bodies. Too old and weak to get out. There were probably more, but I saw all I needed to."

Lora added, "We rode to find Jai Ling and Maddalena, and when we did, they were climbing over the ridge by the river. We saw the fleshers Jai Ling killed, and we killed a few more. Then we went to the manor house and found the room with the hole in the floor. There were fleshers down in a Underground chamber. They didn't move well, not with their feet. We dispatched them with arrows."

"Then we burned it down," Uwe said with a smile.

"I know, leaving a signal for any vampires to follow us with if they choose to," El Erreur said. "And I'm sure the girl was a vampire or a creature somehow tethered to that gristmill."

"But it burned well," Uwe continued.

"Uwe is very good with fire," Trippetta chimed in.

Maddalena snickered, and Nefferi smiled. El Erreur looked them all over.

Finally, he broke the silence and asked, “What happened to the creature in the red cloak?”

“She disappeared into the woods,” Jai Ling said.

El Erreur now had a heightened look of interest as his eyes widened and he asked, “You let her go?”

Jai Ling stared at him before answering. “I shot at her and missed.”

El Erreur looked coldly at Jai Ling. “It is said Jai Ling never misses.”

Maddalena looked; Jai Ling’s eyes were locked with El Erreur.

“I missed,” Jai Ling repeated. “It happens.”

Dioneo finally spoke and said, “Whatever it was, we just need to be careful. Fleshers who can think, who can get into our heads? Maybe they do exist.”

Uwe grunted in agreement.

“And did anyone get into your head, Dioneo?” El Erreur asked.

“Me? Oh no. But don’t forget, there’s not much there to get into. I’m almost a complete idiot, except for the parts of me that are missing.”

This drew small laughter from everyone except El Erreur. He took a deep breath and intoned to the group in his deep voice. “I still believe this was a vampire. Or perhaps Jai Ling was merely distracted. Regardless, we shall note this and be on our guard.”

“There is a village of some size, maybe a thousand or more inhabitants, and approximately two days’ journey north. We will continue there. Lora, send your falcons ahead tomorrow and see if they find any sign of life.”

El Erreur turned but paused and added, “Be cautious, Jai Ling. We would hate to lose you.” Then he and Nefferi went to the dark.

Dioneo grabbed Jai Ling’s shoulder, but she slipped out of his grasp and stormed to her wagon. Some of the others dispersed.

Maddalena sat back down on a log by the fire. Trippetta sat next to her and whispered, "That went well, no?"

I wake up and rise from my blankets. I climb outside my wagon. The sun is shining bright today. Our small group hums with life, with people chopping wood, milking goats, boiling water, cooking eggs. Another day, we are alive. It seems enough to keep these people surviving.

"Fresh eggs!" Bartolome says, coming up to me with a plate filled with two boiled eggs and two spoons. "Here, share with me," he says. I thank him and take one of the eggs and spoons. The egg tastes good. Trippetta comes up with us and offers us salt and some meat, which we both take.

It is a good meal for the morning. An older man and woman are our cooks. They prepare most of the food for everyone. For travelers, we eat well.

"Where is Jai Ling?" I ask.

"Out in the fields hunting and practicing," Trippetta says.

"Practicing?" I ask.

"Yes, I will show you."

She takes me by the hand, and suddenly we are outside the circle of wagons. Our campsite was a small clearing in the thick woods. A few people with the troupe are outside.

"They have pulled up all the traps—at least I think so. I think she goes here."

We walk up through the thin pines that cover the ground. The trail is rocky. At the crest, we hear a voice call, "Well, hello, ladies."

We see Dioneo. He is shirtless and pulling himself up and down by his arms on a tree branch. His body is very still as he raises and then lowers it. He looks silly, but he is unusually muscular. He drops to the ground before us and asks, "So Trippy, what trouble brings you up this way?"

"We want to see Jai Ling," Trippetta says.

Dioneo wipes himself with a cloth and says, "Yes, that would be trouble. She's in a field over there, but be careful. She's practicing her archery skills. I think she's mad that she missed the little red hooded freak." He winks at me.

"Thank you," Trippetta says and leads me further along the path.

Behind us, Dioneo yells, "Jai Ling, your fans are coming. Be careful not to shoot their little arses off!"

We hear his laughter behind us.

We find ourselves walking into a sun-kissed field of short grass. Jai Ling is about thirty feet away, facing us, with a bow drawn in her hand. She is blindfolded.

Trippetta is about to say something when Jai Ling says, "Silence!"

She remains motionless for some time as birds chirp in the background. Jai Ling cocks her head to the side and seems to be listening for something. I can feel her intensity. Then a bird chirps. She whirls around and crouches, firing three arrows, one after another, across the field.

She removes her blindfold. We run to her. She walks away from us, but we are on her heels. I cannot see where the arrows went. Then we approach the other side of the clearing, and I see in the shadows that she has circle targets tacked to trees. Four arrows have struck the targets in the circle, one hit a target outside the circle, and another has an arrow in a tree branch.

"That's amazing!" Trippetta says.

"Four out of six," Jai Ling says. "That means two fleshers would be on us. Not so good, Trippetta. Help me get these out."

We pull arrows from the trees. The arrow I have is hard to remove—the arrowhead is embedded in the trunk. Finally, I get it out. Jai Ling takes the arrow from me and puts it in her quiver. She is amazing. We walk back into the field.

"How?" I ask.

Jai Ling laughs and says, “Magic.”

Trippetta and I look puzzled. Jai Ling laughs.

“No sillies, I’m no sorceress. Just practice.”

“But—you had your eyes covered,” I say.

“You want all my secrets, young ladies? OK, I’ll give you one. It’s being observant. When I posted my targets, I am quiet. I noticed a small flock of thrushes nearby. They chirp on and off, but they make a little whistle when they take off, at least usually. When I go into the field, I take note of where they are and where the targets are. I aim my bow at the birds and then the targets. I focus on their voices and on how much I must turn. Then I cover my eyes, and I wait. I blot every other sound out. When something startles them, they whistle. That sound helps me to track the target. When you girls arrived, you startled them.”

Jai Ling pats my head and says, “Thrushes are little scared cats and they fly easily.”

We’ve reached the middle of the field.

“What’s happening in camp?” Jai Ling asks.

“El Erreur wants us to leave soon,” Trippetta says.

“Of course he does,” Jai Ling says. Then she looks at me and asks, “Did you get something to eat?”

“We had eggs,” Trippetta says. “Bartolome too. They good.”

“Those hens are good for something,” Jai Ling says and pats Trippetta on the shoulder. “It was good of you to take care of Maddalena.”

“She is my friend,” Trippetta chirps.

“And how were your eggs, Maddalena?”

I say, “Good.”

“Did you thank Trippetta?”

I quietly say, “Thank you.”

Trippetta grabs my arm and says, “No need. I told you, we are friends.”

I nod. “Yes.”

“TRIPPETTA!”

Uwe calls. Trippetta smiles at us. Jai Ling tells her to run off. She starts, then turns to wave at me and says, "Maddalena shouldn't be alone out here."

"Don't worry, I've got her," Jai Ling calls back. Trippetta descends the rise we came from.

"They are an odd couple," I say.

"Yes, but they are made for each other. They're the happiest of our lot." Jai Ling turns back to her targets. "One more round, and we'll get going."

I think Trippetta and Uwe are interesting—and strange how they have suddenly become my family.

I miss my mother.

"You practice with the short bow more than the long bow?" I ask Jai Ling.

"For short range."

"You use it well. Why do you like it?"

Jai Ling holds several arrows in her hand. "The long bow can shoot an arrow far. But in close woods like this, you need to shoot quickly. The short bow is best. And this is a good one. Made from ash wood. It's strong and flexible."

"What about a crossbow?" I ask.

Jai Ling laughs. "A complete idiot can use a crossbow. You point it and shoot. It is good for short-range. But then you have to reload it."

"That's what I like about a crossbow." It is Dioneo, riding up to us on his horse. No, it is Jai Ling's horse.

"Did you see Trippetta?" I ask.

"Trippy ran by me a few minutes ago to look for her evil dwarf lover. Can't see what she sees in him with me around. But enough about me. El Erreur wants to get going. You two need to pack up. And," Dioneo says as he dismounts and picks up one of the crossbows hanging off the saddle, "I'll take the crossbow any day."

"A crossbow has a lot of force for short range, but it takes too long to load," Jai Ling says.

Dioneo offers a sly smile. “I’m feeling lucky. Let’s test that again.”

Jai Ling shakes her head and says, “If you wish. Do you see those targets by the trees?”

Dioneo looks over at the tree line and says, “Not really.”

“Let’s get closer then.”

We all walk across the field. Dioneo finally says, “There they are.”

Jai Ling looks at me and says, “Maddalena, you know numbers? Can you count a minute?”

I nod.

“All right. Count aloud to sixty, and we will see who hits the most targets. Agreed, Dioneo?”

Dioneo grabs several bolts from Jai Ling’s saddlebags and says, “Yes. But what if I win? You must promise to marry me, my dear.”

“I promise,” Jai Ling responds, “but if I win, you don’t bother me—not a word—until we reach the next village. Agreed?”

“Get ready to be married, my dear.” Dioneo winks at me and adds, “You already have your flower girl all set.”

Turning to me, Jai Ling says, “Maddalena, start counting.”

“When?” I ask.

Dioneo braces the stock of the crossbow against his shoulder and says, “Now.” With that, he fires a bolt. It strikes the tree, but a bit below the target.

“He cheats too,” Jai Ling says.

I smile just a little as I begin counting.

“One… two… three…”

Jai Ling is methodical, reaching back into her quiver with her right hand, clasping the fletchings, bringing each arrow to the bow, pulling back the bowstring, and releasing effortlessly. Dioneo has the crossbow pointing downward, fumbles with the bolts, and finally loads. He raises the crossbow but shoots before aiming, the bolt flying off to the right.

"You're dangerous with that," Jai Ling says without breaking the flow of her motion.

"Sixty," I say.

We check the results. Jai Ling fired eleven arrows. Nine have hit their circle targets in the center, one is outside the main circle, and one is on the paper but not in any circle. Dioneo fired two shots. We cannot find either bolt.

Dioneo looks at his weapon with disgust and tosses it to the ground.

"I stand corrected," Jai Ling chips in as she retrieves her arrows. "Almost any complete idiot can use a crossbow."

"I'm not a complete idiot," Dioneo shoots back. "Parts of me are still missing."

I notice Jai Ling give him a very slight smile and waves a handful of the arrows at him, saying, "Dioneo, you couldn't hit the side of a castle with a crossbow."

She then whispers to me, "Never trust him, Maddalena."

We begin walking back, all on foot, Jai Ling leading her horse, me by her side, and Dioneo laughing.

"I'm a lover, not a fighter, ladies."

Uwe appears down the path, waving for Dioneo.

"What do you want, you frog?" Dioneo calls.

"A broken wheel," Uwe calls back. "Need your help."

"Is it El Erreur's wagon?" he asks. Jai Ling actually laughs, then catches herself. This makes me giggle. It is the second time I have done so in days.

"No, the Cooks'," Uwe yells.

Shaking his head, Dioneo says, "I guess I need to help that one. Jai, can I use your horse?"

"No, Dioneo. You need the exercise. And don't be so hard on Uwe."

Dioneo replies, "Ahh, well. I bid you, ladies adieu." He runs down the path.

"Jai Ling, why do you shoot so well? Not how, but why?" I ask.

"I had no choice. I grew up in a place where I had to learn quickly," she says.

"Where was that?

"Far from here, very far," she says. "But I'll tell you that story another day."

We reach the descent to the wagons.

"If you want, I can show you how to shoot. It's good to know."

We walk together in silence until we can see the wagons.

"By the gristmill. Why did you hit my arm?"

I am silent. We continue walking. When I reach the wagons, I say, "I don't know. But the girl looked like me. She said she was alone."

Everyone is scrambling to get the wagons in line. Dioneo, Mansa, and Uwe are working on the Cooks' wagon. Jai Ling holds my shoulder, firmly, and pulls my face towards hers. Here face is not angry, but it is very serious.

"I understand. But do not do that again, Maddalena. Not in the middle of a fight. Never again."

The next day, the riding is hard. Heavy rain falls. I stay in the wagon. Trippetta comes by, and we play her game.

Bartolome and I do not speak much. He spends his day playing with small toys given to him by others—usually Uwe. A drum, some carved animals, and a flute. Uwe is always gruff, seeming begrudging, but today he gave Bartolome a carved knight on horseback and a dragon. I suspect Trippetta asks him to. Bartolome plays a game of cats and hounds with Trippetta and I, but he finds it boring and goes back to his own things. He doesn't seem to miss our mother, but at night I hear him cry in his sleep.

Night arrives. Our wagons are circled again, outside a small mountain hamlet. The people from the village have come out to see us. The crowd is small, but it is what we do. Mansa sets the animals outside. Uwe plays flute and Trippetta dances, while many form a small circle and around and clap. Dioneo somersaults in the air and lands in the middle. A chorus of boos follows, led by Mansa.

Dioneo raised a finger in the air.

"I will indeed leave, but first you must indulge me in a song I must sing."

Jai Ling came to Maddalena, who was sitting on a log, and covered her ears with her hands, saying, "You don't want to hear this."

Maddalena pushed her hands away.

"You'll be sorry," Jai Ling chided.

Dioneo began.

"There once was a man from Verona,
Wed to a wife he couldn't control,
and though they owned little, and had no wood to burn,
That dutiful husband did own a solid brass urn,
One day came a buyer,
who saw the man's wife and really desired her,
And the wife thought the buyer could deliver her pleasure,"

The audience laughed and howled knowingly.

Dioneo continued.

The buyer told the husband he desired the urn,
And if it shined bright, he might pay well for it, in turn,
So the husband brushed and scrubbed it so well,
That it shone brighter than any fire in hell,
But the buyer told the husband he'd pay double in price,
If the inside of the urn would shine just as nice,
The wife told the husband,
no greater money could he earn,

so he had better go inside to polish that urn,
And to do so well,
so the man climbed inside that urn,
to clean and to churn,
to make the sale come to pass,
but all the while he was cleaning, the buyer,
was cleaning the wife right up the ass."

This brought groans of laughter and applause, but Dioneo was also pelted with chicken bones and leftover food. Bowing, he said, "A true artist is never appreciated in his own land," and jumped out of the circle.

Jai Ling sighs.

"I told you."

I say, "I've heard worse at the court in Avignon."

I see Jai Ling's eyebrows rise.

I ask, "What do you do when you perform?"

"What do you think?" Jai Ling says.

"Can I help you?" I ask.

"You want to help me, but you do not know what I do?"

"It must be with arrows," I reply. "I need to do something."

"Well, I am always looking for someone to stand while I shoot an apple off their head. Interested?"

I must frown because Jai Ling laughs.

"No? Well, I can use a regular assistant. We'll need to get you a costume, of course. I have a few ideas. Tomorrow morning, we will see what we can find."

Later in the evening, Jai Ling and Uwe tromped through the mud outside the wagon circle, setting traps. Uwe liked to set snares. Jai Ling positioned crossbows and also sprinkled dry leaves around the wagons. The train always pulled off the road so a true pilgrim traveling at night could go by them while staying on the main path, but any person approaching them without welcome would do so at their own peril.

Dioneo rocked back and forth in the hammock he had slung between two wagon wheels. He had strung up a canvas sheet over him and, resting comfortably in his hose and underneath three blankets, he was quite content with himself. There was a slight chill in the air tonight. There was that girl, Rowena. She never said no. He could go to her, but he decided not tonight. Then again—he fell asleep debating the point.

"Yeeaaa!"

Dioneo fell out of his hammock into a pile of mud. The canvas swung back and spilled more water on him.

"Damn it all," he cursed, sitting in his muddied braies and linen shirt.

Jai Ling dashed by him, carrying her short bow, and dropped a heavy walking stick beside him, saying, "Couldn't you have found a better place to sleep?" She hopped over a wheel. Uwe crouched by Dioneo, who slipped on a set of leggings and picked up a walking stick.

"Sounded human," Uwe said.

"That it did," Dioneo muttered. "Let's check your snares."

Maddalena stirred. Trippetta was suddenly beside her.

"We must circle the inside of the camp."

Maddalena followed her out, pulling Bartolome along.

People stirred from their sleep and ran to the perimeter. Most stayed inside the ring of wagons. El Erreur and Nefferi stayed in the middle, holding torches and directing people about.

"We check the edges," Trippetta said. "Only a few go out once the traps are set."

"Who?" Maddalena asked.

"Uwe, Dioneo, Jai Ling, and Lora. Sometimes, Mansa, but he mostly stays with the animals."

The tigers, stirred by the activity, roared from outside the circle.

In the woods, Dioneo and Uwe walked, Uwe holding a torch. The rain was moderate, but Uwe had some concoction coating the top of the torch, so it continued burning. Jai Ling was somewhere out there, but she prowled on her own.

To the side, they heard yelling and the sounds of struggling. Uwe looked at Dioneo.

"I set a snare there."

"Well, in that case, after you, of course."

Making their way over, they found a young man thrashing about, his leg caught in the snare, hanging about eight feet in the air.

"Aiuto, Aiuto!"

Dioneo looked for a moment at the twisting body, then muttered, "Oh hell no."

Uwe asked, "A flesher?"

Dioneo spat back, "No."

"Aiuto!" the boy screamed again.

"Shall we help?" Uwe asked.

"He's beyond help," Dioneo said, grabbing the boy by the shoulders and turning him around.

He was staring into the face of Ricciardo, the boy they had rescued from the arena.

Ricciardo sat by a fire, shivering despite several blankets around him and a cup of tea. Many had returned to sleep, but Trippetta stayed with him.

El Erreur and Nefferi conferenced with Jai Ling, Dioneo, Mansa, and Lora at another fire.

"How did he find us, Dioneo?" El Erreur asked.

Jai Ling answered. "On foot, I'd say."

"He had to have a horse for a while," Nefferi added.

"Maybe," Dioneo commented. "But he doesn't have one now."

Nefferi shook her head. "We don't even get a good horse out of him. But he did follow us, and we're more than twelve days' ride from where we left him. Did you tell him where we are going?"

Dioneo laughed. "My dear Egyptian Highness—with due respect—I have no idea where we are going except north. Maybe the boy's a great tracker."

Jai Ling scowled and said, "Him? He's a pretty boy from court. The most tracking he's ever done might be as part of a well-guarded fox hunt."

El Erreur scanned the perimeter.

"Mansa? The animals?"

"I don't know. The tigers would have a distinctive scent. I've seen dogs who are great trackers. But to come this far on scent? Hard to see that happening."

"But find us he did," Dioneo interjected. "We ran like hell the first day and night, and after we blew the bridge, we've been going slowly. Very slowly. It isn't impossible that we were followed. But why don't we ask him?"

Ricciardo was brought over, where he related his story to the group.

"After you left us, our village was angry. Many of the king's forces were killed in the arena."

Jai Ling interrupted and asked, "Non-soldiers?"

Ricciardo shook his head. "None we heard of. The fire was contained only in certain areas. But our king—you know, he is a barbaric man. His vengeance is—" Ricciardo shook his head.

"Continue, Ricciardo," Jai Ling said.

"The next evening, we were low on water. My grandfather, who you know runs our village, sent me to the stream with two of my friends for water. While there, we heard screaming and the sound of horses. We ran back—there were soldiers from the king destroying our village. Our huts were burned. My cousin, pregnant with a child, was run through the belly. I saw my nephew's throat slit. My grandfather..."

His voice trailed off, and then he continued. "They bound him between two trees and fired arrows at him, in the thighs, the forearms, and the shoulders. He never cried out; he just glared at their leader. Then they fired another arrow into his belly. Let him hang there. A soldier came by me. I grabbed a piece of wood and smashed his head in. Then the others looked my way, but my friends—we all ran. We were separated in the woods."

Ricciardo stared at the campfire. "I don't know what happened next." Ricciardo hung his head. "I'm a disgrace."

The group was silent until Dioneo said, "Doesn't sound to me like there was much you could do. The soldiers were going to do what they did. But I want to know—the leader of the soldiers. Did you recognize him?"

Ricciardo nodded.

"Who was it?"

"The Discourager of Hesitancy."

"How did you get here, Ricciardo?" El Erreur asked.

"Dioneo had told me about the plague and that you were heading northwest to France. I found a horse, and I followed your trail as best I could. I didn't think I would find you, but I had nowhere to go. I asked people—few wanted to help me, but there was talk of a caravan of entertainers going through the region."

Nefferi, standing in the dark, said, "You seemed to have little trouble finding us. And you've been riding since then?"

"I lost one horse, found another, then it threw me. After that, I was just wandering in the general direction." He took another sip of the warm liquid and looked up at the group. "My family was destroyed."

Mrs. Cooke, the aptly named lead cook, gave him a bowl of

broth and stewed meat. Dioneo motioned for Jai Ling to move to a corner. El Erreur watched them drift into the darkness.

"Well, he seemed to have little trouble finding us," Jai Ling said mockingly. "They're real happy with you. Why did you tell him we were heading north?"

"It just slipped out. Never thought I'd see that kid again. Maybe he just got lucky."

"Of course, he got lucky. He stepped into a snare. He could have caught a crossbow bolt through his heart."

Jai Ling peered at the dark woods, then at their encampment.

"With these wagons and all the rain, we're moving sluggishly. Even if Ricciardo did get lucky, someone could be tracking him. If they're after him, they can find us."

Dioneo turned and found Ricciardo right behind him.

"Jesus," Dioneo yelled.

Jai Ling laughed.

"I'll leave you two alone so you can get reacquainted. Nice to see you again, Ricciardo."

She blinked at Dioneo as she waltzed away.

"I am so glad I found you," Ricciardo said. "You are my only friend in the world now."

"My boy," Dioneo said, grabbing Ricciardo's shoulders, "You need to prove your worth to stay here. You're not much of a fighter, and I'm not sure you're the cleverest I've seen. But I think we have a place in our show just for someone with your talents."

The red-hooded girl huddled in a tree trunk, pulling her clothes around her tight. It was twilight. Though she felt restless, she was frightened. Everyone was dead. Perhaps she was, too. But she could still feel some cold. She wasn't dead. But why did she have these feelings to eat? She forced herself to forget her hunger and clutched the scarf the other girl had left.

She was alone and afraid.

"Don't be."

She didn't even know she was talking to herself.

"You aren't. I am."

Voices in her head?

"No, just my voice. You don't need to be alone and afraid. Come down."

She looked down. Her wolves had gone. A woman with flowing red hair and tight-fitting clothes more befitting a nobleman stood at the bottom of the tree, waiving to her.

"You speak to my mind," the girl thought.

The woman responded. "As you can to me. And you can do so much more. Come with me, and I will show you how. You are like me. You see?"

The red-haired woman reached her hand upward, holding a mirror.

The girl looked back and saw the tree branches reflected. Nothing more.

She felt panic.

"Don't be frightened," the woman thought.

The girl climbed down gingerly and said, "My name is…" then her voice trailed off. "I don't know what it is."

"That's all right. My name is Elizabeth. I'll call you—Alatiel. That's a pretty name, don't you think?"

The red-haired woman took the red-hooded girl's hand and thought, "You and I are going to be good friends."

MADDALENA

We go on for several days. Mostly, we must move through the rain. Ricciardo has joined us. El Erreur seems unhappy again that another person is with us, but less unhappy than when

Bartolome and I came. Perhaps he thinks Ricciardo will be more useful.

Everyone must work. During the day, I work with Bartolome and Trippetta, and some other older people, to make arrows for Jai Ling and others. Poor Ricciardo. Dioneo seems to torture him with work continuously, having him fetch him water, shine his boots, and carry heavy weights. But Ricciardo seems most comfortable with Dioneo, so he does as he is told.

Sometimes I play a game with Trippetta. There are a few children much younger than me here, but mostly older people. Sometimes Jai Ling lets me ride on a horse next to her, but mostly I make arrows or stare out the back of the wagon.

Night is a bit better. Jai Ling takes me out and shows me how she sets traps. She instructs me on how to draw a crossbow and lock the bolt. We also found a bright dress that an elderly woman will turn into a costume for me. However, I will *not* let her fire an arrow to knock an apple off my head. Bartolome and I talk a little. He enjoys his toys that Uwe made him.

One day, I am alone in the back of a wagon. We have stopped to get some water. We've caught some in rain barrels, and it has rained much, but today is very hot and sunny. I am cutting wood for arrow shafts. While whittling, I put my knife down. My eyes tear.

Jai Ling finds me in the back. I know she sees me, but I do not look up. She watches me for some time.

Then she climbs in and takes out her own knife, a sharp forbidding dagger, and begins to cut shafts with me. The wagons start up again, and several people run to the back of the wagon to climb in, but they see Jai Ling and go away. Only Trippetta enters. She says she is tired. Jai Ling tells her to go to sleep. Trippetta curls into a ball and pulls a blanket around her.

I wipe my eyes and continue cutting.

Dusk approaches, but while there is still light, we pull aside in another clearing atop a small hill, surrounded by several rocks.

Easy to defend. The rain has stopped. Jai Ling says there is a river nearby where the women will bathe. We are quite excited—it has been a long time since we washed. A group of twenty or so gather and move out. Dioneo asks if he can come, but Jai Ling kicks him in the shin. He howls and jumps on one leg. The girl called Rowena comes up and offers to make him feel better. He laughs, kisses her, and says, "You're my girl." As the two of them walk away, Dioneo waves at us and says, "Have fun, ladies."

This late in summer, the days are still long, and there is still an hour or so of daylight left. Jai Ling leads us to the river—it flows quickly and is rocky, but there is space between it and the forest. I understand why Jai Ling felt this place was good—it has enough room to see parties approaching.

The women hover near the water's edge, waiting for Jai Ling.

"Dive in, everyone," Jai Ling says, "since the water has been warmed. But be back at the wagons before it grows dark. When the sun hits the tree line, everyone is out. We go back together."

I look at the water. Jai Ling gives me a push—a gentle one—and asks what I am waiting for. Trippetta and Lora are there. We all strip and jump in the water. This is the warm time of the year. There is soap passed around. Trippetta has a slender decanter that pours a special pink-colored liquid, which she washes her hair with. She gives me some, saying it smells nice. It does. She also says it is special, that it makes one's hair very strong, and that she should know. I take it and wash. We all laugh.

Later, we are on the banks drying off. I glance and notice scars on the inside of Jai Ling's thighs and arms. These are the round dark circles. Gaviciolis! Buboes. Faint—they are not deep, and one could miss them, but I can see. They are there.

For survivors of the black death.

On the way back, I am next to Jai Ling. We are behind the main group—not out of sight, but far enough that I can speak without others hearing.

"Can I ask you something?"

"I presume a young lady from Avignon knows how to ask a question."

"When we were at the gates of the kingdom, you had to show your body to the guards, and there were no scars on your legs.

"You are observant, my little one. You have lived at the Court of Avignon, correct Maddalena? Have you ever seen women wear fine powder on their body?"

"Of course, for court and high feasts," Maddalena answered. "But my mother and I are poor; we were kept under foot by my Uncle, who saw we were taken care of, but he wanted us out of sight."

Jai Ling seems to listen and think about my response.

"Well, where I come from, we have many powders and ways to color them. Much more so than what is used here. We have powders and gels that look just like the skin. I use it to cover my scars when I need to."

"So..."

"Yes, I did have the plague. Years earlier, it was in my land. That or something like it. I was about your age. I had several things. But those are stories for another day."

More time passes. I miss my mother.

Early one morning, I ride on the back of a horse with Jai Ling. Lora rides another horse. We are scouting where there might be a village. Lora's falcons directed us to this place. How she understands them, I do not know. Our horses quietly go down this narrow path with Lora in front. This pathway seems to be overgrown and not much traveled. That is a bad sign. We come to a clearing, and the first thing we see is a shallow trench filled with bodies. Another bad sign. We give it a wide berth and ride further to find a small cemetery with a combination of old gravestones and recently fashioned stick crosses. The sticks indicate recent deaths, a third bad sign.

Then we find the "village." Two rows of single-story wattle-and-daub houses, with a few other small flint-walled hovels outside the rows. There is no sign of a manor house. There are a couple of latrines outside the rows. The rows are strewn with tools, barrels, wagons, and chickens and goats wandering. We see the back of a person as he staggers into a house. I ask Jai Ling if we should help, but she motions for me to be silent. Lora nods and rides to the other side of the houses. Jai Ling and I ride down one row, very slowly, while Lora rides down the other. A few chickens cluck and scurry before us.

Ahead, at the house farthest from us at the end of the row, a man dressed only in bloodied white braies and covered with sores staggers out of a house. I can see his hands pressed against his face. His body is covered in sores.

Jai Ling stops our horse.

The man collapses to the ground. Three large hogs emerge from the same house the man came from and begin to ravenously devour the man. I am horrified and wince, but I look. The man's body is obscured by the pigs, who dig their snouts deep into him. Blood spurts everywhere. We do not intervene—we know the man is dead.

Suddenly, one of the hogs makes a terrible gurgling, squealing noise, and steps away from the others. It falls on its side and begins to convulse. The other two hogs continue eating until one of them suddenly shudders and collapses, falling on the third one. This third one squeals in anger and finds another spot of the man to eat. As it gorges itself, it too begins to convulse, but it continues. Its front legs collapse, but the pig still keeps gnawing on the body. Then its back legs collapse. The animal is devouring the corpse, even as its own body starts to shake.

Jai Ling whistles, a short two-burst tweet, and turns us around. We meet Lora at the back of the village.

"The plague is active here," Jai Ling says. "We need to stay clear." Lora sees the pigs in the distance and nods.

We journey back down the path we came. Lora raises her right arm out, covered in a leather wrap, and she whistles, a high-pitched one. One of the falcons, the one she calls Francine, alights on her arm. She gives Francine a piece of meat and brushes its beak, speaking quietly. The falcon then takes off.

On the way back, I ask Jai Ling, "Do you think there were any people left alive there?"

"If there are, they are as good as dead."

"The pigs, and that man."

"The black death takes many forms. Sometimes a person can suffer the great mortality for several days and then survive. Others suffer for less than a day and die. Animals eat corpses, but when the black death is most active, it can kill an animal as it is eating. The way the hogs fell, the plague must be very active there. It would be death for us to stay and help anyone."

I am suddenly frightened.

"I am all right?"

"As long as you stay on the horse and don't touch anything, we are all right. But tell me—do you want to stay behind more often and not go on these scouting trips?"

I think for a few moments.

"No. I want to stay with you."

After we return to the troupe, El Erreur decrees that we will continue. We do.

[8]
OUTSIDE PASIZ

NEFFERI'S FINGERS gently tapped Dioneo on the shoulder as she said, "El Erreur says there's a village a day's ride up that road, and you should scout ahead. Pasiz or something. See if you can find some good food for once."

She stood in front of Dioneo, dressed in a gold-laced bustier and a sarong that accentuated her small but curvaceous figure. Dioneo was unloading gear from a wagon.

"Well, if that is what his majesty wants, then I shall obey. But are you coming with me, my dear?"

Nefferi smiled and said, "El Erreur says I should stay back."

"Such a shame. I guess you'll miss all the fun," Dioneo said, leaning toward her.

"Maybe next time," Nefferi said. "Of course, that new boy, Ricciardo, he'll still be here. I just might have some fun after all."

Nefferi gave him a kiss on the cheek and said, "Be careful." Then she turned and sashayed away.

"Hey," Dioneo called to her. Nefferi stopped and looked back.

"I thought Egyptian girls weren't supposed to be so curvy."

Neferri kept walking.

"Quite obviously, Dioneo—you thought wrong."

Dioneo mumbled, "What *does* she see in that old husk?"

From behind him, he heard the reply, "He buys her nice outfits."

Dioneo smiled at the sound of Jai Ling's voice. She was leaning out the back of another covered wagon.

"So, my dear, what are *you* doing tonight?"

Jai Ling threw an unloaded crossbow over her shoulder and said, "I guess I'm riding with you. Ugh, ugh."

Dioneo made his way to Mansa, who was sitting on a wood stump and tossing meat to his caged tigers.

"Your pets must get hungry."

"They eat a lot," Mansa said. "I caught a deer the other night, which made the tigers happy. The black bear is better behaved. But he's hungry too. Don't know how much longer I can keep them all happy."

Dioneo sat next to Mansa and grabbed a handful of meat. He thought of taking a bite when one of the Siberians growled. Dioneo saw the tiger glaring right at him. Dioneo rolled the meat into a ball and gently tossed it into the cage.

"Don't get them angry," Mansa chided.

"Our fearless leader wants me to ride ahead and scout the land," Dioneo said.

"You want me to go along?"

"No. Me, Jai, Uwe, Trippy. I think Jai wants to bring Maddalena."

Mansa shook his head. "Jai is going soft. Maternal even. You might need to marry that woman."

"Me?" Dioneo cried. "Not the marrying type, my friend. Plus, never marry a woman who can break your arse by just looking at you. But uhh—I think you and Lora need to stay alert tonight. I don't know if anything is following us, but—keep your eyes open."

Mansa nodded.

"I will. Just you do the same."

Part I

At the Villa d'Arosa

Gugliemo d'Este was not a bad man. He tried to run his tavern as fairly as possible, charging honest prices for food and drink. The plague had decimated the nearby hamlet of Pasiz, leaving Villa d'Arosa the only place for many miles where one could purchase food or find shelter for the night. While the local populace had been reduced, travelers still frequented the road due to its directness to the Durance River. The Villa d'Arosa was only two miles off that road, and Pasiz another two more miles beyond the Villa. Now no one came to Pasiz, and they hadn't for some time. But for travelers, food and shelter were needed.

The Villa had a few rooms which could be let, but d'Este had grown leery of renting. Too many vagabonds and brigands roamed the woods. He would occasionally let a few people who could pay well and appeared harmless enough. But most he let sleep in the nearby fields behind his barn, where stone fences offered a modicum of protection. With only his family, a stout wife named Ismleda, a young boy named Simon, and a willowy daughter named Elta, left to farm, they were fortunate to keep up enough grain, wine, and some animals to meet travelers' needs. Occasionally, he might have an itinerant worker in search of work or one of the few remaining inhabitants of Pasiz wander in. At one time, you could count on a steady flow of such persons, but now these were rare and unreliable. Fortunately, he had always kept a large stash of chickens and a few lambs. With the need for edible food, Villa d'Arosa had managed to not only survive but to prosper, so much so that it needed to hire men to serve as protectors.

In these times, men came at a cheap price, basically a meal a day and a mug of beer, perhaps some wine which they helped to ferment, and a space in the back of the barn to rest in. These men had to be watched carefully, lest they pursue Mrs. d'Este or their children, especially Elta. So he made allowances when the men took liberties with the local wenches.

Still, Gugliemo felt pity for one particular girl. She looked young enough to be his daughter, though he sensed she was a bit older. She'd been found wandering in the wheat field by his son, Simon. A true wisp of a girl, she possessed long, strawberry-blonde-colored colored stringy hair, pale skin, a slender neck, and a vacant stare. The only item of value on her was a pretty locket around her neck with the name LISABETTA inscribed inside. When found, her clothes were damp and soiled, her feet bare and scarred, as if she had been in the woods for many days. Simon had brought her—led her by the hand, really—to the Villa. The girl was an idiot, capable only of making meaningless utterances of "Eh-eh."

Gugliemo remembered his wife, Ismelda, shrieking that her son had brought the plague to them. They tossed the waif out immediately, but she didn't leave. Rather, she ambled listlessly in circles through the fields around the Villa. When she was found asleep in their barn the next day, Gugliemo noted that she had no boils or boil scars on her, which would be the surest sign of the plague. Reluctantly, he took her back to the tavern and offered her food. The d'Este's were Catholics, after all.

The girl would not touch anything but sat on a stool, rocking slightly back and forth while she clutched her side. Taking pity on her, Ismelda swore and placed some bread on a plate. The child reached for the bread and ate it.

"How do we feed another mouth?" Ismelda asked, more scoffing than questioning.

Gugliemo thought the same thing until Julio walked in, one of his underlings in tow.

Julio had been a brigand, that much was certain, though he never admitted his past. In all likelihood, he had led a small band that was reduced by the plague, and a gang of three could not survive long in the hills today. Gugliemo had made an uneasy alliance with Julio and his two followers, Angelo, a burly dark-skinned Tuscan, and Antone, a young Sicilian with a broken nose and a penchant for fighting, to provide protection. So long as weary travelers came into the area, Julio and his men found little trouble sating their appetites, both carnal and monetary, taking from the pilgrims as they approached or left the villa. Or so Gugliemo supposed.

What he did not see, he did not know.

Gugliemo did not doubt that Julio and his men would kill him if they either knew how to farm and perhaps if they had the key to the box where he kept his earnings, but they needed food, not money. What they had was a tacit agreement. Gugliemo provided food and shelter, and Julio provided protection. That arrangement had lasted for two months when the strawberry-haired child had come into their lives. Gugliemo immediately saw that the girl caught Julio's eye. And her demeanor—submissive wasn't the word. All at once, Gugliemo saw how this girl could help them.

Ostensibly, Lisabetta was kept to clean the tavern. She could eat and sleep as she chose, for she seldom did the former, and as to the latter, she was always in a somewhat somnambulistic state. Mostly, she'd wander off, only to be found somewhere on the property in the morning. As it was, if Julio or the others satisfied their carnal desires, what place was there for Gugliemo to say? Whether or not she had the mental capacity to know what she was doing was not for Gugliemo to decide. Besides, as much as it hurts as a Catholic to say this, better for Julio to focus on Lisabetta than Elta.

So tonight, Gugliemo pushed two mugs of ale, some wine, and plates of salted pork, scallions, and lamb to the tall smiling stranger. Lisabettawiped the main table. She was leaning across it, pulling a wet cloth, when Julio came up behind her and jammed his pelvis against her derriere. Her hips banged forward into the table. But otherwise, she seemed to take no notice.

The tavern was filled with many pilgrims off to Avignon, as well as some scattered travelers. Money and other barter were here to be made. It was noisy and busy. Mrs. D'Este was working the tables along with Simon, while Elta mostly helped with meals at the oven in the back room.

"Two dineens," the stranger said. "That's a bit harsh, isn't it, friend?"

Gugliemo shrugged. "It is a harsh world, no?"

"Still, a bit steep," said the stranger. "How about some Christian charity?"

Gugliemo had only half-noticed the stranger, but his offer to barter drew his attention, and the innkeeper quickly sized the man up. He stood taller than Gugliemo, a good six feet plus, and spoke fluent Italian. Though they were in France, many Italians had settled here, and Gugliemo maintained that atmosphere.

The stranger was broad-shouldered with sharp, distinct features, especially a jutting jaw, and looked like trouble. Gugliemo uttered a deep grunt from his throat, and the stranger was surrounded by Julio and two of his lackeys. Julio, the tallest of the three, still stood slightly lower than the stranger, but Julio's bulk was greater. The stranger looked to his right and left, smiled at each of the men, and turned back to Gugliemo.

"Of course, for a good piece of meat and some tasteful beer, two dineens is a bargain today. Thank you, friend." He tossed the coins onto the table, then, taking his food, said "Gentlemen," and walked away.

Julio watched the fellow retreat to a table at the far corner of the room. The stranger sat with a small party. They had blown out the candles in that area, so they sat in the shadows, but Julio guessed at least one was female, maybe more. None of them seemed as large as the stranger, and he obviously was not looking for a fight.

"He shows us dishonor. Perhaps we should show the stranger how to treat the d'Este family," Julio said. Turning to his lieutenant, Angelo, he said, “Get the others.” The second man walked in another direction. Since arriving, Julio’s gang had increased by two more.

A high-pitched clatter. The sound of a clay plate breaking on the floor.

“Lisabetta Lisabetta!” yelled Gugliemo, “Another plate! Be careful. You are moving me to poverty, you bitch.”

Julio looked at the girl and laughed.

“She needs to be punished again, does she not?” he said and nudged his remaining friend.

Julio glanced back at the stranger’s party. They remained hovering in the corner. Julio laughed. Protecting the d’Este family’s honor could wait. He and his lackey walked over to Lisabetta.

There were two platters on the table. One was filled with half a roasted pork. The other had cooked chicken seasoned with baked scallions, along with a loaf of bread drowned in olive oil. Some pomegranates sat in another copper bowl.

“Eat up, folks,” Dioneo said. “It cost enough.”

They had ridden ahead of the caravan to check out what lay ahead. Dioneo, Jai Ling, Uwe, Tripptetta,and Maddalena. They had followed signs off the main road and proceeded past this tavern to the town known as Pasiz, which had proved to be a near ghost town, decimated by the plague, with a few inhabitants. A poor, emaciated child they’d seen in a field had said there was a smaller village further down the road, another three miles into the valley. They had gone there, only to find it was a true city of the dead, with no sign of life at all. Then they’d made their way back, bypassing Paziz, and found that this villa was the only source of activity in the area. Dioneo had expressed interest in drinking, as usual, and the rest were hungry, so it was worth a stop.

Uwe reached across the table and dragged his plate over. Then he scooped a handful of food into his mouth.

"Lamb," the dwarf said. "I not have in many time."

Next to him, Trippetta sat on her folded cloak, though she still barely reached the table. She corrected, "Inaa long time, Uwe, in a long time."

"Very good, Trippetta," Jai Ling said. "Your tutoring is working."

Uwe tore off a leg of chicken and offered it to Trippetta. With her delicate hands, she took it and began to eat, but then stopped and said, "What about Maddalena?"

Uwe kept eating.

"She feed self," he mumbled.

"Give her some," ordered Dioneo.

"Why me?" the dwarf shot back.

"Uwe, give Maddalena something to eat," added Trippetta.

Uwe grumbled, then begrudgingly threw some meat on the table in front of Maddalena. She did not want to touch it. She thought today was a fast day. But she was hungry. The dwarf's table conduct repulsed her (though he did act kindly to her at other times), the food smelled edible, and her stomach hurt for nourishment.

"Eat Maddalena," insisted Trippetta. "It is important."

"Listen to Trippy," added Jai Ling. "This food is good, and it won't last."

Maddalena reached out halfheartedly and pulled a piece of meat off the chicken bone. It tasted good. She then reached out for the rest and began to gobble it.

"Dioneo, give her some of the fowl," Jai Ling added.

"Why not?" said Dioneo. "I want everyone to eat their fill. And I, Dioneo, shall serve as your server, foregoing any food for the good of the group."

"Shut up and eat," said Jai Ling.

For several minutes, the only sounds at the table were of food being chewed and drink being spilled, the only voice being Trippetta occasionally scolding Uwe about his eating habits. Around the tavern, there was a loud din as it appeared two more groups of pilgrims had arrived to seek food. Gugliemo yelled repeatedly for his wife and children to bring more.

Jai Ling's eyes had been trained across the room, watching a group of men fondling a servant girl. She was passed from one to another as they groped her, reaching up through her chemise, under her skirt, grabbing her wrist and shoving her hand into their britches. No one else in the tavern took notice.

Finally, between bites of mutton and chicken, Dioneo leaned over and said, "Don't get concerned. You've seen that in a hundred places like this."

"It's the girl's face," said Jai Ling. "She doesn't show fear, or anger, or happiness. She has no reaction to them."

One of the men, Julio, the one who'd been closest to Dioneo at the bar, took the girl behind a table and sat her in his lap while hiking up her tunic.

"She can't even resist."

Dioneo waved her off. "Lover, please, let's not get involved."

Jai Ling gave a faint smile and said, "Sorry, *lover*," as she rose to her feet.

The girl was too skinny, Julio thought as he rode her. He wanted a fuller woman. As if any could be found! He was growing tired of her. Of the old man. Of this villa. Of everything. Yes, like Lisabetta, this was convenient, but it was time to do something different. Gugliemo's wife was too much of a hag to be of interest, but there was the daughter, Elta. It was time for Julio to take what he wanted. What did he need Gugliemo for anyway? The wife and the children did most of the cooking. As for farming, the family knew what to do. He had some men here. Plus, travelers often came.

This would provide a perfect locale. No, there wasn't any further need for Gugliemo.

Gugliemo d'Este was serving mead and half-listening to an elderly knight, one eye missing, who was talking mindlessly about fighting for Edward III. Gugliemo noticed a hooded figure walking through the crowd towards Lisabetta and Julio's men. The room was filled with talking and boasting, eating and drinking, and he hadn't seen a person start, but he could tell it came from the table where the strangers sat in darkness. He didn't want any fighting in here, not now. The night was going too prosperously.

Gugliemo intercepted the figure halfway across the room and grabbed a shoulder.

"Hey, you, what are you doing!"

The figure paused.

Gugliemo was about to continue when he felt a sharp pain in his lower right stomach and sputtered, "Oomph A feminine hand was pressing a dagger blade into his abdomen. He reached for the arm, but the figure pressed the point.

"The body is a funny thing. It has many interesting spots on it," the figure said. A female voice. Gugliemo was sweating profusely, much more so than a few minutes ago, carrying food and collecting money. His knees wobbled.

"This one particular spot, which I'm sure has your attention right now, is particularly interesting. Did you know that a one-inch thrust upward, not just inward but upward, and only two inches, mind, a slight turn of the blade to the right, in that spot, will be a fatal blow? But what really makes it interesting is that to an outsider, it's just a flesh wound. And the other funny thing is that it doesn't hurt as much as you'd expect. It's more of a sting. You might sit down and clasp your belly, and someone will come over and start to wash it. But in about six minutes, you pass out, and in another six, you're dead. End of your story."

The figure shot her head to the right, and Gugliemo was staring directly into a woman's slanted green eyes. "Now, *if* there happens to be a good surgeon or a smart barber nearby, you *might* have a chance. *If* he knows to cut at just the right place, one hand length above the cut. It causes much bloodletting, so it scares people.e, but it actually stops more blood from spilling out of the wound. If the doctor works quickly to stitch you, and you have a strong constitution, you have a small chance of surviving."

"But that's what you've got there now, a skin prick. Sit, and you'll just be sore tomorrow. Or I can thrust my knife, and we'll see if you have a good doctor around. What say you, Innkeeper?"

Gigliemo stumbled back and grabbed his side. In the bustle of the tavern, everyone kept to themselves. Julio's group was too focused on Lisabetta to notice. Gugliemo made his way to the pantry behind the main room and sat down. Imelda came over and asked what was wrong. He ordered her to fetch wine and to stay in with him.

Dioneo bit off another piece of bread with his chicken, and speaking to the table generally said, "Well, there she goes. Why couldn't she just sit here??"

Uwe grunted, lamb crumbs falling out of his mouth, and Trippetta ate some grapes.

Maddalena shook her head and asked, "Aren't you going to help her?"

Julio had just finished inside of Lisabetta and lay back in his chair. This wasn't satisfying. The wench just—sat there. He pushed her off his lap, saying, "It's like screwing a corpse." Lisabetta slid to the ground, then grasped the table and pulled herself up.

Angelo, his lieutenant, patted his shoulder and pointed out. Julio had not noticed the hooded figure walk up to his table, but the others had.

"None of you will mind if this girl comes with me, will you?" said a voice in front of him. A woman's voice. Her hood fell such that they could not make out her face.

Julio began to hitch up his pants, slowly, displaying his member to the woman.

"Maybe you are interested in pleasing me and my friends?" he hissed. "Our girl Lisabetta doesn't seem to like us anymore."

"It seems to me that the five of you just aren't enough men to satisfy her." The hood was thrown back to reveal a black-haired oriental woman.

Julio stroked his chin. Two men sat or stood on either side of him, awaiting their orders (though one was an older white-haired man who did not seem to fit in with the group). Would they bear this insult? While the din in the tavern continued, and people pretended not to take notice of anyone else, a few people moved away from the area and furtively glanced up in the direction of the corner table, hoping not to be noticed.

The oriental reached out to Lisabetta and held her wrist. Lisabetta stopped and, while she did not look at Jai Ling, her face indicated some sense of—awareness.

Julio stroked his stubbled chin and laughed. "What do you want?"

"I'll just take this girl with me, and we'll call it even?" Jai Ling responded.

"Who do you think you—" started another man, a wiry, thin fellow named Domingo, but Julio cut him off with a wave. "What is even, pretty girl? You give us nothing in return for the girl. Unless you want to be with her yourself, and let us view, eh?"

Now Jai Ling smiled. "You get to keep your life," she said, releasing the girl's hand and dropping her own arms to her side.

Everyone was silent, and the silence spread around the tavern. First, an insult? Now a challenge? From a woman? Julio's men were genuinely stunned. The only thing holding them back was astonishment at this woman's gall.

Julio himself couldn't believe this woman was challenging them. There had to be an angle, something else going on. But now he saw the woman had taken Lisabetta's arm again and was backing away from them!

"Get her," he said.

Two men, Domingo and Antone, who had been on opposite ends of the group, moved forward on the women. Jai Ling pushed Lisabetta behind her and raised her arms. In her right arm, the dagger, which she had against Antone's throat; in the left, a small crossbow, smaller than usually seen, thrust against the center of Domingo's belly. Both men froze in shock, with a slight spackle of blood coming from Antone's neck.

Jai Ling scanned the group with approval. All were startled, but Julio was most angered.

Jai Ling stepped back. Julio started to rise. Then he began to grin widely, malevolently, and motioned for his men to withdraw.

"Now that I'm sure you gentlemen have reconsidered your decision—most wise, by the way—I will take my leave of you. Good night."

With one hand holding the knife, Jai Ling grabbed Lisabetta's arm and retreated back to Dioneo's table, all the time facing Julio's men. Dioneo and the others were on their feet and went beside her.

"Thanks for your help," said Jai Ling.

"You had things in hand," replied Dioneo. "Thanks for getting us noticed."

"Go now!" Uwe blurted and grabbed Trippetta. In turn, Trippetta reached for Maddalena's shoulder and said, "We go, Maddalena."

The group moved collectively for the door, keeping a wary eye on Julio's table, whose occupants glared back. Julio smiled at them as they left.

Outside, they were in the villa's small courtyard. Finding their horses quickly in the dark, tethered to a nearby post, they began to mount.

"I'm glad we have another mouth to feed," said Dioneo. "I wanted to spend more time fishing; this gives me a reason to do it."

Ignoring him, Jai Ling helped Maddalena to her animal, a gentle pack horse, and then helped Lisabetta up.

"Our new friend is riding with you, Maddalena," Jai Ling said. "Your job is to watch her on the way back."

Jai Ling saw the brooch around the girl's neck and reached for it. She began to flap her arms and cry, "Eh eh eh!"

Jai Ling said, "I won't take it, I just want to look at it."

The girl allowed her to open the locket.

Jai Ling stared at it and said, "Maddalena, read this."

Madalena leaned over and read, "Lisabetta."

"Lisabetta," Jai Ling said. "So that is your real name. Lisabetta, meet Maddalena."

Jai Ling adjusted the saddle blankets on the horse. The girl could at least respond to basic directions. Then Jai Ling added, "Trippetta, you keep an eye on Maddalena while she watches Lisabetta. Make sure she doesn't get in trouble."

The tiny ballerina had already mounted her horse and was beside them. "I do it well," she said.

"I know you will," replied Jai Ling.

Everyone else got up on their horses and readied to ride.

For a secondary road, this was a well-worn path, testifying to the villa's success. Maddalena's pack horse was fairly slow, as was Trippetta's, and the night sky was lit up with a full moon, making the woods somewhat visible (although floating clouds occasionally obscured the moonlight). They rode at a steady pace, Jai Ling and Dioneo up front, the other ladies in the middle, and Uwe in the rear. The party rode south to head back to where the rest of the caravan rested.

Jai Ling looked toward the woods.

"We're being followed," she said. "Not directly. There must be a parallel trail through the woods. They're trying to cut us off ahead."

"We can handle them," Dioneo said. "But having Maddalena and your latest stray pick-up isn't going to help us any."

Jai Ling pulled up the small crossbow she'd had hanging under her tunic and rested it on her thigh. Dioneo laughed.

"Is that thing loaded?" he asked. Before she could answer, he added, "I'm going to ride ahead. You drop back with the girls, maybe six horse lengths. Uwe!"

"Yaa," he called back.

"Why can't that dwarf learn to talk?" Dioneo mumbled. Then he called in a louder voice, "Drop back behind the ladies and watch our rear. And don't fall off your arse, you drunk frog."

"Aaaargh, aaarrgh," Uwe griped, then slowed his horse.

"Only thing worse than an ugly dwarf is an ugly dwarf who's been drinking," Dioneo added, then he moved his horse into the lead.

Jai Ling fell back beside Maddalena.

MADDALENA

It is very dark and hard to see far in this forest. I can't even see ahead with this girl sitting in front of me; she is taller than I, but slim, so I can stretch and peek around her shoulder. The others seem concerned. Jai Ling comes riding beside me, her crossbow out. Trippetta is on the other side, and Uwe is behind. Dioneo is somewhere ahead of us.

Jai Ling and Trippetta look to the right. This new girl just sits behind me.

"Those men from the tavern are coming after her," Jai Ling says.

Ahead, I hear Dioneo's horse neigh loudly. There's the sound of breaking trees and branches. It explodes around us. Jai Ling grabs my horse's reins and pulls us aside.

"Hold, Lisabetta!" she orders.

I wrap my arms around her and use one hand to grab a rein. Lisabetta holds my wrist.

We fall back. There's a wooshing sound. Something immense passes just over my head. More branches are breaking. I hear a cry from Dioneo's direction.

I lose sight of Trippetta. Then a breaking sound in front of us again! NO, behind us! I see Uwe on his horse. Something swings out of the darkness and strikes Uwe's horse on the side. Uwe and his horse are violently tossed to the side. It happens so quickly.

Jai Ling stops us again, holding my horse. She hesitates, looking back and forth.

"Let's talk about a wager now," says a voice from the woods.

Figures on horseback encircle us.

As Dioneo lay hung upside down, his knees curled over some branches, he gazed at the ground below and asked, "Why does this keep happening to me?"

He had sensed trouble on the road and tried to stop his mount, but before he could, the animal tripped on ropes that had been pulled taut across the pathway.

The horse tripped and fell. Dioneo managed to slide off his animal before it crashed to the ground, but in the next moment, something came flying down at him from above. A large tree had been cut and hung by ropes to form a pendulum that swept down, covering the width of the road. Dioneo jumped over his horse, which lay neighing on the ground, its front legs broken. Dioneo yelled at the others to get back. Jai Ling had heard him and retreated. The log was almost upon him, cutting close to the ground. Reacting, as opposed to acting, he leapt up and somersaulted over the flying tree that swept underneath him. Dioneo then hit the dirt, rolled like a ball, and sprang up. The latter was a move ingrained in him from his performances. Had he been thinking instead of reacting, he might have stayed low to the ground. The instant he was on his feet, a second log swung down to the road perpendicular to the other one.

Clever, he thought, and leaped again. But he saw it late, his timing was a moment slow, and he was caught on a protruding branch and flown upward.

The log rose high into the treeline and then came to an abrupt halt as it struck other branches. The jolt threw Dioneo off the log, and he flew backward, finally crashing into a fir and sliding down. He was dazed, but fortuitously came to lock his knees onto some pine branches that broke his fall.

"I'm so tired of this shit," he said.

"I can help your misery." A snake-like voice hissed to his side, so foreign, so unexpected, and so inhuman. shuddered.

Uwe didn't have a clear line of sight up ahead, but he sensed their pursuers were close by. There was some loud shambling and

Dioneo yelling, so he kicked his horse and moved forward to Jai Ling and the other girls. Then there was a thrashing to his right. He turned just before a suspended log swung across the width of the road and struck his mount dead on. From the great snapping noise, Uwe knew his horse's neck was immediately broken. The horse was upended, and Uwe fell to the ground. He tumbled into the woods and crashed through a thatch-covered pit. The dwarf fell face down.

So now here he was, prostrate in a hole, his sides aching. Probably a bear pit, to trap the bastards, he thought. It was totally dark. Things couldn't get much worse.

Then there was a growling noise behind him.

Julio and three of his men had surrounded Jai Ling, Maddalena, and Lisabetta. Up the road, Dioneo's horse was on the ground, baying in pain with its front legs broken.

"Now let's see where we left off," said Julio, stepping off his horse. He had a knife drawn. Jai Ling held the crossbow on him.

"Seeing as it is just you with these other two fine young ladies, all alone in the woods, I thought you would be happier to see us." Julio stepped closer.

"That's close enough," Jai Ling said.

"You're right," said Julio. "It is. You should come to me. On your hands and knees. And suck me and screw me. And when you're done, you'll service my friends. And if you bite any of us, we'll kill you all. Then I'll take back Lisabetta and your young friend there, and you can go. How's that for a trade?"

"I think in two minutes your body will be separated from your balls," replied Jai Ling.

"I don't think so, you bitch" Julio sneered. He cocked his head to the right.

"Let go of her," said Maddalena.

Jai Ling looked over and saw Antone had grabbed Lisabetta off her horse and had a knife to her throat. Maddalena was on her horse, pawing at Domingo's arms.

"Just make it easy on yourself bitch, and be glad we not kill you all," Antone gurgled out.

"Not her, grab the other one!" Julio ordered. Domingo dropped Lisabetta to the ground and grasped Maddalena, pulling her close and putting a knife to her throat. Jai Ling could see the fear well up in Maddalena's eyes.

Julio watched with a smile. "Now you understand, you should not have insulted us in our own house. These," he said, gesturing with both hands, "are our woods."

He now pulled out a knife, a double-edged dagger with a Komodo dragon emblazoned on its hilt. Jai Ling observed a green sapphire serving at its eye.

"Ah, you like my dagger? A gift from a pilgrim to Avignon. She gave it to me after I let her pleasure me with her mouth." Julio laughed. "Enough, bitch, crawl over here and beg for me, or we slit your friend's throat."

Jai Ling had her crossbow aimed at Julio's throat. "Cocky little bastard," she thought. The other two were riding up behind her. Was there one missing? She thought so, but wasn't sure. Reluctantly, she lowered her weapon.

"You don't give me much choice, do you?" she asked.

"No," Julio said slyly.

Dioneo looked back. A man was standing in the trees a few feet from him. He was shorter than Dioneo, appeared older, slimmer too, with a full white mane of hair, and narrow eyes. He had been one of the men with Julio in the tavern. In the moonlight, his entire body seemed to give off a slight glow, all white ghostly apparition save for a trace of pink around the lips.

No—the man was not standing. He was hovering in the air.

Dioneo had heard of vampires who could levitate. It was very rare, they said, and only skilled ones could do so.

After a moment, Dioneo recovered. "Say, don't suppose you'd like to give me a hand there, friend?"

Uwe lay still. He wanted to look up and check the height of the pit walls, but he wasn't alone down here. Bears didn't like to eat dead things they came across, just things they killed themselves, he recalled being told by Mansa. And Mansa should know. The dwarf certainly hoped so as he felt something sniffing around his boots.

"Uwe." He heard Trippetta calling in the forest above. Her night vision was good, and her small stature and dancing ability empowered her to navigate crowded forests quicker than most. She traveled in the direction Uwe had been tossed and was remarkably close to where he'd fallen. But Trippetta was no Jai Ling or Mansa and Laura, all of whom were adept at tracking in the woods. She was a slight and beautiful ballerina, the only thing in the world that mattered to Uwe.

"Uwe," came Trippettta's voice again, now almost on top of the pit. She did see it. She would see it. Wouldn't she? Should he call out?

There was a scratching beside him.

The bear!

Maddalena was also growing tired of being a victim.

Domingo wore a heavy cotton coat, but his hands were covered with slight wool gloves. He held his thumb against the back of his knife, pointed at Maddalena's throat, not across it, and he pressed his hand against her mouth.

Maddalena bit hard onto Domingo's puffy tendon, just below the thumb.

"Shit," cried the brigand, pulling his hand away.

Maddalena slid to the ground.

Domingo was trying to massage his thumb with his free hand, but Jai Ling swung her crossbow and fired. The short wooden bolt blasted into Domingo's throat, the fletchings becoming lodged against his face so that the bolt did not completely pass through his body.

Domingo sat quivering on his horse, his body not yet aware he was dead. Antone stood staring at Domingo, mortified. Angelo, being quicker to realize the situation, jumped on Jai Ling from behind and thrust the small of his knee into her back. Jai Ling had been reaching for her horse's saddle, and both she and Angelo fell to the ground. Her right shoulder was driven into the ground by Angelo. She threw her left elbow back and struck Angelo in the nose. The bandit yelled, and his head jerked back, which changed his body position. With his weight shifted, Jai Ling was able to partially crawl out from under him. Julio, however, had run forward and jumped atop her, grabbing her neck with his large right hand and pushing her head into loose gravel. He was a stronger man than the others and had leverage on Jai Ling.

Julio spat, "Hold her legs!"

Jai Ling kicked Angelo sharply in the face, in the bridge of the nose, breaking it. Angelo yelled, grimaced in pain, and fumbled with her legs. Jai Ling almost broke free, getting one leg out, but then Antone (whom she'd momentarily lost track of) came in and leaped upon the leg. All three men were cursing at her in different Italian dialects. Jai Ling struggled, but the three slammed her back into the ground.

Julio put his dragon-faced dagger against Jai Ling's throat, and she momentarily stopped and smiled.

"Why not let me have your friend first?" Jai Ling spat out from the ground. "Oh, I'm sorry. He's just dead."

"You whore, we're all going to fuck you up the ass!" Julio kept his right hand on her head. They ripped off her cloak. Then he and Angelo shifted positions so that Julio knelt behind her, pressing his dagger into her back. He then untied the drawstring on his britches, dropping them to his knees, and began to tear Jai Ling's tunic.

The figure observing Dioneo hovered above, watching the acrobat caught in the trees.

"Do your companions know they have a vampire for a friend?" Dioneo asked. The creature's expression did not change. The moon was shining brighter now, the clouds having parted, and the forest was eerily bright for the evening. But it suddenly dawned on Dioneo that the entire creature's body really did glow. "Not a vampire," he thought, and as if reading his mind, the creature shook his head.

Not meaning to speak, Dioneo uttered the words, *Revenant*."

The creature nodded and began to descend.

"Well, I feel a whole lot better now. For a moment there, I thought I was in trouble," Dioneo spoke breezily. "It's a good thing for me that your kind only haunt those who hurt them in life, and I never troubled you, did I, friend? So I guess you will lend me a hand?"

The phantom was almost on Dioneo. Its countenance changed from a slight smile to one of aggression and hunger, and it extended its arms for him.

"Well, I'm probably going to die anyway," Dioneo thought. Then he said, "Sorry, friend, love to chat, but I gotta go." With that, he flipped his legs and fell off the tree.

Falling headfirst with his arms extended, his shoulder scraped against something, while smaller branches cut his face. He was falling, but breaking branches slowed his fall. Then the moonlight revealed a fairly straight tree limb. He reached out and grabbed onto it, swinging his body down so he balanced upon another tree limb. Looking around, he couldn't see the undead. Where had he gone?

Uwe's lungs ached, but he did not want to even exhale. The bear was close. Above, the sound of sticks breaking.

"Uwe?"

Trippetta's voice.

Uwe yelled, "Stop!"

The bear growled.

A branch was thrust into the trap.

"Climb," called Trippetta.

Uwe leaped onto the branch and scurried up.

Upon getting out of the hole, he hugged Tripptetta and said, "You better tracker than I thought."

Julio had dropped his pants past his knees and was kneeling dog-like behind Jai Ling, his hands wrapped around her waist and pulling her to him. Jai Ling lay quietly on the ground, Antone and Angelo kneeling on both her shoulders and arms. Angelo had his forearm against her neck, pressing her face down.

"This bitch thinks she's so smart, well I'm going to pull your ass cheeks apart and screw you so hard. Then Angelo, you're next, then—"

I'm sick of being a victim.

"You know," Julio said, breathing heavily, "I'd love to—"

"Aaahrgh!"

There had been a thudding sound just before Angelo yelped and slumped to the side, reaching across for his shoulder. Julio glanced over and saw the younger girl who had been riding with the others standing behind Angelo, holding a round rock with both hands. He had forgotten about her.

The moonlight disappeared behind some clouds, reducing visibility.

Jai Ling pried out of Julio's grasp.

"Get the bitch," he yelled, reaching over to shove Antone back at the woman. But he felt Antone clasp his elbow. Julio looked over. Antone was just a foot from his face, but his mouth was open, and there was a gurgling sound emanating from his mouth. Antone was bleeding from the throat. Julio watched him collapse on the ground, his body twitching in death throes.

This had hardly registered on Julio when he felt a hand grasp at his manhood. Then followed a searing pain in the groin. Julio screamed and fell forward, clasping his testicles, now halfway separated from his body. His face was on the ground, and dirt filled his mouth.

The feeling of hands grasping below again.

"Noooo—" he moaned, and he tried to kick with his legs, but he couldn't see clearly; he was disoriented, he only knew what was happening, and he felt like his groin was on fire.

Angelo was on all fours, his shoulder aching. He had been struck hard between his shoulder and the neck, a hard blow but not one intended to kill. If that had been the object, he would have been hit in the head. Julio lay crumpled in a fetal position, whimpering and clasping his groin, while blood seeped through his fingers. Next to him, Antone lay on his back, blood pooling around his neck. His eyelids had fallen back so that he stared at the unforgiving moon. Domingo's body had fallen from his horse and was a ways off.

Angelo watched the oriental on her feet, tugging her clothes into place. She slid a razor back into her boots. Then she collected one of her knives from the ground, walked over, and picked up Julio's Dragon Dagger.

Angelo tried to remain motionless. He saw the oriental squat down in front of Julio, who was moaning and clutching his groin.

Jai Ling twirled his dagger before Julio.

She looked up. Dioneo entered the clearing from one end. A snap of a twig caught her attention. She spun and saw Trippetta and Uwe coming, each leaning on the other. Jai Ling gave each a nod, then focused back on Julio.

"Nice knife," she said. The newly minted eunuch tried to spit at her but missed.

"Now now now, I told you this would happen. And as my friends seem okay, I guess I can't just kill you. But this knife, I'll take that. It's an honest trade since you killed a couple of our horses. Still, it's a nice knife. I don't think it's fair I leave you empty-handed."

Jai Ling stepped on Julio's wrist and forced some bloodied flesh into it.

"Put 'em to good use," Jai Ling snickered.

Julio uttered a combination of screams and sobs as he clutched the flesh to its former position on his body.

As Jai Ling went away, she muttered, "Yeah, that'll work."

MADDALENA

Jai Ling puts her hand around my head and strokes my hair, saying, “Thanks, Maddie.” I turn away. Jai Ling grabs my shoulder.

“You did a good thing. Now go get Lisabetta. She’s wandered over there. ” I turn to get the strawberry blond girl.

“You’re one of us now,” Jai Ling says. She’s speaking from behind, but I know she is speaking to me.

I am glad we are alive. These men were vile and would have done evil to us. But Jai Ling frightens me. She can be completely cruel and kill one moment, then my friend the next.

Dioneo, Jai Ling, Uwe, and Trippetta stood in the clearing, gathering their animals. Both Dioneo’s steed and Uwe’s corsair had been killed.

“I hope you’re happy, Jai,” Dioneo said. “We lost two good horses for an idiot girl.”

“And we’ll take theirs,” snapped Jai Ling. “Oh, thanks for getting here so fast to cover my ass,” Jai Ling added, then looked at the dwarves. “Are you two all right?”

Trippetta said, “We fine. Uwe fell in hole, and then I looked for bear in hole. I throw branch down, and Uwe climb out.”

Uwe was clutching his ribs

“What happened to the bear?” Dioneo asked.

“I don’t know,” Uwe grunted back. “Trippetta dragged branch into trap. I got out fast as I could.”

Uwe shrugged. “Bones hurt.” He pointed to Angelo, who had crept to the side. “What about him?” asked Uwe.

Angelo remained on his knees, cowering from the group. Julio was bleeding and crying as he clutched between his legs.

“Gather their horses,” said Dioneo.

Angelo began to whimper. “I’m unarmed.”

“What do you mean, friend, you’ve got two arms. Now your boss, he’s got two arms too. He may be deballed, but not unarmed." Dioneo smiled. Julio continued to wail and roll around in the dirt.

"Please," Angelo said. "I ..." and his voice trailed off. There was a pause while the others seemed to go about their business, gathering the horses while Maddalena retrieved Lisabetta. Angelo felt his throat tighten. Surely he and Julio would be killed.

But the young girl came back with Lisabetta. They all gathered their horses, mounted up, and proceeded to ride away, bringing the gang's horses with them. Angelo was left at the side of the road, holding his shoulder, while Julio lay whimpering.

As she rode by Angelo, Jai Ling said, "Don't go piss on yourself."

Then the riders disappeared into the dark.

Jai Ling and Dioneo rode in silence, carefully peering ahead to watch the road. A little while later, they might have heard a cry in the distance behind them that could have been either Angelo or Julio. Jai Ling glanced questioningly at Dioneo.

"Maybe Julio found his missing man," Dioneo said. "He found me—in the woods. That—ouch. My stomach hurts—that log shot me way into the trees. I was hanging from a tree branch, upside down, of course, and like that, he was just—floating there in the air next to me."

Dioneo snapped his fingers.

"A vampire?" Jai Ling asked.

"More ghostly, like a revenant. "Some can blend into crowds. Looked like a refugee from a crusade. Damn, a haunted paladin. It got me pinned in the air, up against a tree. Figured I was done for."

Jai Ling waited for Dioneo to continue, but the acrobat was content to ride in silence.

Finally, Jai Ling asked, "Well?"

"Well? It was funny, Jai. Funny haha. I figured all my problems in this life were finally about to be put to rest. And you know what? It wasn't as scary as I thought it would be. It was like a release. I was going to see if there really is anything beyond this. For a second, I wasn't scared at all."

He again paused, drifting in thought. Jai Ling prodded, "So how come you're here and not back there up in a tree?"

"I fall quickly," he said. Dioneo winced and rubbed his side and blurted out, "My ribs hurt."

"Serves you right for leading us into that trap. Like you said at the tavern, I had things in hand."

A very wry smile crept across her lips as she said this line.

"Jai, you cut his balls off," Dioneo chided. "That's one thing. But then you handed them. That's brutal."

Jai Ling smiled wickedly and said, "Well, now he certainly has things in hand."

Elta, the daughter of Gugliemo and Imelda, was out behind the barn, reaching into the pen for another hen to slaughter. The villa certainly was busy tonight. A fight almost erupted? No big issue. Julio's men on the run? People still needed to eat. As her mother had said, before sending her out, there was money to be made.

She carefully grasped a sleeping chicken and pulled it out from its hutch. The birds had not been disturbed by the commotion at the tavern. The bird began to squawk wildly, but Elta held the throat firm and quickly spun the body around, snapping the head off.

As she turned to leave, she gasped, and the chicken dropped from her hand. The moonlight struck a tall, lean figure standing a few feet from her. He wore the crest of a knight who had fought with King Edward III, and he watched her with one eye. She didn't recognize him; he looked much different than he had in the tavern.

"I'm sorry," he said. "I did not select you. There was another in the villa, a young girl with the strangers who I wanted. But then I learned the ones with her with hunters of my kind, and too strong for myself. I'm sorry."

Elta was too paralyzed with fear to move.

The knight stepped towards her, raising his hands, and small fangs sprouted behind his lips.

"I did not select you."

Lisabetta sat by a fire, naked save for a woolen blanket, her arms around her knees, while Trippetta sponged her with warm water. Maddalena had helped to carry the water over. Nearby, Dioneo lay on another blanket, warm towels over his head and ribs. Jai Ling sat with her legs crisscrossed beside him.

"How's the dwarf?" Dioneo asked.

"Trippetta is fine. Uwe, I don't know. He's around somewhere," Jai Ling answered.

"El Erreur already complained to me," Dioneo said. "Another mouth to feed."

"He sounds just like you."

"Jai, I can't figure out what's gotten into you. You suddenly want to take in every human tragedy we find."

"Look at her," said Jai Ling, pointing at Lisabetta. The girl was sitting on a rock, swaying back and forth. "She's rather pretty, in a coarse way. Different looking with that hair. She might be useful to us."

Dioneo smiled. "You always say that. So you're saying it's good to have another pretty face on board. I can buy that. That's my Jai. But you did call attention to us back there, which we didn't need. And my ribs still hurt. Everything hurts. Next time you want to right the world's wrongs—let me know before you do it."

Jai Ling shrugged. "I'll try to remember that, Dioneo. I really will."

I sense some disappointment that we have not heard from our friend Elizabeth. But please, be patient. She is not forgotten. And she most certainly has not forgotten about Bartolome and Maddalena.

I suspect we shall see Elizabeth and her friends shortly.

[9]
DIGNE LES BAINS

THE CARAVAN CONTINUED through heavy summer rains. They worked their way through the lower Alps valley region. Wooden wheels would slip on upward slopes, and at least twice they had to right wagons that had turned over. Occasionally, another road would drop into the one they were on, or another might fork off, and they might venture down it a ways, but El Erreur kept them going in a north-northwesterly direction, skirting around the base of the Alps but not going into the heart of the range.

The new girl, Lisabetta, usually sat in a corner of the wagon. At different times, Jai Ling, Trippetta, and Lora reached out to her. Mostly all Lisabetta said was a variation of "Eh, eh." On occasion, she would form a few words, but seldom. At night, while food was prepared, she would eat what food was given to her. Mrs. Cooke made a point to have Lisabetta toss scraps to the dogs and other animals near the wagons so that she could tell El Erreur she had a "duty." When the troupe practiced their routines, Lisabetta would sit nearby, perhaps watching, perhaps staring blankly—who could tell what was in her mind?

After what had proven to be three days of long travel in the rain, with nothing but deep woods and slowly ascending earth, the troupe received a respite when the rain stopped. The forest opened. A semi-fortified monastery sat on a hill, with what Maddalena thought were pretty cottages ringing the land around it. Unlike the last village, as they approached this one, some people were working in the fields, cutting down hay.

Maddalena rode on a small pony next to Jai Ling, off to the side of the caravan.

"It is good to see life again," Maddalena said. "So many other villages—it is so sad."

"That is just what happens to a small village when the great mortality strikes," Jai Ling said. "The sickness goes through quickly. Most villages have some survivors, but many are totally destroyed. It will happen somewhere today."

"Have you seen many villages like that?" Maddalena asked. "With no survivors?"

"Enough," Jai Ling answered. "During the great mortality, no place is safe. You've seen at least three with me. All you can do is keep moving."

Maddalena nodded.

"They say even the great city of Florence is littered with ghosts."

"That's what I hear about most of Italy." Jai Ling took Maddalena's hand and added, "That is why we are heading to northern France. We'll outrun it."

"But what about the war with the English?" Maddalena asked.

"We'll turn east long before we get there," Jai Ling answered. "There are many places where we can go. Have you ever heard of Poland?"

Maddalena nodded.

Jai Ling continued. "They say that the plague is not there. They are ruled by King Casimir, who is said to be a just ruler. Maybe they are such good Catholics that God spares them."

Maddalena grew silent.

Jai Ling leaned over in her saddle and said, "Maddalena, I

think I believe in your Christ, at least that he lived. But your Church? They have claimed for so many years to have a direct connection to God. What is the Church doing now? Can they stop the great mortality? Some say it's a punishment on earth for our sins. I'm not sure it is from God, but I don't think it matters. The black death is here, and all we can do is try to outrun it. And from what I've seen, we're not even ahead of it."

So," Maddalena asked, "are you protected? From the black death? Is that why you and Lora always enter the villages first?"

"We go in first because Dioneo is a giant coward, and Uwe follows him." Both riders laughed. Jai Ling paused for a few moments and let her horse carry her, then continued, "I don't know why, but it seems that those of us who survived—we're spared it again. At least somewhat. Myself, Lora—I don't know why. It just seems to be." Jai Ling paused again before adding, "Let's stop talking of it."

In the fields, people looked at the wagons but kept a safe distance. People walking on the roads moved to the side. The caravan continued to roll into the town. The path they traveled led to a solid cobblestone street that went to the monastery in the center of the village.

People seemed more wary of them. The wagons stopped in the town square, directly in the monastery's shadow.

"Hello!" came a call from across the courtyard. The speaker was a man leaning out of a third-floor window of the monastery. He waved at them.

"Hello," the man repeated, "are you entertainers?"

Dioneo brought his horse forward and said, "Indeed, we are entertainers. We are the greatest acrobats, magicians, and troubadours in all of Europe. We've come to your beautiful village to perform as your humble servants."

"Wonderful," the man said, disappearing from the window and then reappearing a few seconds later from the building. A middle-aged man, slightly stout, he was dressed in leather breeches, a woolen tunic, and a felt cap, and ran up to the group eagerly.

"Wonderful to see you," he said. "We have not had visitors in several weeks. Not a group like you. Where did you come from?"

"South," Dioneo said.

"Did you pass through Capreum?" the man asked. "We heard there is much sickness there."

Dioneo hesitated. El Erreur walked up next to Dioneo's horse and said, "We haven't passed any village for several days. How far away is Capreum?"

"Two to three days south. It is small, easily missed. 'Tis well; as I said, we heard there is much sickness there."

"Surely, you must have other travelers come through," El Erreur said.

"'Tis true, usually we have some, but much less over the last few months. The sickness that spreads takes many. We have been spared so far. But our days here are so quiet. Do you bring trade?"

"We do," said Nefferi, appearing from the front wagon. She was dressed in a long, flowing, light-blue chiffon robe, her hair held back with a bronze asp headband, and made her typical regal impression. "But what we trade is entertainment. Perhaps we can barter with you."

The village was called Digne Les Bains, although most called it simply Digne. The monastery was Saint Michelle de Aubney. The man they'd spoken with was named Cisti. His wife was Agnes. A baker by profession, Cisti had been content making his goods and selling them, having amassed enough skill and wealth so that in the not-too-distant past, he was a comfortable leader of a modest guild with the village merchants and tradesmen. As it was, now he was the leader of a loosely associated group who ran the town as best they could. The monastery's official complement had been reduced to three monks and a priest. The rest had been dispatched to various villages in the region. There had not been communication from any of them in weeks. Cisti, on behalf of the main group of town representatives, had asked that the monastery be used as a central meeting place and be turned into a fortification for the entire village, if needed. The monks and the priest had agreed so long as the people respected the piety of the order.

Under the circumstances, they were not in a position to protest. People still went to mass in Digne. The same could not be said in many other places.

Continuing with life while the plague spread around them, the inhabitants of Digne had done a more than passable job of maintaining order in their lives. They had planted appropriately in the spring, fed their animals, and were now in the late summer harvest, so there was some grain and, yes, even meat to trade. El Erreur and (especially) Nefferi negotiated for the group to perform their show. Nefferi was good with Cisti and all men in general, who clearly enjoyed Nefferi's attentions. Agnes, Cisti's wife, seemed more disapproving, but Nefferi was a very persuasive bargainer.

The village had recently been forced to pay a debt, though Cisti was hesitant to discuss the details. The payment had been a combination of gold coins, food, and animals, so the village was reduced in what it could offer. However, there were a few stray horses in the fields, weapons in the monastery, and raw materials. Uwe was overjoyed to find some barrels with sulfur in the monastery's lower chambers. The town's well also flourished, so fresh water could be bartered. The caravan had wine to spare, along with entertainment. A deal was struck. And for the first time in several weeks, the group performed for a paying audience.

MADDALENA

Jai Ling and I walk down a sandy pathway between the priory and the exterior wall of the monastery, near the main entrance gates. We see Dioneo and Trippetta up ahead by a high wall of the monastery. Trippetta is sitting in the sand, her legs crossed, her eyes closed, her arms and her head moving together in a rhythmic motion. She is imagining her dance. She looks so at peace. Dancing is her passion, and she is happy when she does it.

As calming as Trippetta appears, Dioneo is another story. He is working with two parallel ropes, suspended from the high wall. He climbs a rock and shifts his gaze back and forth between the wall and the ground. Then he shimmies up one rope a short way and ties a red scarf to the other rope. He tugs on the rope with the scarf and says, "Ready," and it pulls up and disappears over the monastery's wall.

"What is he doing?" I ask.

"Measuring," Jai Ling said. "They have an act to perform, too. You haven't seen them practice this."

"Pop it!" Dioneo yells upward.

Jai Ling looks skyward and pulls me farther from the wall. "Best to let them stay to themselves."

Just as she says this, a large tree branch flies over the wall. Dioneo yells for us to look out, and he springs towards us. Jai Ling has already moved us safely away, but Dioneo leaps to shield us. Jai Ling firmly pulls me again, and we dodge Dioneo, who rolls into the sand. The branch crashes and shatters where we had been standing moments earlier.

"That could have been my damn head," Dioneo mutters as he gets up.

Jai Ling comments, "With your looks, it could only help."

Dioneo smiles and says, "Ah, Jai Ling and Maddalena, my two favorite ladies." Then, looking at Jai Ling, he says, "Any chance of getting a kiss for saving your life?"

"I think you'd do better to focus on improving your act," she replies.

Trippetta runs up to us and asks if we are all right, and we tell her we are fine. Dioneo then yells to the wall, “Uwe, you ass! You threw it from the wrong spot!”

Uwe’s face appears worriedly over the top of the wall. He waves his hands in frustration. Then he shrugs and disappears from view.

“That’s what they call ‘pop and drop,’” Trippetta says. “Remember I told you about when Uwe and I were in King Frido’s palace?”

“Is it supposed to work like that?” I ask, gesturing to the shattered tree branch.

“Only if we’re very lucky and it hits Dioneo,” Jai Ling says.

“You are so bad, Jai Ling,” Trippetta says. “But they will be ready tonight, you see.”

I notice now that the branch is tied to a rope, and I see the scarf that Dioneo had tied. He tests the rope, and it is firm. Trippetta goes over and tries talking to him, but Dioneo is focused on above.

“I’m coming up there, and I’m going to kick your arse!” he yells, starting to climb the wall.

Trippetta seems unconcerned about the entire event and begins to pirouette on her left foot with her eyes closed.

I whisper to Jai Ling, “He wouldn’t really hurt Uwe, would he?”

Jai Ling laughs and whispers back. “Well, first, I think if he tried, Uwe would rip him apart. And second, that’s just how they work together. They’ll be fine. Just you remember your parts tonight.”

I laugh as well, and we continue walking along the outside walls of the monastery.

The central part of the monastery offered a vast, partly sheltered, rectangular-shaped courtyard for troubadours to perform in. After night had fallen, and the villagers had eaten foods prepared by the

Cookes with a combination of ingredients from Digne and wine from the wagons (for feeding the audience was a requirement), the performance commenced in the courtyard. The villagers lined three sides of the courtyard, while the fourth side ran up the monastery's exterior wall. Even two of the monks came out. Cisti and Agnes sat in special chairs which the troupe carried and set up for dignitaries. The baker and his wife liked the plush down pillows lining the chairs. Torches along the edges were lit, and a couple of the troupe's wagons were strategically placed along the sides.

First up were Uwe and Trippetta and their accompanists. Uwe played various fluted instruments, while Maddalena banged a small hand drum with metal jingles in it. Jai Ling had called it a "tambourine." Several other women from the troupe danced around the edges of the square. Trippetta leapt across the cobblestones, seemingly like a feather. She jumped in the air and kicked her feet. At one point, Dioneo came out and set five hoops mounted on staffs in the middle of the courtyard and lit them on fire. Trippetta skipped through each one, one foot first and the other trailing, doing mid-air splits, her arms gracefully flowing, looking and smiling at the audience the entire time. The crowd applauded greatly. Uwe and Dioneo slipped towards the Monastery entrance, while Rowena, Dioneo's friend, brought out all the children from the troupe. Trippetta, who looked like a child herself, led the children in clapping as they paraded around the edge of the courtyard, waiving at the people and touching hands as they passed. Maddalena hung on the end of the line, then dropped off and went to a wagon by the side where Jai Ling was dressing.

"Our little friend is quite a talented dancer," Jai Ling said to Maddalena. They were in one of the wagons, applying white grease paint to their faces. They could see the show from here.

"She is," Maddalena said, then caught herself. Her friend? She guessed Trippetta was a friend of sorts.

"You asked me about drop and pop earlier. Now watch what happens next.

Rowena led the children off the square while Trippetta went back to the center and bowed again to the crowd.

"Thank you for having us tonight," Trippetta said, her face beaming as she slowly backed to the wall at the end of the courtyard. "We were happy to drop in on you. But now we have to pop out." She cocked her head to the side, smiled, and raised her arms to the night sky.

Dioneo dropped from above, out of the darkness, suspended from a rope tied around his feet, and stopped just above Trippetta's outstretched arms. Dioneo wrapped his arms around Trippetta's wrists, and they both shot upwards into the night.

Those in the audience either gasped or were silent. But a few moments later, Dioneo, Trippetta, and Uwe appeared fromthe Monastery's gate, arm in arm. They took a bow, as the audience exploded with applause.

Mansa and his animals were up next. Two tigers, three bears, some snakes, and smaller animals. They remain chained as he had them walk on tables and pass through hoops. Some of the villagers were noticeably uncomfortable with such large animals roaming their village, but when the act ended, and each animal was properly sealed in their container, their clapping signified approval.

Next up came Uwe, who juggled colorful balls in the air to mild applause. Unfortunately, as he did so, he had a tendency to let his mouth hang open, fully displaying fang-like teeth.

"Poor Uwe," I say as I watch him. "He is very good, but the people seem scared of him."

"Don't pity him," Jai Ling chides me. "If there's one thing Uwe hates, it is to be pitied."

I nod and feel somewhat ashamed. “I don’t pity him, I just wish he weren’t so fearful looking.” I feel worse after I say this.

Jai Ling pats my shoulder and says, “Look at it this way. When he’s with us, he’s with his family. He may be scary-looking to some, but he’s all ours.”

Dioneo bounded into the courtyard, dressed in multi-colored tights and shirt, topped with the motley-colored cap of a fool. He said he would entertain the people with a song. Uwe accompanied him by strumming a mandolin—very badly—and Dioneo apologized to the audience in advance for the bawdy song he was about to sing.

There was a merchant in Arimino,
A man who loved his life,
And who had great wealth, great girth, great age, and so, little strife,
But most notably, oh my, did he have a great wife!

Dioneo told his tale with ebullience. His audience alternately groaned, booed, or laughed with approval. The story told of the wife’s great beauty, boredom with her much older husband, and her wishes for a lover, but she did not act on it. One day, the man heard his wife actually rehearsing her confession in her bedroom, where she expressed her desires for carnal knowledge of a particular young monk in the local abbey. The man, afraid to confront his wife, went to the local clergy for advice and was told he must lie in wait each night to ensure his wife’s fidelity. The man took this advice to heart and vowed to stay by his manor’s door every night to ensure no clergy snuck in.

So he waited by the door,
At night, for many a score,

With a sense of both hate and fear,
but no priest or friar did ever appear,

Unfortunately for the merchant, the young friar who was the object of the wife's affections had overheard the conversation—soundproofing not being a quality well-mastered by the carpenters of Arimino—and decided to take matters into his own hands.

As for the merchant and his wife...
And while I must tell you, dear friends, that though his wife
was never aloof,
What she failed to say,
That while her husband for so many nights by the door did he
stay,
My lady's dear friar came nightly,
Not through the door, but down the roof,
And while the merchant spied the road with strong eye
and ear,
Hemissed that very young fri-ar, in his bed, with his wife, up
her re-ar!

A chorus of humorous boos and throwing of food followed. Members of the troupe gathered the food.

"He is awful," Jai Ling said to Maddalena. They sat on the edge of a cart. Maddalena had changed into a purple gown with sequins on it. Jai Ling wore a purple kimono and had her short bow and quiver slung over her back. Both their faces were powdered with white makeup and black eyeshadow. Both wore their hair wrapped up in chignons adorned with decorative brooches.

MADDALENA

"You look silly," I say.

"So do you."

Jai Ling looks at the crowd.

"The powder on my face actually feels nice."

"It's from the root of the Madonna lily," Jai Ling says. "Very soothing for the skin."

Outside the wagon, Dioneo speaks to the townspeople.

"My dear friends, you are a great audience, and I now present you with your next performance. The most magnificent of archers, the master of any bowed instrument, the Mistress of Mayhem, the very lovely and mysterious 'Miss Mystery! And friend'."

"Miss Mystery," I say.

Jai Ling says, with a sigh, "The people want exotic entertainment. And all we oriental people are so mysterious and exotic."

We come out to applause. Jai Ling bows a type of curtsy, then gestures to me, and I make the same move. Uwe pushes a cart behind us. Some others play flutes off to the side. Dioneo and Ricciardo set up targets against the stone wall back at the far end of the courtyard.

The act displays Jai Ling's prowess with a bow. She uses her short bow to fire arrows in rapid succession at each target, always hitting the center. I replenish her arrows with others from the cart. The people applaud appreciatively. Jai Ling demonstrates other skills. I toss several round rings in the air of various widths, and she fires through them. Dioneo calls for an apple or a pear from the audience, and several are tossed at him. He catches most of them and juggles for a while, to some applause, then begins to make higher and higher tosses with each fruit. When they are at the highest point over Dioneo's head, Jai Ling shoots and splits each piece, and Dioneo eats as many of the falling halves as he can. This happens quickly, and the audience laughs and applauds with real appreciation.

I then blindfold Jai Ling, spin her around, and stop, leaving her left foot at a point we have previously staked out. She shoots several more targets, hitting them square, save for the last one, which she misses by a few hand lengths. The crowd applauds, but there are a few remarks at her miss.

While still blindfolded, Jai Ling raises a finger in the air as if to say "wait". At this cue, I go over and hold Ricciardo's right arm, while Bartolome walks onto the scene and holds the left arm. Together, we lead Ricciardo to a hitching post in front of the stone wall. I hear Ricciardo ask me what is happening next. He says he thought he was tossing the fruit. Dioneo runs up and places Ricciardo's back to the post, and wraps a blindfold around him. Then he binds Ricciardo's hands behind the pole.

"I'm scared," Ricciardo says. "This isn't what was planned."

"Don't worry, it is all for show," Dioneo says, patting Ricciardo on the chest. "And you know we all have to work to make this a success. I told you we have a great role for you. This is your big moment. Trust me, you're in good hands. Now you just stand there quietly. Don't move!"

Dioneo places an apple on Ricciardo's head while Bartolome and I run away.

Ricciardo begins to protest, but Dioneo repeats, "Don't move!"

Jai Ling is standing forty paces in front of Ricciardo, her blindfold pulled back, measuring Ricciardo carefully. Then she momentarily looks at her feet. She shifts her stance and motions for her long bow and an arrow, which I give her. I pull the blindfold back over Jai Ling's. She turns her back to Ricciardo, then draws the bow back, aiming down. There is a collective buzz from the crowd.

Dioneo tells them they must be quiet so Miss Mystery can concentrate.

Ricciardo, now quite nervous, stammers, "Dioneo? What's happening?"

Dioneo is walking backward from him and saying, "Stay there, Ricciardo. And don't move."

As soon as Dioneo speaks, Jai Ling gently kicks my shin. I step back and begin counting softly, just enough for Jai Ling to hear. Underneath her blindfold, she smiles ever so slightly.

"One, two, three."

Dioneo keeps walking backwards and telling Ricciardo not to move.

I reach nine, then I say loudly, "Ten."

Jai Ling whirls and fires her arrow.

It splits the apple just over Ricciardo's head and embeds itself in the pole.

Ricciardo yells, but the crowd's applause is louder. Jai Ling takes off her blindfold, makes a quick nod towards Ricciardo, and extends her hand to me. We both bow. Then we walk over to Ricciardo while the crowd applauds, and I untie his binding and blindfold. Ricciardo's face is ashen. Jai Ling gives him a small round of applause.

Other acts follow. Dioneo appears wearing his multi-colored tights and a purple shirt, accompanied by Uwe. Dioneo calls for a chair and a table. They are brought out to him. He balances the chair on the table, then climbs atop the chair and asks for more. Chairs, stools, and other items are brought out, which Uwe hands to him, and Dioneo continues to pile each atop the other and balance them on the chairs and tables and various other items from the audience. As one is brought out, he places it on top of the other, always staying on top. Finally, a pole is brought out, and he balances himself by one hand on the pole, atop the tower. The audience applauds, and then Dioneo climbs down, disassembling each layer of the tower as he does so. Finally, he does a somersault off the original table and lands on his feet.

"I will admit, he is nimble," Jai Ling says to me.

We have other acts. Nefferi comes out and tells humorous or heartfelt fortunes for villagers chosen from the audience. The fortunes are relentlessly happy ones. Lora and her falcons perform tricks with the assistance of Trippetta. Next, Trippetta comes out wearing a set of leggings and a form-fitting overtunic marked with colorful beads. She sits down in the center of the courtyard and slowly puts her hair up, while Uwe lights several fire pits which he has prepared. Uwe then comes and attaches Trippetta's hair to a long pole. Uwe leans back and lifts the pole with his massive forearms, and Trippetta swings in the air, pivoting around the staff, her body twirling as she holds her arms tight against her chest. The beads of her costume throw off colorful lights from the fire pits that make the courtyard floor sparkle. The audience is truly in awe of this. When Uwe stops swinging her, he gently lowers the pole, and Trippetta gracefully touches the ground, unties her hair, and steps away, bowing to much clapping and the toss of several coins.

I understand why Trippetta is so concerned about that special pink soap for her hair.

Nefferi comes out again and does a dance of one hundred veils. She dances not as gracefully as Trippetta, and I don't think there are really one hundred, more like fifty colorful cloths and sheer pieces of fabric, but the men of the village don't mind. Dioneo appears again with Uwe and Ricciardo, where Dioneo leaps and tumbles over items Uwe sets up. Occasionally, Uwe flips Dioneo into the air. Poor Ricciardo seems a little shaken from his earlier performance and is more of a prop than a participant in the show, someone who Dioneo is thrown over. At the end, Dioneo wraps his arm around both Ricciardo and Uwe, and they bow together.

Lisabetta works with other girls and children to clean up debris after each performance. Our show goes late into the night, and the villagers are pleased. I will admit I have seen troubadours perform at Avignon and other courts in Europe, but our troupe is very different.

At the end, we all line up in the courtyard while everyone in groups appears and claps towards the audience. When it is Jai Ling's turn to be acknowledged, she pulls me forward, both of us still in our make-up, and we curtsy together. The applause is accompanied by whistles, and some food is thrown. We wave our hands, while those who did not perform scramble to pick up the food.

Elizabeth stood in the early morning light with Janosz and Alatiel, staring at a crossroads. She had a strap supporting a large pouch hanging from her shoulder. Something in the pouch was moving. A mixture of mist and fog hung in the air. Before them, a path split three ways: northeast, northwest, and west

Elizabeth stroked Alatiel's hair with a comb and spoke to her mind. "You and I, and Janosz, we can travel in the day. You are the best of us. The others—something about the day seems to make them more difficult. We're getting better, but as a group we move best at night."

Elizabeth pulled a red scarf from her tunic and handed it to Alatiel, who rubbed her face against the scarf.

"So tell me, Alatiel—which way?" she spoke aloud.

Alatiel walked briefly down each path, then returned. She looked into Elizabeth's eyes.

"I don't want you to kill her."

"I won't."

"Will you make her like us?"

"Only if she wants. I want her blood. Hers and her brother's. They will be sooo helpful to me. To both of us. You see, we have the purest blood descended from Charles Martel, a great leader from long ago. He was made like us and given, briefly, the ability to heal his body. If we combine my blood with the children and their mother, I will be able to heal myself perpetually. And you can see enough into my mind to know I will help you to do the same thing."

Alatiel hesitated for a few moments, then walked out to the woods and stopped, letting her hands drop to her sides and closing her eyes. Her body swayed.

Elizabeth could sense Janosz growing restless, but she motioned him to stay with her, and they remained in the shadows of trees.

After some time, a pair of wolves crept out of the woods, warily looking past Alatiel. Scrawny, they looked underfed. Though hesitant, they walked up to her, one to each side. Alatiel opened her palms, and each wolf sniffed. She looked at one, then the other, as they licked her palms. Then they stopped suddenly and ran down the middle path heading north.

Alatiel did not turn around, but she thought, *There. Maybe two days away.*

Elizabeth surveyed the road. Most of her followers were standing in the woods behind her, awake but dormant. She made the command.

"*Lie down*!" She spoke orally and through her mind.

Most of the bodies swung, rocked, and managed to comply.

Elizabeth had discovered that she had mistakenly assumed last year that her fleshers needed to move to survive. They did, if they were fed. But during stretches of hunger, their survival was extended if they rested their bodies during the day. This was a forced rest, no doubt, and without her influence, the miserable creatures would prowl day and night until they dropped. The burning still took place, but the process was delayed by rest. The three sisters had hinted as much. Elizabeth was learning quickly, but there was still much to learn.

Until she could find a better solution, this was how it would be.

Elizabeth walked next to Alatiel and handed her the pouch.

Alatiel peeked in. A small ginger colored coney rabbit, bitten but still alive, was squirming. Elizabeth patted Alatiel on the head, then turned to Janosz.

"We rest today. And tonight we proceed down the northwest trail."

Dawn broke over Digne. Although there had been dancing after last night's performance, people arose to go about their business. Many went to the fields to glean wheat and hay. Others worked on making wine, while others baked bread and pastry. The town had a good well and a strong grape harvest. Nefferi worked out the trades with Cisti, to the slight consternation of Cisti's wife, but overall it was a fair exchange of food, weapons, and other supplies. Uwe got a barrel of his sulfur.

At the urging of Dioneo and Jai Ling, El Erreur had stationed lookouts on the roads leading into town from the south and north. They took four-hour shifts. Dioneo had taken the dusk shift. So, at nightfall, he found himself atop a hill along with two bottles of wine. He had planned to drink to excess and found a place where he could conceal himself. Still, he kept an eye on the road, and after an uneventful stretch, he was eventually relieved by Mansa.

"You look like you kept yourself occupied."

"Me and my friends," Dioneo replied, patting the one bottle still in his hand. "But no sign of trouble. Hey, how about a hand up?"

Mansa grasped Dioneo's hand and pulled him to his feet.

"Try not to fall on your arse on the way back."

"Thanks for caring, Mansa."

Dioneo headed back with a slight stagger in his step and proceeded to the only tavern on the northern side of town.

It was dark now. When Dioneo got to the tavern, it was dimly lit with candles and lightly populated by a few stragglers staying huddled by themselves. At the main table, he asked for a bumper of beer and, being served by a pretty barmaid, he winked and then made his way over to a bench in the corner of the room.

He put his head down to rest. How long, he wasn't sure, but he was awoken by a familiar voice saying, "You perform better than ever, Dioneo."

Dioneo's head lifted quickly.

Across the table sat a slim male, dressed in an olive-drab cloak that looked more like a gown, but with a collar, and a pointed hat on top, its conical end hung down. The collar was upturned, hiding the speaker's face.

"I saw your show. You are such a pleasure to watch, Dioneo. You are a very talented acrobat."

Dioneo leaned forward.

"I'd like to say it's nice to see you again," he said, "but I think it's Sunday and I hate to lie on the good Lord's day."

"It's Saturday. And I thought you had lost your religion, Dioneo. But regardless, I have a proposition for you, if you are interested."

The barmaid came over and brought a carafe of tea. The man looked up and said, "Thank you, dear," and handed her a coin. She thanked him and turned to Dioneo, who also gave her a coin and said, "We're all set. Tend to your other customers."

The woman left. Dioneo saw that under the cloak, the man wore the red motley clothes of a fool—similar to the patchwork pants Dioneo had worn when he sang last night. The man took off his hat and placed it inside his cloak.

"Are you looking for some payment?" Dioneo asked.

"Me? No." The fool shook his head. "I rendered services here, and I was paid." He leaned forward. "You know I honor my obligations."

"Of course you do," Dioneo noted. "And aren't you the slightest bit concerned you'll be recognized here?"

The fool shook his head confidently.

"No, not with these people. They are far too caught up in their own lives. Put on this robe—a drab color, I agree—and they take no notice."

The fool leaned back and stretched his arms above his head

"But I am here to speak to you about another matter, Dioneo. There is word around. Pope Clement is offering a large reward—five hundred florins. Not deniers, or marks, or livres. Florins. Do you know that coin? It is the new one from Florence—all gold."

Dioneo shrugged.

"Money's not worth what it once was."

The fool clasped his hands on the table and smiled. "That may be true. But it will be again. And that doesn't sound like you."

Dioneo took a drink of his beer and said, "Can't spend much when you're dead."

The fool nodded.

"Still, you've always been a man open to a business proposition, Dioneo. And I hear that in truth, Pope Clement will meet anyone's price if they can bring him two children. A boy and a girl. I think their names are—Bartholome and Mary? Or something like that. I can't seem to remember."

"That's interesting," Dioneo said, taking another drink. "I'm sure you can find two children with those names."

"Oh, not just any children. These two are special."

Dioneo shrugged again. "What makes them so special?"

"Oh, it is not clear. But they must be important."

The motley fool leaned further across the table.

"There are others who want them too. There's talk that the children were the only survivors of an attack by fleshers. Now I myself don't know if such creatures exist, but there's talk of a leader of this group. A flesher who controls the others. A woman at that, can you believe it? I hear she wants those children, too."

"Oh, I think we both know fleshers exist," Dioneo shot back. "But they're mindless—they want to eat people like me. Which is surprising because I leave such a bad taste in people's mouths." Dioneo took another drink of beer while the motley fool smiled.

"Funny as always," he said, sipping his tea. "That's why I always liked you. And it is true, the living dead are mindless, or so we think. But there's talk that this woman—I guess she is still a woman. What do you call an undead woman? An unwoman?"

"How about just calling her dead?"

"Ah, you are very funny indeed. No matter. Maybe she exists, maybe she doesn't, who is to say?" The fool sipped more of his tea.

"But do you want to know what else is funny? Those children with you fit the description of that boy and girl."

"Those children?" Dioneo asked. "We have several."

"Yes," the fool said. "Last night, that girl in the danse macabre powder makeup, and the young man who helped with Jai Ling's performance? I see Jai Ling's lost none of her skill, by the way."

"Ahh, you mean Andre and Rose," Dioneo said. "Two annoying brats. Quite worthless. Nobody would pay a dineen for that pair."

The fool sat and put his back against the wall. He placed a flute on the table and began to twirl it with his finger.

"Andre and Rose," he said. "Of course."

"The children you speak of. How long ago were they lost?" Dioneo asked while drinking, but eyeing the flute.

"Not long ago. At the start of summer."

"Well," Dioneo said between gulps, "Can't be any of our kids, they've been with us for years."

"Hmmm," the fool said, still toying with his flute.

Dioneo laughed and shook his head.

"No, no, no," he said. Then, leaning across the table, he added, "And not that it matters since they aren't the children you want, but even if they were, you couldn't take them. Despite your powers —I know you, remember? There are rules, even for you—and as you said, your debt here is paid."

The fool continued to spin the flute on the table. "Oh, I know you too, Dioneo. And you're quite right. I can't just take them." Pausing, he leaned forward. "But you know how I love children. I don't suppose you'd be willing to sell Andre and Rose? I could make it well worth your loss."

Whap! A loaded crossbow appeared on the table, its bolt pointed directly at the fool.

Jai Ling slid onto the bench next to Dioneo.

"Now, my dear, we were just talking," Dioneo said. "Oh, no offense, friend, just—what do you call yourself today?"

The fool stroked his face and said, "Errol. I think that's a good name, don't you? And Jai Ling, it is so nice to see you again, too."

"I can't say the same," retorted Jai Ling. "I guess we know what the villagers paid for." Leaning to Dioneo, but keeping a close eye on Errol and her hand on the crossbow trigger, she asked, "Has he been paid?"

"Oh yes, my dear Jai Ling, in full, have no fear," Errol said. "I was just here to see if we could make a deal."

"Then I make no deal with you," Jai Ling said.

"You should hear me out. It could be beneficial to both of us."

"I make no deal with you," Jai Ling repeated. She bumped her shoulder against Dioneo. "Nor does he. Or anyone in our camp. We want nothing to do with you. Be gone."

Errol sat for several moments staring at the crossbow, then clapped his hands and said, "So be it. I will be on my way. Pleasant travels, pilgrims."

He picked up his flute and sack and stood.

"Perhaps another time," he said and walked out of the tavern.

Jai Ling picked up the crossbow and started after Errol, but Dioneo grabbed her arm.

"That was dangerous," he said.

Jai Ling tried to pull from his grasp, but Dioneo's grip was tighter than she expected.

She glared at him. Through glassy eyes, Dioneo said, "You know there's no weapon made from mortal hands that can kill him."

Jai Ling broke from his grasp and curtly spat back, "You drink too much."

Dioneo said, "I say no to alcohol all the time. It just doesn't listen to me." He got up, but she pushed him, and Dioneo staggered back onto the bench.

Gathering the crossbow in one hand, Jai Ling said, "I'm following him. Then I'm checking with El Erreur to make sure no one's talked to him."

"The Piper's gone," Dioneo said.

"No thanks to you." Jai Ling stormed off.

I sit around a fire with Trippetta, the new boy Ricciardo, and Lisabetta. I can see another fire. Around it is the usual cluster—Jai Ling and Dioneo are speaking to El Erreur and Nefferi, with Mansa, Uwe, and Lora on the edge. I wanted to go over, but Trippetta asked me to play a game, then have some food, then a list of other things, and she finally held my arm and said I had to stay here. I can't hear what is being said.

Jai Ling is angry. She throws her arms up. Dioneo grabs her shoulders, gently, from behind, but she shakes him off. Jai Ling leaves, angrily, with Dioneo following. They pass us, and I hear Jai Ling shouting, "You're all idiots."

I miss my mother. Sometimes we would see the men arguing at Court, or out in a caravan, and there would be shouting. Mother would sing me beautiful lullabies.

Some children and a woman from the village come by and ask to play with us. Trippetta and I join hands and form a circle around a pole with them and begin to sing and move.

"Ring around the rosies
A pocket full of posies
Ashes, Ashes, we all fall!"

Most of the children and Trippetta fall to the ground laughing. I let go of the other children's hands and stand alone.

Once Jai Ling had turned around the wagon on the other side from Maddalena and the children, Dioneo grabbed Jai Ling's shoulders and spun her around. Jai Ling pirouetted on one foot and swung the back of her other foot, kicking Dioneo in the thigh. The acrobat fell back on his rear.

"Ouch!"

Jai Ling sneered. "I could have killed 'Errol' once and for all."

Dioneo dusted off his clothes and got up on one knee.

"Hang on, I'm still a little—never mind. No, you wouldn't have. I may be a little drunk, but I know if you shot him, he'd come back. Not right away, but in some form, he would. And then he'd come after us. And if you settle that temper of yours down, Miss Mystery, you will think straight and remember I'm right."

"So, you just let him walk away?"

Dioneo nodded. "Yes. And it was the right thing to do. You make no bargain with him, and he has no power over you. I'm a little surprised he asked me about the kids."

"They've become our obligation," Jai Ling said.

"Heaven help them."

Dioneo rubbed his backside.

Jai Ling walked into the dark. Dioneo stayed on his knees for a while, then groggily got to his feet. Mansa came beside him.

"I'm guessing she doesn't like our detour to Avignon."

Dioneo shook his head. "Brilliant deduction, my friend. No, she doesn't."

"You sure about that?" Mansa asked. "I mean, going to Avignon and all."

Dioneo gave him an askance look.

"Why is everyone so upset? We pulled those kids out of the river. They'd be dead but for us."

"Actually, it was me and Jai who pulled them out," Mansa corrected.

"Details, my friend. Look," the Piper said, "the pope is offering a king's ransom for those kids. A king's ransom. And it's not like they were running away or we're returning them to prison. Their caravan was heading to Avignon. Maddalena said so. They probably have family there. It makes all the sense in the world to return them."

"You're probably right," Mansa added. "Jai seems upset, though. Did anyone ask the kids if they have family there?"

"They say they have no one. And Jai thinks there's something strange about the reward, that the pope has a hidden purpose." Dioneo put his arm around Mansa's shoulders. "You know what would be strange? If paupers like us hesitated on a chance to make an honest fortune."

"I'm not so sure either, Dioneo. You don't see anything odd about that story of the flesh eaters wanting those kids? That is what the Piper said, right? And with so many children dying from the plague, he wants these children? Why?"

Dioneo laughed and staggered. "Woops. Yeah. He's a trickster and talks in half-truths. But what the hell, fleshers can't track people this far. If there's anything to what he said, if there are fleshers tracking us, which I don't believe is possible, and I don't believe in them having a leader, then all the more reason for us to get those kids to Avignon and be rid of them."

Dioneo raised his fingers in a pose mocking an approaching member of the undead.

An hour before daybreak, there was activity all over camp. Provisions were collected, a few last-minute exchanges were made, and goodbyes were had. Dioneo had managed to find a lady friend in the village late that night, whom Rowena had given the evil eye. One older couple from the troupe, a cobbler and his wife, had decided to stay in the village, and Cisti and Agnes had agreed to accept them. El Erreur was angry. It would hurt to lose a cobbler, but it was a well-established rule of the troupe. Anyone could leave whenever they wanted. Jai Ling had discussed with the couple that no one village was safe with the plague coming and perhaps even fleshers. She asked them to reconsider, but the pair were weary of the constant movement.

Dioneo and Jai Ling had quietly spoken to Cisti and Agnes about concerns over the fleshers and the plague, but they, and the cobbler and his wife, along with the other villagers, were too tired or too afraid to journey elsewhere. They would stay in place, in their homes, and trust in God's providence. Cisti and Agnes both thanked them for their thoughtfulness and offered them a parting gift—an anelace, double-edged, and made of pure silver, along with a protective leather scabbard. Jai Ling unsheathed the blade.

For those of you dear readers unfamiliar with the anelace, as a sword it was relatively short, but as a dagger it was fairly long, and usually with a double-edged blade tapering sharply to a point. While most were designed to pierce an object, some could slice something clean through. This one was made of silver.

"It's one of the sharpest blades I have ever seen," she said.

"It was personal property of Charlemagne," Cisti said. "See, here is the Carolingian Mark."

She pointed to a symbol carved into the handle.

"I'd say it is quite valuable," Dioneo observed.

Jai Ling handed it to the givers and said, "We can't take this for nothing."

Agnes pushed it back to her and said, "Neither my husband nor I are warriors. We prefer to give this to someone who will use it for good. We sense you are such a person."

They said their final goodbyes and left. As they walked back to the caravan, Dioneo said, "We can't take this for nothing? What's gotten into you? That will fetch us some real value. Silver! Charlemagne! One hundred dineens easily."

"All you think of is yourself," Jai Ling said while she hit Dioneo in the rib with the butt of the weapon. He grunted and stumbled forward.

Jai Ling kept walking.

"Question me again, and I'll use the other end."

After some more fond well-wishes, the caravan rolled out of Digne les Baines in the general direction of Mirabeau, a fortified village on the Durance River. The caravan's leaders knew the Durance fed into the Rhone River, and the Rhone River led to Avignon.

What I will tell you now, dear reader, is something the troupe members did not know, and that is, Elizabeth and her followers were only three days behind them. Digne les Bains would be spared, at least from the immediate threat of the walking undead. Alatiel, with her uncanny sense of scent, the sense which endeared her to the wolves, had detected where the caravan was. And Elizabeth, ever the planner, had guessed that the group was seeking quick access to Avignon. She, too had had heard of the pope's reward, from listening in taverns to travelers (before letting her followers feast on them, of course), and she knew what a draw the reward would be, and that the caravan would seek the quickest passage to Avignon. Elizabeth would not pursue down the road the troubadours' caravan had travelled. They would not pass Digne les Bains.

She had found a more direct route to intercept them.

The best way to Avignon was by water. And the best access to water in the region was at Mirabeau. And the quickest path to Mirabeau was a straight line through the woods. Elizabeth and her clan set forth through those woods.

[10]
ANCIENT HOUSES

THE CARAVAN PLOWED through three days of rain, slowly winding up the foothills of the Alps. These were not the Alps proper, not yet, but the topography grew rougher. Then they began a mild descent. On the fourth day, there was a break in the rain early in the morning. A new village appeared

The first thing Maddalena noticed as she saw Mirabeau was its castrum. The fortified Castle Gallic dominated the horizon and loomed over Mirabeau, sitting on a small rise and offering protection and a military position. Beneath it was a cluster of village buildings, separated from the castle by a moat. Like at Digne les Bains, people were working in the fields cutting down hay. Off to the right were the beginnings of the great Alpes Martimes, the highest mountains in western France. Behind all this, the great Durance River flowed peacefully.

MADDALENA

Riding beside Jai Ling, I sense something odd about this place. As we approach, the forest to our sides grows quiet.

"No birds," I say. "No squirrels or chipmunks. No rabbits hopping out of our way."

"It is not uncommon," Jai Ling replies. "They stay away from the loud noises of the city."

"But this is not a large city. More like a fortified castle that a village grew around. And there are people in the fields, but they move quietly. They cut hay quietly. They stack it in their wagons quietly. And they move their stacks quietly."

"Do not worry, little one," Jai Ling says, but I see her rub her fingers against her cheek. Just for a moment. She does that sometimes when she is uncertain. She becomes aware that I am noting it and then stops.

The people do not seem to notice us. Then a young girl smiles at me and comes up to my horse. Others now wave. The people change and approach us, shaking our hands and asking us questions in a variety of French tongues.

Mirabeau was like many large villages in France, more prosperous than most. As the great castle known as Gallic provided the easiest access to the riverbank, the occupants of the castle could charge fares for access to and conducting safe passage over the Durance, and the Durance led to Avignon, the seat of the Catholic Church and the home of the holy seer.

As they rode through the streets, Maddalena admired the town. With cobblestone streets extending in several directions and a clean central way, Mirabeau was actually luxurious. All the people in the streets seemed to be going somewhere. Dogs ran about playfully. Cats lie in windows. Pigs grunted. Yet it was surprisingly clean. The trenches down the center of each street were well maintained, and instead of shit and piss, a steady stream of cleansing water flowed through them.

Looking over the group, Jai Ling said, "Perhaps you are right,

Maddalena. There is something strange here. Everyone is too happy."

"I told you. What do you see?" Maddalena asked.

"These places are run by the Church. Or a military group. There is always a central power in charge. But no one has come out to greet us, or at least warn us off."

The wagons turned a corner and passed under a long, covered stone archway. Riders such as Jai Ling and Maddalena had to slide in behind the wagons or wait for them to pass and then follow. The archway turned to the right, and when they exited, they entered into a large courtyard, one that would serve as a central marketplace. Merchants in booths sold flowers, food, drink, and clothes. Well-dressed women strolled along and picked items of interest.

As the wagons rolled into an open area in front of the imposing round towers of the gatehouses to the main castle, Dioneo brought his horse forward and said, "People of Mirabeau, we are the greatest acrobats, magicians, and troubadours in all of Europe. We've come to beautiful Mirabeau to perform as your humble servants."

"Then you are welcome," came a voice from away.

A tall, gaunt man, not unlike El Erreur but thinner, spoke to them. Clad in a long brown robe trailing to his feet, belted at the waist, and a wide-brimmed hat, he had very clear skin, almost but not quite pale. He stood on the drawbridge, which crossed the moat surrounding half of Castle Gallic.

Maddalena whispered to Jai Ling, "Vampire?"

Jai Ling stared intently at the man, making his way to the front wagon where El Erreur was standing.

"No—I don't think so. Odd, yes, but not a vampire. Of course, there are ways to check. Come with me."

They rode back to get Lisabetta and Trippetta. People from the village were surrounding the wagons, not in a threatening way but with curiosity. Jai Ling scrambled by them and onto one of the middle wagons, gathered a few items and trinkets, including a hand-held cracked mirror.

"That's broken," Maddalena said.

"It is indeed," Jai Ling said. "And it will be some more. Here, Lisabetta, take Maddalena's hand and let's go trading."

Lisabetta held Maddalena's hand, and it seemed to Maddalena that, although she did not smile, Lisabetta's face brightened. Trippetta held a small basket of goods, and Jai Ling placed the broken mirror into it. With Jai Ling leading them, the four women rushed into the growing crowd that clustered around the wagons.

"Trade? Trade?" Jai Ling called out. Trippetta and Maddalena began to echo her, while Lisabetta wandered with them.

With that, the crowd grew. People picked up pieces of jewelry, lace, bows, and other trinkets. Others from the caravan came out to sell their trinkets. Still others sold and bartered from the wagons. Rowena was adorned with necklaces composed of glittering stones. Jai Ling, Maddalena, Trippetta, and Lisabetta worked their way to the front, where Nefferi and El Erreur were talking with the tall, robed man. Dioneo had seen what Jai Ling was doing while he and Ricciardo were also walking among the crowd, shaking hands and offering trinkets.

"Lovely to see you."

"Your town is so lovely."

"What a pretty dress."

Maddalena and Lisabetta were being guided to the front when they walked by the robed man, who had come up to the group.

An elderly woman in a colorful headdress said to Maddalena, "What a nice young girl you are. You are a treasure."

The woman stroked Maddalena's face. Maddalena flinched.

"Oh, I am sorry, I meant no harm."

Maddalena smiled and said, "No harm at all. Thank you. Would you like anything here?"

They traded a small wood carving for a red silk ribbon. It was not an even trade, but it did not matter. Maddalena had been told that the key was to establish a good feeling in the town so they would be welcome. She allowed the woman to tie the ribbon in her hair, giving Maddalena a long ponytail.

Trippetta waltzed along, crying out, "Toys? Flutes? Tambourines?" Young children came up to her, and she passed out her wares.

Maddalena noted how her companion could appear so adult-like at times, such as when she danced, or now, when she was also performing, in a sense. But she was childlike among those she felt comfortable with. Maddalena found herself smiling at the thought of how odd Trippetta and Uwe were, and yet they were perfect for each other.

Suddenly, Trippetta stumbled into Lisabetta (and while Trippetta was many things, clumsy was not one of them), and Lisabetta spilled some of her basket, including the cracked hand mirror, which broke in several more pieces.

"Never worry, never worry," Jai Ling said, swooping down to pick up the items. As she did, she grabbed shattered mirror pieces and directed them over her shoulder at the robed man who was just behind them. His image, speaking to Nefferi and El Erreur, was reflected in the broken glass. Jai Ling picked up other pieces of the mirror and furtively panned it around—everyone cast a reflection.

The elderly woman with the fine headdress stooped next to Lisabetta, gently resting her hand on Lisabetta's shoulder, and picked up some items and put them in the basket.

Lisabetta shifted her shoulder from the woman and cried, "Ehhhh!"

"The poor girl," the woman said. Looking at Jai Ling, who was staring at the woman, she says, "I'm sorry, I meant no harm. I seem to be bothering your girls."

Jai Ling stared at the woman for a few seconds, evaluating her, then said, "It's all right. She's just a little nervous in crowds."

The elderly woman nodded and said, "Of course. I apologize

again." Retreating into the crowd, she added, "Welcome to Mirabeau."

Jai Ling watched the woman disappear into the people. Then she lost her. She didn't sense anything. And yet—

Her train of thought was broken when she saw Lisabetta being buffeted by the crowd.

"Come here, girls," Jai Ling said, holding up a mirror and gathering Maddalena, Lisabetta, and Trippetta about her. They were all reflected, smiling, in the mirror.

Jai Ling said, "There we are—I think we four should form a new act."

France was scattered with communes like Mirabeau—ones that had grown into sometimes sizeable villages, built around a reinforced castle originally made by some land baron. Through a papal bull, the Church often commandeered control of these fortresses, and then the Church controlled the town. In this case, the fortress, Castle Gallic, was especially impressive, with three baileys leading up to the fortified keep. And, of course, good access to the Durance River was priceless.

The man who had greeted them in the field was Roderigo. He told them Mirabeau had been relatively untouched by the plague, and the Church held a solid position here. Roderigo was not an ordained man, but he had the blessing of the Church to maintain the castle as a monastery, and he had under his command a small but well-armed complement of papal guards, roughly forty or so strong—quite an impressive force outside of a major city. The reason for this was unspoken but obvious—this was a great trade route.

"Or it was at one time," Roderigo said, walking along with Nefferi and El Erreur, with Jai Ling and Dioneo trailing them.

They were heading from the central village square towards the gatehouses of the castle.

"Today we do not have so many visitors," Roderigo said.

"But what of pilgrims from southern France and Italy?" El Erreur asked in his deep voice. "Surely there must be many who travel this way?"

Roderigo shook his head and said, "Before, yes, this was a busy hub. You can witness the prosperity of the past. But the great mortality has struck many villages in Italy and France. We here have been relatively fortunate. But also, the Florentines, the Venetians, the Mantuans, they do not care so much for a papacy in Avignon that is removed from their beloved Rome. Many see Pope Clement as nothing more than a French puppet. We, of course, remain faithful. And we welcome devout pilgrims such as yourself. You did say you were travelling to Avignon?"

Nefferi answered, "Yes, we are as pious and devout as any traveler in this world. Indeed, we are journeying there for a command performance. But we always seek to barter along the way. Is Mirabeau prepared to pay for the greatest show it has ever seen?"

Roderigo paused for a moment, then said, "It has been some time since our people were feted by any entertainers. Yes, I believe we can make an agreement."

Walking behind the others, leading their horses through the village, Dioneo and Jai Ling marveled at Castle Gallic.

"It's odd," Ja Ling noted as they passed into the lower bailey, "how wide this castle is."

"The Durance is right behind it. They're protecting as much of the river as they can. It's hard to attack a castle from the river. Almost impossible."

The lower bailey held a number of small houses on its edges, as well as stables and places for livestock. This was a small self-contained village.

"This must be where some of the villagers stay at night," Dioneo said.

"I guess it keeps the wolves at bay," Jai Ling mused.

They continued walking upward and passed through a gateway to the middle bailey.

The middle bailey was smaller and had more barns and stables for animals, as well as what looked like barracks for troops and a few other apartments. Walking along, Dioneo felt a pang of discomfort. He turned to his left and saw a frail, aged man with a long white beard and hair sitting on the ground. The man clutched a walking staff and was staring at Dioneo. It took Dioneo several seconds to realize the man had no legs.

"Poor bastard," Dioneo said, and Jai Ling turned to see the man.

"At least they let them stay here," she said.

The man continued to gaze at them.

Going forward, Dioneo and Jai Ling passed a gateway leading into yet a third upper bailey. As they did, they walked underneath a sharp portcullis, suspended over the entrance.

"That looks heavy," Dioneo observed.

This third bailey had stores of food on the sides. At the far end was a great keep, the largest structure in the fortification, towering with two arsenal towers on the back end.

"Look at the grain silos," Dioneo whispered. "They keep the good stuff close to them."

"And they keep the riff raff out in the outer ring of the castle. Makes sense to me."

They proceeded into Roderigo's study within the keep.

Roderigo was sitting at his desk in a well-appointed studio cut into stone walls, set just outside the main dining hall. Papal guards stood at the entranceways, holding their halberds upright. Roderigo lectured about the history of Mirabeau. El Erreur and Nefferi sat with Roderigo, while Jai Ling and Dioneo wandered through the cavernous great hall. Mirabeau did have a wealth of monetary and other treasures, including food, goods, clothes, and materials. Horses, goats, hens, even pigs. Plus fresh water. A large well existed, and they had built three access points to it, one in each bailey. An agreement for the troupe to perform in exchange for food and coins to buy passage down the river was struck quickly, and it was more than adequate. Roderigo said it was worth paying to bring joy to the people.

"I see it in their faces," he said. "For the most part, God has been kind to Mirabeau, and the plague has spared us. But many of the people of Mirabeau are educated. They have seen travelers come through here over many years. They see what is happening around them now."

"You have been fortunate, in regard to the plague," El Erreur said.

"No doubt due to your piety to God," Nefferi chimed in.

"We are, but we think we are also practical," Roderigo said. "At night, everyone comes into this castle. Everyone. We let no one stay outside the walls. And once the drawbridge is raised, we are sealed in, and guards patrol the castle watchtowers all night. We have found this very practical. You too must stay here in Castle Gallic tonight, if you wish to stay at all."

Nefferi gave a worried glance to El Erreur.

"Of course," Rodergio said, staring directly at El Erreur, "You are not confined here during the day. You are more than free to leave, if you wish. But it is late."

El Erreur stared back, then said, "We will stay tonight and perform the next evening."

Roderigo smiled. "I think you will find our accommodations

more than pleasant. If you have been on the road for so long, you may even decide you wish to stay for a while."

Jai Ling wandered alone through the great hall. It was divided into three spacious chambers. Ornate mahogany partitions rose from the floor to the ceiling. Together, the three large compartments ran the entire width of the keep. She found herself in the room farthest from Roderigo's study, on the western side of the castle. There were two guards in here, but otherwise it was empty. She kicked the colored tiles around the floor.

"Solid marble," she thought. "Expensive."

Long Venetian redwood tables and benches stretched across the hall, sitting on animal fur rugs. Shields and weapons adorned the walls. There were pole weapons—bec de faucons, haches, halberds, and guisarmes. Shields with various crests emblazoned on them. Plus smaller hand weapons—maces, flails, war hammers, and swords. Jai Ling paused to admire a flail, a chain weapon with a large spiked ball attached, and touched the end of a spike.

"Ouch," she said. "They must throw some great parties around here."

On the north wall built into the middle was a great hearth, and to the right and left were large French doors, each with double-paned windows, which overlooked the rear of the castle. Jai Ling was drawn to one such large window, the one farthest to the right of the hearth. The window opened to a small veranda. She rested her hands on a marble balcony, overlooking the rear of the castle.

Several stories below was a crescent-shaped sandy area. Two empty barges lay unattended on the shore. A bulkhead built up with rock and filled in with earth jutted into the river. A cog, a flat-bottomed single-masted boat with a square rig, was moored at the end of this bulkhead. Beyond that stretched a wide plateau through which the Durance River flowed. To her left, on the western side, was a siege engine tower, very tall, and to her right was an arsenal tower. Walls extended from both towers to the water, but the siege tower stood atop a waterfall. Interesting—the moat was designed at an angle that allowed the water to flow through it, then topple over the falls. She wondered if it had been built that way or if it was a natural formation.

For a few moments, Jai Ling just watched the water bubble on —swiftly, but navigable. She recalled the voice of her father—at least, the man she knew as her father. "Flow like water, move like air—" a voice she had almost forgotten.

Unconsciously, she mouthed the words.

"Flow like water, move like air."

"Much on your mind?" Dioneo asked, bounding beside her.

"No. Just the reverse. I'm not thinking about anything. I'm just... emptying my head. Pouring it out in the river."

"If you keep that up, you'll be like me. Empty-headed." He nudged her with his elbow and said, "Of course, I'm not a complete idiot. Parts of me are still missing."

"And you disguise it so well."

Dioneo stood by for several more moments, then said, "The Durance."

"The Durance," Jai Ling repeated

They stared at the moving water for a while.

Dioneo drew a breath as if to say something else, but stopped.

Jai Ling said, "The waterfall is pretty."

"It is," Dioneo said.

After a few more moments, Dioneo said, "I'll see you later."

Jai Ling caught him by the arm. "Look at the keep's walls. They stretch from here all the way down to the shore on both sides."

"You are correct, dear," answered a voice from behind. "Your name is Jai Ling?"

Jai Ling and Dioneo turned to a striking woman, perhaps their age, perhaps a little older, with alabaster white skin and long flowing white hair. Clean, unblemished skin. And dressed in a tight-fitting white gown. The only thing breaking the effect was a black belt buckle, a faint tint of flesh color in the face, and the slightest pink in her lips.

"Yes, Jai Ling. And this is Dioneo."

The woman in white gave them a ceremonious bow, and Dioneo awkwardly did the same.

Rising, the woman said, "Dioneo—yes, I've heard of you. You're entertainers, and you are an—acrobat?"

"Yes, that is true," he answered. "And you are—"

"I am Lady Madeline," she replied. "I am Roderigo's wife."

Lady Madeline stood next to them on the balcony.

"You enjoy the view?" she asked.

"Yes," Jai Ling said. "But we were just noticing the walls."

"Yes, those were built years ago, long before Roderigo and I arrived. The builders knew the value of a landing. Much of the shore along the river is rocky. The waters flow from high in the Alps and carry rock with them. The flow varies greatly, so there are shallow spots and then deep pits throughout. And the river is cluttered with wrecks."

Lady Madeline walked between them and gestured to the river. "The area you are looking at is the plateau of Saint-Sepulcher. We keep this area clear, so it's the best place from here to Avignon to gain water access."

"So with the walls, you provide safe entry to the river," Dioneo commented.

"Our commune has prospered because of it," the woman said. "Until recently. Travel has slowed much this year. The great pestilence covers the land. But like the black death, these times will pass."

Jai Ling gazed at the smooth water.

"It is so calming," she said.

Lady Madeline smiled.

"This time of year, storms can rise quickly. Water builds up in the Alps. This gives us awful floods. I have seen the water cover the entire landing, right up to the keep."

Dioneo quipped, "Good thing I know how to swim."

Lady Madeline laughed. "Have no fear, Dioneo, we are quite safe in Castle Gallic."

"The waterfall," Jai Ling asked. "I've never seen a moat incorporate a waterfall."

"It keeps the water flowing," Lady Madeline said. "An ingenious design from the castle builders many years ago. I doubt we could build it today."

The trio walked back into the dining hall. Jai Ling said, "I noticed you have many different weapons and shields in here."

Lady Madeline gestured to the walls. "Yes, gifts and mementos from travelers who have passed through. We believe some parts of our collection are over two hundred years old."

They saw Roderigo, along with Nefferi and El Erreur, standing in the first chamber, admiring a fresco painting over the immense fireplace built into the wall. Lady Madeline led Jai Ling and Dioneo to them.

"My husband. A humble man, but he is proud of Castle Gallic," Lady Madeline said. "His family has been here for many generations. Of course, the Church owns it, but his family has been the caretakers here forever."

Dioneo and Jai Ling stood beside Nefferi and El Erreur while they all admired the painting on the wall. It was of a noble woman, seated within this room in front of the hearth, her hands folded, a pleasant countenance with the slightest hint of a smile.

"It's you, Lady Madeline," Jai Ling said.

"No, but there is a resemblance," Roderigo said. "The last duchess of Castle Gallic. Before it was taken by the Church. Lady de Medici. She was the second wife of my great-grandfather, Alfonso. They say the artist, Fra Pandolf, spent hours upon hours in here with the duchess, locking every entranceway. Supposedly, it took months to complete."

As the others marveled at the painting, Jai Ling felt light-headed. The figure seemed so lifelike. The countenance had an earnest gaze. Unconsciously, Jai Ling started to reach out to touch the painting.

"Did the face just glance at me?"

The room spun around her, and she stumbled, but Dioneo caught her shoulder.

"Easy there."

"Are you all right, dear?" Lady Madeline asked.

"No," Jai Ling said, shaking her head. "It is so real-looking. I've never seen such a painting—no—wait, I seem to recall something. Who was the artist?"

"Who cares?" Dioneo said. "You need some rest, my dear."

Lady Madeline said, "It is easy to slip on the marble; it is very smooth. We polish it once a week, and it retains its sheen."

Jai Ling rubbed her forehead, then steadied herself. Now angry at what had happened, she snapped, "I'm fine."

In the Duchess's face, she noticed an earnest glance and the faintest trace of a smile.

"I'm sorry," Roderigo said. "I should have warned you all. There is an illusion in the painting. You see, standing where we are, well—walk slowly to your left and focus on the eyes."

Dioneo took Jai Ling aside, but as he did so, he looked up, as did the others.

"The eyes follow you," Nefferi said.

"What magic is this?" El Erreur asked.

"No magic," Roderigo said. "Just the talent of the painter. Fra Pandolf was a skilled craftsman, like many who have passed through Castle Gallic. The best artists always leave a little of themselves in their paintings. But now you all must rest and prepare to spend the night. You will entertain us tomorrow night. Feel free to explore our home. For our part, my wife and I shall have a great feast prepared for our guests."

Shortly thereafter, Jai Ling and Dioneo were walking through the hallways.

"Are you okay?" Dioneo asked.

"I think so," Jai Ling replied. "Back there, the painting startled me." Then, looking at the walls, she added, "Everywhere. So many weapons."

"Most look like they need a little polishing," Dioneo quipped. "Unlike the floor! By the way, you noticed the cog boat and the barges on the shore by the river?"

"Caught my eye," she said. "Enough room for all of us?"

"Maybe. Certainly with the barges. A few of us could take the cog and sail right down to Avignon."

Jai Ling asked, "And then what? Just give the kids to the pope? What do you think he wants them for anyway?"

Dioneo threw his arms out and said, "What do we care? Look, my dearest, according to the Piper, the fleshers want her. He speaks in riddles, but if what he said is true, we can get that ransom they paid for old King Richard."

Jai Ling said flatly, "Don't call me dearest."

They walked further in silence.

Dioneo said. "You're too attached to that girl."

Jai Ling snapped back, "What are you attached to Dioneo?"

Dioneo laughed. "Money. Surviving. What else matters? We haven't much of a life."

They walked further in silence and stopped in front of a triptych, a three-paneled painting.

"I've seen paintings like this before," Jai Ling commented. "What do you see, Dioneo?"

Dioneo paused, stepped back, rubbed his chin, and said, "Another day in the life of another town. Wonderful."

"Ahh, but look more closely, Dioneo. Take a few moments."

Upon closer inspection, Dioneo noted that the "normal" town

contained many abnormal and disturbing images. A dog is eating a woman's body. A man is being sawed in half. Another man being sodomized by a demon. Various other abominations, all subtly hidden in the painting.

"Well, their art is certainly interesting," Dioneo said.

"Yes," Jai Ling commented. "On the surface, everything looks so normal. But when you look closely, it is not what it seems at all."

Elizabeth leaned against a white fir, studying the castle. It was warm today, and she'd already pushed them to walk several hours in the morning through the forest. The problem was simple—the castle was fortified. Once inside, if they got inside, the guards could be overwhelmed. But how to get her group to navigate through the town? How to get through the walls? The town was built close to the walls of the castle, so buildings offered cover (if her idiots didn't give themselves away). But the drawbridge? And how to get the others? Perhaps they could storm the castle, but the bridge would be raised. And water—her followers could hardly swim. Elizabeth thought of waiting to see if the caravan left the castle, but they could easily take a boat out the back and onto the river. No, she couldn't wait. She remembered being so close to Maddalena back at the arena. Elizabeth was too close now to let the children get away.

She'd pushed her group hard the past two nights, perhaps too hard. They looked tired. Yes, they'd found one small group of about forty pilgrims, and that had led to some eating, but they were now over two hundred strong, and the bodies of forty pilgrims did not feed enough (only three of the pilgrims had survived long enough to join their ranks). Right now, she had them rest. They'd wilt in the sun if they came now, and the fields leading up to the village provided no cover. They would be seen, and the gate raised. No, she'd have to think of something else.

Alatiel crept next to her weakly. She still wouldn't kill to eat, and Elizabeth had made sure Alatiel was fed by Elizabeth's own kills. Janosz was also nearby, along with Nicola, Elizabeth's former lady in waiting, and Giancarlo, the former captain of Elizabeth's personal guard, though her memory was a bit hazy on that.

"What to do, Alatiel. What to do?"

She heard, faintly, off in the woods, a familiar voice calling to her.

"Perhaps I could be of some assistance. But please, come alone."

A grin spread across Elizabeth's face.

She turned to the others.

"Janosz, take Alatiel, and both of you look at the castle. Tell me about its structure. I have to go pay a piper for some information. But come back quickly."

Off Elizabeth went.

She returned within the hour.

"Janosz," Elizabeth called aloud. Her lieutenant made his way to her. "Do we still have the barrel in the wagon with the mother's things?"

Janosz nodded.

"Then let's get over there. I have an idea. But I'll need your help, Alatiel."

The group made their way back through the forest. Fleshers moaned and groaned, leaning against trees or lying on the ground. During the last two days of rain, they'd been able to move forward under the heavy clouds, but with this sun, they were listless.

Elizabeth secretly wondered how far she could control them as the lust for flesh became overpowering. She didn't feel confident. When they'd attacked the pilgrims two days ago, she felt them pulling from her. But if she could feed them—that might change things.

Elizabeth asked, "Janosz, Alatiel, did you two find what I asked?"

"Yes," Janosz replied slowly. "There appears to be one near the wall to the sea."

"Which wall?" Elizabeth asked.

Janosz was silent.

"Which wall?" Elizabeth asked again.

"I—cannot—"

"Alatiel, the side where the sun rises, or where the sun falls?"

"Where it rises."

Elizabeth nodded. "Very good. The east side. That's where I will be tonight," she said. "Janosz, be sure you are too."

Janosz slowly nodded.

Elizabeth glanced at Alatiel.

"Alatiel stays at the back of the group until we have opened the gate. And remember—you have more power than you realize."

Nearby stood another flesher, the muscular Giancarlo. It was true, in another life, he had been the captain of Elizabeth's personal guard, who eventually betrayed her. When she had turned him, it was with a ferocious single bite, spurred by regret and anger, but mostly anger. Giancarlo's mind was wiped out, but he still followed her out of some *instinct* that was akin to obedience.

"Giancarlo, you are so hard to read because there is so little to read. But you bring Alatiel in once the gates are secure. Janosz, Nicola goes in with you."

Elizabeth stroked Nicola's hair, saying, "I need you tonight, but I need you to be careful."

The main wagon was surrounded by the most physically fit members of her tribe. Strange how the strongest were the most responsive to her. They had a vague understanding not to allow anyone other than Elizabeth or someone with her to get to the wagon. She climbed in the back, Alatiel in tow. They climbed over clutter until they reached a barrel. Elizabeth took an iron bar and pried the top off. It was filled with a brine-like concoction the sisters had given her.

"Those damn three hags never speak clearly," Elizabeth said. "They love chaos. And so they love us, Alatiel, as we are instruments of chaos. No?"

Elizabeth paused and studied Alatiel's face.

She still hasn't accepted who and what we are.

"Never mind," Elizabeth said, taking out a small compact containing pinkish flesh-colored powder. Wetting her fingers by dipping them into the barrel, she worked the powder into a thin paste and then a lotion, which she rubbed over her face. Alatiel sat cross-legged before her.

"If it looks right, we have a nice warm flesh tone. You need to tell me when it looks right," Elizabeth said. "We don't do well with mirrors."

Alatiel silently watched Elizabeth spread the lotion over her face and arms

Elizabeth then took a small vial of rouge and painted her lips lightly.

"Not too much color," she said. She smacked them together, then blotted them with a soft tissue.

When done, she smiled at Alatiel.

"So how do I look?"

"You are very beautiful."

Elizabeth continued to rub her ears with the lotion.

"You know, you remind me of Nicola before—"

Elizabeth noted Alatiel's sad face.

"But that's no reason I cannot make the party at Mirabeau tonight."

"What party?"

"Oh, a motley fool let me know. He's not like us, but he and I can be mutually beneficial to each other." She began vigorously rubbing her arms and legs with the liquid. After a minute of this, she put a little under her tunic. "It spreads through the body, so you don't have to cover everything," she said, "but you need to get a lot on, especially the parts that can be seen."

Dioneo and Jai Ling walked their horses across the drawbridge, passing over the water moat—a truly deep one, enough to slow down an attacker. After going through the great gatehouse of Castle Gallic, they were in the lower bailey. The walls were high and of thick granite. Up close, they could observe a few small squints and arrow slits, but overall, the fortress looked impregnable.

The land continued to rise as they approached a gateway to the middle bailey. Passing under arcading, Dioneo marveled at the thick-cut stones.

"This thing is well built," he said. "But I've another question for you, dear."

"Don't call me dear."

"Fine, my love," Dioneo continued, "but what do you think of our good hosts?"

"On the creepy side. Not sure who is more so, Roderigo or his wife."

"But you don't sense vampirism?"

Jai Ling shook her head. "No, not that. They're odd, no doubt. And I'm not sure I like coming in here. But I don't see anything we can't handle."

Continuing on, they passed a third gateway into the upper bailey before the main keep. Ricciardo, pulling a pair of pack mules, was sweating profusely. Bartolome was beside him, also holding a rope around the same animals.

Ricciardo came up to them.

"I am so tired, Dioneo."

Dioneo clasped his shoulder. "You're doing hard work. It's good for you, my boy. Bartolome, have you pulled that with Ricciardo all through the town?"

Bartolome, looking flushed, nodded.

"Well, take this and relax for a little while," Dioneo said, handing him a glob of rock candy and taking the rope. Bartolome's face widened.

"Thank you very much!"

He ran to a stone bench.

"That was kind of you, Dioneo," Ricciardo said.

"Get those animals in there," Dioneo said, handing him the rope he'd taken from Bartolome.

"But Dioneo—I wanted to talk to you about the show. When Jai Ling shoots the arrow—I—"

Jai Ling glared at him.

"You have a problem with my aim, Ricciardo?"

"No no no. But it is just that—I—"

"Listen, my boy," Dioneo said. "You are part of the greatest pack of troubadours in all of the Western world."

"And," Jai Ling added, "when you complain, you move from the 'best' column to the 'whiner's' column." She slid her bow out of her horse's side bag and tapped it against Ricciardo's chest.

"Earn your keep."

Ricciardo, with a flummoxed expression, returned to pulling the mules.

After Ricciardo got out of their hearing, Jai Ling asked, "When do you want to stop torturing him?"

Laughing gently, Dioneo answered, "When it stops being fun." He added, "You won't hit him with an arrow, right?"

Jai Ling shrugged. "I haven't yet."

Uwe sat on one of the barges parked on the white sands of the plateau of Saint-Sepulcher. He held three balls in his hands and began to toss them. He had a fourth ball in his pocket that he tried to reach for and enter into the mix, but he dropped them all.

He heard a familiar laugh behind him, and a voice say, "That not toooo bad."

Uwe turned around to see Maddalena and Trippetta walking on the beach. Trippetta said, "I love white sand!" and did a cartwheel into Uwe. He caught her legs in the air, and they both laughed.

"I've never seen you laughing, Uwe," Maddalena said, surprising herself as much as him.

"I used to laugh much," Uwe said. "I was a jester. I played many jests."

"Oh yes," Trippetta added, "Uwe is so good with jests. Maddalena, I tell you, when Uwe dressed up a king and his court as outrangs? It is quite a story."

The laughter left Uwe's face, and he mumbled, "Maddalena does not want to hear such stories now."

Trippetta gave Uwe a hug and ran to Maddalena.

Maddalena quietly said, "You told me that story."

"Oh," Trippetta said. "Then let us cool our feet in the river."

And the three of them did just that.

"You look wonderful," Alatiel said aloud.

Elizabeth eyed her carefully.

"I can't read your mind, but I can read all of your face. What's wrong?"

Alatiel looked away.

Elizabeth and Alatiel began communicating telepathically again.

Come now, Elizabeth thought, *you're the only one I can ask. What is it?*

"There's something—it is hard to say," Alatiel responded. "Your skin looks right, but—I think you can get by most of them. But the oriental woman, when I was hiding from her in a corner of a manor house, passed by me. I was able to shield myself by keeping my body small and my thoughts to myself. But she senses things.

Not like we do, but if you go in and act with them, she will sense you. I know it."

Elizabeth smiled at Alatiel.

"That would be Jai Ling. You only met her once—albeit briefly—and you know about her. Your perceptive powers are growing, Alatiel. That is a good thing. And Jai Ling is someone to be wary of. But I will be prepared for her. I've one more thing to help us."

Elizabeth produced a thin stiletto and went to the largest wine barrel, carefully braced on the wagon, and popped the top off. Alatiel looked inside at a thin greenish liquid—something she'd seen before at the seashore, though she could not remember much more. She looked down at a naked woman's body submerged in the liquid. The body seemed in repose—resting, asleep, with the legs pulled up and the arms wrapped around the knees—but it was lifeless. Still, Alatiel felt a stirring of hunger.

"This is the last part," Elizabeth explained. "The sisters said this would help. You just confirmed it for me, as no one else here could. I need more than makeup."

Elizabeth reached in and pulled out the woman's right arm. Gently, she made a small puncture into the veins at the wrist. Blood began to ooze out of the cut. Elizabeth quickly sucked down the blood for several moments. Then just as quickly, she put the arm back in the barrel and replaced the cover. She saw Alatiel's growing hunger.

"You can't have her—not yet. It would be too much for—"

Elizabeth cut off and doubled over, retching over the side of the wagon onto some of her slumbering guards, who remained motionless. Clutching her middle, Elizabeth crawled out of the wagon onto the ground and vomited more.

"Oh my," Maddalena said, walking into an opulent bedroom. A beautiful double bed with down pillows and comforters dominated the room, but there were other couches and other chairs to recline in. Lady Madeline and Roderigo had offered a few select rooms to the troupe members, and this one was allotted to the ladies if they desired it.

"Do you still want to stay in the wagons tonight?" Jai Ling asked.

Trippetta ran by Jai Ling and did a backward flip into the bedding.

"WHEEEEE," she said. "This is great. Maddalena, we stay here tonight."

"Trippetta, you and Maddalena can share that bed," Jai Ling said.

Lora walked in with one of her bags and, surveying the quarters, commented, "I haven't seen this luxury since Florence."

Jai Ling was going to say those were the days, but she held back. Looking around her, she said, "No other doors—just one, and that window over there."

Lora looked out the window. "Well, we're above an open flat. There's a few shacks on the sides, and beyond that is the river. A small boat docked there. We're okay here. We can throw a rope down if we need it."

Ricciardo carried in some more bags, with Lisabetta trailing him, carrying one satchel. Jai Ling told them to put the bags down by the bed. Then she went to Maddalena and said, "We'll be here tonight. All us girls will be on this floor."

"Rowena too?" Lora asked while unpacking her bag,

"I have no idea where Rowena will be," Jai Ling answered.

Ricciardo asked if he and Lisabetta could take a short walk together.

Jai Ling was about to gently admonish him, but she noticed that Ricciardo looked particularly worn. He was an attractive boy, olive-skinned and black-haired, but a little slender. You could tell he wasn't used to living off the land the way the rest of them did.

Poor Lisabetta stood next to him, staring off to the side, rocking ever so slightly and humming to herself.

Jai Ling asked Lisabetta, "Do you want to go for a walk with Ricciardo?"

Lisabetta ignored her.

Ricciardo took her hand, and Jai Ling saw no protest in Lisabetta's face.

Lisabetta uttered "Eh eh." Ricciardo began to walk out, and Lisabetta walked with him.

"Take care of her," Jai Ling called. "But don't forget. Our hosts are preparing a meal for us tonight. I expect to see a feast."

Dioneo stood on the top of the outer castle wall, looking down through a crenel at the villagers crossing the drawbridge. Uwe stood next to him.

"Can you even see over the wall?" Dioneo asked.

Uwe grunted and pulled himself up with his massive arms to peer through the crenel.

"Everyone coming," he uttered.

"Yeah," Dioneo said. "Just out of curiosity, but doesn't it seem to you that there are a lot more people coming in than there are in Mirabeau?"

Uwe looked puzzled, then said, "They out in fields. Out of town. Come in for night."

"I suppose, you're right," Dioneo said. "Hey, where's Trippy?"

"Playing with Maddalena. They all moving into their rooms for tonight."

A bell from inside the castle began to ring.

"Ahh, Vespers," Dioneo said. "I guess it's time. Let's go."

The acrobat and the dwarf made their way down a tower tunnel and emerged at the east end of the lower bailey, running into Ricciardo and Lisabetta. Bartolome trailed behind them.

"You've made a new friend," Dioneo said to Ricciardo as the bell rang its sixth and last clang. Noticing Bartolome, he added, "Actually, two. And you and Lisabetta actually look good with each other."

Ricciardo blushed, and Dioneo thought—did Lisabetta react? No, it was his mistake.

Or was it?

A crowd milled throughout the bailey.

"There she is," came a voice from the side. It was the woman with the fancy headdress who had touched Lisabetta before. Lisabetta stopped and would not move to her.

"She doesn't seem to like me," the woman said.

Dioneo watched Lisabetta and the woman out the corner of his eyes. The girl—what did she know? She was simple in the head. Still…

Dioneo felt a hand hold his. He flinched, broke the grip, and grabbed an arm before realizing he was dealing with an elderly man.

"Oh. Sorry, friend," Dioneo said, releasing his grip and patting the man on the shoulder.

"No, my apologies," the man said. "My name is Bruno. This is my wife Beatrice." He touched the well-dressed woman, who bowed. Then, gesturing behind him, he pointed to two younger people, also nicely dressed, closer in age to Lisabetta and Ricciardo.

"This is my nephew, Simon, and my niece, Teodoro." The two stepped forward, smiling.

Dioneo introduced each of his party, and greetings were exchanged by all except Lisabetta. Ricciardo shook Teodoro's hand and gently guided Lisabetta forward. She squealed and pulled her arm away. "Please excuse her; she's been through much," Ricciardo said. "She has been badly treated for a long time."

"The poor dear," Beatrice said. "We've all experienced such

suffering. Simon and Teodoro came here from a village in Mantua, which was nearly wiped out by the plague."

"That is far, Mantua," Uwe said.

"It is," Teodoro said, "but the world is not a charitable place right now. You go where you have relatives willing to take you."

Beatrice nodded. "The world has grown mad. Mirabeau is an island of sanity in a sea of insanity."

"At least for the most part," Bruno said, pointing to the middle of the bailey.

Dioneo noticed that the people—the villagers—had retreated to the edges of the square, leaving a great open space in the center. From out of the gatehouse there came a procession of people, walking two by two, each dressed in white or pale-colored robes. Each one's face was covered with a cowl, and they entered the courtyard slowly. At the front of the pack, three men carried great purple banners with gold trim and a cross etched in the middle. The participants were chanting a prayer in Latin. The procession passed through the gateway and proceeded to form a square in the middle of the common.

One robed figure in the middle of the pack slipped off and ran into the castle, towards where the horses, boars, and hens were kept. Dioneo caught her fleeing form.

"There goes one," Dioneo said.

"One what?" Ricciardo asked.

Bruno answered him. "Have you not seen flagellants enter in procession? It is not unheard of for a participant to change his or her mind at this point."

As this flagellant ran by a wagon where Rowena was sitting, her hood fell back. She caught Rowena's eye. A red-haired woman, shielding her face behind her hands. Rowena found it odd how the woman was hiding her face. For a moment, their eyes met, but the woman ran on, and Rowena's attention was drawn back to the square.

The would-be flagellant ran around some buildings to the cool of the horse stables and other animal pens. The late afternoon sun was strong, and though low in the sky, it beat down on this section of the castle, disorienting the woman. Seeing a pen with a covered stable stall in the back, she held up her dress and ran through the mud towards it, pausing at the gate.

While there were several animals around, the street was empty of people. Most of the guards had gone out to watch the flagellants, but then one named Tomas, brandishing a sharp glaive, stopped, placed a hand on her shoulder, and asked her where she was going. The woman spun around much more quickly than Tomas expected and met Tomas eye to eye, inches from his face. Tomas stared into a pair of fiery eyes for a moment—and then dropped dead.

Elizabeth heaved a deep breath, tired, then reached down to drag the body. She pulled Tomas through the mud of a pigsty and into the stable, then covered the body with loose straw. Inside, she felt the pangs to eat. The special blood she drank from Maddalena's mother enhanced and enlivened her. The power of just a sip from the preserved body was stunning. It made her feel more alive than she had since—well, in a long time. She felt she could heal herself. Still, the guard's body was right there.

She fought back her urges. The moment she ate flesh, her glow would be gone, and she could be detected. Plus, her makeup had to remain unblemished. Her plan required her to venture among the castle dwellers.

Elizabeth curled in the stall deepest in the stable and closed her eyes. It would be night soon.

Dioneo rubbed his head and said, "Oh hell no, not flagellants."

Bruno nodded. "They scour the countryside, finding followers, and then arrive here. We see them every twenty days or so."

"Lucky us," Dioneo said. Then, moving to Ricciardo, he said, "Have you ever seen this?"

"No," Ricciardo answered. "But I have heard of them."

"You might want to get out of here."

"No, I want to see."

Dioneo shrugged and said, "As you wish. But—"

Suddenly, Dioneo grabbed Bartolome, pointed skyward, and asked enthusiastically, "Young man, have you ever seen the top of the castle tower?"\

"No, no, not here," Bartolome said.

"Then let's go."

From another balcony high in the castle, Maddalena watched the procession with Jai Ling and Trippetta. The flagellants walked in a large crocodile formation, two by two, their bodies covered with hooded light cloth tunics. They then formed a large circle in the middle of the courtyard. Observers from the castle and village crammed along the edges to watch the spectacle. The banners of the group had been struck into the ground in the center of the circle. The group probably numbered more than one hundred members. Behind them, the great drawbridge over Castle Gallic's moat was pulled up.

Jai Ling says, "Trippetta—don't tell me they're staying here tonight."

Trippetta replies, "I won't tell you."

Jai Ling pats Trippetta on the head." Trippetta does not seem to mind.

In the courtyard below us, the worshippers throw off their cowls, hoods, and upper garments. Many are naked from the waist up. Men outnumber women. A few participants look too young to be there. Each member of the circle stands with his or her arms outstretched and their head facing skyward, forming a small cross.

Many have scars on their backs. Some have a body filled with sores, plague survivors of other illnesses. A few are clean-skinned.

The leader is a large, broad-shouldered man with flowing black hair and a short beard. He looks fierce. I do not like him. He throws his hands in the air and cries in Latin, repeating his words over and over.

While the leader continued his chant, the three men who had brought in the banners walked along the crowd, handing out various whips, cat-o'-nine tails, and other scourges to each participant. As the men walk by a pilgrim, the flagellant solemnly takes the tool with both hands and lowers their chin to their chest.

"Do you know Latin?" Jai Ling asks.

"I studied a little... in Rome," I say. "He is saying a prayer to God. Something like 'Father, hear the prayers of your horrible or despicable sinners and accept our sin offerings.' That's not exact, but that is the idea."

"Wonderful," Jai Ling says. "I'm sure God appreciates this. I don't want you two watching."

She begins to shoulder us away when Trippetta protests.

"I older than Maddalena. You not tell me what to do, Jai Ling. I make my own mind."

Jai Ling is taken aback, and after a moment of contemplation, she says, "You are completely right, Trippetta. Stay if you wish. Do you want to?"

"Oh no, I not like this," she says, and taking my hand, leads me in skipping out of the room. As we go out the door, she turns to me and asks, "Where should we go?"

Ricciardo had also heard of flagellants. Religious zealots who believed in whipping themselves for their sins. The rise of the great mortality, the black death, had seen a rise in the number of flagellants. In his homeland, he'd seen them as part of the king's strange form of justice. Usually, the "justice" ended with men and women being devoured by tigers in the arena.

Yet he'd never seen this. The leader in the middle, the large man with thick black hair and a thicker beard and mustache, completed his prayer and pointed to one of the individuals in the procession, a bearded man standing erect, his gown hanging down from his waist. His age and muscle tone were similar to Dioneo's. This bearded man held his whip with his right hand at his side. Quite suddenly, he commenced screaming in a lower French dialect, "Je suis un pecheur! Je suis condamné!"

He then struck his back with a cat-o'-nine tails.

The man's body shook under the barbs, but he did not cry out. He pulled on the whip and ripped the barbed tails out of his back, then let the whip drop down by his side. Again, he cried out, this time confessing, "Je suis un adultere!" and he lashed himself a second time. Again, he winced, but his legs did not buckle. Ricciardo met his eyes and saw the man's pain. The flagellant pulled out the barbs and steeled himself for yet another whipping.

The man next to him, older, cried in a Saxon tongue that he was a sinner who stole from his neighbor, and he struck himself on the back with a bullwhip. Much more slender and frailer than the first man, this older man grimaced when the whip hit. He raised the whip to strike himself again, completed a weaker swing, and fell to his knees, crying he was a sinner.

The pattern repeated itself among each member of the procession. Some beat themselves repeatedly with a whip. Many collapsed on the first swing, and few made it past the second. Some whips were reinforced with hemp ropes, painful enough, but some were much more fearsome, such as the cat-o'-nine tails with their metal barbs. Some flagellants fainted while waiting for their turn to arrive. One younger woman wearing a pure white gown trembled greatly, then began shaking uncontrollably when it was her time. Her bowels let go, and urine spilled at her feet. Ricciardo watched her—she was just a few yards in front of him, her back basically clean of marks—and he began to move forward when a strong arm grabbed his shoulder.

"Interfere, and they will cut you down," Bruno whispered in his ear. "They are here willingly. They can run, if they want to, but they believe this cleanses their souls. If you stop them, you are an agent for the devil. This is painful to watch, but we must let them suffer."

Ricciardo wished Dioneo were there. Somehow, Dioneo would have an idea. But he had taken off with Bartolome. The girl cried out, "Je suis une pute," and swung a bullwhip against her back. There was a crack. She crumbled to the ground, sobbing. There was a deep gash running down her back, across her buttocks, and down her right leg.

Ricciardo thought he heard a hushed cry from Lisabetta. He reached for her shoulder. She looked away from the square, but kept glancing back. Beatrice touched Lisabetta as if to comfort her, but Lisabetta began crying "Eh eh eh!" and broke away from everyone and ran. Ricciardo pursued her.

As the sun set, the ground of the first bailey was littered with bleeding bodies. The whiteness of their clothing accentuated the bloody sight, and many gowns were piled in a heap in the center of the square. Some of the flagellants assisted in moving the weaker ones to the sides of the courtyard, near some of the houses. A few bodies had been whipped close to a dozen times, usually the strongest among the group, but most had managed no more than four or five strokes.

The villagers left food and water in buckets on the edge of the courtyard, for anyone who wished to take some, but no one could give physical assistance or shelter to a flagellant. To provide more, one would need to be asked, and the flagellants never asked.

El Erreur and Roderigo watched together from an upper room in the massive keep that dominated the rear of Castle Gallic.

Roderigo said, "They refuse any aid from us."

El Erreur nodded solemnly and added knowingly, "They view their suffering as penance to God."

"You must understand," Roderigo continued, "that while we do not encourage the flagellants, we offer them safe haven here and a modest meal. They come at random, but often at the end of the summer like this. We cannot have your performance tonight. We will dine quietly. The pilgrims shall dine by themselves and stay for the night. Tomorrow they shall leave. We can have you perform tomorrow, if that is acceptable."

"It is," El Erreur said. The two shook hands.

Lora stood in the middle bailey looking to the sky. Leo and Francine circled above. Lora held out her left arm, wrapped in a protective leather gauntlet, and made a whistling noise through her teeth. Leo spread his magnificent six-foot wingspan and swooped down, his claws wrapping around the leather. Lora petted his head and handed him a small piece of meat, saying, "You are quite a birdie, Leo, quite the playful one today. Be ready to perform tomorrow." She placed a hood over his crown and then put him in his cage.

The troupe's wagons were being pulled in here for the night. Mansa came over to her from the other side of the courtyard with large chains in his hands.

"I suppose you've heard that we're getting locked in tonight," he said.

Lora, tracking Francine, said, "These quarters seem luxurious enough. It might be nice to rest in a place that's locked and secure for once."

Shrugging, Mansa said, "I don't like it. The flagellants—they're being kept out there." He gestured to the first bailey. "That means if we need to get out of here, they are between us and the drawbridge."

Lora, still looking at the sky, held out her arm and made a different whistle. Francine began to descend.

"If Dioneo and Jai Ling are fine with it, I am fine with it."

Francine landed on Lora's outstretched arm. "Besides, many of us girls are sleeping in the keep. Don't you want to sleep in a luxurious bed? If not, you have been on the road too long, Mansa."

Darkness fell over Mirabeau. Inside Castle Gallic, people prepared for a feast in the great hall. The flagellants congregated in the lower bailey, picking from the food left out for them. Most were in great pain. A few might succumb to their injuries.

The main dining hall of Castle Gallic held many revelers. With the appearance of the flagellants, a certain restraint was deemed appropriate, but with so many other newcomers, a small amount of fellowship was in order. People ate at tables throughout the hall, dressed in the best clothes they had. At the main table, Roderigo wore a magnificent red wool doublet tucked at the waist, and Lady Madeline wore a slim white gown topped with a white steeple cap. They dined with El Erreur and Nefferi at the head table, with others from the village and the caravan joining in. In one corner, Uwe played his flute while Trippetta and some of the other women danced. Two large fires were burning in firepits and roasting venison and boar. In the main hearth, a cauldron had been hung, brewing a passable stew. Cheese and eggs were available, and a few roast rabbits surrounded by strawberries dotted each table. Dioneo held court, telling bawdy stories to a group of mostly female listeners. Ricciardo sat with Lisabetta as they ate gently in the corner.

Most of the children were in attendance, including Maddalena and Bartolome. Trippetta stayed with them. Maddalena wore a turquoise dress and a red ribbon in her hair, the one tied earlier in the day by the strange woman with the fancy headdress named "Beatrice." Bartolome was dressed in a purple doublet and gold silk pants. Both these outfits were provided by Lady Madeline. The children stayed near the main hearth, sitting on the floor and enjoying milk, cheese, bread, and even some sweet pudding.

Roderigo stroked his thin beard, staring through the celebration.

"You seem troubled. Something concerns you?" El Erreur inquired.

Roderigo hesitated.

"By the stables, one of the guards was found dead. No wounds on his body. At least no recent ones. He just died in his tracks. I am having my physician barber examine his body."

"I am sure it was his time," El Erreur said. "That is how the reaper acts. But it is wise to be cautious."

Nefferi clapped during Trippetta's performance, but her keen hearing picked up the conversation. After taking her leave of Lady Madeline and Roderigo, Nefferi quietly made her way to Dioneo and Jai Ling, gathered in the back, and told them what she had heard.

Standing in his acrobatic tights and white shirt, Dioneo took in what Nefferi had said.

"It could be nothing. People die in their tracks all the time. Then again—I don't know. But Jai doesn't sense anything specific about this place."

"And it's not like the place is filled with rats," Nefferi said. "I do not care what others say, more rats, more plague."

"No rats at all," Jai Ling said distantly. "No vermin—"

Something bothered her, but—she could not quite figure it out.

The crowd was calling for the next song, which Dioneo began.

There once was a boy from Mantua,
Who fell in love with a girl from Verona,

Elsewhere, deep in the bowels of Castle Gallic, Elizabeth slipped behind a great tapestry in a hallway far from the great hall. She'd easily slid unseen and opened the lock using her sense of touch and hearing. Down here, it was dank, probably running parallel to the moat. She liked the damp; its coolness was refreshing to her. The passageway was not lit at all. Her night vision was very good, of course, but she still carried a small torch, since she could be blinded in the total darkness down here. The tunnel was clear—no humans, not even a rat. This thought brought a wry smile to her face.

Earlier, she had gone to the front gate to see if she could overwhelm the guards by herself and lower the drawbridge to let her people in, but the hot sunlight had tired her. More than that, though, there was the strain of holding her people back. The mother's blood had enhanced her powers, so she could control her people from a distance, but with the enhancement, she felt her powers fleeing at the same time. Elizabeth had thought of trying to overwhelm the group, but with five armed guards watching her, she might not get them all. No, she would follow her plan.

The tunnel began to rise. She ran a hand along the wall. The slight warming of the stone told her she was coming from below the river line to above ground. This made sense, since this was an escape tunnel, one that opened into the moat on the eastern side. One could slip out of here, let the moat's water carry you to the river, and then float down the Durance. A good design. The Piper had provided her with good information.

She passed a scone which she lit. That might attract someone, but her plan required it.

Then she came to what she was looking for. A door of iron, very thick, covered in rust. It was a single arched portal. A thick iron bar went across. None of this surprised her. The Piper was nothing if not accurate. But the bolt was controlled by a series of dials, one stacked upon the other. Upon closer inspection, she saw there were seven such dials, each one with eight pistons extending from it. The ends of each of the pistons had a different color.

A lock.

Elizabeth placed the torch in a holder by the gate and gripped the pistons farthest from her. They turned with much greater ease than she expected. As she did, she concentrated on the lock, listening for clicks and feeling for tumblers. Nothing. She tried the pistons on the other dials and had no success. The gate would not budge. Elizabeth made several more efforts, and nothing happened.

She had to think. The smoothness of the lock and the tumblers, even after being in this dampness, was indicative of something very well made. The colors were some sort of combination. They had to be lined up just right. The reason they turned so easily was that the innards of the lock were very smooth. She could barely feel tumblers, but she felt just enough movement to know they were there. She could not sense a telltale click of where to stop. The lock was ingenious. There was no key—the only way to open it would be to know the combination. With time, she might be able to figure it out, but—with seven dials and eight handles—what was the formula?

When she was younger, she had formal schooling with a friend. Heloise was the better of the two at mathematics. But the lock had something to do with multiplying the number of handles and dials. Eight handles on one. A one in eight chance of picking the right one. Eight on the second. Eight times eight was sixty-four. Then another eight. She couldn't remember how to manipulate all the numbers, but she knew there were many thousands of combinations. Trying randomly, she might get lucky. Or she might be here all night, and they would be exposed tomorrow.

The Piper also liked to tell half-truths.

For a moment—just a moment—she felt a twang of fear. What now?

Then she smiled. Who would know the combination? She would find out. She'd also find out how true the three sisters' words were. What was the worst that would happen? She would die again and cease to be.

That would not necessarily be unwelcome.

Elizabeth turned and headed towards the lower bailey. In a few minutes, she was there.

Wandering through the courtyard, the smell of blood was strong, almost overpowering. She could taste it. Shadows were encroaching, but she could easily make out the broken bodies on the ground. She suppressed a strong urge to feast. It would be so easy. Too much of a chance she it would create a riot she could not control, and she had to find the Bartolome and Maddalena first. She walked by the flagellant's leader, the wide-shouldered, black-haired wild man. He strode through the group, followed by several followers who looked like they had not whipped themselves. He seemed very sure of himself and bumped into Elizabeth.

"Stand aside, woman."

Elizabeth almost lunged at him, but suppressed the urge. Instead, she lay on the ground and watched him walk away.

She said one word.

"Soon."

Elizabeth collected seven white robes off the ground and slipped away into an empty cottage near the westernmost wall.

In between entertaining his audience, Dioneo excused himself and went to the wine casks, where he filled a golden goblet. He held up the cup and marveled at it.

"A king's ransom, right here in my hand," he said, and took a drink.

Rowena came up to him. He put his arm around her waist and gave her a kiss.

"My dear, I haven't seen you for hours, and I am so saddened by that," he said.

"You haven't been trying very hard," Rowena replied. "Dear."

Dioneo felt a slight push from the side and turned. A ravishing red-haired beauty with porcelain skin, wearing a red dress, had stumbled into him. They exchanged smiles.

"Pardon me," the red-haired woman said. "I think I may have had too much wine."

Dioneo eyed her approvingly. "No need to apologize," he said, taking another gulp of his wine. Rowena looked on disapprovingly.

"Care for some more?"

The red-haired woman seemed to hesitate, then said, "It is the flagellants. They upset me. They upset most of us. I wish they had never come here."

The woman took the glass, and she pulled it to her lips, touching Dioneo's hands as she did so.

Rowena looked at her closely, then asked, "Didn't you come in with them? The flagellants?"

The red-haired beauty took a delicate sip of wine and shook her head.

"Oh no," she replied, "I do not share their beliefs." She laughed and added, "I don't think God wants us whipping ourselves."

"I agree!" Dioneo exclaimed loudly. "What's the point in that? God whips us enough, I say."

The woman held out her hand. "My name is Elizabeth."

Dioneo drew her nearer and said, "My dear, you have the most beautiful skin I have ever seen. Rowena, isn't her skin amazing?"

Rowena made a noise of disapproval and stormed off.

"I'm sorry," Elizabeth said. "I didn't mean to cause any trouble."

"Oh, I think you did," Dioneo laughed. "But never mind, she's like the sister I never had, she's fine."

"Care to introduce me to your new friend?" Jai Ling said, appearing beside Dioneo.

"Jai Ling, meet Elizabeth," Dioneo said. "Elizabeth, meet the love of my life, only she doesn't know it yet, Ms. Jai Ling. Sometimes known as Miss Mystery."

Elizabeth held her hand out, and Jai Ling took it. Nothing seemed particularly wrong. And yet—

"Hello," Jai Ling said.

Elizabeth beamed back at her.

Jai Ling could not recall the woman, but there was something familiar about her.

"Have we—have we met?"

"Not formally. But I have seen you."

Elizabeth stepped back and looked at them both. "You're performers, yes?" Elizabeth asked. "I have seen you before. Dioneo, you are an acrobat, correct?"

Dioneo took an exaggerated bow.

"At your service."

"And a bit of a jongleur, yes? A rather naughty one if I heard you correctly."

Dioneo stood erect and began, "There once was a bishop from Frankfurt—"

"That's enough, dear," Jai Ling said, patting his shoulder. "There's no need to upset anyone further."

Jai Ling smiled at Elizabeth but felt the slightest bit wary at the face that smiled back at her.

Elizabeth said, "And you, Jai Ling—you—you are an archer, yes?"

Jai Ling nodded and said, "Yes, I am."

"It is so nice to meet admirers," Dioneo said.

Addressing Jai Ling further, Elizabeth said, "You are so accurate. How does a woman learn to shoot so well?"

Jai Ling eyed Elizabeth cautiously, then replied, "I'd love to tell you, but it's a long story. Do you have some time?"

Elizabeth gestured behind them and said, "Those children over there—they look so cute. Are they with you?"

"Some of them," Dioneo answered. "When you stay on the road a long time, things happen."

"The girl in the green dress is very pretty," Elizabeth commented.

Jai Ling, now more wary, said, "Yes, she is. You are kind to notice."

Elizabeth added, "And look at the red ribbon in her hair. Such a nice touch. And that turquoise dress. May I see your children?"

Before Jai Ling could respond, Dioneo interrupted with, "That doesn't look good."

Both women looked to the main table. A white-robed and hooded flagellant had entered the dining hall and was speaking to Roderigo. After listening for a minute, Roderigo rose to his feet and raised his hands, at which all music and conversation stopped.

"Our most holy of guests have completed their vigils," Roderigo said. "They have asked us to honor their prayers with our own solemn praise to our Lord, and that we end our modest repast. I ask you all to retire to your quarters. But first, a moment of prayer."

Roderigo then clasped his hands before him and, casting his eyes down, began to intone a prayer to the Father in heaven. Most others complied. Dioneo started to mumble about bullshit, but Jai Ling, head bowed and hands clasped, gave Dioneo a sharp kick to the shin.

"Ouch," he uttered, then assumed the same prayer stance as the others.

Jai Ling kept the red-haired woman in the corner of her eye.

And the red-haired woman was aware of this.

And aware that another had spotted her.

As Roderigo continued a Latin incantation of a Gregorian prayer, he quickly glanced up and scanned the great hall. All were now looking down in reverence, save for one red-haired woman standing near Dioneo.

Her eyes met Roderigo's.

She heard Roderigo's voice in her head.

I know what you are.

She'd been found out. No matter. Roderigo also had plans for their guests here. Elizabeth smiled and thought back to him.

And I know what you are.

Roderigo paused, then finished his praying. Taking Lady Madeline's hand, he bid everyone to leave and retire for the night.

Out in the dispersing crowd, Dioneo looked up, about to say something witty to Elizabeth—she was pretty, after all—but she was gone.

"Missed out again?" Jai Ling chided.

Dioneo shrugged. "Looks that way, and Rowena's angry at me. Guess I'm sleeping in the wagons tonight."

"Where you should be," Jai Ling said distractedly, first checking to see if the children were fine—they were. Then she scanned the crowd.

"Her interest in 'our children' was odd, wouldn't you say?"

"I suppose," Dioneo said.

"Maddalena is staying with Lora and me tonight. Bartolome will be with Uwe and Ricciardo."

Over by the main table, El Erreur and Nefferi exchanged good-nights with their hosts and took their leave. Roderigo looked over the chamber, but the red-haired woman was gone.

Lady Madeline turned and leaned in to her husband, quietly but firmly instructing him, "Find that woman and tear off her head."

Elizabeth, for her part, had lost the children momentarily in the crowd and then saw Jai Ling and Dioneo and the others with them. She moved quickly out of the room. She had to. Roderigo was coming after her.

As she weaved through the crowd, she glimpsed through the double-paneled French doors of a flat-bottomed cog boat out behind the castle. Elizabeth noted it.

A short while later, Uwe sat fuming on his bed. These trappings in this chamber were all right, probably more fit for servants than the royalty, but Uwe was not one for fine things.

Ricciardo lay on his bed and, yawning, asked, "Why are you so upset?"

"I here with you while Trippetta is with the others," Uwe spat back.

"Lisabetta is there too," Ricciardo said. "The girls want to be together. Be happy we have a good place to sleep for a change. Look at Bartolome—he's completely asleep."

Bartolome slept soundly on a cot at the end of the room, still wearing the purple doublet and silk gold pants he'd had at the party.

"You a fool," Uwe said, then threw himself back on the bed. There wasn't much to do about the situation. And now that he thought of it, he did feel drowsy. Sleep came quickly.

The guards on the walls had enjoyed the festivities. Wine and food had been plentiful tonight, and with the threat of the black death always present, any opportunity to indulge was welcome. To the extent any guards bothered to keep an eye out, and there were only two who did, their concern was for the inner courtyard of Castle Gallic. The drawbridge was up, the walls were firm, and though the water in the moat was a little low, the flagellants and perhaps the troubadours posed a much greater threat than anything outside the walls.

At least, that was the assumption the guards made. And as you shall see, dear reader, it was an erroneous one, for they failed to notice a line of a half-dozen fleshers, draped in black shrouds that they had been dressed in by Elizabeth and Alatiel, shambling to the far east end of the moat. Led by the tall Janosz, this group followed their leader to the edge of the moat. Janosz dragged a plank with him. He could keep the others moving in a general direction, and they were drawn by the call of Elizabeth, who was waiting for them on the other side of the door.

Though the guards failed to see this entourage, the flesh eaters were not completely unnoticed. A fool wearing motley clothes sat perched in a white birch on the outskirts of the forest, amused at the sight of the flesh eaters moving as a unit to the castle. What did the others call them, fleshers? The fool always found that term amusing. In Verona, they were called revenants; in Saxony, nachzehrers. Gjengangers in the northern countries. Jiangshi farther east. He'd guessed that Jai Ling had met jiangshi before. The fool thought of them all as moving death. You did not want to come in contact with them, especially in the "dead" of night, like now. Not that they could ever kill him, but they were vicious, and it was painful to have a body torn apart. Elizabeth, of course, was an exception. She could appreciate a good bargain.

In the town, the main group of fleshers was moving death—staying out of sight, huddled in small clusters in houses in the village. They followed Elizabeth. For her to command these undead, she was a powerful sorceress indeed.

Oh, this should be good, the fool thought as he wet his lips.

"Let's hear something—enchanting," he said aloud, and began to play a beautiful melody on his flute.

[11]
THE HOUSE ON FIRE

ROWENA WANDERED through the upper bailey. The portcullis in the gatehouse between the middle and upper baileys had not been lowered, and she could see the cluster of wagons in the next courtyard. Though it was summer, there was a cool breeze tonight. She pulled a shawl around her bare shoulders and turned away.

A young nobleman with beautiful olive skin stood before her.

"You aren't going to join your friends?" he asked, nodding towards the wagons.

"They aren't really my friends," Rowena said. "Just people I travel with."

"I thought you did have at least one friend," the nobleman continued. "The one I saw you talking to at the meal. He's called 'Dioneo'?"

Rowena laughed. "No, he is most definitely not my friend."

The man offered his arm and said, "My name is Christian. Would you like a friend?"

Rowena moved up to Christian and locked her arm with his, saying, "Do you have a place nearby?"

Most of the wagons were formed in a circle in the middle bailey. One, Mansa's, was off to the side where the animals were caged. Mansa had not tethered any out for sentries tonight, as Roderigo had forbidden it. Normally, they would not go with this, but it seemed okay here. The Cookes and their food wagon were over in the corner near the easternmost wall.

Dioneo walked up to one of the wagons filled with provisions and found it filled with sleeping people. Though it was dark, it looked like several of the men had paired off with some local village girls.

"Not my night," Dioneo whispered. He was tired. Gingerly reaching in the wagon, he pulled out a couple of blankets and threw them on the ground near a dying fire by one of the wagons. Dioneo picked up an axe and split the logs into smaller pieces, and stacked them on the fire. At the far end of the yard, he thought he saw Rowena walking into the lower courtyard with a well-dressed man. He was happy Rowena had found someone, but the slightest bit concerned about her walking off alone into that part of the castle.

"Rowena," he called.

She turned her head ever so slightly towards Dioneo, just enough so he could be certain it was her, then grabbed the nobleman and kissed him passionately. The pair passed out of sight into the lower bailey.

"It really isn't my night," Dioneo said.

He lay down on his side and watched the fire burn for a while, then drifted off to slumber.

Jai Ling slept restlessly. Something bothered her, but she was tired. There was a soothing melody in her head, and she found it relaxing. Travel had been hard the last few days and—

Maddalena had said something when they came in this morning. She noticed there were no squirrels, no rabbits.

A shiver shook Jai Ling's spine as she realized what should have come to her much, much sooner.

No vermin. In a town by a river.

No vermin.

Jai Ling sat up and scanned the room.

Lisabetta and Maddalena were both gone.

Elizabeth stopped in the passageway. Deep in the bowels of Castle Gallic, she carried a small torch as before. Even she needed a little light to navigate the complete darkness. For a moment, she rested against the cool wall. Just that sampling of the mother's blood had an effect on her that she never anticipated. She could sense where her people were, and she was still holding them back at the edge of the village. She could help Janosz bring the others to the west wall and wait to cross the moat. It was as if they were beside her. Imagine what would happen if she got the children's blood as well. She corrected herself. When she got the children.

All this was exhausting. At first, she had felt invincible. Not long before, she had to be in close proximity to read and command the most basic of thoughts. Now she held two groups in check, both outside the castle walls. But with each moment, she was feeling the strain and working harder and harder to maintain her control. The minds of her people were not completely empty but overridden with a driving hunger. Driving. Always driving. She was keeping that drive in check, but for how much longer? She knew when she started this would be a temporary empowerment, not something that could last, but her time was running out quickly. While it was daylight, her people rested, and she could too. Now it was late at night. Her kind were in their most aggressive state.

"And so am I," she whispered. But then she chided herself. "You should have grabbed the children in the great hall. You could have turned others and used them and fought your way out."

Then she refocused. She had her reasons.

"Jai Ling was wary of you and might have done something unexpected. There was always the chance that there would be such a feeding frenzy that the children would be devoured. You made that mistake with the mother. You've come too far to let that happen again."

Footsteps on sand behind her made little sound, but she could hear them.

Come get me, Roderigo, she thought. His pursuit strengthened her resolve. She continued as the pathway began to ascend. Back to the door and its intricate lock.

MADDALENA

I am walking through the corridors of a castle.

Where am I? This must be a dream.

Such music. I must follow.

Why?

This must be a dream. I will wake up.

I need to follow. I will wake.

It must be a dream. I must get to the water. NO! Please wake up.

"WAKE UP!"

Jai Ling's senses had just awoken from slumber.

Her inner voice screamed at her.

YOU FOOL! The Piper is calling the children to the river! Maddalena would go this way. Don't make any more mistakes!"

Jai Ling did not hear the Piper's music; only the children did. But from where they slept, the most direct way to the water was down this corridor and out the back and then to the Durance River.

She saw Maddalena walking ahead in the same green dress and red ribbon from the dinner. She was ascending the stairs leading to the great hall.

Jai Ling tackled her at the waist

Maddalena shrieked, "I must follow the music!"

She punched Jai Ling hard, but Jai Ling wrapped both arms around her.

Was that Lisabetta turning at the top of the stairs?

Jai Ling tried to see, but it was too dark.

Maddalena was fighting her. Jai Ling dragged her to the room where Trippetta and Lora were stirring.

"Help me!" Jai Ling yelled.

Atop the stairwell, Lisabetta heard the scuffle below and the cries of Maddalena and Jai Ling. She heard the music of the Piper, but was not possessed by it. *Her*senses had not been dulled.

An inner instinct was driving her.

She had to catch the boy.

Lora leaped to her feet, and Trippetta popped up in her bed.

"Her ears!" Jai Ling yelled, dragging Maddalena onto a bed.

Lora pulled Trippetta off the bed she was on and said, "Find something to wrap around Maddalena's head."

Trippetta was drowsy.

"Trippetta!" Lora spoke sternly. "Find something to wrap around her ears!"

At the call of her name, Trippetta came out of her momentary stupor, sheepishly nodded, and searched the room. Maddalena continued to shriek.

"She possessed," Trippetta said fearfully.

"Get off me! Get off me! I must get to the water!"

Maddalena thrashed and clawed. Jai Ling shifted her left arm onto Maddalena's chest. Maddalena gnashed her teeth. Jai Ling yelled and pushed her forearm underneath Maddalena's chin, shoving her harder into the bed. Then Jai Ling slapped Maddalena's face with her other hand.

"Wake up! Wake up!"

Lora had found a thick woolen scarf.

"Trippy, get behind her and wrap this around her ears!"

Trippetta knelt behind Maddalena's head, while Lora pressed on Maddalena's left shoulder.

The falcons were screeching in the corner of the room.

"Hold her forehead down, but watch her teeth," Lora said, pressing Maddalena's crown into the bed. Jai Ling stopped slapping Maddalena and shifted to hold down Maddalena's right side. Trippetta worked between them, tightly wrapping the scarf around Maddalena's skull.

"That's it," Jai Ling said. All three jumped off the bed. Maddalena stopped thrashing for a moment, looked around—then bolted for the small window overlooking the river.

Lora reached for her and missed. Jai Ling jumped over the bed and grabbed Maddalena's ankle, pulled her to the ground, and forced both her hands over the scarf and Maddalena's ears.

"Grab her legs," Jai Ling commanded. Trippetta and Lora held one each and brought her to the nearest bed.

Maddalena struggled more, but her three friends held hard, with Jai Ling pressing her hands on the scarf against Maddalena's ears.

Lora strained to say, "Who-knew-she-was-so-strong!"

Maddalena thrust her body up and gave an ear-piercing scream, then suddenly became limp. Her eyes closed.

Jai Ling shook her body. No one let go.

Maddalena opened her eyes. At first, they seemed vacant. Her breathing was calming down. Her eyes were darting between Lora, Trippetta, and Jai Ling. Her cheeks were red.

She focused on Jai Ling.

"You're stroking your cheek. You do that when you're worried."

Trippetta and Lora looked at Jai Ling, and she nodded to them. All slowly released their grip on Maddalena, and Trippetta helped her sit up.

"All right?" Lora asked.

Maddalena rubbed her own face while Lora unwrapped the scarf around her head.

"Music," Maddalena said. Her eyes watered. "There was music. I—I—I had to follow—"

"I sorry, I sorry," Trippetta said.

Lora touched Trippetta's shoulder.

"It's all right, Trippetta."

Maddalena's eyes widened.

"Bartolome! He was heading for the great hall!"

Jai Ling was quickly changing into her stocking-net hose, leather boots, and a tight-fitting undertunic. All black colored, of course. She pulled the double-edged anelace out of her bag, the one she received as a gift at Digne les Bains. She sheathed it in its leather scabbard, then she tied a hemp rope around her torso and slid the dagger behind her back, tucking it beneath the undertunic.

"Get everyone up," Jai Ling ordered. "Look for any of our kids. They're being called to the river. Then get to the middle bailey. Be careful. I know where Bartolome and Lisabetta are."

Lora got up and began to gather her things. "The Piper?" she asked.

Jai Ling tightened the hemp around her waist. "No rats in a town by the river. They hired him to clear the rats and did not pay. And he always needs to be paid."

Lora, pulling on the gauntlet with the long leather cuffs her falcons landed on, said, "We all missed it. I'll go with you and—"

"No, Lisabetta can't be far," Jai Ling shot back. "I'll go to the main hall. Your job is no easier. Find as many of us as you can and meet in the bailey."

"We get Uwe," Trippetta said. "He one floor below us."

Jai Ling pointed at her.

"Good idea, Trippy. If you're trapped, get out to the river and make for the boat. But remember that's where the Piper might be calling the children."

"We'll get them," Lora said. She uncovered Leo and Francine, who were more than awake now, shifting back and forth on their perches. Lora opened their cage and pulled the hoods off of each and began to communicate with them as only she could, with gestures and nondescript sounds. Then she inserted her arm out the small window. Leo and Francine took flight.

Jai Ling paused.

Now what? Her inner voice mocked her.

Trippetta was giving Maddalena a drink of water and wiping her face with a wet cloth.

Jai Ling grinned.

"You're a tough pair, you two. Help Lora find the others."

Then she grabbed her short bow and the quiver of arrows she'd left on the bed, paused to say, "We're all getting out of here," and exited the room.

Dioneo awoke from his sleep disoriented. He shook his head and questioned why he was startled. Then he saw an auburn-haired beauty, decked out in only a form-fitting linen chemise and hose, all of which accentuated her curves. She was sitting on the ground next to him.

"Well, hello there," he said.

The woman stroked her hair and said, "I saw you at the hall earlier. You were amusing."

Dioneo grinned back.

"What's your name?"

"Andrea."

"Well, Andrea, you look a little cold," Dioneo observed. "And I put the wood out here in the fire."

"We don't have any extra wood for the fire," the woman said.

Dioneo grinned further. "Poor planning on the part of my friends, even if it is summer. And here I have only got thin blankets."

I'm glad Dioneo saw me leave with this fellow, Rowena thought. *He's too damn full of himself.*

But as she walked through the stone barbican leading into the first bailey, she reconsidered. The flagellants were spread throughout the lower courtyard. There was a bright moon tonight, and it played grotesque games, highlighting the flagellants' white, bloodied robes and their torn bodies. They lay restlessly on the ground, bodies twisted in painful contortions. Some slept. Moans and groans emanated from all over.

As much of an ass as Dioneo was, she'd wished he were here right now.

"Never mind them," Christian whispered in her ear, nodding to the flagellants. "They choose to do this.

She looked at him, and he smiled. "I have a private room just over there."

He pointed to a set of houses on the eastern side.

Rowena thought, *Who needs Dioneo?*

Roderigo had been chasing a phantom under the bowels of the castle's outer walls. He knew what she was. The flesh eater. A wiedergänger. One who could control others of her kind. He knew she wanted the children. She could not have them. At least not here. Castle Gallic was *his* home—*his* people. She had a strong mind—but he sensed she was newly created. He had existed for over two hundred years.

The pathway was ascending to the escape door. Roderigo arrived at that door. Elizabeth was lying on the floor, face down, her red hair a tangled mess, and her left arm limply holding on to one of the combination lock's handles. A small metal sconce by the metal door was burning. The torch she'd carried was on the ground.

"You shouldn't have come here," he said.

He kneeled beside her. Her body seemed frail; her hand slipped off the lock, and she pulled it under her body. Roderigo reached out to touch her on the back. He felt what she had experienced in her last few hours.

"You had a briefly enhanced life. But now it is ebbing from your body."

Elizabeth retched.

"Your body is not a body I would assume," Roderigo said. "So I will release you now."

He turned her over and placed his hands on the sides of her head. "This is Castle Gallic!" Roderigo said and squeezed Elizabeth's temples. He could feel her mentally pushing her back.

Elizabeth broke from his hold and yelled, "No!"

She slid on her back away from him. He advanced on her. She weakly pushed his shoulder, but he tossed her arm aside and again placed his hands on her head.

His fingers pressed into her temples. The veins in his hands and arms began to glow with a green hue, and his eyes filled with green fluid.

"Let yourself go," he said. "Let yourself be freed."

Elizabeth's body twisted in spasms under his hands, and her face stared blankly upward. Roderigo could feel her life force coming out.

Then suddenly he felt great pain. Elizabeth's hands grabbed his wrists, and she pulled herself up so their faces were a mere breath apart. Their eyes locked.

Both their bodies began to shudder.

"When was the last time you were challenged, Roderigo?" Elizabeth asked.

Roderigo gritted his teeth and said, "I am the stronger one!"

Each felt their minds pushing against the other.

"This is Castle Gallic!" Roderigo said and squeezed Elizabeth's head. Clenching his teeth, he muttered, "I am the stronger one!"

Then she shot up and kissed him deeply, holding him in her embrace, staring into his eyes. She saw his pupils widen with green fluid and fill his eye sockets to the point of bursting, and she felt his shock and terror at something he never thought could happen. Her eyes burned orange, and in Roderigo's mind there came one hammering message.

No, Roderigo—I am!

El Erreur sat up in the bed he shared with Nefferi. Like many of the others, he chose to accept his host's hospitality. However, unlike many, he was not resting well. He and Nefferi had not been offered a room in the keep, but rather a small, if nicely furnished, room in the middle bailey. Nefferi had found it only a slight insult, but the room was suitable, and most of the others were in the middle bailey. El Erreur, however, was much more upset.

"This is an insult," he fumed in the dark.

Nefferi, half-asleep, said, "Stop complaining. This is better than any of our wagons. And we're near the others."

"They treat us like vagabonds."

"This isn't ancient Egypt, my great husband."

Nefferi turned on her side. "We *are* vagabonds. Now I am going back to sleep. If you want to keep feeling insulted, do so, but leave me." She buried her head deeper into the pillow. "Down duck feather. Very nice."

El Erreur bristled. In the olden days, even a wife of Nefferi's caliber would not be so insolent to her husband.

But they no longer lived in the olden days.

"You find it amusing we are treated as peasants. You care little for your royal heritage," El Erreur said as he shook his head.

"Right now I care for this lovely pillow," Nefferi murmured. "Now let me get to sleep."

"I often wish that I had never been revived."

After a few moments, El Erreur realized he was not getting any further response from his wife. He got out of bed and paced into the dark hallway. One candle lit the passage, and he took it from its post.

Ahead, he heard what sounded like small scampering feet. He went to investigate.

Lisabetta wandered frantically, voicing her "Eh" in short bursts, touching doors. Her mind was too simple to analyze what was happening, yet something stirred her, and she sensed, on a simple level, that the boy was in danger.

She found herself in Roderigo's study, the corner of the great hall.

Moonlight, in blue hue because of the tint in the glass, shone through the French doors overlooking the Durance River. They had been closed. Between the medium fire burning in the hearth and the moon's rays, she could see the entire chamber. The tables had been cleared, and many of them, along with the benches, had been pushed to the edges of the hall, though a few strays remained scattered on the floor.

A squeaking sound to her right.

Bartolome was working a latch on one of the French doors.

Lisabetta ran across the ballroom floor, sidestepping the long tables and benches in her way. Bartolome pounded against the windows. They would not give. He searched the floor and grabbed a stray mug left behind, and smashed a window pane. Reaching through the broken glass, he worked the latch on both sides and managed to release it, oblivious to the cuts on his arm. The windows parted, and Bartolome crawled onto the veranda. The music was calling him to the river, and he was intent on climbing the wall and jumping off.

He was halfway over the balusters when Lisabetta barely grasped his right ankle and clawed him back. They both hit the stone floor. While it was covered with a bearskin rug, that hurt. They struggled. Lisabetta, getting to her feet, managed to force Bartolome back into the hall.

"Well done, Lisabetta."

They both stopped suddenly.

Lady Madeline stepped into the moonlight, her white gown from the dinner flowing behind her. A single drop of green slime dripped from her mouth.

Roderigo lay crumpled and whimpering. His hands clasped his mouth, where his lower lip had just been bitten off.

Elizabeth was wiping green fluid off her arms and legs.

"This door is an ingenious design," she said, both hands on the lock. "Very impressive. Did you come up with it? Or did you steal the design from some traveler who happened to stop by?"

Roderigo moaned again.

"And what a great idea," Elizabeth continued, staring at the lock. "Putting an escape postern into the moat. You could slip out of here and let the water carry you to the river and float away. Now let's open it."

She grasped the nobs on each handle and began to turn each one, lining them up in the proper order, which she had gleaned from Roderigo's mind. She spoke to him as she spun each one.

"First, blue. Not my favorite color, but it is a start. Next, purple. A royal color. Then green. Or turquoise, if you prefer. I like that word turquoise. Next—oh this one is stiff—orange."

The sound of metal grinding on metal reverberated from inside the door, growing louder with each turn of a dial. Elizabeth felt the lock pulsating beneath her hands, each correct alignment of the rods releasing another part of the lock.

Roderigo began to crawl away.

"Going somewhere, Roderigo? Well, let me see. Next up, white. Ugh, another stiff one. And then violet. That's really creative, you have blue and purple on this rim, and also violet, but you know someone who got to this point might guess it. And finally, last but not least, black. Funny, this combination seems vaguely familiar to me."

After aligning this final one, she stepped back. The piercing screech and squeals of grinding gears and retracting bolts giving way filled the corridor.

Elizabeth went over to Roderigo.

"You lie in wait here like spiders, waiting for flies to fall into your trap. But this fly has teeth, Roderigo. You say you've been doing this for two hundred years, as if the ability to perpetuate your life gives you some special right to keep it. I think you've lived long enough."

Unable to stop himself, Roderigo looked up. He saw the metal door slowly swinging open. Janosz, Nicola, and other fleshers: four males, two females—stood on the other side.

"Welcome to Castle Gallic," Elizabeth said. "We've got some work to do." Then, stepping aside to reveal Roderigo, she continued, "And before we start, I have a little snack here. For energy."

Roderigo pulled himself across the sandy floor. But they descended on him, except for Nicola, who shambled beside Elizabeth.

Elizabeth wiped more green fluid off her hands with a handkerchief.

"What a mess. Anyway, Nicola, we need to find Maddalena and Bartolome. Alive. Let's go."

"Come here, Bartolome," Lady Madeline curled her fingers. Bartolome, still in his stupor, faltered over. Lady Madeline rubbed her hands over Bartolome's face. The boy stared solemnly at her. She walked around him.

"You are so young, Bartolome. And well taken care of. You will do quite nicely for my friend."

Lisabetta grabbed Bartolome by the shoulders and pulled him away, hissing at Lady Madeline. The boy had temporarily lost his drive to get to the water but was now transfixed by Lady Madeline. Bartolome had a green fluid smudged on his cheeks. Lisabetta wiped Bartolome's face with the sleeve of her dress.

"Now that is surprising," Lady Madeline said. "Where are my manners? You're such a dear. Poor Lisabetta."

Lady Madeline reached out to touch Lisabetta's face, but Lisabetta leaned away and hissed again. Bartolome, trance-like, stayed in Lisabetta's grasp.

"You've been wronged." Lady Madeline again reached towards Lisabetta. "For so much of your life, you've been so wronged. Let me help you."

A small amount of green froth was visible in her mouth, accentuated against her alabaster skin. Lisabetta recoiled further and pulled Bartolome with her, gnashing her teeth at Lady Madeline. Bartolome compliantly followed.

"What's going on, dear Lady?"

Jai Ling stood in the dark, just beyond the light flickering from the fire in the hearth.

Lady Madeline beamed. Keeping her back to Jai Ling and looking to Lisabetta, Lady Madeline cupped her hand over her mouth and whispered, "I do think you'll both be useful to us, but right now I have to deal with your friend."

In the lower corridors of the castle, Elizabeth breathed deeply. The spell of the mother's blood was starting to wear thin, but she remained in control of the fleshers at the moment. Yet she would lose them.

Janosz towered over her. He and Nicola had not feasted on Roderigo. The others gnawed Roderigo's carcass down to his bones.

"Come on," Elizabeth said aloud. "We need to move fast before I lose them all."

Her tall lieutenant turned and made a gesture for the others to follow. Refreshed from their quick repas, they fell into line quickly and followed Elizabeth. She had chosen these six carefully—they responded to her directions and were adroit. Thus able to move at a brisk pace, the group made its way through the corridor under the eastern wall. Elizabeth helped Nicola along.

A gaggle of children, boys and girls, raced madly towards them. Elizabeth felt her people preparing to feed again, but she sent a stern mental direction to step aside and let the children pass—not out of any sense of compassion, but of urgency. This was neither the boy nor the girl they wanted. The children ran past, totally oblivious to the group, and Elizabeth saw the possession in their eyes. They disappeared into the darkened recess of the corridor, heading towards the water.

"I'm so glad you got here."

Lady Madeline glanced over her shoulder in Jai Ling's direction. "My husband heard some of the children were running around and sent me to look for them."

The lady giggled and covered her mouth.

Lisabetta was shaking a hand at the lady of the house, but with only one hand holding Bartolome. He broke free and ran from the room.

"Go after him, Lisabetta," Jai Ling commanded, moving through the shadows but watching Lady Madeline carefully. "Get him. Then find Lora."

Lisabetta ran after Bartolome.

Lady Madeline and Jai Ling held each other's gazes.

"Judging from how our children are reacting, it looks like you or your brother forgot to pay one of your debts."

"Oh yes, my brother, he's so forgetful," Lady Madeline said.

Jai Ling stood clutching the short bow in her right hand, with the quiver swung over her shoulder, and the anelace (which frankly, dear reader, she had forgotten about) strapped to the small of her back.

"I meant my husband, of course," Lady Madeline said, laughing, her eyes looking down, her hand covering her mouth. She coughed up green phlegm through her laugh. "Oh, damn. I messed that up, didn't I?"

Her hand dropped, and she smiled again. A little of the greenish fluid dripped on her lips and cheek, and it fell onto her white dress.

"Your poor friend Lisabetta, she is a feral creature, isn't she?" Lady Madeline brushed her white hair, leaving green streaks. She approached Jai Ling, laughing and making animated gestures.

Jai Ling surveyed the room. The windows were locked. Except for the one Bartolome broke. But the interior doors to the hall were open.

"You have some of that feral energy, but much more refined," Lady Madeline continued. "You can't bring yourself to leave because you have questions you need answered. You're asking yourself, 'Why didn't I sense this, and what can she be?' Well, you see, while you were traveling here, I sensed you a long way off."

Jai Ling stared at her advancing adversary.

Lady Madeline waved her right hand. The French doors facing towards the Durance River, the ones Bartolome had opened, slowly closed. Then Lady Madeline waved her left hand. One by one, each of the massive wooden entrance doors swung shut.

"You are very skilled, Jai Ling, very attuned to the other worlds. And I suspect your physical prowess is impressive."

Lady Madeline walked to the hearth, paused, and looked up at the picture of the last duchess of Castle Gallic.

"But you see, if one, like me, knows someone is coming, someone like you, I can block them. You hide yourself well, Jai Ling, but I've been looking for someone like you for a long time. We call you an empath. A strong one. So I did pick you up. And I blocked you. Your friend Lora, too, is another empath, but she's not as sensitive as you. You took some work, but it was worth it. Since everyone relies so much on you, it was easy to deceive them."

Clasping her hands together, Lady Madeline continued. "But

Lisabetta, well, I didn't catch her. The poor thing is so weak she doesn't register, but bless her soul, the girl actually can sense things. Spotted us right away, while you couldn't pick up a thing. She's bewitched, of course. Powerfully cursed."

Jai Ling felt her grip tighten on the short bow, but she restrained herself from moving. She whispered, "La sorcière."

"Not exactly, but for the purposes of this discussion, sure. You were wondering why I let poor Lisabetta go. Well, my friend Teodoro will have her. As for myself, I found someone who suits my needs better."

Jai Ling circled Lady Madeline cautiously.

"You're just letting the Piper have his way," Jai Ling said. "You didn't pay him. That was a mistake."

"He's a nuisance. And that Jiangshi 'disguised' at the party. My God, she's so crude. Roderigo will take care of them. Or I will. But the Piper has no effect on my people."

"Then why bargain with him?"

Lady Madeline continued to gesture back and forth with her hands.

"Because he gets rid of rats, and rats carry the black death, and you see, that does affect my people. We offered to pay him what he asked, but then he asked for more *after* he performed his services. Well, we can't give in to that, can we?"

Lady Madeline clapped her hands yet again.

"But enough of this banter—let's get to business. We can do this very easily, Jai Ling. These bodies my people occupy, they only last so long, and we need new ones. And yours is great."

Jai Ling ran to one of the doors behind her and grabbed the handles—they would not budge. She moved to another and then another, keeping an eye on the lady. Each door was locked. Jai Ling called out—

"Dioneo! Lora! Uwe! Trippetta!"

There was no answer.

"They're resting well, I hope," Lady Madeline said. "A little lemon balm with hops in the beer, a little valerian in the wine, not much, just enough to assist everyone to get to sleep. Not too deep. Our transfer process works best during light sleep."

Lady Madeline remained underneath the fresco, watching Jai Ling maneuver along the edges of the room.

"Oh, check that one, maybe it's open," Lady Madeline taunted. Jai Ling tried each door. All were locked, and she found herself in the corner, in Roderigo's study. Jai Ling looked at Roderigo's desk for keys, then she quickly realized no key was going to help her. Looking up, Lady Madeline, staring and smiling at her, stood near the hearth.

The fire had grown brighter.

With her free hand, Jai Ling stroked her fingers against her cheek.

"Why not hear me out?" Lady Madeline pleaded. "And stop rubbing your cheek like that, that's a bad nervous habit."

Jai Ling froze.

Her breaths were short.

She did not know what to do.

The words of her surrogate father came to her.

"Run to the fire, but from the side."

"Not sure if that's such a good idea, Father."

"Well, you better do something."

Words of an adoptive father. She was never totally clear if this was real or her Qi talking, but the sentiment was true enough. She started towards Lady Madeline.

"That's a good girl. Come closer."

Jai Ling pulled an arrow from her quiver, drew her bow, and aimed at Lady Madeline's body.

"I'm sick of your games, sorceress. My companions are in danger. Let me out of this room."

"Danger?" Lady Madeline said, stroking her chin and looking back to the fresco. "Well, I would say they are in something else right now."

Even with an offer to rest in the keep of Castle Gallic, Mr. and Mrs. Cooke had chosen to sleep in the bed of their wagon. The two routinely arose much earlier than the others to begin food preparation, and Mr. Cooke liked to be close to the provisions, so they'd developed the habit of staying with the wagon. Besides, most others had not been invited to the keep, and so they stayed in the middle bailey. On this night, as usual, the Cookes quickly fell asleep in each other's embrace.

In the darkness, several of the village inhabitants had watched the troupe bed down for the night. In one corner, the frail man with no legs, whom Dioneo had seen when he first entered the second bailey, waited with Beatrice and Bruno, the elderly wife and husband who had spoken with Dioneo earlier. The legless man complained he deserved a better host. Bruno admonished him to be satisfied that, under the circumstances, he was fortunate to be afforded any opportunity. Simon and Teodoro, the young nephew and niece who had spoken with Dioneo earlier in the day, silently lifted the legless man onto a donkey. They then led the donkey up to the Cooke's wagon. The legless man climbed onto the wagon's bow.

With green froth spilling from his mouth, the legless man reached forward and rested his fingertips on Mr. Cooke's temples. The man's frail fingers waivered as his veins pulsed with green. Mr. Cooke's eyes never opened during the entire fifteen-minute process. When it was done, what had been the body of the legless man was crumpled into a leathery ball of flesh, which Simon and Teodoro removed.

The eyes on the body of what had been Mr. Cooke opened. It sat up. Next to him, Mrs. Cooke stirred and asked if he was all right. The body of the former Mr. Cooke took a blanket and quietly suffocated Mrs. Cooke while Beatrice and another woman from the village looked on, patiently waiting for the woman's turn.

Teodoro looked at the wagons clustered in the middle of the courtyard.

"Andrea is going for Dioneo," she said jealously.

"She will not have him," Bruno said. "You know who has been selected for you."

"The idiot girl. Lisabetta. The lady has some interest in that one, I know it," Teodoro said.

"I believe the lady has chosen the oriental girl. A fitting choice, though I suspect the oriental will not be easy prey. But the lady loves her challenges."

Rowena lay nervously on her straw bed. They were inside a house just off the first bailey. Christian shut the door to the small apartment. Rowena saw him pick up a piece of wood to brace the door.

"Why are you doing that?" she asked.

Keeping his back to her, Christian answered, "We do not want the flagellants to disturb us, do we, my sweet?"

Something in Christian's voice bothered Rowena. Good looking or not, she was wondering if she had made a wrong choice.

She just then noticed there were no windows in the apartment.

Down in the middle bailey, Dioneo stroked Andrea's hair, but she pushed his arm away and climbed onto him.

"Hey, there's no rush," he said.

"You have an acrobatic body, so firm and muscular."

Andrea straddled Dioneo's hips and threw her hands around his head. Now it was Dioneo who tried to push away, but her grip was firm.

"Andrea, what's wrong with you?"

Andrea's voice changed to a lower tenor.

"I want you."

"As I want you to, love, but let's—hey!"

Andrea threw Dioneo's shoulders to the ground.

Dioneo thought, *Well, this is different.*

Elizabeth stopped inside one apartment that lined the lower courtyard. She found the blood-stained but still mostly white robes of the flagellants, which she had hidden away. Quickly, she threw them over the others, including Janosz and herself, and tightened the hoods. They were growing restless behind her, but she could handle them. It was the horde awaiting just outside the walls that was so difficult.

Elizabeth opened the door to the lower bailey. The night air carried a heavy scent of blood.

The flagellants lay on the ground in small clusters by fires. Most were unconscious due to exhaustion and pain, though a few just lay down. The leader and some others walked among the group with whips in their hand, as if on some kind of patrol. Were they guarding the flagellants or keeping people from fleeing?

"Go," Elizabeth commanded. Six of her people filed out into the courtyard in a controlled shamble, if that makes sense. No one paid them any attention.

Elizabeth turned back to Janosz and Nicola, who leaned against a wall. Elizabeth closed her eyes and took in a deep breath, and then released it.

She spoke to them mentally. *Nicola, find those children. Janosz, you and I go to that gatehouse.*

"Open the doors," Jai Ling ordered.

Lady Madeline shook her head.

Despite paralyzing fear, Jai Ling aimed at Lady Madeline's heart. Lady Madeline continued to laugh.

Jai Ling pulled her elbow back and shifted her aim to Lady Madeline's thigh, then let go.

Lady Madeline flicked her wrist. The arrow flew to the right, falling harmlessly to the floor.

Jai Ling paused. She was no more than thirty feet from her.

Lady Madeline asked coyly, "Something wrong with your aim, dear?"

Jai Ling quickly fired another arrow at the same thigh. Lady Madeline made another waving motion, and the arrow diverted upward and planted in the ceiling.

"Try a little closer," Lady Madeline said.

Jai Ling drew a third arrow and aimed for the sorceress's midsection, but hesitated. Lady Madeline pointed to her left breast, adding, "Aim for the heart, dear."

Jai Ling fired at the midsection. The sorceress waved her other hand, and the arrow sped into the great hearth where the flames devoured it.

"What the hell?"

"Listen to me."

Lady Madeline wiped the back of her hand across her mouth. Her white dress was now covered with green blotches.

"I'm going to make this easy. Normally, you fall asleep, we get close to you, and we absorb ourselves into your body while you absorb our essence. Some call it chi. You're familiar with it. Ours goes into yours—or yours goes into ours. It can work either way. We model ours on yours, that's how we live. And you're not dead —you're just no more. But we can do things a little differently. We can absorb into someone in a way that's like a sharing. It will still be your body, your memories. You're still you, but you're me as well. I give a little, so do you."

The sorceress looked back at the painting over the fireplace.

"We must reabsorb into another periodically. But when we find a body that has the physical skills we want, we will do this sharing. There are things which the body's muscles and the brain remember together, things that are hard for us to acquire. But it only works if you consent."

Oh fuck this, Jai Ling thought. She ran to one of the great oak-panel doors, pulling and pushing. The panels would not budge.

Lady Madeline sighed, sadly shook her head, and kneeled on both knees before the hearth. Jai Ling looked at the various weapons hanging on the walls until she saw a pole axe. She threw her bow to the ground, grabbed the pole axe, and raced to another door, where she hacked at the handles. Once, twice, three swings, and she was able to knock a handle off. She pulled the other handle, but the door would not move.

Jai Ling felt a burst of heat from behind. Lady Madeline had her arms extended before the great hearth, motioning towards the fresco. Was she praying to it? Or asking for its help? Jai Ling ran to another door and tried jamming the head of the pole axe between the doors. The doors were like living creatures, pushing back. She could not find a way out.

Lady Madeline waved her hand in circles over the flames, which were rising.

They were moving around her.

Not burning her, but dancing. The enhanced fire enveloped her.

Maybe she miscalculated. Burn witch.

The flames formed into a spinning pillar of fire. Jai Ling shielded her face from the intense light and heat. For another moment, she imagined the flames formed into the outline of some outrageous creature—a round ball, with two legs and two appendages, hanging by its sides, and a small, squat head with burning eyes. Then, the fire collapsed and disappeared.

And the room was deathly quiet.

But not for long.

The silence was interrupted by a heavy footfall in the middle of the hall. Ashes flipped up in the air. Jai Ling was puzzled—what was this? The room was empty save for her and Lady Madeline.

Then there was another heavy footfall, accompanied by more ash jumping from the floor, a few feet away from the other. Then another footfall and another.

Something was in the room with them. Something Jai Ling could not see.

But, it was there.

Within their room in the great keep of Castle Gallic, Uwe and Ricciardo slept. Normally, Uwe's snoring would have kept Ricciardo up all night, but they'd both fallen into a restful sleep. That restful sleep was rudely interrupted when Lora barged in.

* * *

Lora, Trippetta, and I are in this room. Ricciardo, startled, pops up in his bed, but Uwe mumbles "Shut up," and turns over on his side. Trippetta runs to him and rubs his back, steadily bringing him awake.

Ricciardo looks at an empty spot.

"Where's Bartolome?"

"The Piper is calling him," Lora answers.

Trippetta adds, "Jai Ling went after him. She brought Maddalena back first."

I nod.

Uwe rubs his head. "The Piper?"

I speak. "The music was in my head, and it drew me. I knew where I was, but I couldn't stop myself."

Lora crouches in front of Uwe. "Uwe! We're in a trap! Get up! We need to get everyone out."

Uwe slides his legs off the cot. Wearing only his britches, he asks, "Jai Ling? We must help her."

"She's the best one of us; she'll get him," Lora says. "Plus, Lisabetta is helping her."

"Lisabetta?" Ricciardo asks anxiously, arising from his bed. "She needs help. She can't wander this castle alone."

"We'll get her," Lora says. Then she seems to notice something, or something just occurred to her.

"We've all been sleeping, too well," she says. "They put something in our food. We need to get outside."

Five guards sat atop the parapet of the gatehouse to Castle Gallic. They had been instructed to stay alert, but their attention was focused inward. The stillness of the village belied any activity there. Yet suddenly there was a cacophony of moaning and groaning from the village. The sounds chilled each guard.

They ran to the exterior walls. The moonlight lit the small area between the village and the moat. Hundreds of flesh eaters were on the mound, advancing on the castle.

The officer in charge, a wachtmeister in the Papal Guards (before he was turned at Castle Gallic), was an experienced soldier named Grumbold in his former life. He had absorbed this body, also of a soldier, years ago. When Grumbold had been absorbed into this body, he had picked up his host's traits, so he had the experience of two soldiers. He did not panic. He was aware, however, of the fear in the others.

One of the younger guards, Lucas, said fearfully, "We are doomed."

"Calm yourself, Lucas," Grumbold ordered. "The gate is up. They cannot cross the moat. Watch."

Several flesh eaters continued marching to the edge of the moat, some reaching out for the castle. While the water in the trench was about three leagues high, the bottom of the moat had been layered with jagged rocks. As if in direct response to Grumbold's statement, fleshers began to tumble into the moat, usually headfirst, their arms flailing as they fell. Their bodies hit the water, and their momentum from the fall often threw their bodies to the rocks. If their skulls were not crushed, the water filled their lungs as they thrashed, and, unable to respond, they succumbed. The water flow carried the bodies to the Durance.

After the first surge fell in, the throng seemed to stop advancing. A few mindlessly still stumbled into the moat, but some began to move towards the approach where the drawbridge would fall if lowered.

Lucas ran back from the wall.

Grumbold looked on the throng in disgust. Yet he felt a mild chill as the horde, a mindless mob, seemed to move as one, with what seemed like some sense of direction.

Almost like they're being led, he thought.

He saw a young girl, eleven or twelve. Most of the fleshers shambled, some ran, some even crawled; they all moved like animals. This girl was standing erect amidst the other fleshers, wearing a hooded cloak. She was not the only girl there, but the others seemed aware of her and did not crowd or walk into her. It was dark, but in the moonlight, it looked like she was staring directly at the top of the gatehouse—at them.

Grumbold muttered, "Stay there all night, sweetie. Even if you have a brain. We will cut you down in the morning." Then, addressing two guards beside him, he said, "Check the drawbridge." The guards went along the parapet towards the gatehouse, in which the winch that held the gate was housed.

"Wachtmeister! Look here!"

It was Lucas's voice. He had gone to the back wall overlooking the interior of the castle grounds. Grumbold told the remaining guard, "Stay here and watch them while I see what that shit wants." Grumbold angrily backed away from the front and went to Lucas.

"Quit shaking," Grumbold scowled. "What do you—"

Then Grumbold looked onto the lowest courtyard where the flagellants had been resting.

Blood was everywhere. It had been before, of course, from the flagellants whipping their bodies. Now, rather than bodies resting in agony, there were bodies atop each other. Bodies gnawing on each other, disemboweling each other, dismembering each other. There were no white robes to be found; they were all blood-soaked. A few flagellants appeared to have been turned and were moving quickly, while others shambled slowly. Some were being consumed. Grumbold noticed several fleshers or flagellants breaking into apartments on the eastern wall. Green and red fluid was everywhere, but it was mostly red.

"They've become fleshers," Grumbold said.

How?" Lucas asked, his voice and body trembling as he viewed the scene.

"Like this."

Elizabeth stepped out of the shadows and bit deep into Lucas's neck, jaws clenching on his carotid artery. Lucas had not been turned by the occupants of Castle Gallic, and red blood burst from his throat and onto Grumbold, momentarily blinding him. He drew his sword and then slashed at the air. Elizabeth chewed on the flesh and sinew. She held Lucas's pulsating body in her grasp. Grumbold wiped his eyes and saw Lucas's body throbbing. Lucas was turning into one of the undead before him.

"Damn you all!" Grumbold said and swung his sword again.

Elizabeth kept pulling Lucas back. His blood was energizing her. She wanted to feed even more, but she desired this boy to be one of them.

"You want him? You want him?" Grumbold cried. "Then have him!"

Grumbold turned to run—and did run—right into Janosz. Elizabeth's lieutenant reached down, grasped Grumbold's shoulder with his hands, and ripped the wachtmeister's head. Grumbold was a strong warrior. It took Janosz almost a minute to fully tear off the head.

Elizabeth was ingesting Lucas's blood slowly. She could feel her blood mixing with his. Lucas was rapidly turning into one of her people. How, she was not sure, but she could bite someone and, if she held back her force, she could turn them quickly.

Using the flagellant's white robes, they had managed to ascend to the top of the gatehouse and overwhelm the two guards at the winding drum used to raise and lower the drawbridge. Then they had come here. One of the guards on the wall had watched their attack in horror and fled. It did not matter.

Lucas stood before her.

Elizabeth pulled Lucas's sword from its sheath, put its hilt in his palm, and wrapped his hand around it. It slid out. Elizabeth picked it up again and said into his mind, *Hold!* Lucas swayed in place, holding the hilt while the point dropped to the floor.

"That will do," she said. Elizabeth walked to Janosz and picked up Grumbold's sword, saying, "We'll try this."

With dead eyes, Lucas followed, his head listing to the side.

The three went back to the room where the winding drum was. Two other guards were dead on the floor—one bleeding green blood, one red. The winch itself consisted of a fifteen-inch-thick hemp rope wrapped around a windlass. The ropes dropped through the floor all the way to the bottom of the Barbican tower and were attached to iron weights and counterweights that raised and lowered the drawbridge, but men had to operate a large wheel to make it work. Normally, it took four men working this pulley system to raise and lower it.

Elizabeth and Janosz grasped the handles—the new one, "Lucas," was too raw to follow her. Janosz had the strength of several men, and it was easier to lower than to raise a drawbridge. After pulling hard, the windlass gave, and the ropes spun around it. Elizabeth heard the high groan of the wooden gate dropping, along with the iron weights rising. Then it stopped abruptly, and as it did, the tower shook so much so that for an instant, Elizabeth thought it might topple.

Just like the door at Sacra di San Michele, she thought.

She ran to the castle edge.

The drawbridge was only halfway down.

Elizabeth ran to the pulleys housed here in the Barbican tower. Something had jammed. Back in the winch room, she saw the hemp rope had been extended.

"Cut it," she commanded Janosz. He took what had been Grumbold's sword and swung it onto the rope. This hemp was stronger than some chains, and it repulsed the blade, but several strands were torn.

"Cut it," Elizabeth repeated, and she pushed Lucas to it. She mentally moved his arms so that he made a swing that hit the rope, not nearly as powerfully as Janosz, but a movement nonetheless. Janosz swung again. They continued at this, Janosz taking mighty swings, Lucas hitting the same area much weaker. The rope began to fray. Finally, Janosz raised the sword high, grabbed the hilt with both hands, and swung down. The rope snapped. The iron weights fell, the iron counterweights rose, and the drawbridge crashed down, crushing several fleshers who did not make any effort to move out of the way. Alatiel, however, had positioned herself beyond the fall of the drawbridge. She pointed into the lower bailey.

Many shuffled. Some crawled. A few ran. Regardless of how they moved, the undead entered Castle Gallic.

Rowena lay nervously on a straw bed. There was a pitcher with water and a basin set on a table beside her.

"Freshen up," Christian said, standing in the doorway, admiring her figure.

She poured some water into the basin. There was no window, and Christian had shut the door to the small apartment.

Good looking or not, she wanted to get away from him.

He turned to her and began to smile.

"You have a beautiful body."

There was shouting coming from the lower bailey.

"Do you hear that?" she asked. "Something is happening."

"Don't be worried, my love," Christian said.

There was a great thud, heavy enough for Rowena to feel the ground beneath her shake. "That sounded like the drawbridge crashing," she said.

Christian said, "We're safe in here."

"To hell we are; I'm getting out of here." Rowena went to the door and reached for the doorknob.

Christian threw her back.

"There's no need for that," he said, green fluid dribbling from his lips. "I need you."

Rowena grabbed the pitcher of water and hit Christian's head. He collapsed on the floor. Rowena ran to the door, kicked the brace aside, and ran.

She was in a small alley between two medium-sized houses. The moonlight was bright tonight, though dark clouds were rolling in. She snaked her way back to the others. After passing some buildings, on her right, she saw a horse stable with a few pigs wandering about, which she recalled from earlier in the day. She ran past it and found herself just outside the gate to the middle bailey.

In his anger, El Erreur had lost his focus and allowed himself to stumble into a dark passage, some sort of escape tunnel that ran along the base of the castle's outermost wall. He had momentarily heard what he thought were children's footsteps and followed them down a stairwell that abruptly ended, but in leaning against a stone block, he had activated a release that slid the block back. He had fallen in. He was not hurt, but it was very dark down here.

Again, he heard the sound of footfalls. Running ones. It sounded like two children coming towards him.

Down in the middle bailey, Dioneo saw a milky-green fluid drip from Andrea's eyes.

"What the hell!" he yelled.

Andrea thrust her hips into his pelvis, then kissed him deeply on the lips. Dioneo rocked back and forth and pushed, but he couldn't shove her off. His arms reached out to the sides when he caught hold of something solid. A rock. He grasped it and struck Andrea's back with it. She shot up and, freeing one arm, flicked the rock out of Dioneo's hand

"Don't you want to make love to me, Dioneo?"

She opened her mouth wider. Dioneo tried to push Andrea off him again, but she threw his arms aside and pressed on him.

Andrea rose for a breath.

"This is less painful if you just let me in." She pulled him up, embraced him, and kissed him deeper. Dioneo was unable to stop her.

He twisted on the ground but could not break her hold. His arms flailed on the cobblestones. His fingers were near a flame —the fire! He stretched and reached for a piece of firewood, then jammed a burning end into the side of Andrea's head. She jerked upward, her eyes rolled up, and her arms slumped to the side.

"Christ," Dioneo called, rolling out from under the limp body.

"Everyone, up!"

He picked up the axe he'd used earlier to cut the firewood and ran to a wagon, the one where he'd stopped earlier that was filled with members of the troupe and local village girls. He looked in and began yelling, “Everybody get up! We gotta—”

There were two pairs of men and women sitting in the wagon, smiling at him. Long strands of slimy green filth were being wrapped up and removed from the wagon by other villagers.

Somehow, he knew. His companions in this wagon were now those slimy husks, and the people staring at him were something else. He backed away and went to the center of the wagon circle, calling, “Is anyone here?”

Over from the lower bailey, he heard mayhem and the slam of the front drawbridge falling. Children from the troupe were running across the yard.

“You kids! Get over here!” he yelled. They ignored him and went by.

“We need to get them,” said a voice. He whirled and saw Mrs. Cooke behind him.

“You’re a lovely sight to see as always, Mrs. Cooke, but we have to gather everyone,” Dioneo said and gave her a quick protective hug, scanning the edge of the bailey.

He felt a clamminess to her body. He let go.

“It’s all right, Dioneo,” Mrs. Cooke said. “I feel wonderful. And you will too. Just let this happen.”

She stepped towards him. Dioneo pushed her back with his axe. He started to swing his axe at her, but caught himself. He ran to the other wagons in the circle and called out.

“Anyone here?”

No one responded, but he saw many of his friends, his companions, sitting in the wagons. All smiling at him.

He backed away, then turned and ran toward the keep.

Mansa ran into him in the courtyard. Dioneo pulled his axe back and stared at his friend.

“It’s me, Dioneo,” Mansa said. “It’s me. I need your help. We have to get the animals.”

Dioneo hesitated, then said, “What about the others?”

"I can't find anyone alive in this part of the castle," Mansa answered. "Some sorcery is taking over."

Dioneo glanced around. Panic set in. Villagers were running helter-skelter. Some members of the troupe—his companions—were moving slowly.

"What the hell?" Dioneo muttered.

Then he looked to the lower bailey.

There was enough moonlight to show the commotion going on there. A few bodies stumbled through the open gateway. Dioneo and Mansa began to move toward them, and then Dioneo grabbed Mansa's shoulder.

"Fleshers," Dioneo said.

"My animals," Mansa said.

More fleshers were coming through the gatehouse into the middle bailey. Fleshers and flagellants who had been turned. The flagellants were only clothed from the waist down, if at all, and some were totally naked. Their grotesque forms twisted in the throng that was passing through the entry.

Most moved slowly, but then one of them, a dark-haired elderly woman, looked directly at Dioneo and pointed in his direction.

"We gotta go," Dioneo said.

"Dioneo! Mansa!" From the opposite side of the courtyard, standing at the entrance to the upper bailey, Uwe was jumping up and down, waving them over.

In the great hall, Jai Ling glared at Lady Madeline, who knelt trance-like before the burning hearth. Lady Madeline slowly raised her hands. Two polearm weapons hanging on the wall began to glow—a bec de faucon, a long pole ending in three different sharpened prongs, and a hache, another polearm weapon that ended in an axe-shaped blade.

These two weapons were taken off the wall by invisible arms

and thrust several feet into the air. A third weapon, a katana, rose from the wall and was tossed towards Lady Madeline. It stopped at her feet. She took no notice of it.

Jai Ling stood watching, feeling her heartbeat.

Then the long pole weapons shifted position. Whatever it was that came out of the fire turned towards Jai Ling.

Jai Ling stepped back and onto her short bow. She picked it up and fired off three arrows into the space between where the polearms were suspended in the air. The bec de faucon and the hache both swung broadly and deflected each arrow. Then the polearms and the footfalls began to advance.

Lady Madeline's eyes were closed, her arms held up in front of her, as if she herself was wielding the weapons. Jai Ling fired another arrow at her, but the hache moved over quickly—much quicker than she expected—and sliced the arrow in mid-air. Jai Ling whirled her head around the room. Again, her instincts were silent.

Any ideas, Father? she thought.

You might want to think about running.

And run she did. Not to the creature, nor Lady Madeline, nor even the giant wooden doors of the great hall, but instead towards the French doors overlooking the water. She could break through the glass panels. After dropping her bow and throwing off her quiver, she leapt up to kick out a glass pane, but the doors swung out and battered her up. She fell to the ground. Quickly, she bounced up to see the hammer head of the bec de faucon coming down on her. Jai Ling rolled aside as the hammer broke the marble floor next to her. She sprang to her feet and ran to the eastern wall, near the study. She could hear the thudding footfalls pounding behind. Among the weapons on this wall, she found a spear with a metal tip. She grabbed it and turned. The pole weapons hung in the air a little further back than she expected. She threw the spear directly between the weapons, and the hache deflected it.

[12]
THE HOUSE IS FALLING

JAI LING WAS PERSPIRING. Having just thrown the spear at the creature from the fire, she grabbed two shields, one a large triangular kite shield with a round top and tapered bottom, and the other a smaller, round targe shield. Both were made of metal. The sharp blade of the hache swung down on her left, and she managed to deflect it with the targe shield. Another swing of a pole axe was coming down on her head, and she leaped to the right. The creature kept trying to lead her into a corner.

Jai Ling had stayed ahead of it, running back to the center of the room. She kept trying to get to Lady Madeline, but the unseen thing always got between them. Jai Ling's breathing was labored.

"Again, you could make this much easier, Jai Ling." Lady Madeline remained seated in front of the hearth, her eyes still closed. "We can do this all night if need be."

Jai Ling had been in tight spots before against the supernatural. But her instincts, her inner compass, were failing her.

Not even there. Bad time to desert me, Father.

She fought back the fatigue creeping in.

The bec de faucon hammer came down again. She blocked with the round targe shield, but it was knocked from her grasp and clattered to the floor. Jai Ling tried to reach for it, but it was kicked across the room by an invisible limb. The clawed prong of the bec de faucon swung again across the side of her body. She blocked it with the kite shield, but the blow tossed her backwards.

Jai Ling raced to the eastern end of the room and stopped at that wall, then turned and pressed her back against the wood, fighting to stay on her feet and not slip down and fall asleep.

Any last advice, Father?

In her head, she heard his voice. Clearer than before. From many years ago. One of his oldest adages.

The quieter you become, the more you are able to hear.

The invisible creature was moving toward her again. How could you become quiet in here?

Breathing deeply, her buttocks slid to the floor. She lowered her head.

Then, one thought.

She doesn't want to kill me.

That took a while for you to realize. What else?

She wants to tire me into exhaustion. Why?

Her father's voice answered. *What does she want?*

My body. She wants to absorb me.

So become quiet, and maybe you will hear what you are not hearing.

Jai Ling thought. And thought.

She dropped the kite shield. Then she crossed both legs, placed a hand on each knee cap, and breathed deeply.

The creature's bellowing roars filled her head.

Calm yourself.

She breathed in through her nose, held the breath, and exhaled through her mouth, but she did so quickly.

The roars continued.

What we think we become. Jai Ling continued to breathe. *Become calm.*

This time, she exhaled much more slowly than before.

The creature's bellows—they seemed the slightest bit more distant. Her shoulders released with her next breath. With the next breath, her legs.

Good. Now, become quiet and listen. Listen.

The creature was still making noise, but it was further in the background. Jai Ling also heard, beneath the creature's bellowing, a buzzing.

The more slowly she breathed, the more the buzzing became like a whoosh of air. It morphed into voices. Loud whispers.

Good. Now listen well.

The whispers. Two voices going back and forth. She could make out words.

"You're losing her." This voice she did not recognize, an older voice, but it contained trepidation.

"No." Lady Madeline's voice was firm but frustrated. "You're losing her." Now with more fear. "I need her body." More argumentative.

Jai Ling listened well. Her senses were alert. The first voice—it was frail. And... ancient.

The first voice started again. "You're losing her."

"No. I need her."

"She's... SHE CAN HEAR US!"

"No. I can—"

Jai Ling resisted an urge to open her eyes. Trusting her senses, she *felt* out the location of the creature. It was hovering about thirty paces in front of her, between her and Lady Madeline—and the great hearth. The kite shield was beside Jai Ling, but she had no weapon.

Or did she?

She took more breaths, and as she exhaled, she swayed back, and in doing so, she felt something pressing against the small of her back.

The anelace.

Keeping her eyes closed, she said aloud, "You said Fra Pandolf was a painter. I couldn't recall before, but now I remember something about him, my lady."

"And what do you remember, Jai Ling?"

"Fra Pandolf was a painter, that is true," Jai Ling responded in a calm voice, breathing deeply. "But he was also a necromancer. A dangerous one. I've heard it said he was as crazy as the mad scholar."

"Your memory returns," Lady Madeline said.

"There was something else I heard. He embedded things into his paintings."

The ancient voice shrieked, "KILL HER! KILL HER NOW!"

Now Jai Ling heard her father's voice. *What do your instincts tell you to do*?

She waited.

Thud.

She heard one footfall from the creature.

Thud.

Then another.

Jai Ling grabbed the triangular kite shield. She ran towards the creature, towards the ashes where it had stepped. The invisible creature raised the bec de faucon. Jai Ling raised her shield to deflect the pole weapon. Instead of coming down on her from the top, the bec de faucon was swung at her in a horizontal motion. This was *not* a swing to tire her but to kill. She threw the shield to the ground and leapt onto it, sliding as the bec de faucon sliced the air just above her. She rode the shield under the creature, and with a pair of ankle kicks, she reached the great hearth. Lady Madeline was moving at her with the katana.

Jai Ling jumped onto the closest banquet table, balancing herself while carrying the kite shield. Lady Madeline swung the katana at her feet. Jai Ling jumped over the blade, which passed beneath her. Jai Ling threw the kite shield at Lady Madeline, who knocked it aside with the sword. While Lady Madeline was deflecting the shield, Jai Ling hoisted herself from the table onto the mantle of the great hearth. Reaching behind her back, she pulled out the anelace.

Jai Ling and Lady Madeline locked eyes. There was no longer bellowing from the creature. No noises. Just Jai Ling on the mantle, looking down at Lady Madeline. Lady Madeline was close —she could reach Jai Ling in a few steps—but they both knew at that moment, Jai Ling was where *she* wanted to be.

"Join us," the lady implored.

Jai Ling turned and, with a great slashing move, drove the anelace deep into the fresco image, at the throat of the Lady de Medici.

Jai Ling was prostrate on the floor. The table she had climbed was flipped over. She rubbed her forehead and then—she noticed a green slime on her hands. Her body was covered in it.

Jai Ling got onto her hands and knees.

What had been an intense fire in the hearth was now burnt embers. Jai Ling could make out Lady Madeline's body on the ground a few feet away, lying in a pool of green, her white dress and hair smeared with the liquid. Her head was twisted around completely and stared lifelessly towards the painting. The katana and the anelace lay on the floor a few feet away.

Jai Ling looked at the fresco of Lady de Medici, the Last Duchess of Castle Gallic. The green fluid had splattered over the portrait, obliterating the woman's image.

But you could see a great hole punched in the wall, where the head had been.

Jai Ling stayed there for several beats, breathing. Then she picked up the katana and the anelace and ran to the other side of the great hall to get her short bow and arrows left in her quiver. Reaching one of the large wooden doors, she wedged the katana into the lock. With a shove, the door popped open. She ran out of the great hall.

Dioneo and Mansa ran across the middle bailey through the gateway and into the upper bailey. Uwe, Ricciardo, and Lora were waiting for them just beyond the entrance to the upper bailey.

Uwe asked, “Others?”

Mansa shook his head.

“Not that I can see. The fleshers have overrun it.”

Dioneo looked backward and said, “It’s a massacre. Never saw this.” He turned to Lora. “Where’s Jai Ling?”

“She went after Lisabetta and Bartolome,” Lora said. “Back in the keep. Trippetta and Maddalena are with a lot of the children we’ve broken from the Piper’s spell. They’re holed up in a room at the back of the keep near the river. But some were drawn outside, and some to the river.”

Lora went to Mansa, and they embraced quickly.

Mansa whispered something to her. Lora nodded, then faced the others.

“The castle is surrounded by fleshers. The Piper is calling the children to drown them. And the people here—we don’t know what they are, but they aren’t like us. The children. They’re. They’re—” Her voice trailed off.

“We have to worry about the living,” Mansa said. “My animals are trapped.”

Lora pushed him back, looked him in the eyes, and said, “Children before animals.”

Each saw the pain in the other’s eyes. Mansa nodded.

Lora said, “Any children still alive are trapped back here in this bailey and the keep. The birds have spotted some of them. We need to get who we can.”

Mansa turned to Dioneo and Uwe. "Can you buy us some time?"

Dioneo put his hands around Ricciardo and Uwe and said, "I think we can do that."

Lora and Mansa went back to the keep.

Ricciardo said, "I thought I saw Lisabetta come out here. I tried to follow, but I lost her."

In the foreground, fleshers were advancing through the middle bailey. They attacked anyone who was not a flesher. A few flagellants had escaped into that middle bailey, but they were weakened from the scourging of their bodies a few hours earlier. Now they moved as lethargically as most of the undead, easy prey for the quicker fleshers. When one of the green-blooded persons was attacked, the fleshers killed and fed, but they did not dwell on that victim for long.

"The green blood doesn't seem to satisfy them," Lora said. "They crave the red blood."

"Well, that includes us, so I suggest we get out of here," Dioneo said.

Most of the fleshers were slowly advancing towards the keep in Castle Gallic, following the scent of the red blood.

Most. But not all.

Dioneo recognized the leader of the flagellants—the broad-shouldered man with the wild hair and beard. He was running through the bailey. A small group of quick-running, nearly naked fleshers was pursuing him. The leader changed course and deliberately ran towards a female flagellant stumbling along ahead of him. Dioneo began to move toward them when the leader grabbed the woman by the shoulders and threw her to the ground, then kept running. The woman was too exhausted to move. The pursuing fleshers fell upon her, save for one thin boy, totally naked, who sped after the flagellant leader.

Dioneo muttered, "You bastard."

The flagellant leader was nearly across the courtyard when he tripped on a cobblestone and rolled forward. He quickly bounced up, bleeding from his forehead, and continued to run, but the slip was enough for the one pursuing flesher boy to overtake him. Both went to the ground. The naked flesher boy climbed on the leader, who held the boy's head back with his hands wrapped around the boy's neck.

The boy bit the thumb off the leader's right hand.

The flagellant leader's arms hooked, and the boy was able to slip from his grip and bite into the leader's right bicep. Blood sprayed. The flagellant leader screamed as the flesher tore out most of the muscle in the arm. Dioneo was surprised the leader had the strength to throw the boy off with his left arm and make it to his feet. The leader even managed a couple of steps before the boy jumped on him again and bit into the right shoulder. The leader dropped to his knees.

Dioneo saw life draining out of the leader's eyes.

Dioneo looked upward. The sharp portcullis which divided the middle and the upper bailey was suspended above them.

"We need to drop that gate," Dioneo said. "That will slow them down."

"It has to be released from above," Uwe said.

"What do you want me to do?" Ricciardo asked.

"Stay here and yell when the fleshers get here, then run like hell," Dioneo advised. "And don't get crushed by the gate!"

Dioneo saw a wooden door in the smaller gatehouse and grabbed Uwe. Clutching his axe, Dioneo sprinted ahead of Uwe over a pile of ropes. Both ascended flights of wooden stairs to the smaller guardroom, where a winch and pulley system smaller than the one in the main gatehouse was in place. This was a large wheel with pistons extending from it and a lever to the side. A coil of rope was nearby.

"This does it?" Uwe asked.

"Let's find out," Dioneo said.

Uwe put down the axe and pulled the lever. The two men

grabbed the pistons and twisted the wheel. The portcullis quickly released and slid in a controlled fall to the ground. It was a latticed grill made of interlocking metal strips wide enough to put an arm through, but not a body.

"Well done," Dioneo said. "Let's get out of here."

Dioneo grabbed his axe and the rope, then ran back to the ground. He struck the grill of the gate with his axe. "This will hold them a bit. Come on."

Dioneo, Uwe, and Ricciardo began to fall back into the main bailey when—

"Lisabetta!" Ricciardo said.

A figure who might have been Lisabetta ran into a small doorway in the northeastern part of the keep. Ricciardo began to go after her when Dioneo grasped his arm and said, "Don't go off by yourself. Wait for us."

Ricciardo shook his arm free. "She needs help." He ran in pursuit.

A few bodies littered the ground. Lora and Mansa were at the other end of the courtyard by the keep, grabbing children and slapping or wrestling with them, anything to bring the children out from the Piper's enchantment. Maddalena and Trippetta were corralling the children for whom the spell had been broken.

Dioneo recalled that those under the Piper's spell had to be brought out of it violently.

I hate that guy, Dioneo thought. Then he said to Uwe, "You help Trippetta. I'll go after Ricciardo."

They both began to go towards the rear of the courtyard. Then from the portcullis, there came a familiar voice.

"Dioneo! Uwe!"

They turned. Rowena was on the wrong side of the portcullis, reaching through the metal bars.

Dioneo looked back at her. He could see fleshers closing from behind.

"Can't save her," Uwe said.

"You're right," Dioneo said, and he turned.

"Dioneo!" Rowena called again.

Dioneo stopped. He turned and ran to the portcullis.

Rowena was sobbing. "I don't want to die, Dioneo, please don't let me die."

Her hand reached out to him through the quilt work of iron bars.

"Don't let me die!"

Uwe came up.

"Let's lift this thing," Dioneo said and dropped his axe. Uwe and Dioneo crouched down and grasped the bars that ran across the bottom of the portcullis. They gave it a mighty heave.

"Pull, you damned dwarf," Dioneo spat.

Uwe gritted his teeth.

They pulled.

They could not move it.

"Too much," Uwe grunted.

The sharp points of the portcullis were driven into tightly spaced cobblestones, and there wasn't enough time nor the tools to dig underneath. Also, two rods on the end of the gate had snapped into cutouts in the jam of the gateway.

"No time to raise it," Uwe said.

Rowena reached through the crisscrossed metal bars and grabbed Dioneo's hand.

"I know you never loved me," she said, not looking at him.

Dioneo grabbed the lattice of the portcullis. "Rowena, you can climb this. I'll help you. Climb."

Rowena sobbed and would not look up, saying, "I can't!"

"You can!"

Rowena slumped down against the portcullis.

Dioneo saw three fleshers closing. "God damn it," he muttered. Then he slapped Uwe's shoulder and said, "Stay here."

Dioneo raced back up the gatehouse. Uwe looked helplessly at

Rowena, just a few feet away, on the other side. A rope was thrown to Uwe. He looked up to see Dioneo smiling.

"Drop and pop," Dioneo said.

They nodded, with Uwe repeating "Drop and pop."

Dioneo went to the other side of the gatehouse and leaned out a window, about sixty feet above Rowena. He tied one end of the rope around his feet and waited. The slack of the rope was taken up. Dioneo tugged on the tight rope, and a little slack was given. He checked the knots around his feet—they were pretty tight. Still, he had tied it quickly.

"Rowena," Dioneo called, "we're going to do drop and pop. You hear me! We're doing drop and pop. You have to stand up!"

"I can't," Rowena sobbed.

"God damn it, get on your feet now!"

Rowena pulled herself up.

Janosz strode through the middle bailey. Even among the carnage, other fleshers parted as he went by, more a reaction than thought, avoiding the alpha predator of the pack. Janosz had enough, and unlike the others, the smell of blood and the sight of exposed flesh did not drive him into a berserk state.

By the high gate—he saw movement. A woman trapped. A man swinging down to her.

With the rope attached, Dioneo slid down the other side of the gatehouse.

"Reach for me!" Dioneo yelled. In the third courtyard behind him, Uwe fed the rope and lowered Dioneo headfirst until he was about twenty feet over Rowena. Uwe was digging his feet into the cobblestones to brace himself as he slowly but steadily continued to lower Dioneo, watching that he did not drop him too fast.

Rowena was still crying, face pressed against the metal bars. Dioneo saw two or three male flagellants—now full-fledged fleshers—closing for her. One was running ahead of the others—the one whom Ricciardo and Lisabatta had seen as the first flagellant who whipped himself that afternoon.

Uwe tightened the rope and dropped Dioneo just above Rowena. Dioneo reached his hands out. Rowena still held the bars.

"Don't look around," Dioneo yelled. "Give me your hand!"

"You don't love me," Rowena said, looking aimlessly into the stone. "You never loved me."

"Rowena, God damn it! Reach for me!"

The closest flagellant flesher, who bore a passing resemblance to Dioneo, was a few feet away.

Dioneo pushed off with his legs from the portcullis and swung out, while on the other side of the wall, Uwe pulled with his great forearms. Dioneo flew across the gateway, suspended by the rope. Rowena reached up with one arm. Dioneo grabbed her with his left hand. Uwe saw this and pushed even harder on his thighs, finding purchase for his feet in the spaces between the cobblestones, and pushed himself backward. Dioneo and Rowena were carried up.

Now you must understand, when Dioneo and Uwe practiced their moves, they used pivots and pulleys to get leverage. Right now, this was just Uwe pulling up both bodies over a wall with his arms and legs—not much of a pivot.

Rowena was still crying.

Dioneo was breathing heavily.

"Look at me, honey. Just look at me."

The rope slipped in Uwe's hands. Dioneo and Rowena slid down, but Uwe caught the rope.

"Uwe!" Dioneo yelled.

Uwe leaned so his back was nearly on the ground. One foot

after the other, he began pulling them back. Rowena was several feet off the ground when the flesher who looked like Dioneo reached the portcullis and jumped, grabbing onto Rowena's left foot. She screamed and twisted, but Dioneo had her hand.

Uwe moved further back. Dioneo, Rowena, and the flesher ascended. The flesher could only grasp Rowena's foot, but he could not bite her.

Dioneo grabbed Rowena with his other arm and said, "Kick!"

She did, and the flesher fell on a pair of other fleshers who had reached the portcullis and were pawing upwards.

Rowena's grip shifted in Dioneo's hands. They were wet with perspiration.

He looked at her, their faces only a couple of feet apart.

"Honey, you need to work with—"

Rowena's hand slipped through Dioneo's.

Her body disappeared under a pile of fleshers

Except, amidst the group, there was one tall flesher. Unlike the others, he stood erect, square-shouldered, rigid posture, and he was glaring up at Dioneo.

Their eyes met.

Dioneo looked away and pulled himself up to the gatehouse. Rowena's screams mercilessly followed him. He picked up the axe he had left and ran down the other side and out to the courtyard, not looking back.

Uwe met him.

"I-I—" the dwarf stammered.

"Not your fault," Dioneo said.

"Nor yours," Uwe grunted.

"Never said it was." Dioneo was bent over, holding the axe across his knees, catching his breath.

Mansa, Lora, and Trippetta had gathered more children together at the foot of the keep, along with some stray adults from the troupe, and were heading inside.

"Come on," Uwe said. "We get out of here now."

"You go help them," Dioneo said, pointing towards Trippetta. "The place is surrounded. Get to the Durance. I'll get Ricciardo and meet you there."

"I lost Maddalena," Trippetta said. "She was with me as we were moving the children to find more. We got separated."

Everyone was silent until Dioneo spoke again.

"Get to the boat on the other side of the castle. Try to find Maddalena along the way. Ricciardo and others ran over there. I'll try to find them."

No one moved.

Dioneo pushed Uwe.

"Get out of here. I'll be right behind you."

Uwe nodded. The group gathered the children and went back into the keep. Dioneo gathered his wits. He saw the wagons of his troupe were ablaze, burning everything they had.

The portcullis was down. But the fleshers would soon find ways through the wall and invade this, the upper bailey. And the fleshers didn't seem to discriminate in who they ate.

Dioneo was heading where he'd last seen Ricciardo heading when, out the corner of his eye, he saw Nefferi. She was struggling across the bailey in only a nightshirt, half-carrying, half-dragging El Erreur draped over her shoulder. Their leader's head was hanging down, far too down, and his arm looked as if chunks had been torn out of it.

"What the hell is she doing?" Dioneo muttered. Then he began to sprint towards her, waiving his free arm and yelling, "NEFFERI! GET AWAY FROM HIM!"

"He's my husband!" she called back.

Dioneo never quite knew if they were truly revived Egyptian royalty. But Nefferi was always a practical one. Couldn't she see what was happening?

El Erreur's body spasmed, his head shot up, eyes closed in pain. His head then slumped down again. Nefferi stumbled, but stayed upright.

"DROP HIM!" Dioneo yelled. He had almost reached Nefferi when the inevitable happened.

El Erreur raised his head—Nefferi was looking forward—but this time his eyes were crazed, large black pupils—the eyes of the undead, wild with hunger.

His jaws bit deep into Nefferi's neck.

Nefferi cried in pain and fell to her knees.

Dioneo reached them and, with a swift kick to the head, knocked El Erreur off of Nefferi. Their leader, the man who had planned so many of their escapades, was now a flesher, skin and blood hanging out of his mouth. El Erreur crouched on the ground, studying Dioneo. Dioneo drew back his axe to swing, but hesitated—was there any sense of life in there? El Erreur had never been close, but they'd been through much.

El Erreur launched himself.

Dioneo swung his axe. El Erreur's skull split like a piece of firewood in an explosion of bone, flesh, and brains.

Beside him, Nefferi lay on her back, her body in deep convulsions.

Between breaths, Nefferi said, "He-was-my-love-forever." Then, with even more effort, she uttered, "S-s-save-your-self."

Dioneo looked skyward. Clouds had come in. A slight mist was falling. He swung the axe into the ground several times, creating small sparks, and he took deep breaths.

A voice in his head (and with so many voices in people's heads, dear reader, you should know this really was his own common sense) asked, *and what are you accomplishing now?*

"Dioneo." Nefferi's voice was a whisper. She was shuddering on the ground. The nightshirt had crawled up her waist, and she had lost control of her bodily functions. "Don't-let-me," was all she could muster.

"Nefferi," he said weakly. "I can't."

Her head rolled to the other side, her eyes open.

Dioneo saw her pupils shrink.

"Nefferi," he muttered.

He watched a spark in Nefferi's eyes fade. But then the black pupils grew large. Quickly.

Even with her eyes changing, with blood spurting out of her mouth and from her wound, Nefferi – the real Nefferi - managed one word.

"P-P-Please."

Dioneo did what he had to.

Where am I? Where is Bartolome? Lisabetta was just with us. Where is she? I must find my brother. He's still hearing the Piper.

I'm high up in the castle keep.

Wait, there's a doorway.

I-I don't hear anything on the other side.

What was that sound?

It's from the stairway underneath.

I'm going outside.

Ouch!

That silly red ribbon gets caught on the door.

It's raining. I'm wet. This foolish dress is not easy to walk in.

I can see the troupe's wagons burning. There are many fleshers. Everywhere. So much blood. I feel sick. I must get—where?

MADDALENA.

That's not me.

MADDALENA.

Stop.

There's a hooded figure. She's standing on the building next to us. I am on a dais at the edge of the keep.

She is wearing a white cloak like the flagellants had, but it is completely blood-stained.

She tosses back her hood.

I've seen her.

The parapet along the castle wall runs between us. If she jumps onto it, she can reach me. But I can make it back to the doorway—

"Maddalena. Don't run."

I stop. She is speaking out loud.

The voice.

She is the Romani woman I met. Near the caravan. Months ago. But it seems longer.

Before the attack on our caravan.

"You once asked me to pick you a flower," I say. "A red firethorn. And I did. I pricked my arm, and you licked my arm and healed the cut. And that night, you attacked the caravan. And my family. Just like now."

"Yes. And no. Not like now," she replies. "I was still learning to control the others then. But now I am stronger. Observe."

A horde of fleshers appears behind her. They look hungry and start for me, but the woman raises a hand. They stop.

"Come with me, Maddalena. I can protect you and your brother. I can protect you from the Black Death."

"What happened to my mother!"

The woman searches for words.

"You killed her."

The woman strokes her chin. "No. I know it is hard to comprehend. To you, your mother would appear dead, but Maddalena, I can show you so much. She is not really dead. She is preserved. Her blood gives life. As does yours, and your brother's, and mine. There is so much more to the world than what you know. You'll see she is alive, but in a different way. I can protect you from the Black Death. I don't want to hurt you. We are so closely related. Just give me the chance to show you these things. Look inside, you'll realize the truth of what I say."

I am frightened. Yet somehow, when she says we are related, I feel -

A hand grasps my shoulder.

"Maddalena. Get behind me."

Jai Ling stood on the parapet of Castle Gallic's keep. Below her, the troupe's wagons were burning in the middle bailey. The decapitated bodies of Nefferi and El Erreur lay next to each other.

Fleshers were progressing unimpeded over the drawbridge and the gateway to the middle courtyard. The portcullis to the third and highest bailey was closed, but with no one stopping them, the fleshers would find a way through.

Jai Ling held the katana in one hand. Her bow and quiver hung off her shoulders.

Maddalena was clutching her waist.

On the opposite building stood a white-robed figure, watching her.

Maddalena whispered, "Jai Ling. She's the one who attacked my caravan. She's the leader."

"I know," Jai Ling said. "Her name is—" Jai Ling cocked her head. "Elizabeth, isn't it?"

"Very impressive," Elizabeth called across the ramparts.

They stood staring at each other as the rain began to intensify.

"I've seen you," Jai Ling said. "Not just tonight, but before. And not at a show. In the other city."

"Yes, you did. I was weak, and you heard my thoughts."

Jai Ling kept her sword towards Elizabeth.

"You want the children," Jai Ling said. "You can't have them."

Elizabeth turned her face skyward and let the rainwater gently wash blood off her face.

"Run back and find your brother," Jai Ling ordered.

"Not without you. I'm—"

"GO."

Jai Ling felt Maddalena release her and heard feet splash in the puddles back towards the doorway.

Elizabeth shook her head.

"Have it your way."

Elizabeth motioned with her hand. Three fleshers charged along the top of the curtain wall in her direction.

Jai Ling jumped down onto the same parapet as the advancing fleshers and drew her arrows. Her first one struck the lead flesher, a male, in the kneecap, and he fell forward. The other two, also males, ran into the first one and stumbled. Jai Ling then fired three direct shots, striking each flesher in the forehead and piercing their skulls. She moved forward on the walkway and used the katana to slice off the heads and spear them into the courtyard, just to be sure.

Now Elizabeth sent a pair of women fleshers from the same direction as the other attackers. Jai Ling drew an arrow and waited until they were within a few yards, then hit the first one square between the eyes. The impact propelled the flesher over the curtain wall and outside the castle. The second got closer. Jai Ling hit it with a swing of her sword. That body fell into the courtyard.

Elizabeth sighed. "Very impressive. You're bleeding, by the way. You should wash those cuts. Bad things happen when you let cuts stay open. Put alcohol on them. It seems to help."

"Why do you want them—those two—so badly?" Jai Ling asked.

Elizabeth wiped her face with her hands and turned back to Jai Ling.

"I respect you, so I will tell you. Those children, I, and their mother, are the purest blood descendants of our ancestor, Charles Martel. We creatures, our bodies burn. We are dying. But with just a lick from Maddalena's blood, I felt healing. Another sip. Larger, from their mother, and I was able to pass before you tonight, and you did not know who or what I was. The three sisters have promised me. If we join the bloodlines, I can regenerate my body. I can pass that on to others of my kind. Plus, the mother's blood enhances my mind. Just watch."

Their eyes locked. Jai Ling felt a searing pain in her head. Her sword fell from her hand. She covered her ears.

I don't want to hurt you, Elizabeth spoke in her head. *And I don't want to hurt the children. I really don't. Give them to me. I promise, I'll keep them as they are.*

The words seemed to be more penetrating as she spoke. Jai Ling glanced back, not looking at Elizabeth's face. The pain was most intense when their eyes met.

They will need someone to watch over them. That can be you, Jai Ling. And your friends. We can work together. Don't fight me, Jai Ling. Join me.

With everything she had, Jai Ling ran back. The more space she put between herself and Elizabeth, the pain of the words diminished. She reached the top of the keep and ran to the rear of Castle Gallic overlooking the Durance. There she found the coil of rope she had left earlier, secured to a stone gargoyle, and threw it over the side. She wiped her hands, grabbed the rope, and started to belay down.

I'm running. Where is everyone? These stairs keep curling and going on and on and on, and it is so hot from the fires and—

"Hey, you!"

Lora has grasped my wrist. Others are with her.

Dioneo walked cautiously but urgently through the narrow passageway, axe in hand. It sloped downward, the perfect place for a trap. The fleshers hadn't gotten down here... yet. But they were coming. Didn't seem like Roderigo's people—whatever the hell they were—were immune from the fleshers. At least there were some torches down here. He reached an intersection, right and left disappeared around corners, and straight further down. Where had they gone?

Ahead, from the dark descending path in front, he heard yelling that sounded like Ricciardo's voice. Clutching the axe with both hands, he proceeded forward.

There was a set of thick granite steps. At the bottom was a torch which he removed from its sconce. He was in an oval-shaped room with several alcoves built into the walls, covered by iron bar gates.

There were coffin-shaped boxes in the alcoves.

"Burial crypts."

Ahead, the sounds of Bartolome's voice and perhaps the babbling of Lisabetta.

"Jeez," he said and went forward.

Turning a corner, he saw Lisabetta and Ricciardo wrestling with Bartolome within one of the crypts. There was a sarcophagus in the middle of the room, with a statue of the Virgin Mary carved on top. One small torch burned in the center. Several other tombs were cut into the walls. The crypt Bartolome was in went back and off to the side, but it was too dark to see how far it went in that corner.

Bartolome was whipping his body about, and Ricciardo and Lisabetta struggled to hold him. He had lost his purple doublet and the green silk pants and was in his braies and an undertunic.

Dioneo said, "Under other circumstances, this would be terribly amusing, but for now, stop screwing around and get that kid!"

Ricciardo's eyes lit up. "You're here!"

"Yeah, well, we're getting out of here," Dioneo said, entering the crypt gate. "Grab that kid and let's go."

Lisabetta was trying to reach Bartolome, who was pulling at the back wall of the crypt. Suddenly, she jerked her head and whirled around, pointed to the door and screamed, "EI EI EI!"

Dioneo swung his axe at whatever was behind him. The axe head clanged off the crypt's iron gate, which had just been shut.

Standing outside were Bruno, Beatrice, Simon, and Teodoro.

The same group who had met them hours earlier in the lower bailey.

Dioneo grabbed the crypt gate handle. It was locked.

"We've been waiting for you," Bruno said.

Simon, although larger than Bartolome, was wearing the purple doublet that Bartolome had at the dinner. He pointed at Bartolome.

"That one is mine."

"I don't know what you things are," Dioneo said, "but if you haven't noticed, you've lost your castle. We need to work together to get out."

Bruno, tall and statesmanlike, pressed his fingers together.

"He's right," Teodoro said.

"He is mistaken," Bruno said. "We have sealed the entrance-ways. We've been waiting for them to come here."

Then he addressed Dioneo.

"We do not have to leave. We have only to survive. Your bodies are perfect for us. When we have them, we will merely hide and wait out the flesh eaters. They are mindless, save for their leader. They will move on from here in a day or two or three. And then we will reclaim Castle Gallic."

"You've got a few flaws in that plan, friend," Dioneo laughed, despite the circumstances. "The one who thinks. I met her tonight. Pretty and smart. She shredded your defenses. And she wants to get that boy." Dioneo pointed at Bartolome. "So we'd better work together to get out of here. Besides, don't you need to touch us? That's not happening, old man."

Beatrice went to Bruno and said, "He's a vibrant one. You've chosen well, my husband."

"We are patient beings," Bruno said, sitting down. "You are the ones who need to eat. Your fatigue will eventually overcome you. And we shall be waiting."

He waved his hand.

All torches went dark.

Dioneo swung his axe at what he thought was the lock to the gate. His axe hit something—he saw a spark—but the lock did not break. He repeated the action several more times. It was hard to hit the lock in total darkness. The bars in here were reinforced, stronger than they should be for a damp crypt.

"Bastards," he said.

Dioneo sensed panic rising in Ricciardo, right next to him. He grabbed Ricciardo and, using the axe as a walking stick, they made their way to the back of the crypt.

"I'm frightened," Ricciardo whimpered.

"Who isn't? Speak quietly. Get to the ground and reach around till you find something. "

They lowered to their hands and knees.

The floor was cold, composed of loose dirt and gravel. Dioneo felt something like a tool handle. Rubbing his hands over it, he thought it was a small pickaxe, probably used to hollow out tombs in the walls. He pushed it over to Ricciardo.

"Take this," Dioneo whispered.

"And do what?" Ricciardo asked.

"Poke around with it. Where the hell are Lisabetta and that kid?"

"Lisabetta was struggling with Bartolome back here. He was pulling something from the wall. Then I looked back at the gate. "

Dioneo felt the wooden coffin in front of him. He pried off the cover and reached in and felt nothing.

"Bartolome pulled this out and slipped in behind it," Dioneo said. "There was something back there. They didn't just disappear. Check the walls."

They had to fumble around the coffin. It shifted and made some noise, and both men were startled. It took a little longer to maneuver around than one would think. But crawling on their bellies, they circumvented it.

Ricciardo pushed the pick into the tomb walls and scraped stone. "It's solid," he said.

"Check the whole thing. Lisabetta and Bartolome didn't just disappear. Must be a way."

In the distance rose the sound of fleshers groaning nearby. The darkness accentuated the noise.

Teodoro's voice said, "They've gotten in!"

Simon's voice said, "We have to run."

"Stay here," came Bruno's voice.

"Where can we run?" Beatrice asked.

Teodoro was crying. Then there was a running sound. Maybe another running after her.

A moment later, footsteps running back

"They're right behind—"

The darkness was punctuated with an explosion of noise. The growling and wallowing of a hoard of fleshers was distinctive, and they were r there. Just a few feet away. The sound conveyed very clear images in his head. Teodoro's limbs were being ripped apart on the other side of the crypt gate.

Dioneo foze, just for a moment. Ricciardo said, "There's a hole back here."

Dioneo crawled right past Ricciardo and reached out.

There was indeed a hole at the base of the tomb wall. It must have been hidden behind the coffin.

Ricciardo was breathing heavily. Dioneo clamped his hands over Ricciardo's mouth and whispered.

"Shhh. The Piper is calling kids to the river. They'll find the most direct way they can to get there. Bartolome found a way out. Hold that pickaxe, and I'll take mine, and follow me."

"We don't know where it goes."

Behind them, the screams and worse, the eating sounds, continued. The crypt door was being pushed against.

"Those doors aren't dungeons, and the fleshers smell us. Grab my boot and follow me in. You want to stay, stay. I'm not waiting for you."

Dioneo crawled into the hole. Though in total darkness, He

moved without hesitation. There could very well be death waiting in this passage, but there was certainly death coming from behind.

He was in a crawlspace with stone on all sides except the dirt floor. Probably an escape tunnel dug years ago. He just hoped it went somewhere.

There was a weak tug on the back of his foot.

"Keep up," Dioneo said. He hoped it was Ricciardo he was talking to.

MADDALENA

After Lora found me, I helped her gather the other children. It was a madhouse. Lora had used her birds to scout the rest of the castle, and we rescued who we could. Uwe and Mansa held the children, while Lora, Trippetta, and I shook them until the spell was broken. In the panic, I didn't think; I did what I was told. The entire area is overrun with fleshers. We made our way through the keep to the river. Uwe, Mansa, Lora, Trippetta, and I, along with other children and some of the other adults from our troupe, have made it to the back of the keep and out here. The rain is light. Lora's falcons circled the castle and flapped at a few more children, stopping them from jumping into the River. I'm glad we saved some. The cog boat was lying unguarded at the end of a bulkhead, and we reached it. In the air around us, we hear the growls of the fleshers.

The cog is the only choice. The barges are sitting on the sand, and it would take too much to move them.

We crossed the bulkhead and made it on the boat. There are a couple of fleshers on it, but Uwe and Mansa dispatch them.

God, why are you doing this to me? I am devout, I say my rosary. I have always attended Mass. Why do you torture me?

There is not a strong wind, but there is a breeze and a current.

The boat should go. There are two long quant poles in the main hold of the cog.

Grabbing one such pole, Mansa says, "We're going to need these."

Both Uwe and Mansa push the quant poles against the bulkhead.

"There may be others inside," I say.

Everyone looks back at the castle. Pockets of flames are burning in many places, including the siege tower and the arsenal towers. There is a black smoke hanging in the air. It is raining, which holds the flames down, or the entire castle would be engulfed. The castle is a grave. My brother. Dioneo. Jai Ling. Ricciardo and Lisabetta—poor souls both. The Cookes. Neferri. El Erreur. Rowena. All dead?

Lora rests a hand on my shoulder. "Trippetta is helping the children put up tents, Maddalena," she says. "Go help her."

"I need to see if anyone else is coming," I say.

"I will watch," Lora says. "Go help Trippy."

"I need to watch for my brother," I say. It is not that I do not trust Lora. But I must look.

Out of the way we came, one of the guards is running. He is wounded, but he yells for us to wait, that he is all right. A gateway in the arsenal tower—the one to our left—is torn aside. Fleshers burst out, and they see the guard. They pursue. Some of the pursuers are slow, but some are not. The guard looks back and then trips on the sand. Two fleshers pounce on him.

Mansa and Uwe push both their setting poless gainst the bulkhead, and Lora unfurls the last mooring rope. The cog slides along the sandy bottom of the river. For a moment—but just a moment —we are stuck. My heart jumps. Uwe and Mansa make massive pushes on the poles, and the flat bottom of the boat slides over the sandbank and reaches deeper water. I have traveled on cogs. They do not need much water to float in. The Durance is wide. We catch the current and begin to sail away.

"JAI LING!" I cry, pointing. She is running from the siege tower on our right, heading for the bulkhead. A pair of male fleshers emerge from the siege tower and chase her. They are fast. Fleshers who attacked the guard are still outside, and they are eating him. Jai Ling and the ones chasing here are heading for the bulkhead, which we are pulling away from.

Everyone on the boat is yelling for Jai Ling to run.

Do we have any bows? We look around. None can be found.

Jai Ling runs faster than her pursuers. She reaches the end of the bulkhead at the same time as the two fastest fleshers. Without hesitation, she dives headfirst into the water. The fleshers follow her off the bulkhead. Jai Ling does not appear. The fleshers thrash about in the water. They claw for purchase and find none. The current is stronger than I realized, and both fleshers disappear under the water. Then Jai Ling breaks the surface, close to the boat. She swims after us. We are picking up speed. I grab one of the ropes used to anchor the cog and throw one end to her. Jai Ling reaches it. I am holding it. Then Mansa is with me, as is Lora. We pull Jai Ling onto our boat.

The mist turns into rain again. On board, we put Jai Ling under a tarp that Trippetta has raised. Jai Ling lies on her back, eyes closed, breathing heavily. Lora comes over with some blankets, and we begin to dry Jai Ling. Jai Ling raises her head and sees most of us on the boat—there is no cabin, just the hull, and a small upper platform deck at the rear.

Eyes closed, and breathing with effort, Jai Ling asks, "Others?"

Her voice is weak. Her body is cut and bruised.

Lora ever so slightly shakes her head.

"Sorcerers," Jai Ling says. She lies back and closes her eyes. "They blocked us. They trapped us. They..."

"It's a slaughter."

Carmen Teresa watched the fires burning at Castle Gallic through a long cylinder with convex lenses on both ends, which made images seem closer. It had been invented by an unusually talented member of the coven. The rear of the castle was relatively flame-free, but a great black cloud of smoke hung overhead as fires burned throughout the lower and middle baileys. A few dozen people had barely reached a small cog boat and made it into the river, but now hordes of fleshers walked listlessly along the riverbank of the Durance, proving conclusively they had overrun the entire castle.

"Was the girl on that boat?" Raphael asked.

"I'm not sure," replied Carmen Teresa. "I think so, but there were several children. It was hard to make them out. The woman who outran the fleshers and dove into the river seemed quite fit. And she looked oriental. That would match what the sisters said was the girl's protector."

Federigo said, "I wouldn't trust the sisters. Ever."

"They are known to play games," Carmen Teresa said, "and I do not trust them either. But we lost Cesare. He's around here somewhere, but if he reached his lab, which I suspect he did, the sisters are the only card to play." She handed the cylinder to Federigo.

"Take a look. Do you think anyone else got out of there alive?"

Federigo peered through the device. All he saw were fleshers falling upon a few humans who had made their way to the river, only to find there was no boat but an army of the undead waiting for them. He put the cylinder down.

"I think not."

They stared some more at the fires. Raphael broke the silence.

"So, what now?"

Carmen Teresa said, "If the boy or girl is in there, they're dead. If either made the boat, they have a chance. Cesare will want to find that girl, especially if the boy is dead. Elizabeth will too. I don't think we have any choice but to intercept that boat."

She turned to Raphael.

"Go calm the horses. The fires may make them nervous."

Raphael went to the night mares they had left tied up a short way off. Carmen Teresa and Federigo lagged behind.

"You're so sure Cesare wants to find the girl," Federigo commented. "Why?"

"He wants her for a number of reasons. She's currency. Both the flesher woman and the pope want her. So Cesare wants her enough to come out from where he's hiding. We find her, we'll find Cesare."

"It won't be easy to find another boat," Federigo said. "But why does the woman want the children so desperately?"

"I don't know." Carmen Teresa pointed with the viewing device at the burning castle.

"Suppose you were a flesher—a super-intelligent one. Like her. She's out there. You're dead. And you're always dying. Eventually, the bodies fall apart; that's why they haven't overrun us yet. Why would you want to reach a particular child?"

Federigo shook his head. "I'm lost."

"This woman is smart, Federigo. And driven. There's something about those children that will help her. And think about this. She carts around the mother's body. Why?"

Federigo shrugged. "Impossible to say."

"True, but I think it has to do with her survival. There's something about the children and the mother that will help her. Fleshers don't survive long."

Carmen Teresa pointed to the river.

"The Durance curves southwest before it turns and meets the Rhone. The cog is a slow boat. They'll travel downriver well, but when they reach the Rhone, they will be going against the current. If we ride hard inland, and they don't get much wind, we can catch them after they turn onto the Rhone and are close to Avignon."

"And then what?"

Carmen Teresa looked skyward. The rain had stopped, and the moon shone down.

"Then we'll see."

Using his axe in front of him, Dioneo crawled through the dank blackness of whatever tunnel they had found. Ricciardo followed, dragging the pickaxe. How long or how far they were there, neither could say.

Ricciardo whispered, "Do you see the others?"

"Just keep moving," Dioneo snapped back.

"But how could they—"

"Bartolome's mind is bye-bye. He's following the Piper. Which is good for us. He's being drawn outside; he'll find a way out of here if there is one. And Lisabetta doesn't have enough wits about her to be scared. Now be quiet, or I'm leaving you behind."

But then Dioneo paused. "I see something up there. Move quietly."

Ricciardo said nothing, but Dioneo could hear him furtively crawling behind him.

Dioneo reached what seems to be the end of the tunnel and peered out cautiously. The sound of water flowing in the dark. Dioneo paused for his eyes to adjust. There was a bit of moonlight inside here. "Here" appeared to be an underground alcove with a high ceiling. A natural cave in the rock. Some moonlight from the harvest moon was coming in through a hole in the rock.

Dioneo could hear whimpering. Something was curled in the shadows just outside the light.

"Lisabetta?" Dioneo called. "Bartolome?"

He heard Lisabetta's familiar, "Eh Eh."

"They're here!"

Dineo climbed out of the hole and onto sandy ground. He even turned to pull Ricciardo out.

Lisabetta was rocking Bartolome's limp body in the sand, before a pool of water. Both of them were wet. Beyond the pool was a great gaping hole in the wall, with water falling outside. At first, Dioneo thought it was rain. Then he realized the water was cascading down.

They were underneath the waterfall on the western side of the castle.

Ricciardo and Dioneo went over to Lisabetta and checked the boy. Bartolome was pale and cold. Ricciardo gently turned his head and saw a bruise over the left temple.

"What happened?" Dioneo asked.

They were surprised when Lisabetta splashed the water violently, and she made a chirping noise.

"Easy, easy," Dioneo said. He looked back to the hole they had crawled out of, then checked the sand. He stepped a few feet into the water, then slid, but caught himself.

"Very slippery," he said. "Look. Bartolome was being called by the Piper, like all the children. When the Piper plays his flute, children are in a trance; they follow wherever he is calling them to. That's how Bartolome found this passageway. The Piper brings children to water. Something about drowning them."

Dioneo looked toward the hole and the falling water. "Bartolome got in here, and he went into the pool because that waterfall is on the western side of the castle. Beyond it, we can get to the river. That's why he was drawn here. But he hit his head on the rock. Lisabetta found him. She pulled him out of the water."

"So Bartolome—drowned?"

Dioneo said nothing.

"Let me have him," Ricciardo said gently, reaching out to Lisabetta. She looked at him—yes, she focused on Ricciardo—and she let him take the boy. Ricciardo pulled Bartolome out of the water and laid him in the sand. Kneeling over the body, he pinched Bartolome's nose and began to breathe into his mouth.

"What are you doing?" Dioneo asked.

Ricciardo raised his head, took Lisabetta's hands, and placed them under Bartolome's neck.

"Hold his head back like this," Ricciardo said. Lisabetta was compliant.

Ricciardo breathed into Bartolome's mouth again. Then he began to push down on Bartolome's chest. Lisabetta became agitated, but Ricciardo reassured her, "It is all right, it is all right."

"We've still got to get out of here," Dioneo said, and he began to wade into the pool.

Ricciardo repeated this breathing and pushing on the chest. Bartolome's chest abruptly lurched, and he coughed up water. He waved his arms and made choking noises, but Ricciardo and Lisabetta sat him up. Bartolome coughed several more times.

Lisabetta gave a cry of glee and patted Bartolome's back. She clapped, then grabbed hold of Ricciardo's hand.

Ricciardo beamed with pride.

Dioneo stopped, turned to survey the situation, and then remarked, "Je-sus. Ricciardo, for once, you are actually useful. How did you do that?"

"It was taught to me by my father. He was a healer."

"Well, I hate to spoil this tender moment, but I hear some noises coming from the hole."

"They can't be following us!" Ricciardo said.

"Why can't they?" Dioneo turned back to the water. "That's the waterfall. Our way out."

"Can you be sure?" Ricciardo asked.

"Only one way to find out."Dioneo took more tentative steps. "It's slippery here. I can see how Bartolome fell and hit his head."

Dioneo waded farther out. The water rose to his thighs. He reached the wall of cascading water, looked both ways, then disappeared to the right.

Lisabetta was rubbing Bartolome's chest and back, and the boy was still spitting water. Ricciardo looked around.

The three of them were alone.

They waited.

Would Dioneo come back for them?

There was increasing clamor from the hole they'd exited from.

"Time to go," Dioneo said, emerging drenched from the water wall. He spoke as he walked to them. "Hold hands and get over there. There's a small ledge outside, just under the waterfall. Grab Bartolome. We'll get on it and jump. You'll pass through the falls and land in the river."

Ricciardo and Lisabetta pulled Bartolome to his feet and guided him into the pool.

"Where am I?" Bartolome asked groggily.

"He's himself!" declared Ricciardo.

"Brilliant observation, my boy," Dioneo said, stepping onto the sand.

"We have to flee Bartolome," Ricciardo answered. "The fleshers are after us."

Dioneo picked up the pickaxe and handed it to Ricciardo.

Fearful, the others hesitated.

"We're in the middle of the falls," Dioneo said. "It's about thirty feet down. The ledge is wide but a little slippery. We leap into the falls and land in the river. Ricciardo, you lead. Use the pickaxe for balance; it's heavy at the end. Put Bartolome in between, and Lisabetta on the end."

One of the undead peered out of the tunnel hole. Dioneo recognized the man. It was one of the same undead flagellants who had killed Rowena. It scrambled out and fell on the sand.

"I'll take care of this—get going!" Dioneo said, pushing them towards the falling water.

Lisabetta grabbed Bartolome's hand. She gestured to Ricciardo and pointed to the aperture underneath the waterfall. Ricciardo nodded and took Bartolome's other hand.

The trio entered the water and moved towards the waterfall.

Behind them, the creature got up and moved after them. It was emitting muffled gargling noises.

Dioneo approached the flesher slowly. "So much for being penitent, buddy."

The flagellant stumbled in the sand and fell to its knees. Dioneo swung his axe and struck the creature in the neck. The creature was thrown down but was still moving. Dioneo tore his axe out of the neck.

"This is for Rowena." He mashed the creature's skull with the butt of the axe, making a pulpy mush.

Dioneo stopped.

From the tunnel. More sounds.

More fleshers coming.

"Time to go."

Dioneo waded through the water, using the axe for balance. Stepping through the opening, he found Lisabetta and Ricciardo on the ledge just under the waterfall, Bartolome between them. Dioneo came beside them, reaching into the falling water.

"Hey, perfect temperature. Like we're all getting first shift in the bath tonight."

Then—

"Join hands."

They did.

"We go on three. One... Two... Three!"

They jumped forward together.

[13]
THE HOUSE HAS FALLEN

THE FOOL LEANED back on a tree branch and listened to the cacophony of screams and growls floating through the night air. Beautiful.

It was always good to be paid. It was how he lived. But if he were honest with himself, this is what he really loved. What made him feel alive. The sounds of agony. Oh, sometimes the wail of parents just discovering the loss of children was as intense, but this was good. Mirabeau had been turned into a virtual torture chamber, with a confluence of parties—fleshers and flagellants, witches or whatever they were, peasants and troubadours. He couldn't claim all the credit for it, of course; much of it was just fortuitous. But the rules had been followed. He had performed a service asked of him, and he had not been paid. That pompous Roderigo had been so haughty. What if the price were raised just a bit? No matter. The fool claimed what he was entitled to. No more, no less.

He sat there for hours until the screams subsided. When he was finally satisfied, the fool slid down the tree and set forth to another distant town where his services had been requested.

"WHERE ARE THEY!"

Elizabeth raced through the top of Castle Gallic's keep, Janosz following. Yes, her plan had worked, but again, they had not gotten what they came for. All this carnage—where were those children? She came across an old hag crouched on the ground, gnawing on the neck of a boy about Bartolome's size. Though the body was covered in blood, she could tell the boy had been wearing a red doublet and silk pants. Hadn't Bartolome worn something like that tonight? His was purple, but was this one blood-stained? Fear shot through her. Elizabeth grabbed the hag's shoulder and tossed her back towards Janosz, who caught her in his massive hands. Elizabeth then turned over the boy's body. The face was gone.

She checked the doublet.

"It's bloodied all right, Janosz. But it's magenta. This wasn't Bartolome's."

The woman flesher snapped her jaws at Elizabeth.

"Rip her head off!"

Janosz dutifully complied.

Elizabeth took the head by the hair and went to the curtain wall overlooking the three baileys of Castle Gallic. She hurled the head out into the courtyard. The decapitated head bounced off bricks far below, cracking as it did, and rolled into a drain.

"You must think," Elizabeth said aloud. "They were both sleeping in here. That's why you planned this. Where did they go?"

All around her were mindless creatures feasting. It was a crazed orgy, just like at Prince Prospero's castle, a place she had once called home. This was the hardest time to control them, when they were at the height of their feeding and blood flowed seemingly everywhere. This was maddening.

There were good things. When her people attacked tonight, they moved under her guidance, her control, in coordination, in planned movements. They encircled their prey, who were almost always too overcome with fear to react. There were a few exceptions, of course. Jai Ling was quite lethal with her weapon. Elizabeth had to admit she was impressed with how quickly Jai Ling struck down five fleshers with arrows. She had gotten away. And Dioneo? She was not sure what happened to him, but he had the nine lives of a cat.

Elizabeth's tribe had grown tonight. The flagellants had been particularly easy targets, and most of them were rapidly dispatched, but the leader and a few others had turned. Some of the villagers, too. Not everyone had been overtaken by those sorcerers. However, most of the inhabitants of the castle, whatever they were, didn't turn. Thus, they became food. Elizabeth looked down at her own body, covered in blood, both green and red. Some of it was hers—she herself had been cut several times.

None of that mattered.

As close as Maddalena and Bartolome had been, she did not have them. She raised her face to the night sky, letting the drizzle fall on her face. The water felt cleansing, washing the red and green blood off her skin. Janosz stood silently beside her.

"All this has been for nothing, Janosz. Nothing at all."

She pulled at her hair and held a fistful of red strands. She opened her fingers and watched the rainwater wash the hair from her hand.

"If there is a god, Janosz, he's laughing at us."

She heard some feet sliding behind her. Nicola, head slumped to the side as always, and dragging one leg behind, reached her mistress.

Elizabeth gently stroked Nicola's hair.

"Still my loyal lady in waiting. We need to fix your leg again, Nicola. I'll make another splint."

Nicola did not raise her head, but she did raise her right hand.

In it was a red satin ribbon.

Elizabeth looked at it. Suddenly, her eyes widened.

"Janosz," she said hurriedly, "get Alatiel here now."

With the scent of the ribbon, Alatiel led them through the castle and into the great hall. Elizabeth knelt beside the body of Lady Madeline.

"I sensed she was the strongest of them, Janosz. Roderigo was strong, but his sister was even stronger. There was quite a battle here. This had to be the work of Jai Ling."

A gust of wind blew open one of the French doors. Alatiel took great notice of that.

"What is it, Alatiel?"

Alatiel rubbed the red ribbon on her face.

"We should go to the river."

The group made its way down until Elizabeth, surrounded by Janosz and Alatiel, stood on the sandy shore of the plateau. Nicola wandered nearby with others.

Alatiel stepped from the sand into the Durance River.

Elizabeth grabbed her arm.

"Wait. Do you want me to—"

"No," was Alatiel's response.

She closed her eyes and stepped further, allowing the river to flow against her knees. She felt a bit off balance, but she wanted that. It helped her mind to drift.

After a while, she waded back.

"So they are on the water?" Elizabeth asked.

Alatiel paused.

"I think so. There are many scents here. Hard to separate them."

Elizabeth turned to Janosz

"We had them, Janosz, and they escaped on the water. Seems familiar, doesn't it?"

Nicola stumbled to them.

"Dear Nicola, what is it now?"

Nicola stared blankly. Elizabeth saw she was dragging something behind her leg.

"What have you got there—"

It was a purple doublet which Nicola held in her right hand. Grasping the jacket, Elizabeth quickly brought it to Alatiel.

"Check this. The boy Bartolome wore this earlier tonight. Can you find him?"

Alatiel held the torn garment against her face, along with the red ribbon she'd been given earlier. "Several have worn this," she said.

"Keep trying," Elizabeth pushed. "Think of the girl, Maddalena. The ribbon is hers. The boy Bartolome wore this at the dinner. The red-blooded smell different than the green-blooded, don't they?"

Alatiel rubbed the garment over her face. Then she entered the Durance River up to her thighs. This time, the water did not hamper her. She kneeled on one knee and liked the sensation of the kneecap burying into the sandy riverbed.

"The boy's scent. Yes, it's more like the girls'."

Alatiel stayed for several minutes, as the water flowed around her. Elizabeth stood a few feet behind her. One or two fleshers wandered near, but Elizabeth telepathically forced them back.

"The boy is on land, on our side of the river," Alatiel said, pointing. "The girl is on the river, traveling faster, but the boy is closer, moving slowly."

"Are they both alive?"

Alatiel listened to the waters.

"I think so."

Elizabeth scratched her chin, then paced on the beach.

It came to her.

"There was a cog here before that's gone. They must have reached it. Maddalena is on it with the others. Bartolome was cut off or couldn't make it."

She turned to the western wall of Castle Gallic, burning in the night.

"But Bartolome got out. He's not too bright. He must have had help." Her eyes lit up. "It must be Jai Ling or Dioneo. They're the only ones who would help that useless boy. One must be with the boy and one with the girl. But the boy is on foot. Even if he has help, he can't have much. He's out there. Following the river. And I think I know where they are both going."

Elizabeth lost track of a flesher who was approaching Alatiel. Alatiel abruptly turned her head, just enough to see the flesher out of the corner of one eye, and made eye contact. The flesher wobbled and fell into the river. The waters, although shallow, covered the body and carried it off.

Elizabeth ran to Janosz and clapped her hands on his shoulders.

"Just like before, Janosz. The race is still on!"

MADDALENA - OUR FINAL LOOK

Jai Ling stirs. She sees me and rubs a finger against my face.

"You lost your red ribbon, little one."

I hold her finger. "We'll find another."

"That's my girl."

She smiles and drifts off.

Lora kneels next to me.

"Maddalena, watch over Jai for a while, ok? Then go help Trippy."

I nod.

Lora walks to the back of the boat towards Mansa. The falcons, Leo and Francine, follow at her feet.

The cog sails along with the current. Mansa is in the back, steering. Lora rests her head on his shoulder. I think she is crying. Francine and Leo are silent, perched on the boat's railing nearby.

On the other end, Uwe and Trippetta are comforting the children.

I have lost my brother. And others.

I wipe Jai Ling's body with a wet linen cloth.

She sleeps.

EPILOGUE

And so, dear reader, daybreak is coming, so we must end our story.

Maddalena, Bartolome, Dioneo, Jai Ling, and their companions—and Elizabeth and Janosz, and Alatiel—their stories continue, but my tale tonight is through. I am afraid it is time for you to leave.

A few parting words? Let me think. Ah yes. Unbeknownst to any of the participants in our story, many miles to the northeast, altostratus clouds were rolling through the night, over the uppermost regions of the Alpes Maritimes. Even this late in summer, there are still ice dams at the highest part of the Alps, but they are close to the end of their life. And at just the right moment when the heat meets the winter-like upper cold atmosphere, the clouds will unleash their burden, dropping heavy rains onto the various bodies of water already trapped in the glacial regions.

This will add to the great pools of water being held in check by those ice dams, between the alpine and the glacial regions. As more rains fall, the waters rise, slowly eroding those ice dams.

The flood season is coming.

ABOUT THE AUTHOR

WILLIAM J. CONNELL is currently a practicing attorney in the great states of Rhode Island and Massachusetts. He has also worked as a public-school teacher in the areas of Special Education and History in the same states. He enjoys writing on a wide variety of topics. Most of his non-fiction material is in the legal field, and his work has been published in many law journals, most frequently in The Rhode Island Bar Journal. His fiction tends to run to historical adventure, which reflects his love of teaching history, mixed with elements of sci-fi, classic literature, and horror thrown in for good measure!

Besides being a member of the Wild Ink Writing Family, for which he is most grateful, he has had fiction pieces published by The Ravens Quoth Press, Godless Publishers, Culture Cult Press, and Underland Press. He likes to spend time with his family and Lulu, the family's green-cheeked conure. His author/writer website continues to be a leading example of why you should not do one yourself unless and until you know what you are doing.

www.ingramcontent.com/pod-product-compliance
Lightning Source LLC
LaVergne TN
LVHW050929080826
845145LV00001B/266

* 9 7 8 1 9 6 4 8 8 5 6 2 9 *